TOUCH AND GO

THAD NODINE

TOUCH AND GO

UNBRIDLED BOOKS

This is a work of fiction. The names, characters, places and incidents are either the
product of the author's imagination or are used fictitiously, and any resemblance
to actual persons living or dead, business establishments, events,
or locales is entirely coincidental.

Unbridled Books

Copyright © 2011 by Thad Nodine

Library of Congress Cataloging-in-Publication Data

Nodine, Thad R.
Touch and go : a novel / by Thad Nodine.
p. cm.
ISBN 978-1-60953-061-7
1. Blind—Fiction.   I. Title.
PS3614.0374T68 2011
813'.6—dc23
2011030865

1   3   5   7   9   10   8   6   4   2

BOOK DESIGN BY SH · CV

First Printing

For Shelby

TOUCH AND GO

ONE

Before we left California, we lived in a hodgepodge of a house where you couldn't get anywhere without walking around something else. Isa and Patrick slept in a rear room you had to walk outside to enter. Their two foster kids had small rooms along the hallway, but you had to walk through Ray's tidy nook to get to Devon's burrow, with its piles of denim, t-shirts, and rumpled magazines. I lived in a tiny room off the kitchen.

Summer's liberties had helped the kids loosen up with us, the way a common change of routines draws people closer, but by August the heat of Burbank didn't feel much like freedom. In a couple of weeks, Isa, Patrick, and the boys were driving cross-country on a family vacation of sorts, to visit Isa's dying father in Florida. I wasn't planning to join them. At the time, I didn't think of us as family so much as people who needed each other. I can admit this now: I was still in love with Isa.

Most people walk on autopilot. For me, steps understand; I navigate based on the supervision of surfaces. From the bus stop, our driveway was five paces past an odd slant in the sidewalk, which had been lifted by a tree that no longer existed. We didn't have a front path leading from the street, just a wide expanse of concrete where the trucker who'd lived there before us used to nose right up to the house. With all that driveway, the hardest thing for me to find was our front door in the stucco wall. There was no stoop, just a threshold.

On a sweltering day in the second week of August 2005, Ray guided me up the driveway, my hand gripping his thin shoulder, both of us hopping. Sweating. Laughing. Catching our breaths. As he reached for the doorknob, I stiffened at the sound of Isa's voice inside. "Isa" is pronounced with a long *i* like "Isaac," even though it's short for Isabelle. I'd always liked the way her voice warbled when she was upset, but that day, I bristled. I'd just lost the only real job I'd ever had, a part-time gig at the community paper, and I didn't want to face anyone—least of all Isa, who could always see through me.

The editor who had laid me off had been at the newspaper one week. When I'd walked into his office, his keyboard clattered in spurts by the far wall, so I knew he was facing away from me, typing at his computer desk. I cleared my throat; his keys stopped. The rollers of his chair whisked a moment and halted as he came to his desk, which lay between us. Two hard wooden chairs faced the desk and had their backs to me—assuming he hadn't rearranged the office. It was our first one-on-one.

He offered a half statement, half question, as if he weren't sure how to handle me: "There's two chairs in front of you?"

I should have set him at ease, saying something light and funny about sight, but I was self-conscious myself.

Mostly I'd been assigned profiles of local personalities that I wrote based on phone interviews. For people who were quirky or had an eccentric setup, I'd hire a cab to visit them, bringing along my digital recorder and laptop. I'd ask about their place, pictures on the wall, anything unusual, so I could fake a visual setting. The previous editor had insisted on that: readers need visuals.

But the people I interviewed were interested in nonvisuals. "You can't see at all?" they'd say. "But you get around so well." They liked listening to my screen reader on my laptop, the electronic voice that droned out my typed sentences at various speeds. And they asked how I knew where my cursor was on the screen. I tried showing them by having them close their eyes and listen to the computer read through options on a website as I dragged my finger across the touchpad. But it took too long to explain, so I learned to deflect the first rounds of questions. "Space is an abstraction," I told them, "based on the relationship between local objects." I got that from Einstein. I can't pretend to understand the science, but I like the idea of the space between us being illusory. I don't know how any of us find our place in this world except in relation to others.

After finding the two wooden chairs facing the desk, I folded Charlie—my cane—and laid him in my lap. He collapses like a tent pole, with an elastic cord inside, and opens solid, yet flexible. I faced to the right, trying to hide the scar that scampers from my forehead, behind my dark glasses, and onto my cheek. How many times had Dad told me: "Look at a man square. People get jittery when your head drifts." I took off my Western hat—a Bandit whose stiff Cattleman crown protected my head from branches and overhangs—and laid it on top of Charlie. Running my fingers through my hair, I braced myself and faced the editor full-on.

He wanted to know how I got from interview notes to finished copy, so I started telling him about getting quotes on my recorder and taking notes on my laptop, which I would listen to with my screen reader.

"What a memory!" he interrupted, followed by a long pause. "To listen to your notes and then type the article from scratch."

The truth is I listen to my notes more than once—particularly quotes. But I didn't want to dampen his praise.

"What about the visual details you put in? You know, what the guy looks like. The books on the shelf." He ran his words together and stopped—the same way he'd typed, I realized. "How do you come up with those?" he blurted.

I didn't want to blame his predecessor; wouldn't that seem a cop-out? I shrugged and said calmly, "I ask questions. People tell me things. I report them."

"How do you know they're telling the truth?"

"Same as anyone," I suggested. "I cross-check facts. And I touch things to verify."

"The view out a window?"

"These are profiles," I said. "Not attack pieces." My voice sounded sluggish, so I sped up, trying to match his confidence. "Why would people lie about things like that? I cross-check when there's a reason to."

Behind me in the newsroom, keyboards blazed. The full-time reporters. Hard news. What a poser I was.

"You're young," he exclaimed. "You're a good writer. I can use someone like you."

As if I didn't have a job already.

He described the benefits of freelance. The promise of doing a variety of assignments. The ability to pitch stories to multiple editors. "I like your early articles, those profiles of bums and addicts. That prostitute." He paused. "The later ones have been soft. Don't you think?"

My head drifted as I thought about that; those stories did have an edge. I'd written them after graduating from Channel House, a recovery home. I'd hung out in Hollywood, interviewing any drifter or street performer who'd talk to me. "I used a tape recorder," I offered. "That's how I did those stories." I realized I was gripping the armrests. I faced the editor and tried to relax.

"There you go," he said. Papers shuffled on his desk. "I want to see stories like that. You'll get an extra week's pay. After that week, give me a call and we'll talk about articles."

"You don't want anything next week?"

"Consider it severance pay. The least we can do."

I knew I should press him: Why not two weeks' pay? Why was I being laid off if he liked my writing? But I didn't want to jeopardize the relationship. I let my face drift. "Freelance again," I said.

"Welcome aboard." His chair rolled back, and his hands thumped the desk; he was making sure I heard. When I stood and extended my arm, he grabbed my hand and shook it.

I stepped out of his office feeling stung and numb, swinging Charlie back and forth along the short aisle between desks, stepping briskly, wanting to disappear. Since I'd never been given a desk or computer, I'd always felt like an interloper anyway. I knew most of the reporters, but it wasn't as if we confided. Even as I scuttled toward the stairs, I wanted Helen in sports or Cameron at the city desk to call out. Helen's keyboard clacked. Cameron bantered on the phone. I hurried on. Ex-addicts excel at that, rushing into the pain we long to escape.

My pal Charlie led me downstairs and out the office door, into the bedlam of pedestrians bent for home. Footsteps spat across concrete at odd angles. A stroller nearly clipped me. August is usually a slow month on Glendale sidewalks even in late afternoon, but I was jostled along and held up short. I scurried too quickly, mishandling Charlie and striking his tip along the edge of storefronts on my right. He didn't complain. I blustered across alcoves as the heels of my Western boots echoed the recesses. I found myself clenching my jaw. Before I came to the street corner, I had to huddle in a doorway. How many counselors had told me to stop and breathe—breathe, for God's sake—when I got like this? Holding Charlie against my chest vertically, his tip resting on the concrete and his rubber grip pointing up, I lifted my hat to rake my fingers through my hair. I took off my dark glasses to wipe my face with my forearm.

It was a part-time job anyway, I told myself. Eight hours a week. Hardly paid anything. Hack writing in a dying industry. But it was the best job I'd ever had. In San Francisco I'd been stuck in data processing, taking orders over the phone back when those jobs existed on this side of the Pacific. Writing for the community paper was the only gig where I hadn't felt hemmed in by blindness. The fact that it was part-time and low pay—that this was all I could get—what was the point of remaining sober? I'd struggled to stay clean for twenty-seven days shy of two years. Even on the best days, I found myself longing for a whiff of crack—just a small rock to take me away. Today I needed to get home before I did something rash.

I reached Charlie forward and set off for the street corner. When his tip caught on my left, my opposite hip glanced against something: a parked bicycle? It didn't fall. I knew I should slow down, but I charged on, driven by the risk of dawdling, as if I could hear my personal triggers—click, click, click—snap toward relapse.

Cross-traffic signaled the end of the block. I made my way left and should have waited for the light's cycle as footsteps ran past me across the intersection. Instead I hustled from concrete onto the gentle slope of road pavement, swinging Charlie back and forth. A horn blared on my right. A man yawped, incoherent. Charlie found the opposite curb, and as I stepped onto concrete, a car whizzed behind me. I turned north and caught an MTA bus toward home in Burbank.

When I got off downtown and the bus pulled away, the sidewalk felt forlorn after the bustle of Glendale. A woman's heels disappeared around a corner. A man's shoes scraped away and then back, pacing. Diesel hung in the air. The longer I waited for the Empire line, the more the shame began to gnaw at my stomach. There'd been rumors for months that the paper would be downsizing, and the new man had started with me. I could get that. But he'd done it by questioning my accuracy. He'd laid me off by saying, "Welcome aboard." And I'd folded like a wet leaf.

I turned away from the sun, away from the noises of the street, my crown sweating inside my hat. I had about an hour until the N.A. meeting at Victory Church, but I was two blocks from the tinkling of highballs on a bar. I thought about calling my sponsor, but my neck tensed into knots. I pressed my thumb into Charlie's rubber grip past the point where my knuckles hurt. My left foot tapped the ground as I stood still as a bum. I dreaded seeing anyone and was afraid of being alone.

A bus hissed, releasing a whoosh of air. Doors clattered open. My face was wet with sweat. I turned and stepped forward. "Empire?" I called.

"Kevin!" Dotty barked from the driver's seat, which groaned as she shifted her weight.

Charlie's tip glanced against the side of the bus, then found the doorway. I stepped in, relieved and panicked to be heading home.

"Why the face?" Dotty said. "What happened?"

I forced a smile. "Just got a freelance gig," I said, my voice high-pitched and cheery.

"That's what I'm talking about!" she said, her voice gruff. "Good for you!"

I sat against a window and laid my hat on my lap. I'd been fired before. Laid off. Let go. Of course I could adapt. I was only twenty-seven, for God's sake. I'd used crack for less than two years; I was not one of those rigid ex-addicts.

When I got off the bus at Lincoln Street, I set out along the sidewalk in an obstinate rush, tilting forward, a right angle to Charlie's line swinging back and forth down to the concrete. To my left, from the open door, voices buzzed from inside the local bar.

"Hey, partner!" a man stammered from somewhere near the doorway, his tone open, friendly.

I frowned. From the hot sidewalk, I smelled bratwurst and old urine. My head throbbed. I kept charging. Halfway down the block, I struck the outside of my right ankle midstride against something hard as hell—a shopping cart, which clanked as it pitched over the curb into the street. Stupid-ass cowboy boots, I thought, grabbing my foot, wincing, hopping in circles on my other foot. Charlie clattered to the concrete, no help at all.

"Kevin!" Ray called from across the street—or in the street. "You okay?" His voice was unmistakable—high-pitched and concerned. He was twelve years old and had just begun to open up after ten months with us.

It happens to me a lot: private moments turn public all of a sudden.

"Watch out for cars!" I called back, still stooped, balancing on one foot, holding my ankle.

Ray was already pattering next to me, forever running and fidgeting, ten steps ahead of my thoughts. "You look funny!" he said, giggling. He didn't care that I was blind. He wasn't ashamed of my scar. He didn't know I was a failure. In that instant, I saw myself from a kid's perspective: hopping. I dropped my foot and tugged him against me, my arm around his slim torso. He wanted none of that; he pulled away quickly. In the house, away from people, he loved to be coddled, but not out on the street, where someone might see him. He was small, but he was going into seventh grade after all.

I heard him folding Charlie. Then he brought my palm to his near shoulder and set off guiding me home. I squeezed gently, enjoying the familiar curve of his thin collarbone. That's one way I know people, by the rhythm of their shoulder or elbow as they settle into a gait. I tried to match his short, quick steps. Ray doesn't like to lead so much as he likes the attention of being followed. After a few strides, he started hopping on one foot, laughing, and I started hopping as well. Before I could help it, I was laughing too.

TWO

As Ray and I hopped up our driveway, panting, the strike of his shoes and my boots echoed from the stucco siding. I heard the lilt of Isa's voice inside, which made me plant both feet on the ground. With Ray tugging my arm, however, I didn't have long to linger. If I didn't tell anyone, I reasoned, how could Isa know I'd been let go? Ray pushed open the door.

"I don't want to travel with that thing," Isa sang out, her voice restless and uneasy. "It's morbid. It gets in my head."

As I stepped onto the threshold behind Ray, nudging him into our stale air conditioning, he resisted. I wanted the escape of my room, but now Ray wouldn't budge. Our front door opened to a seam between kitchen linoleum to the right and family-room carpet to the left, as if the doorway had been built before the rooms were laid out. To the right of the entry, a spot where the linoleum buckled meant two steps to the kitchen table, plus three more to my room, depending on the odd chair in the way.

Before us on the linoleum lay a startling sight, I know now. But at the time, I assumed it was Isa's tone that made Ray hold back; he hated confrontation. His mother had died almost a year ago, and his dad was in Soledad, a maximum-security prison—that was how he'd come to us.

"It's a business investment," Patrick said irritably. "Every time I have a breakthrough, every time I show initiative, every time I come up with an original idea to put food on this table, you have to bring me down. Have a little faith, for God's sake."

Patrick was thirty-eight and was always trying pyramid schemes and so-called business investments to get rich quick. For the past six months, most of 2005, he'd been trying to sell prefabricated homes, but they hadn't taken off as quickly as he'd expected. Before the modular units, it had been Japanese kitchen knives, which he'd bought below wholesale, from an importer facing bankruptcy, and tried to sell to housewives. He still had sixty in slim wooden boxes in the hallway. Before cutlery, it had been obscure bones, most of which he'd bought in Mexico and smuggled across the border for resale as juju, or fetishes, to fortune-tellers and kooks, as far as I could tell. He'd participated in an archaeological dig in Mexico years ago and claimed to have smuggled Aztec jawbones into California for a professor. He said he carried stingray barbs, python vertebrae, and coon bones, but I never trusted what was in the cardboard boxes stacked in the corner of his room. Once, when he was away, I opened a box, expecting to find human-like tibias or femurs, but the bones I felt were thin and brittle, gritty, like whittled chunks of chalk.

This was soon after we'd moved in together, Isa, Patrick, and I. When they were applying to be foster parents, he hid the boxes from the people at Children and Family Services and said he was an underemployed cook, which was true; he's the best cook I've ever known. He'd studied to be a chef somewhere back East or in the South—he was always vague about where. Before Isa and I met him, he worked in some top kitchens in L.A., but he could never keep that kind of job, where he had to get along with lots of people in a crowded space and submit to a chain of command. He started doing speed and blow to stay on top of things. And when he was high, he couldn't stop his mouth. He would make snide remarks that undermined the head chef or humiliated his coworkers. That's what he told us at Channel House.

As I look back now, I sometimes wonder: if Patrick had been able to run his own kitchen—if he hadn't stumbled into the consequences of his own youth—then maybe he'd be a more generous man.

But I doubt it.

"Of course I have faith in you," Isa said to him, her voice thicker than before. "But I'm not talking about business. I'm talking about Daddy."

"Sweetie, this is what he wants," Patrick said, almost pleading. "Something handmade. Wooden. You told me so yourself."

Their voices came from the kitchen, from near the table. I heard no footsteps; no one seemed to be moving or acknowledging Ray and me in the doorway.

"I ain't going to Florida," Devon declared from the opposite direction, from the family room, somewhere beyond the couch. "With or without that thing."

What thing? I wondered. What had Patrick taken up now? I took a step past Ray along the seam between the living room and kitchen.

"Let's see what Kevin thinks," Isa said, as if I'd just appeared.

"Kevin," Patrick said sarcastically. "Now there's business savvy."

"Why can't I stay home with Kevin?" Devon complained, trying to sound tough but coming off as whiny. "I'm off probation. I passed every class last year. I hooked myself a job. You guys treat me like a sucker." At sixteen years old, he was taller than any of us, six foot two, and bony at the elbows but filling out his biceps. "Black as Mississippi mud," Patrick had told me several times, though how would I know that color?

As I took off my hat, a hand touched my arm, startling me. Then I smelled Isa's perfume. Woody. Like sweet wine.

Sometimes I hear people's steps, sometimes not, depending on the room, the footwear, and my focus. Ray was easy to decipher, with his quick, fidgeting steps. Devon usually dragged his feet, shuffling in long strides, as if the bother exceeded the effort—unless he was wearing flip-flops, and then he slapped the floor, which gave the same long strides a sense of urgency. Patrick's pace I couldn't predict: brisk and controlled one moment, silent and cunning the next. When Isa was wearing her wedge sandals or boots, she walked with soft thuds I liked to hear. But when she was barefoot, she could slip up on me, like Patrick could, but with different effect.

Ray leaned toward Isa as she hugged him with a flourish. I'd always loved that about her, the way she could dote and incite with a touch. But I pulled away, not trusting my reactions. She tugged me toward her and gave me a quick hug, brushing her side into me, setting off tingles. I couldn't help it; my head drifted as I thought of my lost job. Would I ever be able to sustain myself? Would I always be dependent?

"What's the matter?" she said. "What happened to you?"

I collected myself, stiffening. "Nothing. What? Nothing. What are you guys talking about?"

Ray swept by me, disappearing. Was he still holding Charlie? I closed the front door.

"You never listen to me!" Devon complained. "I ain't going!"

"You raise your voice once more . . ." Patrick said, letting his threat hang there.

Patrick was always threatening without filling in the blanks, so he couldn't be held accountable. He called himself a Christian Libertarian; I don't know if he invented the term or got it from somewhere, but it gave him a belief system (after the recovery home, anyway) that was open and rigid at the same time. As a Libertarian, he believed in maximum freedom—under God, which was the Christian side of the equation. Take it or leave it; it's up to you whether you want to be saved, but don't try to butt in on Patrick's freedoms. For him, free choice was the right of all Americans to make their own stupid mistakes and be damned to Hell if they didn't correct their ways. That was the genius of the American Christ.

Yet he expected us to do as he said. He loved to talk about smuggling of all kinds, ripping off the government, treating neighbors with respect so long as they stayed on their side of the fence, obeying the laws that mattered, patrolling the borders of this great country, and leaving a better world than you inherited. He wasn't muscular so much as solid. He had a shotgun locked in his closet. I'd felt the threat of his grip on my arm plenty of times. I still think of him as sinew and gristle.

Isa, on the other hand, was a dream I couldn't make real and couldn't quite get over. In the doorway, she took my hat from my hand. I meant to touch the small of her back but found her hip instead so that half my hand felt her soft skin, the other half touched her belt and hip huggers. I knew I shouldn't, but I couldn't help myself: I dipped two fingers just beneath the waistline of her jeans, aware of Patrick in the kitchen. Could he see? Was he looking at his wife? It had been over a year since I'd touched her like that, and I'd never done it in front of him. I chided myself even as I relished the touch of her warm skin. Hadn't she just brushed her body into mine? Why couldn't I be affectionate and flippant too, particularly now, after losing my job?

"You can't make me go," Devon muttered in a low voice that was plenty defiant. "I'm staying with Kevin."

Back then I knew Devon better than Ray, even though Ray had lived with us a month longer. I liked playing guessing games with Ray and listening to the pitter-patter of his steps; I helped put him to bed almost every night. But he was reluctant to say much, so I gave him space. People told me he had a winning smile.

Devon, on the other hand, was a verbal jouster who liked to go at it, which played to my available senses. When he first came to us, he kept to himself—who wouldn't with strangers? He grunted when spoken to, but that was the same as most teenaged boys I'd been around. As soon as he began opening up, his attitude got under Patrick's skin, but it didn't bother me, though I'll admit I never saw his grimaces or gestures. He started calling me Cowboy Bob, but that didn't get a rise out of me. "Watch out for my shit-kickers," I told him, smiling and raising my boot. "They have a mind of their own."

After a couple of months, I could tell I unsettled his preconceptions. I wasn't a threat, for one thing, or an authority figure. Yet I wasn't a kid either. I had a marginal status of my own. And I was a reporter—he respected that. He started saying I had mad skills getting around. "That shit's harder than being black," he admitted.

"What color are you again?" I said.

He didn't respond right away. Then he said, "People see you. You got that white cracker thing going even if you can't see it. It's like a virus, the way it spreads. Gets in everything." He could be perceptive and articulate that way. All year, in his school essays, I tried to help him draw that out, when he would let me.

Devon had been with other families before he lived with us. His mom had been sent to minimum security at Chino for identity theft, and she had two more years to serve. He hated but had never known his father—a white guy who'd screwed his mom and left them both. About a year and a half ago, when he was a skinny fifteen-year-old, he'd tried to take on a football linesman at school who had called his mom a whore. The white kid beat the shit out of Devon, giving him a black eye and a bruised rib. But it was Devon who got busted. A blunt—a cigar hollowed out and filled with weed—fell out of his shirt pocket during the fight. Those few grams on school grounds, his testy demeanor, and a host of priors sent him to Juvenile Camp for six months.

When he came to us, he was transferred to Monterey High, a continuation school. In the second semester—the recent spring—an English teacher found that if he let Devon read about rebels and strife, he'd stop challenging everything under the sun and focus on the readings, which sparked other kids' interest. Devon devoured *The Autobiography of Malcolm X, One Flew over the Cuckoo's Nest,* and *On the Road.* I listen to books all the time. When I was a kid, cassette tapes from the library saved me—mysteries at first and then anything I could find, as long as it had a story that took me places. Sometimes Devon and I would sit and talk—"choppin' it up," he called it. We'd start with whatever he was reading and end up arguing about politics or race or religion. He began to figure out how to come around the other side of an argument instead of attacking full tilt all the time. But when he got backed into a corner, he liked the shock of a personal affront. "You are one well-read ex-addict," he told me once, "if you count shit like books on tape."

Those quips pissed off a lot of people, but they made me smile. They endeared him to me, and I often found myself wanting to protect him—tough as he pretended to be—from Patrick's quick tongue and oddball needs.

Still standing in the doorway with my hand on Isa's hip, I heard from the kitchen the crisp sound of a page turning. Patrick sometimes read at the kitchen table, arcane books about outlandish thefts from archaeological sites or the battle to secure the border. But if he was reading now, I knew it was for effect: Was it to piss off Devon? Or to feign indifference to my touching his wife? Or to hide his anger at Isa?

I swept my hand up to Isa's back just before she pulled away and I was left standing alone, without Charlie or my hat.

"It'll be good to get out of L.A.," Patrick said from the kitchen table. He probably had his back turned, his head in the book. "You'll learn something about yourself."

"Right," Devon scoffed. "From adults like you."

"Don't push me, boy," Patrick said evenly.

"Don't call me 'boy'!" Devon said slowly, mimicking Patrick's tone.

They had never come to blows, but they'd blustered plenty lately.

"Stop it, you two," Isa said.

Patrick turned another page. "You're still a boy," he said dismissively, "whether you like it or not."

"Kevin," Isa said, "come look."

"Like I can see."

"You know what I mean," she said lightly, trying to distract everyone, I knew. That was one of her blessings: her generous spirit, the way she tried to bring us all together.

I walked across the linoleum toward my room.

"Stop!" Patrick called.

The stiff toe of my boot struck, not hard but squarely, against something heavy. Thank goodness for my dumb-ass boots, I thought. My foot didn't hurt at all.

Devon laughed.

"What the hell!" Patrick said. His chair scraped on the floor. "I bet you chipped it."

I leaned down, reaching. It was a massive box of some kind. Almost up to my waist. Wooden. With carved patterns on the side.

"Look at that smudge from your boot," Patrick said.

"What is it?" I said.

"A coffin," Devon said sarcastically. "He wants to take this dog to Florida."

"Look at the carvings!" Patrick said. "One of a kind. Hand-carved maple. Her dad said he wants something different. Not those ready-made boxes that cost a mint and have shiny handles." He spoke rapidly, the excitement real.

"Kevin," she said, "don't you think it's morbid to take it to Daddy?"

I crouched and felt along one side: varnish or lacquer made the surface slick and smooth. My fingers traced a raised cross with intricate embedded patterns of lines and angles. Its juncture was encircled by a halo. Along the edges of the cross, the wood was chiseled away like little waves.

"Wow," I said.

"How much did it cost?" Isa asked. "You promised not to use the credit card anymore."

"That's the beauty," Patrick said. "His estate will pay for it. We're going to make money on this baby. We can't lose."

Beyond the cross, I touched a horizontal figure carved in relief, wings outstretched, feet protruding from a flowing frock, a long trumpet from its mouth. "An angel," I said. I brought my fingers over her slowly, across the feathers of her wings and the folds of her frock. Her hair blew back as if in a breeze. Her eyes laughed, her cheeks full from puffing the trumpet. I liked that; she felt alive.

"I'm going to sell them to funeral parlors," he said. "People are going to love these babies. And I've got the sole franchise."

My fingers came across Ray's small hands; he was feeling the casket too. I thought about his mother, gone less than a year: Had he seen her in a coffin? As I gripped his hand softly, he pulled away like in the game we sometimes played—grabbing hands at the kitchen table. Or was he upset? I couldn't tell.

"What's inside?" Ray said.

Patrick ignored him. "What do you think, Kevin?" He wanted my approval.

Past the angel, there was a second cross. Symmetrical. An angel in the center, with an ornate cross on either side of her. "Where'd you get it?" I asked.

"An old carpenter in the San Gabriel Mountains. You should've seen all the coffins he had lying around. Like a museum. And sculptures and weird old things. He even had bones."

"Stop it!" Isa said. "You're not selling bones again."

"It won't open," Ray said.

"There's two latches," Patrick said.

I heard two crisp snaps as the telephone rang.

"Wow!" Ray said.

"Looks like Christmas," Devon said, laughing.

"That is so cheesy," Isa said. "It's tasteless."

"That's why I love it," Patrick said. "It'll sell."

As the lid had opened, a string of pin lights that were nestled in the seams of the fabric had flashed on inside the coffin. But I didn't know that then. I thought they were talking about the material.

The phone rang again.

I felt the cushioned fabric inside. Satin. Soft as clouds. My fingers brushed against Ray's hands, which flitted about, but I didn't feel the pin lights.

"Fine," Isa said. "Sell them around here. We're not driving this to Florida." Her voice shifted to her phone politeness: "Hello?"

"The carvings feel great," I said to Patrick, "but you can't take this to her dad. It's rotten luck. He's not dead yet."

"What the hell do you know?" he said.

"Quiet!" Isa boomed. "It's Daddy!" Her voice turned to sugar: "Don't say that, Daddy. You'll be fine."

We could all hear the tinny voice of the old man raving: "The steroids they've got me on. Plugged up. Jesus!"

"We'll be there soon," Isa said. Her voice was thin now, precarious.

"It'll be too late!" he said. "You're always too late, Isa."

What a bastard, I thought.

"We got you a casket like you wanted," she offered. "It's beautiful."

"I won't have those metal boxes!" he said. "I need something that rots, goddamn it. I'm going to buy it myself."

"It's handmade, Daddy," Isa said. "Wooden. Daddy!" After a moment, I realized she was sniffling. "Why does he always hang up?" she said.

Patrick didn't move; I could hear him breathing next to me. I wanted to walk over and hold her, but how could I, with him there? Instead I felt with my foot for the bulge in the kitchen linoleum. Then I beelined to my room and shut the door on them all.

Over the next week and a half, I kept up the facade of working for the newspaper, which was easier than I had expected in a house of distractions. Most of the time, Ray stayed at the Boys and Girls Club a few blocks away, where he could play basketball and air hockey with kids his age. Patrick was either on the phone or making the rounds to funeral parlors in Betsy, his old Taurus wagon, with the foot end of the casket sticking out the back. For several days, he tried to sell his one-of-a-kind coffins; then he tried to place them on consignment. He found the funeral industry to be a tight bunch.

Devon slept mornings; most afternoons, he worked at Target, his summer job. At night, he started pleading with me to run off with him. "Come on," he said in the bathroom as I was brushing my teeth one night. "You're sick of living here too." For months he'd been borrowing my laptop and fooling around on the Internet, meeting people online through Friendster and Myspace. He wanted to run with me to San Francisco, San Diego, or Las Vegas—or wherever his online friends claimed to live. Ray's quick footsteps found their way along the edge of the room.

I didn't tell Devon it was a dumb idea. Or that I'd get arrested for kidnapping. I rinsed my mouth and put my toothbrush on my shelf. "Go to Florida," I said. "You'll come back here, and before you know it, you'll have your high school diploma. You'll find out soon enough how hard it is to be on your own."

"I ain't going to Florida," he said.

"Quit using 'ain't.' You might like Florida."

"I'm down with Florida; it ain't that," he said. "It's getting cooped up with this family." He shuffled into the hallway and stopped. "One day you'll wake up, and I'll be gone. You too, Beavis Butthead."

"I'm not Beavis Butthead," Ray said from the hallway.

During those weeks, Isa would go off to bed with Patrick, but in the middle of the night, she'd slip from the back room around to the kitchen. I wasn't sleeping well either, so when I heard a chair scrape on the linoleum, I'd get up, make tea, and sit with her, both of us hunched over the table. As everyone else slept, she would grip my hand, telling me how much she needed a listener; why couldn't Patrick listen like I could? When she clutched my palm against her belly, my fingers tingled from her warmth. I breathed the salty sweetness of her skin.

Sometimes her hands trembled, and we sat in silence. Other times she raved in whispers about owing her life to Daddy—he'd saved her so often when she'd been lost. She told me stories about growing up in Florida—being spied on by her younger brother, doing art projects with her mom, and being groped at the real estate office by Daddy's partner. Then she'd ramble and fret about wanting to bring Daddy peace. Her anxieties seemed minor compared with her depression the winter before, when she hadn't gotten out of bed for two weeks. She lay unresponsive that time, sullen, as I tried to get her to sit up and drink tea or eat a cracker. I wanted to help her this time too; I knew Patrick didn't have the patience.

I met Isa almost two years ago, when I came to Channel House, and I got to know Patrick about a month later, when he was admitted. I had just turned twenty-six, was about ten years younger than they were, and was the youngest person there. I first heard the lilt of Isa's voice in group counseling, but I first spoke with her in a hallway, where she stopped me with a soft hand on my arm. I knew who it was before she spoke; back then she wore a cheap fragrance several traces too sweet.

I turned my face to hide my scar.

"You don't have to be shy with me," she said, bringing my chin forward with her hand. "You're quite striking." I drew her hand away from my chin because I wanted to touch her fingers, which were thin and long, with fingernails bitten too short. Her palm was soft.

"Do you know me?" she said.

"Isa," I said.

She brushed full into me, enlivening my chest with her breasts before stepping back. "You're cute when you blush. Do you know what I look like?"

I savored the lilt in her voice and her friendly laugh, but I figured she was playing to an audience, so I waited for the chuckles of others.

There were none. No sounds of people at all. But still I couldn't let myself relax. "Is that important," I said, "how you look?"

"You're right," she said. "It's more important how we feel." She lifted my hand to her face and dragged my fingers through her hair. She let me feel her long neck and the way her throat trembled as she laughed. She traced my hand along her shoulders, arms, and thighs. Her skirt clung to my fingers as if the material were on my hand instead of her hips. My fingertips tingled, and my breathing quickened. She had on a halter top that was open in back and held her breasts like pendulums; I knew because she traced my fingers along her stomach and up under the fullness so pliable and resistant through the thin cotton—all of which made me grin like a goof.

"You're cute," she said again, as if surprised. "You don't get to see anything; you might as well touch." The way she laughed made me feel included.

I was touching the roundness of her hips when footsteps approached. "None of that at the House," a counselor said. "There's plenty of time after you're clean. After you respect each other. After your graduation."

"I respect him already," Isa said. "Do you respect me?"

"I do respect you," I said.

"You know what I'm talking about," the counselor said.

Everybody at Channel House loved Isa; all the men did anyway. She liked to command attention by blustering into rooms. She and Patrick were drawn to each other as soon as they met; even I could tell. Patrick was a lot more fun back then, always making jokes. He was also more open about himself, but that's the nature of a therapeutic community. When we were making moral inventories of ourselves—the fourth step—he admitted that he was weakest when he pretended to be strong. He chronicled the boozed-up fights he'd gotten into over nothing, the jobs he'd lost because of coke, the insults he'd thrown at people he loved. That was why he got tweaked all the time, he said, because it allowed him to forget his own mistakes and believe that everybody else was fucked up, not him. Isa loved that kind of honesty. She flirted and put him off, and he treated her like she was the world. He handled me like a kid brother, bringing me in on his secrets; he didn't compete with me like he did with everybody else.

Isa and I graduated about six weeks before Patrick did. We got a place together, the two of us, a rental I called a deficiency because it was so small. Ever since I'd graduated from college, Mom and Dad had been badgering me to get a caregiver, someone to at least read my mail and help me pay my bills. I had a settlement from my accident—my blinding when I was a child—that my parents had managed when I was growing up. They got control of it again after my freefall in San Francisco, where I lived for just over two years—long enough to lose my job and my apartment. During the last six months, I lived on Casey's couch and in the back of TBone's van. They watched my back, and we all used my money. After Casey died, Dad had to fly out, bail me out of jail, and drive me down to Channel House in Burbank. When I graduated from the recovery home and still refused to move back to Greeley, Colorado, they got this advice from everyone: don't give a crackhead any money. They insisted on paying my bills directly.

So I set up Isa to be my caregiver, and we invented a clean history for her. She had to interview with my parents by phone, but they took to her like everybody else did. They started sending her my monthly checks for room and board, plus a hundred dollars for helping me—as if I needed her help. The payments roughly equaled the interest from my account; I had to find my own income to purchase anything else. Mom flew from Colorado once to check on things, which I resented because it was obvious that she didn't trust me. Or Dad didn't. We had to hide Isa's stuff and pretend she lived elsewhere. It made me feel like a kid.

Isa got a job waiting tables right away, but I couldn't find work. I'd majored in journalism in college, and I'd written pieces of my life story at Channel House—as part of my moral inventory. I'd always liked writing, so I started doing street interviews along Hollywood and Sunset Boulevards, drawing from my experiences in San Francisco. I wrote several profiles of street characters, and the editor of the community paper printed one. When I came home and put that money on the table—it wasn't much, but it was something—it was like we were together, Isa and I. I would change in the bathroom and sleep on the couch, but she could get dressed anywhere. She'd say, "It's too hot for clothes," or "All my panties are in the wash, so I'm getting some air." We went to N.A. meetings every day, and that was when she started trying out churches and born-again revivals. She needed something, she said. Something to believe in. I'd hear her pull on a dress and take it back off, and I'd catch a drift of her hair just shampooed as she walked to the mirror. I love the swish of clothing against skin.

"How's this look?" she'd say.

"It makes you look thin," I'd say, or "I like the green one."

"There isn't a green one," she'd say. "Look at you cultivating your trousers. You better go in the bathroom and elongate."

On days when I was glum, she'd sing, "What can you see, Kevin? What can you see?" and I'd tell her things to lighten our mood: "I see a rose blossom opening its folds. I see a fog bank shrouding the moonlight. I see a butterfly unable to land." They were visions, mostly, things I'd listened to in books and couldn't quite picture.

Sometimes she'd let me massage her, unless I got fresh with my hands, which she'd slap away. "You're my temptation," she'd say. "But you know I'm waiting for Patrick. We need to get you a girl." I had girl-friends in college, I told her, and a few one-nighters when I lived in San Francisco. But she knew I hadn't been with anyone since.

During those nights at the kitchen table—with Isa obsessing about her dad and me feeling weak after losing my job—my affection for her began to simmer again. I'd succeeded in pulling away from her about the same time Ray and Devon had come to live with us, but now I felt myself sliding back. I told myself I didn't love her even as I hungered for her verve and lack of restraint. I knew she was married and it was hope-less, but I was a fool. When Isa quivered and leaned against me, I tried not to feel the wisp of her hair on my neck or the prick of her fingernails on my skin. I tried not to sip the scent of bath soap mixed with perspira-tion on her arms. I did press my fingers against the silver cross on her breastbone, letting my hand touch the swell of her breasts. I massaged the tense spots along her shoulders and neck. I rubbed her forehead and temples. All to calm her, I told myself, not to caress her skin. She needed me.

As she worried and fussed, I excused her childish tone and her dips into born-again language. "With God's grace," she whispered, "I'm go-ing to bring Daddy the mercy of Jesus to heal his judgmental nature. When people are tired of being broken and sick, Kevin, they're ready for the spirit of God." I knew lots of people who'd come out of recovery clinging to faith—even Patrick had his version. If God could dampen her bipolar swings, I thought, so be it.

It never occurred to me, in the midst of my compassion, that I was the one wracked with self-deception. I was always on the verge of letting her know about my job, but the moment never seemed right. I told myself I could live with Isa without loving her, even while pretending I could love her without showing it.

From those frustrating nights, I felt hungover during the days, and I grew more anxious about being left in the empty house as the day neared for them to drive to Florida. I could cook and care for myself; it wasn't that. I was worried about keeping myself from relapse, particularly since I didn't have a job. Each day my freelance work took me to avenues where people were using all the time. The more I spoke with street performers and the homeless, gaining their confidence for the interviews I would need for my articles, the more difficult it became to refuse their offers of nips and tokes. I felt my resolve slipping, so I attended daily N.A. meetings again.

I drafted two articles within ten days of being laid off: one about a sax player who'd lost everything in a fire and another about a seventeen-year-old girl from Indiana who'd run away to Hollywood and couldn't go back home. I didn't like either story; they offered only darkness. But I called the editor during that second week and left a message every day for three days, telling him I had the stories he wanted. He never returned my calls. On the fourth day, the afternoon of my twenty-eighth birthday, I called Cameron, the city reporter, who told me the editor wasn't taking any freelance.

I heard myself thanking him. When I hung up, I threw my cell phone across my room into the wall.

The front doorbell rang. After a moment, it rang again.

"Get the damn door!" Patrick yelled from the kitchen.

"You get it!" Devon called from somewhere else.

Tossing on my bed, I convinced myself I was glad everybody was leaving for Florida the next day. Think of the quiet; I'd have two weeks to decompress from their stupid dramas. I should have moved out months ago, I told myself. What the hell had I been thinking, letting myself get sucked in by Isa's needs again?

When the noises and smells from the kitchen could no longer be ignored, I resented in advance the cheap birthday card that Isa and the others would give me. The cake. The stupid song. If they remembered my birthday at all.

After a while, the kitchen quieted abruptly; feet shuffled outside my room. Then they banged at my door, laughing. I turned away on the bed, facing the wall, gripping my hands into fists. They came in uninvited, singing "Happy Birthday" out of tune, all except Isa, whose melodic voice I resented all the more. Devon poked my ribs, trying to make me laugh. I gritted my teeth. Ray scampered onto the bed.

"Get up!" Isa said.

I put on my dark glasses and faced them.

Ray hung around my neck, hugging me, bringing out a quick smile despite myself. They laid boxes all over my bed, startling me. I let myself breathe.

"Look at your clothes," Isa said. "You never buy anything."

Ray helped me open each box. They made me stand up and try on four shirts, including a seersucker that caught the hairs of my chest.

"Where'd you get the money?" I protested, but they ignored me.

"No more Cowboy Bob," Devon said. He tugged me down on the bed, and I let them pull off my socks, though I pretended to struggle when they tugged at my jeans. They had me stand in my boxers so I could try on two pairs of baggy shorts that reached below my knees.

"Volcom," Ray said.

"Sounds like a planet," I said, though I knew it was surfwear. I couldn't help smiling.

"Pull them down low," Devon said, "like this. Show the top of your boxers."

As if I didn't know the style.

"I got you some new boxers with little surfer men," Isa said with a friendly laugh. "But you have to try those on yourself."

"These shorts are way too big," I complained.

"They're perfect," Isa said.

They showed me how I could fit Charlie, folded, into the wide pockets of the shorts, though he protruded out the top. They had me sit on the bed so they could put sandals on my feet.

"Huaraches," Ray said.

"They're Mexican," Patrick said.

"Warachas," I said.

"Huaraches," Ray corrected.

Devon put a cheap straw fedora on my head that was a touch big. I pulled the front brim down to hide my scar, and he lifted it back up, at an angle.

"There," he said. "That looks better."

I pulled it back down.

I grew up wearing Western gear in Colorado. I gave it up for army boots and black shirts when I started smoking weed in high school. About two years ago, when Dad bailed me out of jail in San Francisco, he didn't lecture me about how bad I smelled or how skinny I was. He didn't ask how I'd sunk so low so fast. We didn't talk about what drugs I'd used or how long I'd been on the streets. He didn't know how to talk about that stuff. He called ahead and got me into Channel House in Burbank. When he drove me down from San Francisco, we stopped along the way and he bought new clothes for me: cowboy boots and hat, as if I were still in middle school.

In my cramped room, I turned around in my new clothes and walked a few paces, feeling exposed without my Western boots, my toes unprotected from chair legs. And I missed my Bandit with its stiff Cattleman crown; I hated bumping my head. But my new clothes were cooler and more comfortable. I held up my arms and stamped my feet. I liked the feel.

"He looks like a tourist," Isa said, laughing.

"We should have gotten you Ray-Bans," Devon said. "You still look like a geek in those big glasses."

I smiled. "I don't know what to say," I said. "Thank you."

"And this just came," Isa said. "It's from your parents." Ray helped me open the box. We reached in and pulled away the Styrofoam.

"What the hell is that?" Patrick said.

It was a Braille note-taker. Small, compact, perfect. Shaped like a large book but much lighter. Not quite as long as a regular keyboard. For almost a year, I'd been trying to convince my parents to buy me one from my own account; they cost over four thousand bucks. There were eight keys on top, plus a spacebar and some function keys. Along the front, beneath my wrists as I rested my fingers on the keyboard, was a one-line display where refreshable Braille dots would pop up in a row so that I could read what my fingers had just keyed in. No monitor needed. For the first time in my life, I could take notes without turning on a laptop. I could write from and edit my notes. I could read quietly. I could feel every comma and punctuation mark.

"I spoke with your mom a few weeks ago," Isa said. "I told her this was the one you wanted."

The irony suddenly overwhelmed me. To receive this—after losing my job as a reporter, after being rejected as a freelancer—was too much. I had to turn away—not to hide my scar but to wipe my face.

"Tell him," Ray said, excited. I pulled Ray to me and hugged him.

"We want you to come to Florida," Isa said.

Not a chance, I thought. No way.

"We know about your job," she said. "There's no reason for you to stay."

I was pissed suddenly—that they'd pried into my life. What right did they have? And I was insulted that they'd kept their snooping from me.

"I saw you hanging out on Sunset with those bums," Patrick said.

"I wasn't hanging out," I said. "That's my beat!"

"I called the paper," Isa said. "They said you didn't work there anymore."

"Come on," Ray said.

"I'll go if you go," Devon said.

Isa sat on the bed and hugged me, but I wasn't pulled in. Where would I sit in the car—in the backseat with the kids? What if I sat next to Isa all day, feeling her thigh against mine, her hand on my leg, with all of them in the car? I imagined Patrick always controlling where we stopped, what we ate, and when we went to the bathroom. "I need some downtime," I said. "This'll be a good trip for the four of you."

"I ain't going, then," Devon said. "You already know what I'm going to do. Just don't be surprised."

"Let's eat," Patrick said, ignoring him.

"You're coming!" Isa said. "We're not leaving without you."

They paraded me to the kitchen, where Patrick served my favorite meal, chicken and yellow rice, which made me imagine Mom back in Colorado; she always gave me an early taste on a hot wooden spoon.

"I'm starving," Devon said. He was always eating; he'd grown three inches in his nine months with us.

We dipped our heads as Isa thanked Jesus for the food we were about to eat and for keeping Daddy well in Florida until she got there in time to save him, please Lord, as he'd saved her so many times, amen.

All through dinner, Ray asked questions about the trip. Patrick described cactus standing like sentries in Arizona. Thunderstorms rolling across New Mexico mesas. The friendly people in Louisiana. The unhurried sweep of the Mississippi.

"What about Texas?" I said. As a kid, I'd had a wooden puzzle of all the states. I could name the capital of each one.

"And Alabama," Isa said. I'd forgotten that Alabama touched the Gulf.

"We're going to blast through Texas at night," Patrick said. "You won't even see it."

"Wait until you float in the Gulf in Pensacola," Isa said. "There's so much salt it holds you up like a cork. And it's so warm, when you float in that water, it's like the womb again. Everything feels right."

Her eagerness surprised me; she hated the beach in California, claimed the water was too cold.

"Of course it feels like a womb," Patrick said. "It's where you were born."

"She was born in the Gulf?" Devon quipped.

"We're all born in a gulf," Patrick said.

He brought out homemade chocolate mousse for dessert, with three candles that I had to blow out before they sank.

The chocolate astonished my mouth.

"Why's it called 'mooooooose'?" Ray said, laughing.

"Look at this!" Devon said, smacking his lips. "It's as black as me."

"You're a mess," Isa laughed.

"It's the French word for foam," Patrick said.

Was he making that up? He was always so sure of himself, I never knew when to trust him.

"You should both of you go to college," Isa said. "Like Patrick."

Had he gone to college? I thought he'd gone to chef school.

"Right," Devon said, "so we can be unemployed cooks and sell coffins."

I expected Patrick to snap back, but he kept his cool.

It was I who lost perspective. In a moment of chocolate weakness, I thought about my new note-taker and pretended *that* was why I needed to join them. I imagined Patrick selling a handmade casket to Isa's dying father, the old man ranting as Isa floated in the womb of the Gulf, Devon goading the others into something rash, and Ray pitter-pattering along the edge of the fray. If I couldn't come up with some edgy articles about this family journey, I decided, then what writer was I?

THREE

The next morning I stood in the doorway in my new shorts and sandals, chilled by the dawn air and irritated at myself. Our bags were already packed in Betsy's hold, and the casket was lying atop the old wagon at a tilt, gift-wrapped inside a big tarp with plenty of duct tape. Half an hour earlier, the boys and I had helped Patrick cover the bulky box as it lay on the driveway. I didn't like the idea of transporting the thing, but I did my part, holding a corner of the tarp against the side of the box and feeling the contours of the relief carvings. Suddenly Patrick tugged the tarp out of my hands and pushed it aside, the stiff material crinkling—a sound I always found satisfying, like popping a sheet of bubble wrap underfoot. But the abrupt noise spooked me now.

He clicked open the lid and whispered to us not to tell Isa.

Devon laughed. "I forgot about the lights."

I couldn't help reaching inside, where my hands found the string of small pin lights, growing warm, tucked into the crease of soft fabric around the base of the casket. I pulled my hands away. Jesus, I thought. Lights in a casket! And the casket for an old man not yet gone.

I'm not one for empty decorum, but there are limits that shouldn't be pushed.

"Never mind the lights," Patrick said brusquely. He brought to my hand a large canvas sack. Within it, I realized as Patrick pulled it open and I reached inside, were several zip-lock plastic bags. He opened one, and we all passed around a small, prickly bone about the length of my fingers. He's selling bones again, I thought, shaking my head. And this time from a coffin.

"Coon bone," he said, though he wouldn't tell Devon, when Devon asked, what a coon bone was, or what was in the other bags. I pretended I didn't care, but Devon took the bait, asking him who would lay down for some janky bones.

"Gamblers," Patrick said, his voice tinged with enthusiasm.

"Where we going to see gamblers?" Devon said.

"You'd be surprised."

"What do they want them for?"

"Luck."

Devon pressed him, but that was all Patrick would say.

Gamblers, I thought, trying to take it in stride. I'd never been to any of those Indian casinos.

We used half a roll of duct tape to make the tarp cling to the casket. Next we hoisted it onto Betsy's roof, careful not to bump anything. There was only one crossbar in the roof rack, the back one, so the coffin tilted forward. Patrick lashed the casket to the crossbar and sent a second rope in through the front of the back doors and around the top. He rolled towels around the two ropes to protect the wood. He tried to show Devon how to tie a trucker's hitch on the back rope and a carrick bend on the front, but Devon wasn't interested. It made me think of Dad, who'd tried to teach my brother, Larry, how to tie knots but had never bothered with me.

"That's a good tilt," Patrick said proudly. "More aerodynamic."

"Looks like shit," Devon said. "We look like hillbillies."

As we waited for Isa, I stood in the doorway, stewing about Patrick's stupid plans: Lugging a casket cross-country. With impertinent lights inside. And bones—Jesus, the bones!

But I was also annoyed with myself for being ensnared by this trip. And for breaking my cell phone the day before; now I'd have to travel without it. Deep down I must have known why I was going, yet still I clung to my delusion about writing some articles. I even made a vow, as Isa rustled in the kitchen behind me and Patrick shuffled around Betsy before me: I resolved to keep my distance from them both. I would be a reporter, a witness. I'd have to comfort Isa and suffer Patrick from time to time. But I would not get pulled into their vortex.

It's startling to me now, how good I was at self-deception.

Devon's flip-flops slapped the driveway as he approached. "Lighten up," he said, jiggling my arm. "Why you always playing the worried white boss?"

I shook my head and couldn't help but smile. "You're the one worried about how Betsy looks," I said.

"That's more like it," he said, slapping his flip-flops down the driveway. "You got to let things go."

Betsy's motor rumbled, stopped. Caught and revved. "Get in!" Patrick yelled.

Nobody got in, so far as I could tell. The pitter-patter of feet came up the driveway, and Ray leaned against my side, sleepy, so I put my arm around him, trying to feel better about going. It was about the kids, I told myself. I'd hang out with the kids.

"What's the racket!" Mr. Grenadier yelled from next door. "Turn off the damn motor!"

"Isa!" Patrick yelled. "You're waking the neighbors!"

"Let's go!" Isa declared, pushing Ray and me out of the front doorway. We hurried into the backseat as Isa locked the house and jumped into the front, filling the car with her woody perfume. Patrick gunned it, throwing my head back and spinning Betsy's tires. Isa shrieked and laughed as her door slammed shut. The old station wagon bounced into and out of the gutter and swerved to the right into the street, pushing Devon on the backseat into me and me into Ray, who was pinned against the door, all of us laughing, even Patrick, with his rapid-fire chortles sounding like a machine gun. A horn blared on our left: Caution! Welcome! How dare you!

Betsy bounced, but the casket seemed to hold.

"We're tipsy," Patrick said.

"Seatbelts on!" Isa sang. She turned and reached between the front seats to slap our knees and scratch her fingernails like rain under the hems of our shorts and along the insides of our thighs, making us squirm. I felt my penis quiver.

Patrick accelerated up the ramp to the 5.

"Ray," he said, "don't hang on the rope."

I reached forward and up toward the ceiling. The taut rope that came through the car and ran around the casket sagged with Ray's movements, then twanged as he released. The kids leaned out, the wind whistling a long ssshhhh around heads or arms. The tarp fluttered above.

"Seatbelts on!" Isa bellowed this time. They dropped back into their seats, and we tugged at the belts, poking each other with elbows.

We had to be back in two weeks for the kids' school and Isa's job. Patrick and Isa had about fifteen hundred dollars, they'd told me, enough to visit Isa's dad and see some sights on the return. But it wasn't enough for motels—about a hundred dollars a day—and it's not like we had a tent, not that you'd need more than boxers and a mosquito net along Interstate 10 in August. As part of our living arrangement, Isa was supposed to cover monthly room and board for me, but I told her I'd get my own food on the trip. After all, they'd bought my new clothes—or so I thought. I started with seven twenty-dollar bills in my wallet and ten fifty-dollar bills clipped in the zippered pocket inside my suitcase, money I'd saved from my job. I didn't have a credit card. I fold fives in half across the width; tens in half along the length; twenties in half first along the length, then across the width; and fifties in half first across the width, then along the length. It's easy to remember because five and fifties are similar, as are tens and twenties. Ones aren't folded at all.

When the sun moved to the windshield, warming my face, I knew we were heading east on the Ventura Freeway. "What a beautiful dawn," I said, though I knew the sun was higher than that in the sky.

"You can't see it," Ray said.

"What can you see, Kevin?" Isa teased. "What can you see?" I hadn't heard that phrase in a long time—not since we'd lived alone together.

"I see a road that goes to Florida," I said, smiling. "I see an old man who's happy to see us."

"You do not," Ray said.

"Sure I do. I even see his dreams. Last night he dreamed he was dying. But today he wants to go swim in the Gulf."

"For reals," Ray said.

Sometimes I joked too much for Ray, so the two of us had a deal: whenever he said "for reals," I had to tell the truth. "You already know what I see," I said, laughing.

Ray loved to imagine nothingness.

Devon groaned. "Not again."

I spoke slowly: "I see absolutely nothing. Or nothing absolutely. I see neither darkness nor light."

After a moment, Ray said, "I always see black and bits of color."

I knew he was closing his eyes.

"You have to imagine," I said. "Back before there was light, there was no darkness either. There was just the heavens and the earth." I'd never liked that first paragraph of Genesis, which says there was darkness before God summoned light. That's how I knew, even as a kid, that the Bible wasn't written by God. It was written by people with sight.

I was born with vision but lost it in an accident when I was five. After I was blinded, I still had visual memory as a child growing up, but by the time I arrived in Burbank, I could remember only a few broad sweeps: The flatness of a prairie. The expanse of a mountain dwarfed by sky. I could remember Grandpa's barn looming above me, the huge span of the open barn door, which I always associated with the rich smell of manure. Picture what you can remember from age five without the benefit of someone having snapped a photo; the few wisps I can generate are hazed in the fog of a dream, in murky shades—no colors or stark whites.

I can't remember faces, including my own. I can recognize with my fingers Mom's high forehead and quick dimples, but my mind won't connect the dots to construct a likeness. To this day, I can maneuver each turn from our street in Greeley to our front door, but I can't picture the entryway. I can identify instantly the pattern of wood grain on my chair at Mom and Dad's kitchen table, but I don't try to sketch it in my mind. For me, chairness is nonvisual; it's the feel of a seat connected to four legs and a backrest.

Many children who lose their eyesight have its memory fade in adulthood, as the brain no longer receives light sensation and begins to dedicate its functions to other senses. At least one fleeting image, however, has come back to me since I got clean and sober, so maybe part of my loss came from the drugs. As I was getting out of bed one morning in Burbank, I recalled an indistinct image of Mom turning and pausing in her bedroom, looking away from me. I sat on my bed and thought about Mom a while, but my other memories were sightless: her heels tapping across the hard porch, her fingers gripping my hand, and the smell of peach cobbler in her apron.

When I was a teenager, I still had visual dreams, but not anymore. Now my dreams are multisensory except for sight: Voices call out, but I can't scream. Or I'm naked in the commotion of a trolley that smells of Dad's hair gel. Sometimes I recognize footsteps or the clutch of a hand on my shoulder. I caress a woman's thigh as she laughs. I taste oysters. A man hits me as I reach. How do I know it's a man? He smells rough. Or maybe I recognize a place—a fluency with the coarse fabric of a cushion beneath my fingers, the smell of leather, or the sound of my boots on Mexican pavers—but I don't quite know where I am.

After we merged onto I-10, I reached over the backseat and felt for my backpack, pulling out my note-taker. The night before, when Devon had helped me test it, I'd talked to him about describing things on the trip for me: the visuals I thought I'd need. But after I told him I wasn't bringing my laptop along, he got pissed at me and refused to help with anything. "Forget it," he said. "I'm not describing a thing for you." He loved roaming the Internet and posting comments about how fucked up the world was. And he blamed me for keeping him out of touch on the trip.

"Show us your new toy," Isa said, twisting in the front seat.

After I showed them the keys for typing and the strip along the bottom for the Braille display, Ray and Devon ran their fingers along the display line.

"I haven't typed anything yet," I said.

"Ah," Devon said. "No wonder I couldn't read it."

"You can't read Braille," Ray blurted.

"It has a voice reader too," I said. "Let's try one. Tell me what the dawn looked like."

"That's over," Ray said. "It's day already."

"I know. Tell me what it did look like."

"It was orange and yellow like cotton candy."

"That's good," I said. "I like that." I pressed the keys, and Ray and Devon felt the dots pop up along the display line:

"It tickles my fingers," Ray said.

"Here," I said, "push this button. You'll hear what I typed."

"Wait," Devon said in a deep, authoritative tone. "I think I've got it." He was still feeling the Braille display, trying to convince Ray he could read it. "Something about orange and yellow and cotton candy."

Ray ignored him. He pushed the button, and the mechanical voice rushed through its monotone. "That was too fast," Ray said. "What did it say?"

I slowed the speed; he pushed the button again, and the voice intoned, "The pre-donn smog glowed like cot-ton can-dee at the fayr."

"That's not what I said," Ray complained.

"That's what writers do," Devon said. "He's conning you into describing stuff for that article about us."

"What article?" Patrick boomed. "What the hell are you writing in that thing?"

We sat silent for a moment, startled. I knew these clashes would come, but already? An hour from Burbank?

"It's not anything real," Isa said. "He's just writing stories about himself. Aren't you, Kevin?"

"Like those articles he got Devon to write?" Patrick sputtered. "About the teachers?"

For an assignment at school, Devon had wanted to write about teacher-student relations, so I'd let him borrow my digital recorder to record what teachers said in class. He got outrageous quotes: put-downs and name-callings to get kids to behave. Instead of just handing in a paper, he turned it into a newsletter for everybody to read. It caused an uproar and almost got him suspended. The teachers denied what they'd said, but then he produced the recordings. It made his newsletter a huge hit and made him want to be a reporter.

"If you put me in that thing," Patrick said, "I'll throw it in a river. I'm not kidding."

I remembered my vow to myself not to get sucked into his squalls. I took a deep breath and spoke evenly, like none of it mattered to me. "It's a journal," I lied. "I'm just writing about myself."

"That cost over four thousand dollars," Isa said. "You better not throw it in a river. He'll walk out. His parents will sue us."

"Look how you got him in trouble," Devon whispered across me to Ray.

"I did not," Ray said. "You did."

"Maybe he should walk out. He can take care of himself."

"Of course he can," Isa said. "But this setup is good for everybody."

I felt like a kid, the way they were talking as if I weren't there.

"Listen to me, Kevin," Patrick said loudly and slowly. I figured he was looking at me, glancing over his shoulder or in the rearview mirror; I was sitting in the middle of the backseat. I took off my dark glasses and faced straight ahead so he could see where the sweeper wire had etched an *S* across my crumpled eyebrow, down through my eyelid, and into my cheek. I'd never excelled at pressing myself on others, but over the past year, as Patrick had become more controlling, I'd found an approach that allowed me to hold my own: I would remind him one way or another that I'd already been cut to the core and survived.

"Parents or no parents," he said, "money or no money. If I find you're writing about me, that thing's going out the window. Or you're going out the window, and I'll sell it."

"It's not about you," Devon said.

Patrick swerved onto the shoulder, throwing us all to the left and then forward into our seatbelts as he braked and Betsy kicked rocks and dust into the dry heat of California's summer. The car slid to a stop and everybody was breathing hard and a cloud of dust enveloped us and whirled in through the windows, smelling like tires and sweat and asphalt, making me sneeze once, then again, into my hand to keep the mucus off my four-thousand-dollar chronicler. Patrick twisted in his seat—the vinyl creaking—and spoke across me into Devon's face, cars whizzing past us on the freeway: "How the hell would you know?" He waited a full half minute to let that sink in, Devon fidgeting beside me, knowing better than to mutter a word, the dust settling as an acrid taste in my mouth. Ray sat as still as stone on my left. "You think I'm an idiot doesn't know you and him sat up all last night figuring out how to download between that thing and his laptop? Blind man can't write on his own."

My jaw clenched. My breathing stopped. "Fuck you!" I wanted to say. I wanted to reach over the seat and grip him by the throat. But I suppressed all that. I kept my vow; I remained quiet. I would not let him get to me. Not already.

"You listen good, Devon," Patrick said. "Not everything's on the up-and-up. Somebody with your record ought to know not to write stuff down. Don't give them anything to pin on you. Don't show your tracks. Tell it by word of mouth. With your history and the color of your skin, you better learn that and learn it well. You'll know soon enough how fast you can lose what you've got."

What a paranoid son of a bitch, I thought. I forced myself to breathe.

"And you listen, Kevin." He spoke so close I could smell his sour face and the dank coffee from his gums. "You'll have to get your own ride in the middle of the damn desert if I find you've got a hand in writing about me." He turned away, sitting squarely in his seat. "And put your glasses on. It's not right to have to look at a man without an eyeball."

I faced straight ahead at the rearview mirror, defying him to look. And I thought, I'm going to focus the damn articles on him. Just to spite him.

Isa got us back on the highway with her effervescent and disabling goodwill. She reached back between the seats, tapping on the note-taker with her finger: my cue to slip it into my backpack.

Looking back, I don't mind so much that Patrick insulted me. But I'm still pissed at myself—my blood boils—for not standing up for Devon right there. Maybe I could have brought things to a head a lot earlier.

All across the desert, Betsy's air conditioning kept shutting off, roasting us, and then coming back on, only to bake us again later. The radio had been torn out by a thief the year before, leaving a hole in the dash. Without music, there was no escape. Searing winds blew the car around and shifted the casket on top. Twice, one of the towels above flapped and fluttered; Patrick cursed, pulled off the freeway into the shade of a gas station, and fiddled with the ropes, which were stretching in the heat. Each time we stopped, we would pile out and dawdle at the back of the minimart in the coolness of open refrigerators until the clerk told us to buy a soda or close the damn doors. I loved my huaraches and shorts and couldn't imagine wearing jeans and boots.

When I was six years old, after I got out of the hospital and my body started to heal, I wore Western boots and a hat because I loved being a cowboy, not to protect my toes and head. I had visual memory then, of course, and I was intrepid in our neighborhood. I used a hockey stick to get around, dragging it against fences and along the ground like any kid would. I didn't care if I banged my shins. The houses were packed pretty tightly. It was second nature for me to learn the dips and ledges in sidewalks, the location of a tree trunk or a bush near a friend's yard, the contours and length of his driveway, and whether it was two or three steps up to the door. I knew all that before I knew anything about sweeping with a cane. "Hey, cowboy!" Dad would call out. The cowboy with the hockey stick, that was me.

When I started school, a year late because of the accident, Dad wanted me to go to Cameron Elementary like other kids; he didn't want me surrounded by blind children in a special school. That summer before my first school year, Mom and Dad would argue after I was supposed to be asleep, but sometimes I would lurk in the hallway, listening.

"He gets around fine!" I remember Dad saying. "He might as well get his licks now."

"You don't see him all day, by himself."

"You watch," Dad said. "He'll come back helpless and feeling like a misfit."

A few days after my seventh birthday, Mom drove me three hours south to a school for the deaf and blind, and I hated it before I got there.

For a bunkmate, I was paired with Matthew, an eight-year-old who could see billowing clouds of color in a world that moved: to him, our bunk bed keeled like a boat, parked cars loomed from fog, people floated like ghosts. I got the top bunk because he was afraid to go up there. On the first night, he cried, missing his mother, so I climbed down and got into bed with him, comforting him, allowing us both to sleep. The next morning, he pushed me aside in the bathroom. "You can't see as well as I can," he said.

I convinced myself that I hated blind people. In the second week, my dessert started to disappear off my tray as I was eating. After a few days, I learned to put my cookie or brownie in my pocket as soon as I got it. And by the end of the third week, I learned the shuffle of his step and would slap his hand as soon as he came around. "You're getting smarter," he said. "My name's Charlie. When I was new, a kid did that to me. Taught me how to listen."

Charlie was a couple years older than I was. He could see splinters and shards of objects in the corners of his eyes, and he helped teach me the real way to cane, sweeping back and forth: don't tap, touch. It was easy for me to coordinate my feet with the sweeping. I already knew how to listen for the echoes of my own footsteps on walls and overhanging roofs; that was another benefit to cowboy boots, the hard heels and soles. One day, as we were walking along the periphery of the school grounds, he offered to take me around the block.

I paused, of course—going across the street was against the rules.

"Get out of Braille Jail as often as you can," he said. "Otherwise you'll always be blind." He pushed the button at the traffic signal, and when the tune came on, we walked slowly across, our canes outstretched. My heart was in my throat, but I learned to relax. He explained how he created a tactile map inside his head every time he went anywhere. "Only it's not a map," he said. "It's life size. And you fill it in with sounds and touches as you go, so you can always get home. Feel this: that street curb. That's when you turn right. Feel the wind? It's coming from behind. Hear that car going by? That means we're heading along the sidewalk fine." We turned at another street. "Now the sun's on your face."

We were almost back to the crosswalk when bicycles clattered from behind and skidded in front, stopping us. Maybe two or three bikes.

"Look," a kid said, "it's the freak show."

Charlie grabbed my elbow, and we caned around them quickly. They zoomed by us laughing, slapping me hard on the shoulder.

"Hey!" a kid said, his voice rough.

"What a wimp you are!" another one said, his pitch higher. "You gonna let him do that?"

"I'm gonna beat his ass," the first kid said.

"I got him with my stick," Charlie whispered to me. He was the first person I knew who called it a stick.

The bikes skidded out ahead and started rattling back toward us.

"Here's the crosswalk," Charlie said. I heard him hit the button. Then he pushed me behind the pole and I prayed for the sound of that song as we huddled together, waiting for the bikes. I didn't hear any cars. I decided we should run for it: dash across the street to the safety of the school. But I was afraid of moving and of standing still. I didn't know what to do. As I faltered, the first bike was upon us. I tensed and prepared to jump into the street. I felt my friend lunge away from the road just as the bike approached. The bicycle crashed: bam! A kid yelled.

"Charlie!" I said, panicking.

The other bike crashed. The song came on at the crosswalk. A hand was suddenly at my elbow, pulling me across. Then he swiped my cane from my hand. "Hold on to me," Charlie said. "We gotta go faster."

"Are you okay?" I said.

The kids behind us were moaning.

"I poked my stick in his spokes," he said.

By the end of the day, they traced the broken cane to Charlie. "I'm getting out of here," he whispered to me in the bathroom that night. "No more Braille Jail. They're looking for you, but I didn't tell them who."

I was terrified they would find me. Charlie was gone the next morning; I didn't get to tell him good-bye.

By the time I came home for Thanksgiving two weeks later, I'd convinced myself I couldn't bear the school. I told my parents I was bolder than the other children there. I could do things they wouldn't do. And I said the teachers kept us inside to protect us. I knew that would get to Dad, the idea that I was being coddled. But the truth was, I was homesick. I missed my pal Charlie. And I was terrified of the kids on bikes; I dreaded going out anywhere, certain they'd track me down. On the Sunday my parents were supposed to drive me back, Mom and Dad sat me at the kitchen table and gave me the choice. I never went back. I named my stick, and every one since, after Charlie.

My parents got me a tutor, Mary Robinson, who helped me with schoolwork every weekday afternoon from first through ninth grade. She taught me Braille. For several years after my blinding, I was bold, even reckless, around my neighborhood, with plenty of bruises and scrapes to show for it. I didn't use my cane much except at school. I rode my brother's skateboard while poking my hockey stick out front. Sometimes I rode his bike and crashed into bushes, fences, and walls. I bounced on my pogo stick for hours in place.

By the fifth grade, however, I had gotten left behind so many times by neighborhood kids that I began to turn inward. I also became cautious and quiet as I grew more accustomed to accessing the world through my ears. Listening is not passive; I had to focus and concentrate and invent the world from what I could hear. That was when Mom started getting books on tape from the library, and I started listening to stories whenever I could. I loved books not because they let me escape but because they showed me the world. The Jupiter Jones series got me started; Jupe was a fat kid, an outcast who didn't have money but was smart as hell. He could fool adults and solve mysteries they couldn't solve because he thought about things differently.

In middle school, as kids started picking on me more, I kept to myself until shyness became routine. I started wearing dark glasses to cover my scar, and I ditched my cane whenever I could. I avoided going out on my own. Dad pressed me to do things outside, but he was gone all day. It was Mom who helped me in stores, showed me how to open plastic wrappers when I got frustrated, or took me to doctors and specialists. At night, Dad would drill into me how difficult the world was for a boy like me—that was his phrase: "a boy like you." My parents never used the word "blind." I couldn't just be mediocre, he said. I had to excel at whatever I chose. That was the only way I would ever support myself. Even then, I sensed that that was how I could gain his respect, by not being a drain on society.

One afternoon, I overheard Dad demanding that my tutor stop pushing me to use my cane.

"It's about being independent," Mrs. Robinson said, "getting around on his own."

"They make fun of him," Dad said. "He gets around Greeley fine."

"He gets around the neighborhood," she said. "He doesn't strike out into new places anymore."

"This is about your movement, isn't it?" Dad said. "You want to show the world how many people there are without sight."

"It's not about a movement," Mrs. Robinson said. "It's about Kevin accepting who he is."

Dad just about lost it then. And my tutor almost lost her job.

Later in Burbank, as I was getting to know Ray, I wondered sometimes, when he grew quiet or distant after he'd been running around only moments before: Had Ray come to us at the same stage I'd been in—those middle school years—when I'd stopped being intrepid? Maybe it was a projection on my part, that parallel between him and me. But the thought always made my heart sink because I didn't want him to hide inside himself, as I had. And I didn't know how to help him.

After lunch, the temperature was 104, and Betsy got a quart of oil and a gallon of water. "You think the heat'll warp the wood?" Patrick said, coming inside the store where we were loitering.

"What is that thing?" a man said, his voice rattling like pebbles. "Looks like a coffin."

Nobody spoke for a moment. Maybe we shouldn't have wrapped it so tightly, I thought.

Then Patrick tried to sell him one: "It's a handmade, one-of-a-kind casket. Everybody's buying 'em. You can't get 'em in a funeral parlor."

Before I got into Betsy, I made the mistake of laying a hand on the coffin's tarp. I jerked my hand away; the thing almost burned my skin.

"I hate that ugly box," Isa said. "I can't even look at it."

When we were back on the road and the desert furnace came through the windows, my sweat evaporated at the same rate as I perspired. As far as we knew, we were driving until Patrick couldn't drive anymore, which depressed us all, I think: the hot road ahead. My skin felt tacky and smelled salty. Devon pushed away my leg whenever it touched his, but Ray couldn't stop moving. He kept bumping up against me with elbows and knees. He had grown some during his months with us, I realized.

Late in the afternoon, just before Phoenix, Isa said she hoped we could stop at her brother's place in Tucson for a night—which was such good news it even got Devon asking questions. She hadn't seen Robert in four years, she answered, since before she was clean and sober. No, she didn't have any other brothers or sisters. Yes, he had a family: June, his wife, and Alexis, his teenaged daughter. Yes, he knew about us; she'd talked to him on the phone a couple of times over the past year. No, he didn't know we were coming. Then she started mumbling to herself in her thin, anxious voice, asking Jesus something or other—I couldn't quite hear.

"Enough questions!" Patrick declared.

I was glad to hear Patrick come to her aid.

We were quiet after that. I remembered that Robert was the younger brother who'd badgered her and spied on her as a kid. I knew he was a successful contractor and that she felt inept in comparison with him and his family. But I'd forgotten he lived in Tucson.

We pulled up at Robert's place after six, but it still felt like 100 degrees as Betsy tick, tick, ticked in the heat. The AC hadn't kicked on since Phoenix. We hadn't eaten since Quartzsite, just this side of California. Now that we'd gotten it into our heads to spend the night, the thought of being turned away and driving on toward Florida was out of the question.

I don't remember stepping out of the car, just holding Devon's strong, bony elbow along a curving walkway as his body loped forward and his flip-flops slapped the pavement. We followed the gentle thuds of Isa's wedge sandals. Ray's steps chattered far ahead, even in the heat. Behind us, Patrick's rubber soles came in even paces, always so damn certain. Charlie, folded into sections, protruded in a lump from my pocket and pressed into my leg as I walked. Devon hardly broke stride in rambling up a set of oddly deep stairs, where I had to quicken my pace, stuttering a step and a half for each stair. We shuffled across a large expanse of stone or ceramic pavers until we stood in a cluster before what I assumed was a front door, the five of us standing there as if the door would open of itself. None of us wanted to press Isa to act; we knew she felt unsound. In the silence of that scorching portico, how was it that I felt responsible, as if this were my younger brother and I had gotten us into this bind?

After a flurry of short breaths, Isa stepped quickly forward and told us to "smile natural," as if there were such a smile. I thought of what Patrick had told me on the roadside outside Burbank: blind man can't write on his own. I pressed my lips together and dipped my head to the right. I let go of Devon's elbow, nudging my glasses up my nose and lowering my brim to hide my scar, berating myself for hanging on to this family, for not staying home. Inside the house, chimes set off the yapping of a little dog, mocking us from the other side of the door.

"He must be one rich motha', your brotha'," Devon said, but he offered a quick, good-natured laugh.

"Stop it," Isa said, edgy. "Don't talk like that here."

Ray fidgeted like a terrier, moving about the porch and brushing against my arm. Heat radiated from some wall to our left, sucking moisture; even in the shade, I withered. As the door chimes trembled to a stop, the high-pitched yaps fell away. I made myself breathe.

"That's one big-ass door," Devon said.

"I said don't talk like that," Isa said, her voice cracking.

"Like what?" Devon said.

"Ruff!" Ray snarled, which got the yaps started again inside.

"Stand still, Ray!" Patrick said. "You're making me hot."

Leave him alone, I wanted to shout. Let him be himself, you son of a bitch! But I caught myself, closed my mouth. I shook my head and breathed. I was beyond this, I decided, outside it all.

That's how selfish I was.

Still the dog yapped, with pauses between fits and bursts.

"Should I ring again?" Isa said in a high, nervous pitch as she shifted from one foot to the other.

"I'm starving," Devon said.

"Why would anyone live in Tucson?" Patrick said, disgusted.

The heat didn't so much oppress as drain me; I could feel my lips parching. Again I made myself inhale.

Just then the door scraped fast across its threshold, and the yaps circled in a frenzy.

Isa gasped. "Oh my gosh!" she said. "Robert! You scared me."

Her brother. Was he holding something? Doing something? What had startled her?

From the doorway, Robert exhaled a miserable groan that blended into "Isa."

A cool slant of air drifted across my ankles. I've waited on plenty of thresholds hoping for the kindness of others. Standing on Robert's pavers in the bald heat of Tucson's summer, I didn't know what he looked like, how he stood. But I imagined how we appeared to him, his degenerate sister's ragtag troupe: a Mexican kid, a black teen, a sightless ex-addict looking who knows where, and two born-again sinners posing as parents. He knew the baggage we bore.

"Don't bother with introductions," Patrick said. "We're brothers!" He let the brother bit burrow beneath Robert's skin.

Somehow the dog stopped barking, making silence deeper.

With a forced giggle, Isa clapped her hands and seized the moment. "Robert!" she said. "Praise Jesus you're here! We're on our way home to Daddy and just stopped by for a night. You look great." She swished up to hug him or peck him on the cheek; I'm not sure. But as quickly as she'd thrust herself on him, she took a step back. From her pace, I could tell she was in self-protect mode, staving off insecurity by ramping toward one of her highs. "You've never met Patrick," she blurted. "This is our little Ray. Look, your dog likes him! And this is our teenager, Devon." Isa has always been generous that way, claiming us, trying to make us family though only she and Patrick shared a name.

"Come on, Kevin," she said, grasping the back of my left arm, her palm tacky against my skin. She didn't mean to, but she pulled me off balance. I stumbled, mouth open, pitching to my left and forward but catching myself before I fell. Charlie sprang from my pocket, releasing and clattering on the tiles. As my hand flew out, it pressed into softness between her thighs. Isa giggled as I pulled my hand from her leg.

The dog started yapping again.

Patrick chortled. I should have laughed too, but I was too self-conscious. I straightened, embarrassed. Isa clung to my arm, her hand trembling as if she might collapse without contact. I stood tall and dropped my shoulders to show strength of mind. I tried not to think about my scar.

"This is Kevin," Isa said. I reached out to shake Robert's hand.

"Who is it, Robert?" a woman's voice called from inside.

Patrick's footsteps—the rubber soles—flashed into the house, vanishing, leaving the rest of us to swelter in the heat, suspended.

Ray was squatting next to me, fiddling with the dog. "Are we staying?" he said.

"Shut up!" Devon said. "You're going to blow it."

My right hand still hung in the air, so I moved it down to Ray's shoulder. Isa handed Charlie back to me, opened fully, so I held him upright like a staff, his tip on the ground, his grip in the air. I relaxed my jaw when I realized it was clenched.

Isa offered a nervous laugh. "I'm sorry we didn't call first," she said. "How are June and Alexis?"

Still Robert didn't answer. Devon shifted his feet. The dog panted.

Across the street a car door slammed, and a man's rough voice called out, "Robert! Sorry to hear!"

From inside the doorway, a trace of garlic cooled to my nostrils. Still nothing came from Robert; I was certain we wouldn't stay.

"This isn't a good time," Robert said finally, his voice dead serious. "You can't visit right now. You can't be here. I'm sorry."

I thought of walking back into the sun, stooping into the backseat, and spending the night at a rest stop: the sweltering seats, the suffocating air. Even my eye sockets felt dry.

Off to our right, a camera clicked rapid-fire.

"Hey!" Robert said.

The clicks fluttered on.

"Get off my property!" Robert yelled. Then he stepped among us and herded us toward the door, his hand on my back. Ray scampered ahead as the dog yapped. I swept Charlie back and forth, feeling the threshold through Charlie's touch and stepping over it into coolness. The door slammed behind, footsteps dispersing helter-skelter on hard stone: marble? As I pulled the artificial moisture deep into my lungs, I felt blood pulsing in my temples.

We were in.

FOUR

Robert's house was alive with activity that I didn't try to pattern into space. The slaps of Devon's flip-flops disappeared. The dog yapped and yapped, his toenails ticking on slick stone and mingling with Ray's laughter. Every pore on my skin came alive to the cool air.

Robert called out, "I'll be damned! A photographer just . . . There he is on my lawn."

Isa's soft thuds scampered off. A trace of woody perfume hung in the air.

A woman's sharp heels clicked briskly, then changed to strokes on carpet. Jewelry jingled. "Pistol, stop that!" she commanded. "Robert, where's your manners?"

"How did Jerry Linneman find out?" Robert called. "That's what I want to know. Not even in the paper yet, and already the neighbors know."

As the barking subsided, a TV popped on nowhere close. The smell of onions got me licking my lips. I could hear a pan sizzle.

Isa greeted June, Robert's wife. An air-conditioning unit kicked on and settled into a hum. Faintly, a toilet flushed, upstairs perhaps. The acoustics were tricky.

I laughed for no reason. It felt good to shake my belly.

Eventually Isa brought me onto the springy carpet of the living room, where she sat on a couch but I stood with Charlie, after sitting all day in the car.

"I'm calling the cops," Robert said. I could hear fabric being rustled. Everything felt and sounded like money: heavy and lush.

"Calm down," June said. "I'll call the police in a minute. And don't close the drapes. They can't get a picture inside until the lights go on. If our curtains are pulled now, we'll look like drug dealers."

Robert groaned, throwing himself onto a stuffed chair or couch, which gasped under his weight. "What are you really doing here?" he demanded.

"Isa, you'll forgive Robert," June said. "He isn't himself."

"That's okay," Isa said. "I've seen him like this before."

"Don't start with me," Robert threatened. "You show up without even calling."

There was a pause that felt more uncomfortable the longer it lasted. I could hear Isa fidgeting on the couch, so I allowed myself to feel sorry for her; I assumed she was edgy and tense.

Robert let her know we could stay one night, but we couldn't go outside.

"I already told you," Isa said quietly—trying to calm herself, I knew. "We'll be driving on tomorrow morning."

"What's that on your car?" he blurted. "It looks like a casket."

As Isa explained the coffin to him—not Patrick's business attempts but the old man's ravings on the phone—Robert said he'd gotten earfuls about the same thing. But it was stupid and arrogant, he said, to pick out a coffin before somebody died. He badgered Isa about her job and the kids and how much the state paid for foster care. She answered and deflected as best she could. To help her out, I sank beside her on the sofa, whose cushions were so soft they swallowed me; I had to shift to get my balance. June fiddled with ice and glasses—from someplace behind us—and tried to change the subject by asking about Patrick, who seemed to have disappeared into the kitchen.

"He likes to cook," Isa said, as if that explained him.

When Robert stood and shuffled around our couch, his chair sighed from the loss of his weight.

"You don't need another," June said, her tone sharp, like fingernails.

He said he did.

As I sipped the sparkling water, I tried not to think about the clean taste of a vodka tonic.

"What's going on?" Isa said. "That hubbub outside."

Robert grunted—he was back in his chair—but didn't speak.

"You better get used to talking about it," June said. "He's over his head in some business deals." She was standing beyond Robert, and her voice sounded like she was turned away; perhaps she was looking outside.

"I'm not over my head," Robert said quickly. "It was a business trip. Those allegations won't stick."

"Of course they won't," she said matter-of-factly.

Again there was a pause. Ice swirled in Robert's glass.

"You already owe us six thousand dollars," Robert blurted.

"Robert!" June said.

"She promised never again."

"I'm not here to borrow anything," Isa said. "Daddy helped me so many times . . ."

"Thank God he stopped loaning you money."

It was painful to sit in the room, the air felt so tense. I fingered the fabric of my new shorts and wondered where they'd gotten the money for my clothes. I knew Devon wanted all kinds of things: an iPod, a cell phone, and new kicks, which was what he called sneakers. Ray never seemed to want anything.

"This time I'm going to help Daddy," Isa offered. "We're going to save his life." The way she said it, all buttery, I felt sorry for her.

"You're going to upset him," Robert exclaimed. "Except this time it really will kill him."

Isa's breathing seemed to quicken, and I couldn't help it: I reached to calm her, touching her near forearm and then laying my palm on her knuckles. I thought she'd be fretful, her hands flitting—but they were motionless. Strangely steady. As Isa began to tell about our drive through Arizona, it occurred to me how calm her voice had become now that she was inside the house. I'd misread her, I realized: Robert, with all his badgering, was the one unbalanced. She was the older sister after all, and he the younger brother.

I'm ashamed to say that it pissed me off, her self-assurance; I wanted her to need me. I pulled my hand from her arm, and as I leaned away, the cushions sucked me in. I struggled to sit up.

"Tell me about Isa," I managed to say. "What was she like growing up?"

Robert obliged. "She was a nightmare," he said pleasantly, his tone completely different, as if he were reading to a child from a picture book. "The smartest kid in the class. She was in theater. Art. French Society. Everybody loved her, and she soaked up all the attention she could get. Everything was Isa, Isa, Isa. Even after Mom and Dad split up." Ice swirled again in his glass. His voice became even sweeter, almost sappy: "Then she got into drugs in college, and Mom and Dad ran off to Gainesville to help her. Didn't they? And Atlanta. And Los Angeles. For years they would fly out and bring her home. It's the only thing they did together after they divorced. They consoled Isa. Confronted Isa. Tried to buy Isa into stopping." Even with his put-on voice, a tinge of bitterness came through. "None of it worked. She lied through her teeth."

I wasn't surprised. I'd suspected she was a captivating child. And I knew she'd been rescued before. When I was in San Francisco, after a year and a half of smoking crack, I had to be rescued too.

"Happy now?" Isa said derisively to me. "Is that what you wanted to hear?"

I looked away; I didn't want to acknowledge anything.

"I'm not ashamed of any of that," she said. "I've changed now that I'm with Jesus. That's not me anymore. Why don't we talk about you, Kevin? Why don't you tell us why you came on the trip?"

"Stop it," I said.

"Oh," she said. "You just want to hear about me." As she leaned toward me and touched my hand, I sank away from her. She spoke into my ear, "You want me to tell them how you lost your job? And how you were so depressed I stayed up with you night after night? No way we could leave Burbank without you. You would have relapsed. You do need a caregiver after all. That's why your parents pay me."

My breathing quickened. My jaw tensed. What she said about my parents—and that I couldn't be left on my own—made me cringe. But since that was too painful to think about, I clutched at her suggestion that *she* had nursed *me* those nights at the kitchen table. I tried to stand too quickly and sank back into the cushions. On the second try, I got my feet beneath me and extended Charlie in several clean snaps. "I stayed up those nights to help *you,*" I said coldly. I wanted to tell everyone how fragile she'd been, but I caught myself.

I swept Charlie back and forth off the lush carpet and onto marble, where I came around a corner and leaned against a wall. It hit me then that Isa's little announcements were not secrets—not to Patrick and the kids. They all knew: Kevin can't be left at home. He can't keep a job. He can't survive on his own. We'd better get him some new clothes and fool him into coming along. Watch him, don't let him relapse.

I found a doorway along the wall and retreated into a bathroom—the only place I ever seemed to find privacy. For several minutes, I ran warm water across my hands and onto my face. Why couldn't my body be deadened like the dullness along my scar?

At first I couldn't concentrate, I was so angry. Yet after several minutes of standing at the sink, it dawned on me that I *had* been depressed those nights at the kitchen table. And beyond that, I admitted to myself: I'd been in love with Isa all that time. Or infatuated, actually. Engulfed. Each day I'd pined for her touch. Her mindless caress. Her impetuous embrace. What a fool I'd been.

But still I didn't understand how mixed up it all was: our version of love and caretaking and vulnerability. All I knew was that I couldn't live with her anymore, not if she stayed with Patrick. It was over, I told myself. Over. No need to talk this through. She was too rash and impulsive; it wasn't worth the drama. Standing there, I resolved: on the way back to Burbank, I would tell her, and I'd have to tell the kids too, that I was moving out. They could visit me—the kids, that is.

As I walked out of the bathroom, I didn't dawdle; the last thing I wanted was to suffer Isa's apologies. Why had I gone into the living room anyway? Hadn't I told myself, just that morning, that I would hang out with the kids? I set off toward the sounds of TV, which brought me deeper into the smell of tomato sauce, onions, and garlic. From slightly above and to my right, however, came gentle steps down stairs. I stopped and turned. Bare footsteps I didn't recognize scurried past me with a flood of sour, sugary perfume. Alexis, I decided, Robert and June's teenager.

"Which way to the TV?" I said, though I could hear it myself.

"This way," she said, still walking. I respect that about kids: no introductions. If you want an explanation, they expect you to ask. After about ten paces following her, I stepped from marble onto soft carpet, springy under my feet. The sounds of TV surrounded me. I lost her footsteps in a rap song.

"Over here," Devon said. I turned to the right and found the back of a big stuffed chair, a La-Z-Boy that jiggled as someone squirmed. The music pounded. It felt good to stand and just relax a while. I tried to identify Alexis's fragrance that hung in the room, like Pop Tarts but bitter too.

"You look funny in your new stuff," Ray said to me. He was the one squirming in the La-Z-Boy, but his voice came from down by the carpet.

"Why don't you sit right-side up," Devon said. He was sitting beyond Ray somewhere.

"Why don't you quit staring at her," Ray said.

"Why don't you shut up," Devon said.

The TV was pumping Eminem.

"Check out my upside-down muscles," Ray said. His arms were skinny but had some strength; he'd been doing push-ups and chin-ups for three months. "Hey!" he said. "Gimme back the remote." But he didn't move.

"What are you here for anyway?" Alexis declared in a tone I recognized from her mother, like fingernails tapping aluminum. She struck me as preppy. Coiffed. Manicured. Her voice came from near Devon's. Were they sharing a couch? Or was it a cluster of chairs facing the TV?

"Isa's dad is gonna die," Devon said. "She wants to see him before he goes tits up."

"Granddad," Alexis said. "Very funny."

"That makes us like cousins," Ray said. His voice still came from the floor.

"Don't be ridiculous," she said.

"I can do seven chin-ups," he said.

"He didn't say we *are* cousins," Devon said. "He said we're *like* cousins."

"We're foster cousins," Ray said.

"There's no such thing as foster cousins," she said.

"We're foster brothers," Ray said.

"Shut up," Devon said.

"Why don't you change the channel?" Ray said.

I could feel the bass vibrating in the floor. Then Eminem: "Will the real Slim Shady please stand up. Please stand up."

"You're an only child, aren't you?" Devon said, as if she had a contagious disease.

"Ray," I said, trying to change the subject, "aren't you getting a headache, upside down like that?"

"How do you know I'm still upside down?" he said, his voice coming from down by the floor. I hadn't spent a lot of time with Ray when he was around other kids, particularly girls. It struck me how talkative he was.

"What do you care if I'm an only child?" Alexis said. "Where are your real brothers and sisters?" She emphasized "real."

"We don't have any real brothers or sisters," Devon said, drawing out "real" as if the word extended forever.

"My mom died," Ray said. He said those words so quickly, innocently, it was startling.

"Oh," Alexis said.

"And my mom's in jail," Devon threw in quickly. "Is that what you wanted to know? Is that what you're after? Does that make you feel better?"

"You're the one started it," she said. "You said I was an only child like I was spoiled or something."

"Of course you're spoiled. Look at you. Look at this huge TV. Look at your parents. Your dad wasn't even going to let his sister spend the night on her way through town."

"Yeah, well, why didn't she like call first?" she said.

"Why don't you change the channel?" Ray asked again.

"Why don't you shut up?" Devon said.

A Green Day video came on, and I couldn't help but smile. After being with adults, it was a pleasure to hear the kids.

"No time to search the world around," Ray sang, "'cause you know where I'll be found."

Devon shifted channels, one ad to another.

"Hey!" Ray said. "I like that song." As his body shifted, the back of the La-Z-Boy sank; he was right-side up.

"At least you're going on vacation," Alexis said, offering a short burst of a laugh. "I'm sick of Tucson. You guys are lucky you live in California."

"Lucky?" Devon said. "Face it, we're pariahs." I don't know how he came up with that word, but his voice was lighter, less aggressive.

"Whatever," Alexis said. "I want to live in California." Her voice sounded present, instead of drifting down from above.

"You don't even know what 'pariah' means," Devon prodded.

"I've been studying for the SAT," she said. "It means loner or rebel or something."

"It means outcast, but what would you care about that?" he goaded. "What are you supposed to be, goth? You've never been oppressed."

Goth, I thought. And I'd imagined her as preppy. I'd had a girlfriend in college who was goth.

"Oh, that's your problem," she said. "I've oppressed you somehow, because I'm white."

"I saw how you raised your eyebrows when you came in," Devon said.

She started laughing in a knowing way, as if this were all a joke and she was in on it. "Maybe you ought to tone down your look," she said.

"Yeah," Ray said, trying to be included.

I heard Devon slip forward, pop Ray, and fall back into his chair.

"What'd you do that for?" Ray said.

"You think you're the only one who's oppressed?" Alexis said. "Everybody's oppressed one way or another."

"You think you're oppressed?" Devon bantered. "For what? For being anorexic? You've probably got a boyfriend who likes you skinny. Look at you! You do have a boyfriend!"

"You better shut up," Alexis said, her voice deep, gritty. "You better shut up right now."

"What's anorexic?" Ray said.

I didn't hear Devon this time, but Ray screamed, "Devon keeps hitting me!" He jumped on Devon, yelling, and I could hear him batter

Devon with his fists. Devon pushed him off, half mad, half laughing, and then they were both on the floor, tussling. I came around the La-Z-Boy and reached in, leaning forward, but I was useless; I couldn't grab anything. My jaw got whacked, which jerked my head back and threw my glasses off. Alexis giggled, and the two brothers struggled, rolling and wrestling, Devon holding Ray down, all for the attention of a rich white girl, I assumed, who was full-out laughing, maybe trying to forget that bit about anorexia. I sat on the edge of the La-Z-Boy and, leaning back, reached with my legs, trying to push Devon off Ray, but he brushed my legs away.

As Ray screamed, I resented that the grown-ups had to scurry into the room: June's heels on marble, the soft thuds of Isa's sandals. I felt worthless—unable to contain this on my own.

"Boys!" Isa said.

The phone rang. "I'll get it," Robert said.

Devon was laughing in fits, which only infuriated Ray. Suddenly here came the dog, yapping and yapping.

Someone slammed down the receiver so hard it could have broken the phone. "Bastards!" Robert said. "How'd they get our home number?"

When Devon let go and started to slide away, Ray clung to him. Isa and I pulled at Ray, but he wouldn't let go.

"Don't answer the phone, dear," June said. "Let the machine get it. Pistol, come here!"

We finally dragged Ray from Devon, who was still laughing.

"Stop laughing!" Isa said.

Ray and Isa sat together on the floor, panting. Alexis handed my glasses to me, and I thought about the scar coursing like a river from my eyebrow to cheek. But she didn't say a word.

I was finished with them all, I decided. It was past time to move out.

"Dinner is served!" Patrick proclaimed.

I put on my glasses. Where was my hat? I hadn't noticed that it was gone too.

"Look at you, with your hair mussed up," Isa said. "What, were you fighting too?"

I felt their sudden glances just before the kids laughed, the grown-ups laughed, and, rather than shouting at them all, I allowed myself a feeble chuckle. We laughed not because it was funny but because it let everybody off the hook; it enabled them to look at each other and move on. As they walked toward dinner, I said I'd be there in a minute. The TV popped off. Maybe I stood up too fast, for I felt light-headed. As I plopped back down on the carpet, I felt the bitterness coming on. How had Devon and Alexis connected so fast? Their conversation seemed to have turned in an instant. I reminded myself that vision isn't just a social act but also a greedy one—and aggressive as well. Didn't my world expand a touch at a time, whereas other people could glance at each other, collect information from a smile or smirk, and, with hardly any imagination, assume they knew the next step in the game? I was exhausted.

And I am alone in my world, sitting on the wood floor, my back against a wall. I am six years old, and my father looms tall just from the strike of his boots on the floor. I don't lift my head. Why should I? It's many months after my accident, so that I know, yet don't understand, what it is to see nothing. Dad says nothing. He hitches up his pants with the butt of his crumpled left hand, a shuffling of clothing and an altered step in his walk, sounds I recognize at age six but no longer see: Dad hitching up his pants.

He startles me by slipping me his left hand for the first time ever, the crumpled one, the hand he won't talk about so that it's become a void, a silence, a broken bird. As I turn my palm, I know immediately what I hold. I caress his dead left hand with the whole of both palms and the length of

each of my fingers and thumbs. I drink up the touch of taut muscles that
make up Dad's forearm and wrist and the calluses on the butt of his hand
still good enough to prod a stubborn steer or pull a rope with a crooked twist
of his wrist—snippets of stories he's told me, though he doesn't like to talk
much. I trace the dells between each useless knuckle and the bony contours of
each lame finger, all of them stiff and crooked as if lassoed and wrapped by
twine invisible to touch. It's a connection only Dad and I have; I sense that
from him. It's a message, that hand between mine, of how you tough it out,
create calluses wherever and however you can, and move on.

The touch of Ray's fingers on my shoulder pulled me back into common sense. I reached up to grip his hand, so slender and soft as he tugged me up and handed me my hat. I found his shoulder and neck. As we set off toward the smells of dinner, he took two steps for every one of mine.

It was about a year before my accident that Dad had his, when he was a ranch foreman outside Greeley. He and his crew were separating cattle for medications, using a new squeeze chute they weren't used to. One of the cows went berserk in the chute and pinned Dad's hand between bars, crushing it so badly it never regained strength.

I hadn't thought about Dad's hand in a long time. Walking with Ray to the dining room, holding to his thin collarbone, I was grateful for the warmth of his skin.

I barely had time to sit at the table before Robert, with a half cough and stammer, started to say a few words, but Isa exploded into prayer as if she'd just gotten the calling. She thanked and praised the merciful Lord who came to us through Jesus Christ, asking His blessing for the food on this table and all tables throughout the world and for the health of those around those tables, not pausing as the phone rang, using it to pace her rhythm, asking for His healing mercy for Daddy's recovery in what would not be his final days, praise the Lord, whose sacred touch she felt each day all day, now of all times, seeking His special favor for Daddy's health through the power of love and affection within the network of family all in Christ, Christians, amen.

At first I was appalled by the transparency of her vanity, by her need to show her brother how she'd changed—as if prayer were proof. Then I realized: of course! This was Isa now. It was I who'd refused to see her. How many times had I ignored her born-again language back in Burbank, all that about saving her Daddy through Jesus? How deeply I'd preferred the Isa of a year ago.

The phone rang again.

"Damn that phone!" Robert said. I was stuck between them, with Robert on one side of me and Isa on the other. I could smell whiskey on his breath as he began to grumble, so I knew he was leaning forward, looking past me at Isa. "If you think for a minute," he griped, "that you can waltz home now and just talk about Jesus. After all you've put that man through! And get written back into his will and life insurance policy. After all I've done to help him. Even from way across the country . . ." He paused as if uncertain where to go.

"Stop this, Robert," June said. "Not at the table."

Of course, I thought. It wasn't just the coffin. Or a family vacation. Or that the old man was dying. We were the poor relations. And we were heading to Florida for the old man's money.

I kept my head down and felt with my fingers: spaghetti on the right side of my plate and salad on the left. I bit into some garlic bread. It was as if all the emotional drama were behind me. I was starving suddenly, and the bread tasted divine.

The phone's next ring was cut short by June's voice on the machine, followed by a beep. A woman's voice came on, deep and soothing, offering to tell Robert's story the way Robert wanted it told, the way it should be told.

Robert stayed seated.

"At least they don't have your cell," June said.

I let the smell of pasta sauce, garlic, hot bread, and salad vinegar guide and lubricate my taste buds.

"This is delicious!" Alexis said.

Isa exhaled loudly. "Robert," she said, "it's not about his money. I want you to know that up front. Things have changed. I'm going to pay you back. You'll see."

"It's about his approval, isn't it?" he grumbled. "You want Dad's approval before he dies. And you know the sign of his approval has always been money."

"That's not true," Isa said.

"Abe's a romantic," June said, drawn into the conversation despite herself. "If you can get past his ploys and deceptions, it's usually about a woman."

"Who's Abe?" Ray said.

"Granddad," Alexis said.

"The man who ran off with his secretary," Patrick said.

"Stop it," June said. "Enough."

It was an open secret about Isa's family: her dad had slept with his secretary and had been divorced promptly by Isa's mother, Rose.

We were quiet then, chewing, save for the ringing of the phone. It was a man's voice this time, telling Robert they were running a story he wouldn't like. Did he want to correct the record, get his story out while there was still time?

"How did they get our number?" Robert said. "Ten minutes ago they didn't have it, and now they all do."

"It's embarrassing," Alexis said.

"We'll talk about it later," Robert said curtly.

It struck me that families start a lot of conversations they never quite finish. Devon asked for the bread.

"How long will you be on the road?" June asked.

Isa finished chewing. "About two weeks. We're going to see Mom as well."

"When's the last time we went on vacation?" Alexis said.

"Yellowstone," Robert said. "Three years ago. You got mosquito bites all over your throat. Remember?"

"I saw them shoot that cow."

"I told you she was too young," June said.

"She was thirteen," Robert said.

"They hoisted it up with straps," Alexis said. "They put a handgun right up to its head. When they shot it, I thought it was gonna be the gun that was deafening. But it's like you could hear the cow sag in those straps. It was eerie, that sound."

"In the end, gravity wins," Devon said.

"When they cut it open, you could see grass in its stomach."

"Please," June said.

"I mean, it looked just like from the lawn mower."

Devon laughed.

"I grew up around cattle," I said. "My dad's an inspector in Colorado."

"Cows have four stomachs," Ray said.

"Please!" June said.

Devon laughed again, and Alexis did too, a quick burst that seemed to connect them.

"We should do another vacation," Alexis said warmly. "They get to go on vacation. We never do."

"This is my first vacation," Ray said.

"Listen to this—from my daughter, of all people," Robert said. "You're engaging in conversation. You're complimenting the dinner. What's gotten into you?"

"I think it's a good idea," June said.

"What?" Robert said.

"Vacation," Alexis said. "Ever heard of that?"

"Are you kidding me?" he said. "You said never again. Not with your parents."

"You work all the time," Alexis said. "That's why we haven't gone."

"You do need to get away, dear," June said. "Especially now."

"You both do," Alexis said, her voice serious and somber suddenly. "You never do stuff together. You're always arguing."

Nobody said a word. Silver clinked on porcelain plates. I would have liked to know the looks around the table.

Finally the doorbell chimed, which set Pistol into a yapping frenzy that reminded me of standing in the heat of the doorstep. Robert pushed his chair back, but June said, "Let me get this."

I picked at the salad with my fork, but the lettuce kept falling off, so I used my fingers. We ate in silence until the click of June's heels returned. "It was the police, dear," she said. "There's not much they can do."

"What! He was on my lawn! That's trespassing." The phone rang again. "Damn the phone!" he said, breathing hard.

June began, "I bet your blood pressure—"

"I'm not going to run from this," Robert interrupted.

The phone rang again.

"Nobody's running anywhere," June said.

"Jeez, Dad. We're talking about a vacation, not a major life event."

On the answering machine, the old man's voice, strained yet persistent, called out, "Robert! Where are you? Don't worry, it'll all be over soon!"

"It's Daddy!" Isa said.

Robert pushed back his chair and hurried across the floor.

"I can't find my will," Abe called out. "Isa's coming out here, thank God!"

By the time Robert picked up the phone, the old man had hung up. "Why won't he call my cell?" he said. "He never calls my cell."

"Let's go see Granddad," Alexis said in a voice that was too cheery. "Is he really going to die?"

Her tone made me wonder if that was what she'd been setting up all along, a way to hang out with Devon.

Robert paced back and forth. "Why doesn't he answer?" he said.

"I don't mean Florida," June said. "We need to go someplace else. Someplace relaxing."

"Can we drop this?" Robert said. "Can we just have a regular dinner and eat our food?"

"This is the best dinner we've had in a long time," Alexis said. "And I'm not talking about the food."

After dinner, Patrick brought our luggage in from Betsy. Robert and June quarreled in the kitchen. I avoided Isa—and maybe she avoided me. Devon and Alexis wouldn't let Ray hang out with them, so Ray and I explored the house together. He put on a blindfold, and we both let Charlie lead us around, Ray swinging him wildly as I held to his shoulder.

"Try to touch, don't tap," I said, thinking of my first pal named Charlie.

In the upstairs hallway, Ray got going too fast, so I decided to let go and wait against the wall. On his way back, he blundered into me, and we both fell down, laughing. For several more trips down the hallway, I became his obstacle until we tired of that. In our bedroom, as Ray jumped back and forth between the twin beds, laughing, Pistol came in yapping, so Ray chased him down the hallway.

I pulled my note-taker from my backpack and sat on the bed, beginning where we'd started, in Burbank. I left myself out, of course; this was not about me. After Ray showered, he described the desert for me, a gas station, and Robert's tiled front porch. He said that when Robert opened the door, his eyes bugged out and his skin looked like frozen fish. "White," he said. "Whiter than you."

That got me wondering. I'd heard plenty about what Devon looked like, but Patrick hardly ever talked about Ray. "What color's your skin?" I asked.

"You don't know colors," he said, not in a dismissive way, just stating what he knew. I associate things with color but can't envision a hue. I know that tree trunks are brown. Some houses. Some shoes. The sky is blue. Grass is green except in California, where the hills are golden.

"Tell me anyway," I said.

"It's the color of sand," he said reluctantly.

"I thought sand was white."

"It's kind of complicated. There's different colors of sand."

"Bedtime," Isa said from the doorway. "We've got a long drive tomorrow."

"I like that, sand," I said, but Ray had already moved on.

"Are they coming to Florida?" he said.

"They're thinking about flying," she said, "so maybe we'll see them."
That surprised me.

As Ray brushed his teeth, Isa sat on the bed next to me. She told me
she was sorry for the things she'd said in the living room. "But I was mad
at you," she said, "for getting Robert to talk about that old stuff from
the past. You don't know what it's like—he's so judgmental about everything. He tries to make me feel small and unimportant. Whenever I talk
to him, I have to go inside myself and be strong. That's family."

It's not that I didn't believe her; I know we're all different around
family. I just wasn't interested anymore. She could be whoever she
wanted, I decided. That would be fine with me.

"I see you're still mad," she said.

"Hey," I said, trying to be light, "I'm just along for the ride, okay?"

"Maybe I'm not as smart as you," she said, standing up, "but don't
belittle me."

I didn't know what to say, so I didn't say anything.

She hugged Ray in the bathroom, told him good-night, and went
off to look for Devon.

I lay there a while, unable to think or write. When Ray called me
over, I got down on the carpet and tucked him into a sleeping bag. He
started describing his mother, which shocked me and pulled me out of
my funk. He'd never done that before. What he liked to remember
most, he said, was the smell of her hair after a shower. The taste of her
fresh tortillas. The way she rubbed his back at night. The way she
blinked her eyes when she smiled.

I was used to Ray leaning up against me, leading me around, playing games, and asking questions—but not this. I squeezed his arm. "Great descriptions," I said. "It's like I can feel her."

He kicked the sleeping bag half off. "I forgot to bring that picture of her," he said.

"Then it's at home," I said. "Waiting for you. She loves you."

"Tell me who," he said. That was my cue. Though he was probably too old for it, I'd been putting him to bed for months, and the routine made us both feel good. It helped calm my nerves at the end of a day.

"Close your eyes and take a big breath," I said, "the biggest eyes and the biggest breath in all of Arizona." He turned on his side, yawning, and I rubbed his back and neck, feeling behind his left ear for the keloid scar my fingers were used to, the tough, irregular tissue where he must have had a nasty cut before he came to us. His chest expanded as he took another breath. I drew closer to him and whispered slowly, "Your mom loves you in heaven. In everything you do, she loves you and misses you. Your dad loves you in Soledad. He wants to see you every day." I paused. "Isa and Patrick and Devon love you. Kevin loves you so much. Tubba the frog loves you from heaven. Tía María and Tío José love you. And now Robert and June love you."

"They don't love me," he said.

"Sure, they do. If only they knew how. And Alexis loves you too."

As Ray's breathing eventually settled into sleep, I found my own breathing easing. I realized how much the kids helped me escape my own angst—most the time.

About fourteen months earlier, when Isa had said she wanted to sign up for foster kids, Patrick and I had both been against it. We were all living together by then at the Lincoln Street house, but I didn't plan to stay long. They weren't married, but a couple of weeks after he got out of Channel House, Patrick drove us to Las Vegas, where the two of them had a ceremony—just like we were going to the movies on a Friday night. "Witness this!" Patrick kept saying all the way out of the chapel. "Watch me kiss her." He loved that, having a blind witness.

I had planned to move out by the end of the month, but the editor of the community newspaper offered me a part-time job the next week, and I got busy learning that routine. Patrick let it be known that he didn't want kids at all, so eventually Isa started the paperwork for foster care without telling him, and she got great references from her pastor, the Channel House director, a lawyer at her church, and her boss at the restaurant where she waitressed. It took several months for her to get final approval. Her steady job helped, as well as her experience and income as a caregiver for me. I was surprised that neither Patrick nor she had a drug bust or a theft on their records. Just some disorderlies for Patrick—drunken in public, that kind of thing. They took my fingerprints too and later asked about my suspended sentence for grand larceny—I'd been with Casey after he'd stolen some jewelry. I also had two possessions of marijuana, both misdemeanors, one in Colorado and one in California. I guess they needed foster homes in Burbank because I got clearance. Isa signed the papers for Ray in October 2004. Within a month, Patrick got Devon lined up—because, I assumed, Patrick liked the payments from the state.

With Ray asleep on the floor, I got back into bed just as someone burst open the door and threw something next to the wall. "There," Devon said. "I brought it in."

"And brush your teeth," Isa said.

"Watch out for Ray," I said. "He's over on the floor."

"Are you blind?" Devon said. "The bathroom light's on."

"Very funny," I said.

"What are you and Alexis doing?" Isa said.

"Choppin' it up," he said.

"Don't you do anything with her," she warned.

He grunted. Water ran in the sink.

"And don't stay up late," she called before she closed the door. She was staying down the hallway with Patrick. I didn't often think of her as a mother, perhaps because she wasn't as engaged with the kids as I thought she could be. I was glad she was trying to set limits.

Devon shuffled through his duffel bag. "What's up?" I said.

He grunted.

"You going to bed?"

"I'm pissed at you," he said.

"What for?"

"I ain't got time right now," he said, opening the door to leave.

"Don't use 'ain't,'" I said.

The door didn't close, so I assumed he was still there.

"Go on," I said. "Tell me."

"You don't represent yourself. You let people walk all over you. You don't stand up for anything. You got those clothes now. I ain't got shit, but I represent myself. Why don't you be somebody?"

He'd been storing it up. "You're talking about Patrick in the car."

"I'm talking in general."

I fought the urge to say I was sorry; the last thing he wanted me to do was apologize. "All right," I said. "I might as well tell you: I'm done with them. So what's the point of arguing and fighting with Patrick? What the hell difference would it make?"

"Props," he said right away. "You got no props."

He was saying he didn't respect me. That nobody respected me. That I didn't respect myself. It hurt, hearing that from him. I felt kicked in the gut. "You can take your props," I said gruffly, "and shove them up your ass."

"That's better," he said. "That's what I'm talking about." After a moment, he added, "What do you mean, you're done with them?"

I didn't want to go into that; I didn't want Ray to find out I was moving out. "What do *you* mean, you ain't got shit?" I said, even though I knew: the iPod, the kicks, and the cell phone he wanted.

"Don't use 'ain't,'" he said slyly. After a pause, he added, "Girl's got crazy game. Don't be surprised. We might run tonight."

"Stop it," I said.

The door closed. He was gone.

As I tossed about in bed, I didn't worry about Devon and Alexis running. They'd met each other hours ago, for God's sake. No way he could get her to run. What nagged me was Devon's comment about props—because it brought me back to losing my job and not standing up to my boss.

I realized that in one day on the road, I'd managed to piss off Patrick, Isa, and Devon. I remembered their displays of cheap bravado: Patrick's outburst in the car, Isa's prayer at dinner, and Devon's tussle with Ray in the TV room. I thought of reeds bending but not breaking in the wind, and the strength of roots holding down the reeds—and the force of the wind itself, blowing. I was tired of being the reed.

Yet strangely for all the tumult, I was glad to be away from Burbank, outside my routine. There's something heartening and exhausting about relationships on the road, I realize now—the way new molds reveal worn-out patterns. I hadn't traveled much, and I found myself liking the feel of it, the freshness. I fell asleep within half an hour, which was quick for me.

Sometime in the night, Devon got into the other bed. I only knew because there he was in the morning. He told me later—somewhere near Fabens, Texas—that he started out resenting Alexis, her pampered life and candy perfume. But he loved how she didn't back down. The way she raised her black eyebrow when she smirked. The luxury of her green eyes. All night he felt guilty just for holding her and swapping secrets and wanting to run with her—as if he weren't allowed to fall for a white girl.

FIVE

We said good-bye to Robert and June in the foyer the next morning as Ray cavorted with Pistol on the marble floor. The reporters seemed to have dropped away now that the morning news was out. There'd been hushed discussions in the house, but I avoided them; I figured I'd learn about it soon enough in the car. Devon and Alexis seemed to have vanished, so far as I could tell, except for several gulps at the breakfast table and a flurry of steps back upstairs, after which Robert let on that they were not coming to Pensacola, not this week. And by the time we drove back through Tucson, he said, they'd be off somewhere—maybe Santa Fe or Sedona. So it really was good-bye.

"Devon!" Patrick yelled back into the house. "Let's go! Get your damn bag!"

I'd expected Patrick to roust us early. But he didn't want to get to Texas before sunset, he told us, so we could be through it by sunup and miss the whole damn misfortune of a state.

As we stepped onto the stone portico, I was shocked by the heat of Tucson at ten in the morning. I had to catch my breath. But as Ray led me down the stairs and along the curved walkway, I liked the cool texture of my new seersucker shirt against my chest.

We threw our luggage into Betsy's hold and piled into the hot seats, all of us except Devon. Patrick revved the engine and called out, but to no effect. Isa's woody perfume drifted into the backseat. She even turned and slapped our bare thighs. Yet I didn't feel the slightest urge or pang. What a relief, I thought, to be beyond all that! What a waste of energy, those complications of desire for a woman I could never attain. Even the morning heat heartened me. I'd stand my ground, I told myself. I'd earn some damn props.

Patrick started banging on the horn, and after a while flip-flops came slapping in big, happy strides toward the car.

"I forgot about the stupid coffin!" Devon said, his voice bubbling over as he jumped in next to me. "We look like idiots."

"Go get your damn bag," Patrick said.

Devon's flip-flops laughed all the way up the walkway.

"Isn't love enormous?" Isa said.

"That's not love," Patrick said. "Those kids have no idea about love."

I had to duck so Devon could throw his duffel bag over the back-seat. Then he took a long time out on the sidewalk with Alexis.

"Enough, you two," Isa said. "Let's go."

Alexis made a big deal about seeing us at the Redneck Riviera within days—no matter what her dad said.

Devon jumped into the backseat and shut the door.

"We'll all go swimming in the Gulf!" Isa called to Alexis.

Patrick kicked Betsy into gear and gunned it, pressing us into our seats and then jerking us to the side as he screeched around a corner. Devon held his place—he was too big for games now—but I slid into Ray, who giggled and laughed. This time I could hear the creak of the casket as it surged in the ropes.

"You better watch out," Isa said. "That thing's moving up there."

I reached forward and felt the taut rope that wrapped inside the car and looped up around the casket. The rope dipped as Ray hung and snapped as he released. Ray leaned outside so the wind whizzed through his hair.

"Seatbelts on!" Isa sang.

I learned about Robert's dilemma after we bought the *Daily Star* at a rest stop about an hour east of Tucson, where Devon said the huge rocks were insane. Ray wanted to climb on them, but Patrick wouldn't let him—just to be in control, I figured. But looking back on it now, I wonder: maybe they were dangerous.

"What's it look like?" I asked Ray, to distract him.

"Boulders up on end," he said. "They're dancing."

"That's great," I said, taken by his sharp metaphor. "I'm going to use that." But his footsteps were already running. Gone.

"Nice hat, scarecrow," Devon said.

When we got back on the freeway, Isa passed the newspaper into the backseat. Devon and Ray couldn't believe Robert's picture in his front doorway—right on the front page.

"Those are the bug eyes we saw," Ray said.

Somehow the camera angle missed us completely, Devon told me. "'Bribes and Brides,'" he began reading. "'Double Jeopardy for Contractor.'" The gist was that Robert had purchased plane tickets for at least two state politicians. There appeared to be proof of that, but the article never said what he'd gotten in exchange. Influence on state contracts, supposedly. The story led across the border, to a villa on the outskirts of Nogales that was owned by Cowboy Dove, a company that hooks up single American men with Mexican brides. There was a question as to who paid for services in Mexico. The politicians—one was a widower, the other divorced—had no comment. A foreman who used to work for Robert called him an egomaniac and said his business was a mess. He had no cash flow, the man said, and was being sued by homeowners in a Tucson development whose houses leaked around every window. And the kicker: the paper ran a picture of Robert on an inside page, showing the back of a naked woman who was sitting on his lap. Robert was grinning, Devon said.

I felt sorry for June and Alexis.

Patrick said, "None of it matters about the politicians. It's the money. Your brother's broke."

"It's about time rich people get what they deserve," Devon said.

"People in glass houses," I said.

"Exactly," Devon said.

"I mean you," I said. "None of us are saints."

"Blessed are the poor in spirit," Isa said.

Devon mumbled something I didn't want to hear.

I was glad to be driving away from Robert's house. We probably did look like misfits, with a casket wrapped and tied at a tilt on an old Taurus. We didn't have money. We argued too much. But compared with what Robert and his family were going through, our trip felt like a vacation.

We stopped for a late lunch in Deming, New Mexico, where we found a hole in the wall that served enchiladas with green chili as sweet as sin, with a kick that kept you filling your water glass. At the counter, the owner told us proudly, in a gravelly voice running without a pause, that he bought all his chilies from a family who'd been growing and roasting them in the valley of the Rio Grande since before the Civil War. The grandmother of the family—la abuela—was now blind but still ran the operation. He gripped my arm and said, "Green chilies strengthen the heart, and God fortifies the soul." I could hear him thumping his chest.

I was thankful for the quickness of Isa's blessing: "For our safe trip to visit Daddy, in Jesus' name in Christ, amen."

I can't count the times when, as a child, I'd prayed for partial vision: to be able to see flickers of movement. I used to pray for low vision because I didn't think I qualified for the miracle of full sight, having lost it already. Asking for low vision was like praying for an Erector set or a bowie knife; it was in the realm of what God might grant a kid from Greeley, Colorado.

As we ate, Isa was cheery but not as manic as she'd been, content to let others hold the floor. I remember being proud of her for that. Devon couldn't stop eating enchiladas, but he couldn't eat as many as he wanted because his lips were on fire.

"That reminds me," Isa said. "One of our brake lights isn't working."

Patrick, obsessed with the green chili, scampered up to the counter to ask the owner if he added sugar. As soon as he was gone, Ray said the smell of warm tortillas made him sad because it reminded him of his mom in the morning.

I hadn't thought much of what it meant for Ray to live with us—to lose not only the intimacies of his parents but also the cultural anchors he knew, so that a trip to a restaurant brought painful memories.

"That means your mom loves you very much," Isa said warmly. "Every time you smell tortillas, she's thinking of you in heaven."

"I forgot to bring her photo," he said. "I don't have her with me."

"Your mom can see you always," Isa said. "She's always with you."
I liked that; Isa sounded like a mom herself.

Outside the restaurant, Isa's cell phone toned "Für Elise." "Daddy!" she said in a singsong voice. There was a pause, then "Daddy! We'll be there in two days, tops." She started pacing in short, rapid steps. That was how fast she could swing into anxiety.

"We are so weird!" Devon said, walking off along the sidewalk. Ray's steps scurried after him.

"Daddy!" She flipped the cell phone closed.

As Isa tried to reach her father again, I drifted in the same direction as the kids, staying along the sidewalk in the slender shadow of a building until a hand grabbed my elbow, stopping me: Patrick's sinewy grip, his thumb pressing into the soft spot above the bone. I tugged, and he released.

"I know she likes you," he whispered. "There's a lot between you."

"There's not. Not like that." I was relieved to be telling the truth.

"It's okay," he said, as if I'd agreed with him. "We both want what's good for her. I'm telling you because I'm seeing some early signs: she's going up and down, and she's being tough on herself. She likes attention and all that when she's with people. But you know what she's like at night, when she can't sleep. She's been through a lot, you know that. Seeing family is hard on her."

For a moment, I was taken back to Channel House, when Patrick used to confide in me. It had been a long time since he'd shared anything like that. "She needs you," I said. "You should listen to her more."

His shoes stammered as he shifted his weight. "I don't have the patience you have. You help keep her balanced. She needs that. And I appreciate it. The less said about all this stuff, the better. But I wanted you to know."

I thought about my father, who never talked about emotions.

"Sometimes I overreact," he continued. "I know that. Like in the car yesterday about your writing and stuff. Isa got all over me about that. You're teaching the kids, I can see that. Just don't write about me."

It hadn't occurred to me that I was teaching the kids. That was how poorly I saw myself.

"Okay, then," he said, walking away, as if we'd come to some understanding. I stood for a moment, dumbfounded, wishing I'd confronted him about Devon and Ray. "Patrick," I called.

"Yeah, what?" he said, not far away.

A car with a booming bass drove by.

"The kids," I said. "You ought to loosen up some. Give them more space to do things their own way." It sounded wrong as soon as I said it.

"Don't tell me how to parent," he said coldly.

Honestly, I never thought of him as a parent. I thought of him as a guy trying to make a buck and hold things together. But as I look back, I think he was trying to parent, and what mattered to him most was respect. He wanted people to defer to him.

Ray's steps scampered up, rescuing me. "Ice cream!" he said, drawing Patrick and me toward a Dairy Queen, where Devon joined us in line. We all ordered ice cream except Devon, who got a cheeseburger and large fries. "What?" he said. "I'm still hungry."

"When I was a kid," Patrick said, "there was a place across from the beach that would make me bacon burgers before they were on the menu."

I could tell he was proud of that, of being a local boy somewhere. "You grew up near the beach?" I said.

"A block from the shore. Biloxi."

"Sounds like detergent," Devon said with a good-natured laugh.

"Where is that?" I said. "Mississippi?"

"Look at those men," Patrick whispered. "Smugglers."

We were standing at a counter licking ice cream while Devon ate his burger; they were looking out through glass.

"They could be dealers," Devon said.

"Unlikely," Patrick said. "The deals aren't made in Deming. They're smugglers. This is straight north from one of the best crossings there is. All kinds of drugs come into Deming. But they move on."

"They've got bank," Devon said, "that's for sure."

"You ought to pay more attention," Patrick said smoothly, enjoying Devon's interest. "There's guns here too—mostly going south. El Paso's another crossing, but border patrol is better there, so things cost more. Rolex watches. Gucci bags. All kinds of things come across that border."

He was so comfortable talking about this. What a change from our conversation about emotions. "You mean fakes," I said. "Counterfeit."

"Don't tell Isa. There's no reason to worry her. I'm not doing any of that anyway. But it's always good to know how to make a buck. I was going to buy cigarettes in Phoenix, where you can get them cheap from the Indians. But they're already cheap as shit where we're going. So I'll buy some cartons on the way back and sell them in California, where they're taxed like crazy. It's easy money."

"Cigarettes aren't taxed in Florida?" Devon said.

"They're not taxed much all over the South."

Great, I thought. We're driving bones east and cigarettes west. "What are you going to carry the cartons in?" I said. "You won't have the casket."

He didn't answer. He said Isa was waving for us to go.

Tumbling into Betsy, we squirmed like pirates, Devon, Ray, and me, the backseat scorching our bare legs, the three of us gasping. The kids rolled down windows to let in and out the oppressive heat. Patrick backed up. Waited. Waited. As he screeched forward, turning and kicking stones, Devon succumbed to the pleasure of falling into me, and I leaned into Ray, pinning him giggling against the door.

After about an hour, thunder started to rumble, and Ray got excited watching for lightning and counting the distance until the boom sounded: one–one thousand, two–one thousand, three!

Patrick said, "Here it comes."

Raindrops popped on the windshield. Then a splatter of drowning noise enveloped the car in coolness as the kids rolled up their windows and then rolled them back down and popped off their seatbelts and thrust their torsos out, laughing, and I leaned over and stuck my arm outside into complete and utter wetness stinging my skin. A crack of thunder exploded so close I tensed and ducked and we all pulled back inside, their wet bodies falling and sliding against me, all of us dripping, laughing, my ears ringing.

"Seatbelts on!" Isa sang. We clicked on our belts.

When I asked Ray what lightning looked like, he said you can't see it when it's close. It strikes too fast. That surprised me—thunder bellowed louder the closer it was.

"But in the distance," he said, his voice high-pitched and excited, "it's like a tree upside down. You can see the trunk and the little branches flash down to the ground. By the time you see it, it's gone."

I took out my note-taker and started to register that. "That's good," I said.

"You gonna write what I said this time?" he said—which reminded me of his cotton-candy sunrise and his boulders dancing on end.

I tried writing a while, but my new toy was so easy to use that I got frustrated by my own inabilities. My ideas strayed. My descriptions sounded bland. Nothing came together. I put the note-taker away. As we barreled along the Rio Grande heading southeast toward Texas, Ray's head pressed against my shoulder, Devon snored lightly, and my head dropped against the seat back. I woke to the sound of Isa's faltering voice and the throb of a dream: I was reaching for the softness of a dress that drifted in a breeze, billowing unseen. I felt wisps of fabric—more like a scarf or sari than a dress—on my cheek, but though I stretched my arms, it eluded my reach, its silk brushing the tips of my fingers, like the curves of a woman's hips.

"I don't think we'll see them," Isa said.

Even in dreams, I thought, I couldn't quite reach what I sought.

"Don't kid yourself about Robert," Patrick said. "He's going to beat us there by plane. He's going to cheat us out of the will. He needs the money."

"I'm not going there for the money," Isa said emphatically. "I'm going there to help him."

Ray nestled his head against me, waking.

"People are suing him," Patrick said.

"Look out!" Isa said.

Betsy lurched, and we pitched forward, the click of seatbelts locking. Since I was in the middle, I only had a lap belt. Ray sat up. I put my glasses back on.

Isa told us the traffic was El Paso. It was almost six-thirty.

"Welcome to Texas!" Patrick said. "I'm gonna drive all night. When you wake up in the morning, you can say, 'Hello, Louisiana!'"

After we got going again, Patrick started quizzing the kids about U.S. rivers: The only major river that runs north? The largest river by volume that flows into the Pacific? The names of states the Mississippi borders or flows through? The river in North America that separates two countries but will never keep out Mexicans?

Here comes his rant on immigration and the border, I thought, cringing and thinking of Ray, whose grandparents had slipped across that border looking for work. I wondered how Patrick could be so interested in the smuggling of bones and guns and merchandise yet be so adamant that people shouldn't come across.

But Patrick didn't rage about immigration. He stepped on the gas, then slowed. "Why doesn't that damn car pass me?" he said.

"I'm hungry," Devon said.

That was when Patrick braked ruthlessly, pitching us into our seatbelts, for what I don't know: another car, a truck? My stomach leaped to my throat.

We got slammed from the back so hard that my head must have jerked back; it happened too suddenly to feel. A cracking boom exploded in my ears, making me deaf in slow motion fast. Shards and bits of something blasted over me from behind as Betsy swerved one way and jolted the other, skidding and turning briefly, tilting, languishing, then stopping dead, a horrible ringing in my ears.

For a moment, we all sat in shock.

Ray started screaming. My head pounded. I felt nothing else. Isa moaned sorrowfully, like a lame cow. Was I moaning too? I don't know.

I remembered to breathe. The back of my neck and head felt like it had been hit by birdshot. I felt my head with my hand; there were diamond-shaped bits of rough safety glass in my hair. So far as I could tell, though, I wasn't bleeding. I reached for Ray to check him, feeling his neck and face. He screamed and screamed.

"Are you okay?" I said. "Ray!"

"Asshole!" Patrick said. "Goddamn jerk!" Then he was all business. "Is everyone okay? Ray, Devon, Isa, everyone check in."

"I'm okay," Devon said.

"Okay," Isa said.

"I'm not hurt," I said. "I'm okay."

Ray's scream came down an octave. I realized again that my ears were ringing.

"Ray," Patrick said, "where does it hurt?"

"I think I'm okay," he whimpered.

"Thank goodness for seatbelts," Isa said.

As Patrick pulled Betsy over to the shoulder, something dragged on the road at the car's rear, making a gruesome screech. We unbuckled our belts. Ray clung to me.

Patrick jumped out of the car. "You goddamn idiot!" he screamed. "You were tailgating for miles!"

"Hold on there, partner," a voice said. "What'd you brake for? There weren't no call to brake like that."

"I was getting you off my ass!"

"That strategy didn't work too good," the man said.

Cars and trucks whizzed by us. "The back window's smashed," Devon said quietly from the seat next to me. My stomach began to turn. I had to stumble over Devon's legs to get out: headfirst, hands down on the gravel, my legs coming after. I crawled in the rubble and retched, heaving up barely anything, we'd eaten so long ago. My right leg began to twitch. My head felt woozy, and all sound fell away.

I'm in an alleyway in San Francisco, where I crouch between ledges, twitching, panicking, too high, clutching my buddy Casey—skinny guy, frail—who's convulsing in my arms, his legs jumping, his arms jerking, and his head jolting in spasms as no one can do on his own. I've already been up, away from him, running, yelling for an ambulance, using Charlie folded in fifths to bang on doors, yet no one will answer until glass breaks.

"Hey!" someone calls from inside.

"Call an ambulance!" I scream. "There's a man out here dying." And I know an ambulance will come.

Two days later, Dad will pay my bail and drive me to Channel House in L.A., where I will meet Isa and Patrick. In those counseling groups, I blame myself: if I can see the window in the door, and if I don't break that window, does the first 911 go out for an ambulance instead of the cops? How is it that even when I take action, I lose, I fail, I cause harm?

I'm crouching in the alley with Casey, holding him as he trembles and jolts, willing him calm, talking to him, waiting with him. I hear sirens of the ambulance coming. Footsteps are running. I get cracked on the head, jerked up, thrown against a wall, and hauled off to jail. It's my last touch of him—no good-byes for Casey, except in the convulsions of my dreams.

When I was at the treatment center, during all those self-writing exercises, I began to realize that if I hadn't acted at all in that alleyway, if I had remained still except to hold Casey in my arms, I would have been with him when he died. Maybe I could have comforted him. At least I would have had that memory. How is it that fools are always bustling while the quiet man leaves nothing undone?

When I could, I joined the others huddled on the side of the freeway in gravel and sand. Ray was still in shock, so I held him cross-legged in my lap. I don't think he knew where he was; he was listless mostly and otherwise tried to lunge toward the car, but I held him tightly. I rocked him calmly, which helped to soothe my stomach. I massaged the back of his neck. I hummed a few songs I'd often used to put him to sleep—until a panic overtook me at the thought of losing him, and I hummed an upbeat version of "I've Been Working on the Railroad."

Isa tried to calm Patrick, but he paced back and forth. Whenever she spoke to him, he flew into a rage.

I found myself twitching again.

After about twenty minutes of sitting, Ray felt better and my stomach settled. Still, the cops hadn't come.

"Look at the sunset," Isa said, trying to distract us. "It's about as beautiful as you can imagine, Kevin."

The thought of cotton candy was sickening.

When Ray crawled into Isa's arms, I stood and shook my legs, trying to get the blood flowing. Devon and I explored the damage to the cars: The man's Volvo appeared okay except for its front bumper, the grille, and one headlight. Betsy's rear door was smashed in—a large depression. Her rear window was shattered, and her bumper was half on the pavement. The ropes up top were taut; Devon said the casket looked fine.

"Of all the rotten luck," Patrick whined.

The air cooled as night fell. We were sitting together in the sand beyond the shoulder of the road, Ray in Isa's lap, when car tires crunched behind the Volvo.

"About time," Devon said. We all stood. I kept a hand on Ray's shoulder.

As soon as a car door opened and steps sounded on gravel, Patrick began, "This man here—"

"Just a minute, sir," a man said, cutting him off. "Let me make sure everybody's all right." His steps crunched toward us, and he had us walk around to make sure we didn't need medical attention.

"You a blind?" he said.

A blind what? I wondered. "Yes," I said. "You a police?"

"Texas Highway Patrol."

When Patrick started to talk, the patrolman cut him off again. Then they walked around the vehicles, silent except for footsteps—and the cars whooshing by.

"His brake lights weren't workin', Tony," the man said.

"What!" Patrick said. "You know this guy?"

"And he braked fer no good reason. He didn't have no call to do that."

"He plowed into me!" Patrick said. "My brake lights are fine!"

"Doesn't matter who I know and who I don't," the patrolman said. "We're going to test your taillights."

"They're smashed!" Patrick said. "Of course they don't work now."

"That one isn't. What's that up there? Is that a coffin?"

There was a pause. "It's a handmade, one-of-a-kind casket," Patrick said. "I'm selling—"

"What's in it, sir?" the patrolman interrupted.

Only then did I think about bones in ziplock baggies inside a burlap sack. No matter what Patrick had told us in the driveway back in Burbank, who knew what kind of bones they were?

"Nothing," Patrick said. "Not a thing."

We all followed the patrolman's steps as he approached Betsy. My jaws were clamped together—all my muscles were compressed. I tried to settle them by loosening my fingers and shaking my hands, getting the blood flowing again.

"You got a license for that?"

"For what?"

"You can't cross state lines with a deceased unless you have a license."

"But there's nothing in it, Officer," Isa said. "We're taking it to my father in Florida. He's on his deathbed."

"You're going to have to open it, sir," the patrolman said.

"That's a search," Patrick muttered. "You can't make me open it."

"The hell I can't. You already told me it's a coffin. That there's probable cause."

Patrick shifted his weight and finally said, "Fine!" But he fiddled with the ropes forever, pretending he couldn't get them untied.

"I've got a knife if you need it," the trooper said.

We had to pull down the casket and plop it on the dirt. Patrick tugged at the duct tape to unwrap the tarp.

"Can I go?" the Volvo man said.

"You stay put, Cecil," the patrolman said.

"If this thing gets damaged . . ." Patrick said, but didn't finish his sentence.

"Wow," Cecil said. "That is one fine-looking casket."

"I'm selling them if you want one," Patrick sneered.

"Open it," the patrolman said.

"I teach anthropology," Patrick lied, "at a community college."

"Patrick!" Isa said. I recognized the panic in her voice. Back when Patrick was selling bones, he always pretended to be an anthropologist, to give himself authority.

I heard the two snaps of the latches, but I didn't hear the lid open. Ray jumped back into me, startled—as if he hadn't seen inside before.

"That's really bright at night," Devon said.

"Never seen a coffin light up," Cecil said, chuckling. "That is one nice effect."

"I told you I sell them," Patrick said, proudly this time.

"What's in that bag?" the trooper said.

"Animal bones," Patrick said with an air of importance. He rustled with the burlap; I could hear the bones shake.

"How do I know they're not human?" the patrolman said.

Patrick let out a quick burst of laughter. "Look at them. Careful, they're brittle." After a moment, Devon handed me a skinny, prickly bone; it felt the same as the ones he'd shown us in Burbank. "There isn't a human bone like this. Ever hear of a coon bone?"

Cecil let out a big guffaw. "Coon bone! Haw!"

"Gamblers wrap a dollar bill around it and tie it with red thread," Patrick said. "It brings them good draws and lucky rolls."

"What?" the patrolman said.

"It's the penis bone of a raccoon," Cecil bellowed. "That's what a coon bone is."

I almost dropped the bone from my hand.

"That's right," Patrick said, warming to Cecil. "They bring good luck because they're as big as the dick bone of a bear. On a little raccoon. Lovers wear them on a necklace."

I put the frail bone into my shirt pocket. I'd heard a lot from Patrick about bones, but never this. Was there such a thing as a penis bone?

"Some people call it a hillbilly toothpick," Patrick said with a fake laugh.

Cecil guffawed.

Isa tried her open, airy laugh to bring in the patrolman.

"I don't know what you're saying," the trooper said, dead serious. "I'm going to confiscate this bag to see what we got here. We might have to tow your car. And you may be partly at fault depending on your taillight."

"My taillights worked!" Patrick yelled. "And he rear-ended me!" He paced back and forth. "He'd been tailgating for miles."

"Patrick!" Isa said. Devon, Ray, and I backed away from the car, away from the interstate. I had one arm around Ray and my other hand hooked on Devon's elbow.

"Sir, you're going to have to calm down," the patrolman said firmly.

"Like hell!" Patrick said. "You guys are friends, you two. Gimme back that bag!"

There was a pause I didn't like. A silence looming.

"You know what I don't like about Texas?" Patrick sneered. "Texans!"

"Patrick!" Isa said.

There was a series of grunts and shuffles and moans that didn't sound like Patrick or the patrolman, but who else could it be?

"Stand back!" the patrolman ordered.

Devon told me later: Patrick thrust himself at the officer like a penguin, over and over, keeping his own arms at his side.

"Patrick!" Isa said again.

There was a thud as a body—or both bodies—hit the ground.

"Okay!" Patrick said.

"He's got Patrick on the ground," Devon said.

A car pulled up, no siren, wheels skidding on gravel.

Patrick and the patrolman were panting.

A door opened. "Tony!" a man called. He came running. "You okay?"

"I'm fine, Sheriff," the patrolman said, still panting. "It's under control." He read Patrick his rights.

"I'll go," Patrick said. "I don't need your damn handcuffs."

"Hold your hands still," the sheriff said. I heard some metal clicks. "There, ya bastard!"

"I'm not payin' no goddamn tow fee," Patrick said.

"The hell you won't if you want outa my jail," the sheriff said. He spoke slower than the patrolman, with a deep drawl.

"Then by God, I'll eat your grub till I rot."

"Well, it's some mighty fine cui-zine," the sheriff said. "You'll see that yourself."

Steps crunched across gravel to a car door opening, then slamming shut.

"There ya go, ya bastard!" the sheriff yelled. He came crunching back to us. "Excuse the language, ma'am. You saw him resistin' arrest."

"You weren't even here," Devon said.

"Devon," I said, "be quiet."

"He was just flailing around," Devon explained. "He wasn't hitting anybody."

"You shut the hell up," the sheriff drawled. "Excuse the language, ma'am."

"Sheriff, see if the car is operable," the patrolman said. "And check the taillight."

In the darkness, the sheriff asked me to pull the car forward.

Devon laughed.

"He's a blind," the patrolman said. "See if she can do it."

"Well, I'll be damned," the sheriff said.

"Take your light off his face," Devon demanded.

Again I told Devon to be quiet.

"You lookin' for trouble, boy?" the sheriff said. "Ring my bell once more and you'll be sittin' in the back with Mr. Jail Cui-zine over there."

I held to Devon's arm, expecting him to lash out over being called "boy." But he just grumbled as Isa walked with the sheriff toward Betsy, which started up right away. I worried about her behind the wheel; she didn't like driving, particularly in strange places. As the car pulled forward, there was a loud scraping again.

"Hold it!" the sheriff said. "I got it." There was a loud wham! and something metal hit the ground.

"The bumper," Devon said.

"Taillight doesn't work," the sheriff called.

Just before the sheriff drove off with Patrick, we walked over to say good-bye through the closed window.

"Don't worry," he yelled. "You can do it. Betsy'll run fine. Use your credit card if you have to. I'll be out tomorrow."

"We'll make do," Isa said.

"Devon," he yelled, "make sure you lash it good on the roof."

Still my leg was twitching, so I shook it some.

I thought Isa would cry when the sheriff pulled away, but if she did, I didn't hear it. She stepped right over to the patrolman, saying what a shame it was the way Patrick had acted and thank goodness the patrolman was there to help us. "We don't have much money," she said, "but the Lord will provide if you can help lift the coffin onto the station wagon. It's for Daddy."

I imagined her reaching and touching his hand. I imagined him leering at her breasts.

We didn't bother with the tarp—Devon, the patrolman, Isa, and I. We grabbed four handles and hoisted it up. "You get along good for a blind," the patrolman said.

"A blind what?" I said.

"A blind man," he said matter-of-factly. "I've seen folks with two good eyes can't do a thing after a crash like this."

Devon and I did the best we could tying the casket on, but there was some slack, and we forgot about the towels to protect the wood, so we wedged them around the ropes after the knots were tied. We were brushing glass from the backseat when a truck pulled up behind us, its motor rumbling. A door opened and thudded shut, the engine still on. Someone walked toward us.

"Evenin', Tony," a woman said. Her gruff voice reminded me of Dotty, the bus driver in Burbank.

"Hey there, Mabel," the patrolman said.

"Damned if that don't beat all," Mabel said. "Somebody in that coffin up there?"

"You been watching too much TV," the patrolman said.

The woman chuckled. "Kind of spooky, though, ain't it, settin' up there all tilted on that old busted-up wagon?"

"All you get is the bumper," the patrolman said.

"Been that kind of day," Mabel said. I heard her drag it to her truck.

Isa got behind the wheel and started Betsy again, with Devon in the other front seat. I sat in the back with Ray, who seemed better; he could answer questions.

"Get off at the first exit," the patrolman said. "That'll be Fabens. There isn't much there, but you can get back toward El Paso on State Road 20."

"We'll be fine," Isa said. "Where do I find my husband tomorrow?"

"County jail in El Paso. Get your taillights fixed."

As she drove, I was proud of her strength, the way she was stepping up for the kids. She seemed to relax into her role now that she was in charge. Ray hung on the rope that ran through the car and I tugged down on it too to make it tighter. On the roof, one of the towels started flapping, then quieted completely. Devon laughed, and Ray said the towel was stuck on the grille of the patrol car behind us. Our exhaust came in through the smashed rear window, nauseating me.

"Betsy's running fine," Isa said. "Praise Jesus that none of us is hurt. Who cares about some dents?"

"Dents?" Devon said. "Betsy's busted up. The back door won't open. No rear bumper. There's glass pellets all over the suitcases."

The other towel started flapping.

"It's a miracle the casket is fine," Isa said, as if that was what she'd been talking about.

"I think I'm getting sick," Ray said.

"Stick your head out the window, honey," Isa said. "Breathe some fresh air."

As we dropped off the highway and slowed, we could hear the casket slide forward. We pulled over, pushed the casket straight, and tried to tighten the ropes, but we couldn't get the knot loosened on the front line.

"Look for a church," Isa said. "A church with a light on."

"At ten o'clock at night?" Devon said.

"God grants miracles," she said.

Before we knew it, we were through town. Isa turned several times and wound along rural roads that smelled of fertilizer mixed with our exhaust. I pulled down steadily on the rope that ran through the car, to keep it taut.

From the creaking of the roof, it seemed the coffin was inching cockeyed again. "What'll we tell them?" I said.

"We'll explain what happened. We're on a journey to visit Daddy, who's dying. We'll ask for a place to sleep, just for a night, like Joseph and Mary. I'll say we believe in God the father, the maker of heaven and earth. My name is Isa that comes from Isaac of Abraham." She wasn't making sense. Her voice had risen to that excited pitch.

"I thought your name was short for Isabelle," I said, trying to throw out an anchor.

"Good idea," Devon said. "We'll drive up with a coffin and say Abraham sent us. They'll think we're crazy."

"You'll see," she said triumphantly. "We'll just tell the truth."

Was she ramping up or calming down? I couldn't tell. "I hope we find something soon," I said. "This exhaust is making me sick." A sharp pain began to stab the base of my skull, whether from being rear-ended or from pulling down on the rope, I didn't know. Lao-tzu says that adversity comes from having a body; without a self, how could there be bad luck?

I released the rope—not to relieve the ache but to rid us of the coffin.

I felt a tender hand on my arm.

"You okay, Ray?" I said.

"Did we almost die?" he said.

"No," I said, grasping his warm fingers. "We're alive. And we're all fine."

"God wants us here for a reason," Isa said. "We have to trust the Lord Jesus."

"There's one," Devon said. "There's a light on over there."

Isa slowed. "Voice of God Church of Christ," she said. "That's perfect."

"It looks like a barn," Ray said.

"It's a warehouse," Devon said.

After we pulled up and Isa turned off the car, we sat a while gathering courage. I rubbed my sore neck with one hand and held Ray's fingers with the other. The engine ticked. Crickets crackled as if they'd been in my head all along, only I hadn't been listening. How could there be crickets in the desert?

"No reason to say anything about Patrick for now," Isa said as she got out of the car. "No reason at all."

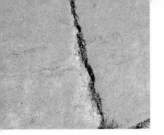

SIX

We stood restless on a concrete slab at the Voice of God Church of Christ, hesitant to knock on the door. From our left, a dry breeze blew the smell of wet fertilizer. I rubbed my neck. The world spun a little, almost tipping. A mosquito bit my forehead; I slapped too late. Where had the crickets gone? When Ray leaned into me, his back to my front, I felt my foot tapping the ground again, so I stilled it by shifting my weight and draping my left arm around him. Devon stood on the far side of Isa, who stepped forward and rapped three times on a door so defiant that her knuckles barely made a sound.

"Relax," Isa said. "We're in God's house." But her voice was thin, apprehensive.

"That's what I'm afraid of," Devon said.

I straightened behind Ray, standing tall and softening my shoulders, trying to show strength of mind. I was the man among us.

"It'll be the night watchman or janitor," Isa said. "We've got to look safe so he trusts us. Take off your hat, Kevin, so he can see that you're blind."

My disability had become an asset.

I don't have much faith in humankind's image of God, though I'm drawn to the impulse. I'd attended Isa's Bible Church a few times in Burbank. It was housed in a converted auto-parts store, on a concrete slab like this one. The Pentecostals joked and jostled even as we stumbled over their legs to take our seats in folding chairs. It was a far cry from the Presbyterian church my family had attended in Greeley when I was growing up, with its carpeted aisles, rows of pews, raised altar, and hushed tones. But the smells were the same: perspiration and perfume, farts, the food people had had for breakfast.

"This *is* a barn," Ray said.

"What kind?" I said.

"How many kinds are there?"

"Dairy, grain, horses. Wood, tin, rock, and lean-to."

"It's a warehouse," Devon said. "It's some kind of concrete."

"Well, it's a church now," Isa said.

My grandpa's barn had a gambrel roof, the classic Dutch barn shape, and vertical board siding. It held horses and bales of hay but was built for cattle, with its long troughs and hay bins for feeding and gutters and drains in the concrete subfloor to wash out the muck. After my accident, I used to sit alone in the loft, listening to the horses munching and stomping below, an owl hooting now and again above, and sparrows flickering into nests, their flits like whispers to my ears. I couldn't hear the cats until they were next to me purring or until they pounced on a mouse. The first time I heard the scuffles of a cat's paws about the floor, I didn't know he was playing with a mouse, tossing it. I knew that later, when the mouse lay limp and wet in my hands.

Ray shifted his weight, which worried me; he wasn't skipping around, animated. I remembered how listless he'd been on the shoulder of the interstate. I stepped forward around him, felt the rough door, and pounded with the side of my fist, making a clattering sound as the rough door hit its jamb.

"Look at you," Isa said. "Thanks."

I stood beside Ray and waited, hat in hand.

The hinges of the door squeaked. I smelled ammonia. I considered thrusting out my right hand but thought better of it, not wanting to appear aggressive. "Hello," I said.

"Yes?" a man said. From the source of his voice, he seemed tall.

"We're sorry to bother you," I began, "but we've had a car accident."

"We are children of Christ," Isa said quickly. "We're traveling to see my father, who's dying. Can we sleep here in God's house? You don't have to worry. We'll be gone in the morning before the minister returns."

The man released a deep-belly chuckle. "Even the pastor mops the floor," he said.

"You're the minister?" Isa said. "I'm so sorry. You're here so late." She mentioned the accident and told him how far we'd come, and how far we had to go. She introduced each of us, though not herself. She said faith had saved her life, and it helped her get up every morning. By the end of her short talk, she was hugging him, and he welcomed us to stay at his home.

"This is Isa," I said.

"Isa is for Isabelle," Ray said, "but you say it like Isaac."

"Shut up," Devon said. "He doesn't care about that."

The man let out his chuckle again, deep and welcoming. "I'm Pastor Curt. You say it like a K, but it's spelled with a C." He had a slight Texas twang.

He put some things away while we waited outside, relieved. Yet as the four of us walked to the car, I realized Ray was still clinging. I had

Devon and him stand next to Betsy, and I felt all over their heads, necks, and shoulders. "Anything tender?" I said. Ray giggled; Devon resented the attention.

"I think I'm still in shock," Isa said abruptly. "I can't relax. All of a sudden I can't stand the sight of that thing up on Betsy. If it wasn't for that thing . . ."

"Your hands are kind of moving," Devon interrupted.

I found her hands, which flitted about like sparrows. I pulled her several steps away from the kids. "You're doing a good job," I said. "You found us a place to stay. As soon as we get to the house, you can lie down."

"I don't think I can take it anymore," she whispered frantically. "I don't know what to do. I don't think I'm going to make it. Oh, my God, I can't stand that coffin up there. It's morbid! Like it's waiting for one of us. Hold me." She pulled me to her, her body pressing against mine. She dropped her head onto my shoulder, clenching all her muscles and squeezing the air from me. I hugged her as tightly as I could. Then she relaxed her muscles, sagging into me.

"That's right," I said, supporting her weight. "Breathe."

"When I close my eyes, everything's moving, and it's my fault. I know it is."

She seemed to be falling apart, now that we'd found a place to stay. "It's not your fault. Everything will settle. Give it time."

Her body shuddered against me, and she tried to pull away, but I held. "I've done a terrible thing," she said in a breathy whisper. "You don't know what I've done."

"We've all done things," I said.

"I can't get away from it."

"What?" I said. "Tell me."

Before she could say anything, long steps approached. If we could just make it to the house, I decided, she'd be fine. As we turned toward the car, the pastor said we couldn't bring the coffin with us; his wife wouldn't have it.

"Thank goodness!" Isa said. "We've got to get it off. We're driving it to Daddy. We'll come back and get it, I promise! But I can't stand the sight of it right now. Not tonight."

She walked off somewhere, I didn't know where, but she refused to sit in the car as Devon, the pastor, and I struggled with the ropes. We got one knot untied, but the other was so tight that Pastor Curt had to get a knife. The three of us slid the big box off the roof, careful not to smash a corner on the way down. Ray grabbed a handle as we carried it behind the church into an open shed. I was glad to be rid of it too, if only for a time.

"I've seen coffins," the pastor said, "but never one quite like this. The carvings are remarkable. Do you mind?" The latches clicked loudly as he opened it.

He let out a friendly chuckle. "That's quite an effect."

The lights.

As we got back to Betsy, Isa approached, and I held her hands together in mine; her trembling had settled some. She said she could drive but relented quickly when Pastor Curt insisted. I sat in the back with the kids and collapsed into the vinyl seat, exhausted yet restless. My body wouldn't settle. I felt like I was coming down, speedy from crack and needing something to help me let go. My jaws were clenched. My hands were in fists. I took several deep breaths.

"Why is it called the Voice of God?" Ray asked. What made him ask that? Had he read it again on a sign? Or was he picking up Devon's attitude?

"We seek the truth of God through Jesus' words," the pastor said.

"I can't wait to lie down," I said, trying to deflect the conversation. I didn't want to get into religion with a Voice of God pastor, not at ten o'clock with everybody on edge.

"What makes you the judge of truth?" Devon challenged.

"Devon," I said.

"How does anyone know truth?" the pastor said right away. "How do you know it?"

"What I see with my eyes," Devon said.

"What about Kevin?" the pastor said.

"You know what I mean," Devon said.

"You mean through experience," the pastor said.

"Okay," Devon said.

The car slowed and turned, then gained speed again. The pastor said, "We all know things we've never experienced. And we don't understand even everything in this car." His cadence was slow and soothing. Again we turned, Betsy's tires crunching on gravel. The car stopped, and the motor shut off. I heard him twist in the front seat. "Devon and Ray," he said, his voice facing us, "here's something I believe is true: the voice of God speaks through you. Through each of us. It's up to us to find that truth and bring it out."

Isa started sobbing, big, wholesome sobs. I leaned forward and put my hand on her shoulder, which was trembling. "Isa," I said.

"It's just the accident," she wailed. "I'm such a mess. I'm sorry."

"Kevin, is it okay if I sit here with Isa for a little while?" the pastor said in a steady voice. "Why don't you take the boys in? My wife, Andrea, is there. Just introduce yourselves. We'll be right in."

"She's all right," I said, to comfort everyone. "We've been in an accident, that's all." Then we slipped outside. All three of us were relieved, I think, to be out of that car.

The house was set back from the driveway about the same as my parents' house in Greeley, with a similar curve to the walkway, the same two stairs up to the door. I'd planned to turn and wait there on the steps with the boys, but the front door opened. I was clutching Charlie's grip so tightly that my fingers hurt.

"Well, hello," someone said in a high pitch. The pastor's wife, I assumed.

"You must be Andrea," I said.

"And you must be blind as a bat," she said, tittering. "I'm no girl. Come in."

I was confused. What did that mean, "I'm no girl"? I tried to explain who we were and how we'd met Pastor Curt, but whoever it was—male, female, I was no longer sure—stepped out and grabbed my forearm, pulling me into a house that enveloped me in the rich aroma of home-made soup, pork perhaps, onions. Suddenly I was famished. We hadn't eaten since Deming—and a few hours ago, I'd thrown up on the side of the road.

"Come in, boys," the voice said. "He does that all the time, bringing home stray cats. That's how I met him. You can't see a thing, can you?

The kids walked in behind me.

"My name's Carlos." Still the high-pitched voice. My hat was lifted from my head. "Look at you in those glasses," he said. "You have that chiseled look. I like that in a man."

"You're gay," Devon said.

"Well, aren't we one happy family," Carlos said. "Black, white, and brown."

I started laughing. I couldn't help it.

"Don't mind Carlos," someone said from behind him. "He's harmless." A warm tone, hospitable, with a tinge of Spanish accent. Deeper than Carlos's voice. Scratchier. Man or woman? I knew better than to guess.

"Excuse me," Carlos said. " 'Harmless' is not in my vocabulary."

"This isn't what I expected in a minister's house in Texas," I said, still chuckling.

"Well, that's a good thing, honey," Carlos said. "That's a good thing."

"I'm Andrea," the second voice said.

Again I tried to explain why we were there, and again I was interrupted.

"Come on," Andrea said. "I have a pot of posole on the stove."

"Posole," Ray said, excited.

"I'm starving," Devon said.

As we walked across carpet onto linoleum, Andrea began to fuss over Ray, and the two of them spoke rapidly in Spanish. From the echoes, it seemed like one big room: water splashing in a sink, bowls scraping on a tabletop, silverware clinking, and Ray's footsteps disappearing into the clutter of movement and meaning and safety.

Charlie found my way to the table, where I sat without thinking. My mind shut down a while. I was startled when Andrea served me steaming soup and Carlos thanked God for the food on the table, the health of those around it, and the hope of compassion around the world.

I picked up my spoon in a daze, the world around me spinning, but someone slapped my hand softly, reviving me.

"No," Andrea said, laughing, "it's too picante. First you crumble this cheese into the bowl. I'll help you so the others can see. Then you spread around the sliced cabbage. And green onions. And avocado." She handed me some chips. "Now crush chips between your fingers and spread them on top." She handed me a lime. "Squeeze in some lime, and you can eat. Without all that, it's too spicy."

I liked the way she prepared my meal while seeming to care for the others. As I dug my spoon into my bowl and lifted it up, bits of things fell from my spoon, so I leaned over the bowl to bring my mouth to the spoon. First I felt the raw cabbage against my lips, then the warmth and flavor. I could taste pork chunks, salty broth, cabbage, and lime. Then the chilies hit me: my tongue, the roof of my mouth, even my lips were on fire. The back of my hand hit my water glass and spilled it.

"I told you it's spicy," Andrea said, laughing.

"You got that right," Devon said. I could hear him gulping down water as someone wiped my spill with a towel. My face was sweating.

"More cabbage and chips," Andrea said. "And have a tortilla. That helps more than water."

As I ate, my body calmed, yet the room still moved from time to time, spinning. About midway through our soup, the voices of Isa and Pastor Curt drifted inside just before the front door opened.

"Good!" the pastor said, entering. "You're all eating."

"Not me," Carlos said. "I dined at the earlier seating."

"Isa?" I said. "Are you okay?"

"She went to the bathroom," Curt said. "She'll be fine. She's in a bit of shock."

Withdrawing to the bathroom was a good sign for Isa; it meant she cared what she looked like. When she joined us, she said she didn't feel like eating, which made Andrea fuss over her more, making sure she had something in her bowl. After a bit, Isa exclaimed about the heat of the soup. Later she said suddenly, "I'm doing fine. I just needed to talk. I haven't seen a minister in a while."

"Like two whole days," Devon said.

When I finished my posole, my belly felt warm.

The pastor spoke in Spanish with Andrea and then divvied up the beds, asking Carlos to sleep on the couch. "Isa and Kevin can have Natalie's room," he said. "She probably won't be back until morning; she won't mind. The kids can sleep in the garage."

I sat up, tense; he'd put me in a room with Isa. Yet why should I be surprised? Of course he assumed we were together.

I waited for Isa to shift the rooms around. But she thanked him and said, "Kevin, I need your support tonight. I'm still in shock."

My heart raced. What did that mean, that she needed my support?

"Who's Natalie?" Devon said.

My pulse thumped in my temples. Had Devon missed the sleeping arrangements? As the others talked about where we were traveling and what had happened, I couldn't hold a steadfast thought. I worried about Patrick; what if he found out? But that wouldn't happen, I decided. I wasn't about to sleep alone in a room with Isa. I rubbed the ache in my neck. My forehead popped with sweat. I drank some water.

I'd slept alongside her once in our little deficiency in Burbank, before Patrick was out of Channel House, when she'd been overwhelmed by—what was it then? Fears that she wasn't good enough. That people didn't love her. That Patrick wouldn't want her. We'd both slept through the night. Harmless.

And what about all those nights the past two weeks at the breakfast table? Hadn't I been alone with her then as everyone slept? Patrick must have known about that. Or else why would he have said—just that day at lunch—that I helped her stay balanced? Hadn't I withstood those nights, as she brushed herself against me? Afterward, yes, I often withdrew to my room to bring myself off. But what was the harm in that?

It occurred to me: What if Patrick didn't get out of jail and we needed to stay a second night? How would we explain that to the pastor and his wife? Then I thought, what if Patrick got out early and somehow found us sleeping together?

That fear startled me: Had I decided to sleep with Isa?

When we left the table, I was a jumble of indecision. To avoid Isa, I walked outside with the kids. Since Betsy's rear gate wouldn't open, Devon pulled our bags over the backseat. Pellets of safety glass lay everywhere, but they didn't cut. Isa and I were the only ones with hard suitcases—the firm sides helped me organize and locate my clothes.

Devon carried Isa's luggage down the hallway as I dropped my suitcase and backpack in the living room; I didn't want to commit to her room. Ray led me from the kitchen linoleum through a doorway and down a couple of steps onto concrete. Carlos followed and started up an air-conditioning unit, which rattled before settling into a low buzz. He was staying just a few more days and didn't mind giving up the garage, he said.

After he went back into the house, I explored the room with Charlie, searching for a cushion or something else to place on the concrete floor. There was nothing but the double mattress, which was directly on the floor and was pushed up against the wall.

"What are you doing?" Ray said.

"Want to sleep in Isa's room?" I said.

"No way. She scares me when she gets like that."

"Like what?" I said.

"When she gets all sad and cries."

"You've seen her like that before?"

He didn't answer, and I didn't press him.

Footsteps shuffled down the stairs—no flip-flops. "This is my side," Devon said, opposite where Ray and I were. Something heavy thudded onto the concrete by the bed: his duffel bag.

I left Charlie leaning against a wall as Ray and I walked up to the kitchen and along the seam of the living room carpet to my suitcase. I took out my bath kit, and we walked down the hallway to the bathroom door, but the shower was already running. Isa, we assumed—so we walked into her room.

"I'll sleep on this carpet," I said, to make sure Ray knew.

"When I close my eyes," he said, "I still see flashing lights. Blue and red. Going 'round and 'round."

Poor kid, I thought, all the crap he's been through today. We sat on the bed and I rubbed his forehead. "Take deep breaths," I said. "That'll help."

A door in the hallway opened, and a moment later Isa breezed into the room, smelling of shampoo and soap. I could feel my pulse quicken.

"That feels better," she said, rustling through things.

What was she wearing: A towel? A nightgown? A shirt? "I better sleep out in Betsy," I said, standing.

"The mosquitoes will eat you alive," she said. "I need you. Don't we need him, Ray? Isn't he a good balance for all of us? Aren't you glad he came?"

Balanced, I thought. Wasn't that the word Patrick had used? He must have gotten it from her.

"Then I'll sleep on the floor," I said, retreating after Ray into the hallway, where I vacillated outside the bathroom door, waiting for Ray to pee. Moments later, as we brushed our teeth at the sink, I was still distracted. Could I sleep in the same room with Isa? Would Patrick believe that I'd crashed on the floor? Ray stood on tiptoes and reached up so we would bump elbows, my right with his left. His giggling made me smile.

Thinking back now, I have to laugh at myself, how apprehensive I was about everything. What should I do, and when? What shouldn't I do? It was always Ray's soft touch that helped me lighten up.

Back in the garage, as Devon took his turn in the bathroom, I sat on the mattress next to Ray, my legs stretched out on the concrete. He rolled away from me; I was not prepared for what he said.

"Mom hit me once, the week before she died."

I heard him clearly, but I had to fight the instinct to ask him to repeat it. His parents had made crystal meth, for God's sake. His mother had died in an explosion, which had burned the house while he was at school. His dad survived with severe burns but was locked up afterward, so Ray lost everything. All he had was the picture of his mom that his aunt and uncle from Mexico had snapped years earlier, during a visit. As I rubbed his back slowly, I remembered the way Andrea had fussed over him when we'd arrived, and the Spanish they'd spoken together.

"Tell me about it," I said.

"I don't want to talk about it." He put his feet under the thin sheet, and I pulled it up over his chest.

"I know you don't. It's scary." Through the sheet I rubbed his legs for a long time, down where the growing pains always were, along his shins and just above his ankles.

"They used to do drugs," he said, his voice steady but thin. "I found needles sometimes. At night Dad would get crazy and yell at her. It wasn't her fault. He'd hit her, and she'd scream at him. I used to think she hated him. I'd go in the closet and hide under my blanket and think that tomorrow we'd get away, Mom and me. Sometimes I'd cry, and he'd yell at me to go to sleep or he'd come shut me up." His legs twitched under the sheet. "But I couldn't sleep. I was scared of him, and I couldn't sleep."

I leaned over and hugged him. "I'm here with you." He was still facing away from me.

After a while he continued, "He never hit me. But I thought he was going to. I told Manny I fell."

Manny was Ray's case worker at Children and Family Services.

"And that's what I told those lawyers. They wanted to blame it on Dad. But it was Mom."

I rubbed the muscles along his spine, waiting.

"Can you scratch?" he said.

I pulled down the sheet, put my hand under his t-shirt, and scratched lightly with my fingernails, all over his back the way he liked.

"It was just one time and Dad wasn't there and she was mad at me because I wanted something to eat. I could see the drugs in her eyes. I wish I could've made some money or something. She said all I did was eat stuff and want things. It was the drugs. She had those scabs on her face and neck. Her eyes wouldn't look at me. They wouldn't look at anything."

I waited, not sure what to say. I'd felt those scabs on Casey in San Francisco—and TBone too, a big Sumatran that everybody clung to; his guitar riffs brought bills from tourists at Fisherman's Wharf and Union Square. I never did meth, and I refused needles, but that didn't make me better than any other addict who needed a fix and then threw a fit and hit somebody afterward. When I was on crack, I was a different person. I threw things and wanted stuff and stood up to people—no more blind misgivings. I had my share of fights with Casey, who always just took it as I railed against him, lashed out, struck him, and thrashed at myself afterward, the whole dismal cycle of cruelty and self-abuse, because that was what it eventually came to the next morning or afternoon: the self-hatred and self-blame and sense of failure.

I rubbed Ray's neck behind his left ear, where I felt the raised keloid scar. "You want to tell me about it?" I said.

"That's all," he said.

"Where did she hit you?"

He wouldn't say anything else. I rubbed his face, along his jaw. His lips were pressed together, the brave little guy; he wasn't crying.

After a while, I said, "Grown-ups don't always do the right things. They don't always say the right things. Your mom is so sorry that ever happened. She loves you, and she's sorry. It was the drugs; it wasn't her. It was drugs."

"You used to do drugs."

"Drugs messed up my life. I'm still trying to get over it."

He lay very still. "Why did you do them?"

I told him I was confused.

"That's what scares me most," he said, "when grown-ups are confused."

"Are you scared now?"

"I don't think so," he said.

I waited. "If you were scared now, what would you be scared of?"

"Patrick," he said right away.

"Why?"

"I don't know."

"Has Patrick ever hit you?"

"No."

"Has he ever threatened you?"

"No."

"For reals?"

"Well, just like he has with everybody else. Remember when he pulled the car over and yelled at Devon and you?"

"Has he ever hit Devon?"

"I don't think so. He grabs Devon sometimes."

"Does that scare you?"

"I don't know what he's going to do next."

I felt myself breathe. "I know what you mean," I said. "But you know what? I promise I'll protect you. And so will Devon. No matter what anybody says, you tell me if anyone ever hits you or hurts you. Do you understand?"

I was pretty sure he nodded. I put my hand on his head.

"You promise?"

He nodded.

"I thought you were nodding. Are you trying to sneak a nod on a poor blind man?" He nodded again. We'd played this game countless times. "Poor blind man. You hold your head still, do you hear me?" He nodded and nodded. "You know what happens to anybody who nods to a blind man?" I tickled him with one hand and tried to hold his head still with my other. We rolled around the bed, twisting the sheets sideways, him nodding and me tickling and holding his head until we were breathing hard. But still we weren't laughing.

We lay there, settling.

"Now, close your eyes," I said, "the biggest eyes in all of Texas." He rolled away from me, on his side the way he liked. "Take a big breath," I whispered, "the deepest breath in the Lone Star State."

His lungs expanded and his shoulders relaxed. He yawned.

"Your momma loves you so much," I said, "and she wants to say she's sorry from heaven. You're a good boy, the best boy. She never wanted to hurt you. She didn't mean to do what she did. She remembers how much she loves you. And it's so much love that it fills up heaven and spills down here onto earth, and that's what that thunderstorm was today, all of her love."

"That's not true," he said.

I told him how much his dad loved him, how sorry he was about what happened. And I went through the litany of everyone who loved him: Isa and Patrick and Devon and I. I remembered his aunt and uncle, María and José, in Mexico. When I stopped he piped up, "And Robert and June and Alexis."

"And Robert and June and Alexis love you. And Andrea and Pastor Curt and Carlos."

I sang softly, "She'll Be Comin' 'Round the Mountain." Footsteps slipped down the stairs, lighter steps than Devon's. Isa's voice joined me singing, barely more than a whisper. She sat next to me on the mattress, her hip against mine, her hand trembling as she touched my shoulder, her skin smelling of soap from her shower. By the end of the song, his breathing had changed; he was asleep, out cold, one leg sprawled to the side.

"You're so good with him," she said. I wondered how long she'd been watching from the doorway. I could hear her hands quivering in her lap, so I reached to calm them, laying my hand on hers—but I felt as if I were somewhere else, outside my own body. My senses felt deadened, like the nerve endings along my scar. When she leaned and hugged me, her breasts through her cotton chemise brushed against my body, but I felt no tingles. No yearning. No desire. Maybe I was too exhausted after the conversation with Ray; I was still startled by what he'd told me. Maybe it was the car crash. Or maybe it was true after all, what I'd been telling myself: that I was no longer interested. In any case, I thought, it was a good sign to not be aroused by her.

"He's seeing flashing lights," I said, to have something to say.

"You're lucky to see nothing. You don't see demons when you close your eyes."

"That's what you see?"

"I'm going to keep the bad things out of my mind," she said. "Like that accident. That's behind me. Jesus died for my sins, Kevin. That's what Pastor Curt helped me remember. If it weren't for my faith . . ." She didn't finish her sentence. I could feel her arms trembling. "You're a good man, Kevin Layne. You have compassion. Sometimes I think I fell for the wrong guy."

I tried to pull away, but she held on.

"Don't get me wrong," she said. "I love Patrick. He's stayed with me even when I've been down."

She drew away suddenly and stood, just as footsteps shuffled down the steps. "You feeling okay?" Isa asked. From her tone, I knew she wasn't talking to me.

Devon grunted. Maybe he nodded? After Isa walked into the house, I stood up from the mattress and shook my legs, letting the blood flow back into them.

Devon shuffled through his bag and then said, "You're not really gonna sleep in her bed, are you?"

"I'm sleeping on the floor. Or in Betsy."

"Good idea," he said. "Patrick will kick your ass."

I picked up Charlie and started to walk toward the stairs.

"I'm sick of this shit," he said. "This is your last chance. I'm running tonight."

I stopped. I could hear him shifting around on the mattress, so I walked around and sat on his side, where he was lying down. I waited, trying to figure out what to say. I couldn't imagine him running from here, of all places: Fabens, Texas? But I knew better than to dismiss the idea. I thought of the five hundred dollars tucked into my suitcase, and the six twenties in my wallet. "Got any money?" I said.

"Thirty-eight dollars."

"Where you going?"

"Out of here. Who cares? Maybe I'll hitch back to Tucson."

Right, I thought. Back to Alexis. Tonight. After all this.

"I spoke with Alexis," he said.

"How?"

"Isa's cell. Just now, while you were with Ray."

That was kind of Isa, I thought, to let him call. I asked if they were coming to Florida.

"She doesn't know. She can't convince her parents."

I waited, but he didn't say more. "You've known her for one day," I said.

"Two days: yesterday and today. And I can't get her out of my mind. She has this way of squeezing her lips together when she's about to cry. She dips her head to the side when she's mad. And she's smart, even street smart. We came so close to running last night. So close. You don't even know."

I'd never seen him so innocent, so removed from his cynical self.

"I hated her at first," he said. "That candy perfume—Sweet Tarts—and her rich fucking parents. But I liked the way she didn't back down."

Sweet Tarts. *That* was her perfume.

"When I sat next to her at dinner, as pretty as she was, all that blond fucking hair and black makeup, I peeked at her skinny white legs during the prayer, and you know that shit, they won't love you like a black girl? That popped into my head, and I felt guilty for liking her. Like I wasn't allowed to."

We sat silent a while; I knew better than to prod.

He took a deep breath. "Then after dinner, she started telling me stuff about her parents arguing and blaming each other and not talking to each other for weeks, until she refused to eat for four days, and that was like a year ago. They're still mean to each other, and she has trouble eating. That's why she's so skinny. At night she dreams of pizza and cookies." He inhaled. "Nobody ever told me secret shit like that before. I don't know, she looked so scared. So I told her everything. I told her what a shit life it is to be a foster kid. I told her I didn't know anything about my dad except that Mom hated him and he was a white guy who got her pregnant back East and then brought her West and dumped her when she had me. I even told her how much I missed Mom. How smart she was—she could speak five languages: English, French, Spanish, Portuguese, and Italian. How when I was little we used to go to the movies on Fridays after school and sneak in milkshakes. I never told that to anybody. And then I felt bad because I realized I was talking about food. And she had a eating problem."

Still I waited.

"I even told her how scared I was. To be alone. I don't know. I told her I grew up hating my dad. I told her to forget about her parents; what the fuck! It's not her fault, all their fighting. She should just fucking eat.

I said if I ever found my dad, I wouldn't starve myself. I'd kill that motherfucker. I'm going to shoot him."

"Devon," I said.

"It's true. He never wanted me in the first place. I was an accident. He wanted to abort me; that's what Mom always said."

Jesus, I thought, what a day for this kid too.

"He never did shit for me. He never sent me a goddamned birthday card. But you know what? I didn't care until Mom was gone. Now I hate the bastard. He wasn't *there*; I was the one who was there when the cops came for her. I was the one who couldn't stop them. I told Alexis what it's like to have cops in your house pinning your arms behind you, pushing your head into the floor, taking your mom away. And Mom didn't even get upset. She was calm. She was telling me she loved me. Telling me to be strong. But I was screaming as they pulled her outside. I was yelling and kicking as hard as I could."

Devon is so tall and so smart I usually think he's okay, he's growing up, he'll be all right, he doesn't want anybody to touch him. But he's a kid, just sixteen years old. I laid my hand on his arm. He turned away, and I rubbed the muscles from neck to shoulder: so strong, so taut. He sniffled and his shoulders shook as he tried to hold back tears. Despite his attitude, he seemed to do the right things, though maybe for the wrong reasons. And he was harder on himself than on anybody else.

"Devon," I said, "just like you told Alexis: you're not responsible for your parents."

"I'm their fucking mistake."

"You're not. You're the best thing they ever did together." I waited several minutes, just sitting there as his breaths evened out. "Call Alexis in the morning," I said finally. "Tell her you'll see her in Tucson on the way back to California." I paused, but he didn't say anything. "Or talk her into Pensacola. You can see her there."

"Her mom doesn't want to go."

"You never know. They need the money. Robert doesn't want Isa to get the old man's estate."

"That's what this trip is really about, isn't it? Getting that money."

I let the idea hang there so he could see a hope of Robert going.

"Go away," he said after a while. "I'm sleepy."

I squeezed his arm. "How do you fall in love so fast?" I said, chuckling, trying to lighten things some. But in truth I was floored. How many hours had they been together, eight? And somehow they had connected.

As I stood, I couldn't help wondering if that was what he'd wanted all along, for me to talk him out of running. Had I talked him out of it? Would he still be there in the morning?

"You're a good kid, Devon," I said, just in case.

He didn't respond.

Charlie led me up the stairs and into the kitchen, where I closed the door behind me. What a day, I thought, leaning back against the door and feeling my world spin. I released my clenched fists and massaged my arms. My head fell back against the door, and the impact of the collision on the highway jolted me again, sending shivers through my body. Casey came to me, his body shuddering in my arms in that alleyway. So I pushed into space—sweeping Charlie back and forth, my neck throbbing and my legs sagging. I wasn't about to sleep in Betsy's backseat. I'd take a shower. Isa would be asleep. I'd crash on the carpet. People could think whatever they wanted.

I carried my suitcase and backpack into Isa's room. She didn't stir as

I opened my case, lifted the lid, and felt inside: shirts folded on the left, pants on the right, and dirty clothes rolled up along the bottom. I checked my cash in the inner zippered pocket. I didn't count the bills but felt the clump of fifties clipped together: folded in half first along the width and then the length. I took off my seersucker shirt and didn't bother to roll it. I carried a clean pair of boxers into the bathroom, where I lost myself in the shower, holding to the tiled wall and letting the water soothe my neck, the blood pulsing behind my eye sockets so that the room didn't spin as much as throb. As I succumbed to the gush of water along my neck and back, my dream returned from Betsy's back-seat before the crash: my fingers sensing yet not quite touching the silk of a woman's garment billowing in a breeze.

For six weeks in high school I'd had a girlfriend, Julie, who used to drive us to the reservoir on April evenings, where we'd park and get high. I'd reach beneath her bra and hold her breasts, rubbing and caressing and cajoling as they seemed to scamper beneath my touch. My fingertips would literally tingle. She wouldn't let me unzip her jeans, but I could slip my hand down along her belly and explore her curves. "It's like your fingers can see," she said, squirming and panting. But in May she went to the prom with Steve Carlton, who lived down the street. I was crushed. High school was over.

A few years later, at the state university in Greeley, I met Renee in bowling class, where I aligned myself by the thundering pins. Her friend told me I should ask her out, so I asked Renee to the movies, which she thought was hilarious—a blind guy at the movies. We dated for about half a year; she was the first besides Mom to feel along the length of my scar, but she traced it as if it were a treasure, an *S* she said stood for "scare." "Scarce." "Scandal." And "striking." "That's what you are," she said, "striking." She called herself "plain Jane," but she didn't feel plain to me. I loved the way her hip jutted up when she lay on her side. We were both virgins, so we tried every position we could think of, but what she liked best were my fingers, like little penises, she said, so nippy and sudden and abiding. After about six months she drifted away, though; I never quite knew why.

When I was a senior, just before I graduated, I had sex with Crystal, a girl I'd known for years who could see shapes and contours, no details. She was younger than I, brash—a goth. On weekends we did lines of coke in her dorm room, and she would slam me with sex that was so raunchy and wet and wonderful it left me catching my breath. After three weeks she left me; she said I was too dependent on sighted people. "Quit pretending you can see," she told me. "Use your damn stick. Get around on your own. Don't wait for your mom to pick you up."

I took her advice, but not until after college, when I moved to San Francisco. I still hid my scar, but I finally basked in being blind. I carried Charlie everywhere and got around on my own. I knew the buses and streetcars like clockwork. I found a job at the phone company, where I took orders over the phone and the callers had no idea I was blind. I let go. I unwound. For the first time since I was a little kid, I did what I wanted without thinking. And I fell fast and hard.

After my shower, I walked into Isa's room in my boxers, pausing, listening to her breathing; she was fast asleep. My neck throbbed; my back was stiff. I threw my clothes on my suitcase and slipped into the comfort of the bed. Isa shifted but didn't wake.

I'd like to say I dreamed. Sometime in the night we came together, Isa sobbing and inarticulate. I was lying on my back when she threw her arm across my chest. I rolled away from her; I'd awoken already stiff.

"She's standing by the closet!" she declared, her voice unsteady. "She's watching me."

"There's no one in the closet," I whispered.

Isa sat up. "There she is. Jasmine! Don't go! Oh my God, she's gone!"

"It's a dream," I said. "Let it go."

"It's not! She was here. Jasmine!" She flopped back down and latched on to my back, pulling at my shoulder, so that I lay contorted, with my torso facing up but my pelvis shifted away from her, shielding myself, hard. She touched the left side of my face, my good side, with her fingers. "Kevin," she said, sobbing. She clung to me. Her breast, loose inside her thin chemise, brushed my chest.

"Everything's okay," I said. "It was a dream."

"It's not a dream," she moaned. "It's real. I've made a terrible mistake."

"Breathe," I said.

"Just hold me. Hold me. I can't sleep. There's voices. I can't sleep."

Her arm and shoulder and breast were already resting on my chest, so I slipped my near arm under her rib cage. Her silver cross dropped onto my skin. Quickly she brought her thigh over me, trapping my penis, pressing it between her thigh and mine, making the thing shiver and leap. My legs twitched and quaked. She reached into my boxers and grabbed me, tugging, her hands not quivering like before but firm now, knowing. She tugged and pushed and tugged again so that it was my body that shuddered, not hers. I surrendered my hips, unsteady and impatient, and they swiveled toward her. With one arm still underneath her ribs, I brought my other hand around, holding her as she wanted. She pressed into me, breathing harder—or had she been panting all along?

On and on she ground me with her hand and then drew her fingers away, letting go, but I flapped up against her hovering thigh, alive and flourishing. "Kevin," she said, "I need you. Hold me tight. Hold me."

"Oh, my God," I said, pulling her toward me and touching the side of her face, her cheek full and hot as she breathed on my fingers, on fire, a fever. Or was that just my own heat pulsing in my hand? Her neck seemed to run forever from her chin to her rib cage to her breast. How long her neck! How high her small ears. How lithe and vulgar her throat, trembling as she said, "I need you, Kevin. I need you." And in the dead of night I needed her too; this was everything I needed. I wouldn't stand back and witness anymore. We pressed on, her leg lifting, and I was between her thighs, her hand slippery, guiding me, the space there engulfing imagination, both of us thrusting, suspended, my body and hers, moving in rhythms that she knew and I sensed, carrying us past consequences. For a long time I breathed and couldn't catch my breath, my hands on her hips like faces, caressing and mouthing and smelling the tender contours of her moist skin as she rocked and shuddered and moaned, "Kevin, Kevin." And me, oblivious and omnisensory, panting, "Isa."

SEVEN

I slept undisturbed until I roamed the edge of consciousness, tossing. Vaguely I became aware of a stabbing pain between my shoulder blades and a constriction to my knees. As I rubbed my neck and pulled up my boxers, I woke with a start, realizing where I was and what we had done. Beside me, Isa inhaled steadily, serene. After a moment, she inhaled again. I couldn't hear her exhale. She seemed to be sucking up my air. My heart raced. I thought of Patrick in jail. My gut turned. I slipped onto the carpet, bringing my pillow with me. I lay on my side, facing the wall, curled up, knees to chest. I didn't have a shirt or any cover at all. Did I love her? I had to decide! Did I? Otherwise, no one needed to know.

Then I remembered what she'd said to me about falling for the wrong guy. What if she loved me? What was I to her?

Someone opened the door, stepped into the room, but made no sound otherwise.

Ray, I thought; he must have had a nightmare. I was thankful to have dropped to the floor. What if we hadn't had sex and I had still been in her bed? Wouldn't that look worse than this? That was how pedantic I was.

I remained stock-still. I thought he would approach, but he walked out and shut the door.

I wondered what time it was; how close to dawn? Then I realized: it wasn't Ray. It was Devon. He was stopping in before running away—or deciding whether to run. I was doubly thankful to be on the floor. Or had he seen me at all? How dark was it in the room?

I wrestled with myself over whether to get up, whether to stop him. Maybe he *should* run, I decided, to get away from these adults. What kind of example was I anyway? What did I know about how to act? I cringed and pressed my knuckles into my cheeks: hello! Hadn't Devon told me just last night that he had been an accident? What if Isa got pregnant?

I got up in a stupor. I wish I could say I tried to stop Devon. But that wasn't why I stirred. I stood because I realized I could join him. I could get away before she awoke. It was implausible. Unrealistic. But it got me out of the room, stumbling down the hallway in my boxers without Charlie, stopping, listening for a moment in the living room, hearing Carlos breathing on the couch. Was Devon already out the front door, gone? I walked barefoot along the seam where the living room carpet and kitchen linoleum met, the fabric warm, the linoleum cool. I opened the garage door, stepping down the stairs and around the mattress, where I leaned down, reaching, and felt Devon's legs. He was in bed. Asleep.

My heart sank, and I tried to understand what that meant. If I was willing to run, did that mean I didn't love her? Or did it mean I was a coward, unwilling to face Patrick?

I knew only one thing: I felt like shit.

I wandered back up the stairs to get some water. As I stepped from the concrete of the garage landing and onto the give of the kitchen linoleum, I heard what, exactly? The sniffles of someone in the kitchen. Isa, I thought. Someone crying softly, not sobbing. I stopped, listening, aware of myself standing in my boxers, my hair mussed, no hat, no glasses, my right eye socket collapsed on itself, my scar raking an *S* through my right eyebrow and cheek like Moses parting the Red Sea.

"I saw you walk into the garage," a woman said, her voice soft and firm. "I like those surfer boxers." She chuckled.

I hadn't known I was wearing them: the boxers Isa had given me for my birthday. My stomach twisted as I thought of Isa reaching inside, grabbing me, pulling. Why couldn't I turn back the clock?

"I couldn't sleep," I said, feeling sheepish and pissed at myself at the same time. Furious, actually. How could I have done it? Yet strangely, it felt good to stand almost naked before this woman.

She blew her nose. "You're blushing," she said.

Instinctively I thought about turning to hide my scar. Instead I kept my face still. She was at the table, I decided, probably seated. If she could see me blush, she could see my scar. "How can you tell?" I said. "Is it light outside?" I wanted to know the time.

"The sun's not up," she said, "but there's a glow. I feel like Baby Bear. Someone's sleeping in my bed."

The room I'd slept in, I thought. She was the one who'd entered and left as I lay on the floor. I remembered what Pastor Curt had said—that someone would return in the morning—but I couldn't remember her name.

"You were crying," I said. She didn't respond right away. I thought I'd gone too far.

"How well do you see?" she said.

I liked her quality of voice, its shifting tones and inflections. "Not at all," I said.

"Do you want to sit?" Her pitch dropped at the end, making it more a suggestion than a question.

I asked if she'd mind getting me some water. As I sat at the table, I was aware of her moving about on the other side, running the tap, setting the glass before me. I wanted to ask again, why was she crying?

"My grandmother went blind," she said. "It makes me smile to think of her."

Despite her confidence, I could hear a constriction to her voice, as if strained through a sieve. "How old was she when she lost her sight?"

"In her seventies," she said. "When I was a kid, we used to take long walks and I'd describe things to her. She could see shapes. Can you see shapes?"

I shook my head.

"I'd describe this or that, but all she really wanted to hear about was the men. We'd walk along the sidewalk, and as men approached I'd describe them. She wanted to know the color of their hair, how it was cut, what they were wearing, but mostly their eyes." She chuckled again.

I smiled. "Sounds like a dirty old woman."

"I thought she was elegant; she had such a flourish. She was Lithuanian, from Chicago. It all seemed very thrilling and grown-up to me. She never cared about the men's age. But she always wanted to know about their eyes: Were they laughing eyes, or serious, or ironic, or tragic? Those were the four choices. And I had to tell her from a glance. She told me to stay away from serious eyes and laughing eyes and to look for irony."

I imagined that Isa had all those looks, depending on the moment. "Tragic eyes were okay with her?" I said.

"Tragic eyes show depth," she said. "Laughing eyes harbor lies."

What about me? I wondered. Did I have a look? I took a sip of water. "Irony is telling a blind man about the importance of eyes," I said, smiling.

There was a silence so complete I felt bad. "I'm sorry," she said.

I realized she thought she'd insulted me. "I was trying to make a joke," I said.

"It's been a long night," she said thinly.

I drank half the water and set down the glass. "It can't be much worse than my day yesterday." I thought about getting into Isa's bed. "We were in an accident on the freeway."

"Who?" she asked.

"The family I'm traveling with. We met Pastor Curt at his church afterward, and he let us spend the night."

"That sounds like Curt," she said. "My friends were arrested last night, out near the border."

"We had someone get arrested too," I said, then remembered we hadn't told anyone about Patrick. I made a note to myself: no more of that secrecy. This morning I would talk about him so it wouldn't look like I was hiding anything. "How did they get arrested?" I said.

She didn't answer for a while; I waited. Finally she drew in a breath. "It's not really about that," she said. "I mean, that's not why I was crying. I can't stay here anymore."

"At Curt's?"

"Curt's. My job. Maybe El Paso." She said she'd moved to El Paso with her boyfriend. They'd broken up a month before, but they were still working at the same place, which complicated everything. She was staying at Curt's until she figured out what to do. "But I don't have a car. It's a mess."

Outside, a rooster crowed but stopped midway, as if he didn't trust this dawn.

"Do you still love him?" I said.

She didn't respond right away. "I don't think so, but I get torn up when I'm around him."

That made me think of Isa and me. "Does he have ironic eyes?" I said.

She started laughing. "Definitely not," she said, laughing harder and in a brighter pitch than her voice, a roll that ended in a funny wheezing whistle running downscale, a "wheeeew" that sounded so crazy after listening to the lyrical rhythm of her voice that it made me open up and laugh too.

"Lord have mercy," Carlos sang in his alto from the living room, "you children are exhausting."

I'd forgotten about him on the couch.

"What's with that whistle?" I said, still laughing.

"People tease me about it, but I can't help it. Well, I guess I could, but it's how I laugh."

I liked that.

"I like the way you show your scar," she said. "I bet that's not easy."

I didn't tell her I usually wear dark glasses and a hat. I felt outside of myself, unchained. "I'm Kevin."

"Natalie Mick. Nice to meet you." She stood and moved about the kitchen, opening and closing cabinets.

"What got you started?" I said. "What was so funny?"

She stopped. "The thought of him with ironic eyes," she said. "He's so serious and driven." She closed a cabinet. "Damn!"

I smelled coffee grounds.

"You a mess, girl," Carlos said, suddenly in the kitchen. "I'll make the coffee. Go lie down or something."

"Put some clothes on," she said, teasing.

"Why?" Carlos said. "He can't see a thing."

"Is he naked?" I asked, laughing.

"He's got boxers on," Natalie said, "same as you."

"But not those surfer-boy boxers," he said. "I got to get some of those."

"Maybe I should get dressed," I said, but I didn't move. There it was, unbidden: the thought of Isa's room.

"How'd you get your scar?" she said.

Her question was so quick it threw me off. Lots of people want to know if I've always been blind. When I tell them I lost my sight when I was five, they feel compelled to ask how it happened, as if they'd been suckered into the question. No one had ever asked how I'd gotten my scar. "You don't need to hear that," I said. "Not with all that's going on."

"I want to. Tell me."

I hadn't talked about my blinding in a long time. "It was ages ago."

"Tell me about it."

So I began. I was five years old, I said. It was the height of spring—late May—in Greeley, Colorado. I was excited that I'd learned to ride a bike, and I was riding with my older brother, Larry. He was behind me; I was out in front and proud of myself. I was flying, and it was the freest feeling in the world.

When Carlos set a cup of coffee before me, I made the mistake of pausing; my eye sockets started to well up. I couldn't help it. In that instant, sitting nearly naked at that table before strangers, I felt like a failure—all the mistakes I'd made since that day as a kid on a bike.

"I'm sorry," I said. "Just a minute." I wiped my eyes.

"It's okay," she said. "You don't have to."

"No, I want to," I said. "It's just been a while since I told it." I felt for the cup and drank some coffee. I barreled on: "My brother Larry had gotten a new bike for his birthday. I was riding his old one. I surprised everyone when I rode it so young. Dad had just bought me a shiny new bell. We were riding down our street, back from Ollie's house, and I was ringing the bell with my left thumb, and Larry was behind me, saying something, so I turned my head to look back at him. I couldn't hear what it was with the wind in my ears. We were in front of our house by then. If I'd turned into our driveway, I would've been fine. But I didn't; I kept going. Up ahead a city street sweeper was backing up. You know, with those metal wire brushes on rollers? I was looking back over my shoulder at my brother as he screamed. Maybe I turned my head to see the truck and its whirling brush coming at me. But if I did, I froze. I forgot how to brake."

Maybe Natalie thought I was going to well up in tears again because she walked around the table and put her hand on my forearm. She smelled like the desert, not hot or dusty but open and robust. I don't know if it was the soft touch of her fingers on my skin, or the strangeness of travel, or the telling of my blinding for the first time in a while, or another layer of fog lifting from my junkie brain, or the emotional and physical exhaustion of the day before—or all those together, or something else beyond me: God's grace, if there is such a thing. But there at the table I suddenly remembered and pictured in my head the warm shade of orange of our home—none of the house's features, no roof, door, or windows. Just the looming color, as if it were a direction rather than a thing in itself. Orange.

I'm sure my mouth was open.

"Oh, my God," I said. "I remember the color orange. I remember what it looks like."

Natalie gripped my forearm; I pressed my arm up into the touch of her palm.

"What do you mean?" Carlos said. "You don't remember orange?"

"I don't remember colors. Not since I was a kid. Our house was orange. Mom used to joke about the color, how the neighbors said it looked like a pumpkin. It's like I can sense that orange in my head."

"Can you see at all?" Carlos said. "Can you see anything?"

"Go on," Natalie said. "I want to hear all of that. But first tell me what happened."

I took a sip of coffee. A rooster crowed again, longer this time. I heard creaks from the house awakening. "Mom told me that Larry saw the truck back up over me. He saw me get sucked under by the tube sweeper, the brush on the back that rolls around and around. Later the driver said he'd missed something and was going back to get it. I fell to the left as the brushes and the undercarriage rolled over my torso and crushed my face and body. All my brother could see was my skinny legs and feet sticking out and kicking. The truck stopped and pulled off me and by then I'd stopped kicking and my brother kept screaming and the guy jumped out, and that's what Mom saw when she came running out of the house: the man standing, Larry screaming, and me crushed on the street."

I stopped to sip coffee. Natalie's hand was still on my arm. Carlos sat down across from us. All of us sat there breathing.

"It crushed the right side of my face, including my eyeball and eye socket. On my left side the blow to my forehead caused my optic nerve to swell up inside the bony canal at the back of the eye socket. The optic nerve literally strangled itself. So I lost light perception in both eyes. But when I woke up after the operations, it wasn't my eyes that bothered me. They didn't hurt. Everything else hurt. I was in a body cast, and my head was all bandaged up. Over the next weeks I found out my neck was broken. One arm was broken. My collarbone. Several ribs. My hip.

They had to reconstruct the right side of my face. I could move my left arm at the elbow, so I used that hand to feel the outside of the body cast. When I first woke up, I thought, That's why I can't see, there's a cast on my head. Mom kept thanking God I was alive, but I didn't think about life or death. As a kid you expect life; you are life. After a few weeks, I just wanted to get out even though I was still in all kinds of pain and I couldn't move at all. I told Mom I had to get out so I could ride my bike and do stuff with Larry. That was when she told me there was something wrong with my eyes that the doctors couldn't fix. I said, 'Okay,' but I didn't know what that meant. Pain was what I was reacting to then, and if it didn't hurt, I was okay with it. I didn't think much beyond that. In the hospital as I got better, I hated not being able to watch TV, but I learned to listen to it. And Mom read to me a lot. I learned how to eat my food okay. It wasn't until later, when I got out of the body cast and started moving around and then went home, that I began to realize what it meant not to see. But even then I had no idea. You can know things with your head but not understand them at all."

"You can see things and not see them at all," Carlos said.

"Why didn't you have plastic surgery to fix that scar?" Natalie said. She let go of my forearm, dragged a chair closer, and sat down.

"I did, but I gave up after a while. I had so many operations, so many doctors. They had to rebuild that side of my face. My left eyeball is intact. But on the right side they had to put in an implant because my eyeball was crushed. And the muscles around the implant got infected, so they had to take it out and put in a new one."

"Show me," she said.

"You sure?" I said. "Are you a doctor or something?"

"Community organizer," she said.

I hesitated. The round implant inside is covered by tissue and muscles. Since there's no artificial eye covering the tissue, my right eyelid is sunken, and when I open the lid, the inside looks somewhat, I've been told, like an eyeball covered with red blood vessels, with no pupil, no iris. Eerie.

"Show me," she said.

Twisting toward her, I opened my eyelid with my fingers, revealing the red, glistening tissue.

"Where's the implant?" she said immediately. Not even a gasp.

"Under the muscles. You can't see it. But that's what makes the tissue rounded, like it's over a ball."

I turned toward Carlos.

"That's okay, sweetie," he said. "I don't need to see that."

I laughed and released my lid. "When the new implant took," I said, "I went through all kinds of artificial eyes. They're like big contact lenses that sit over the tissue and are attached to the implant. They're supposed to look like real eyes, but I could never get used to them; they hurt and got dry and made my eye itch, maybe because I don't tear much on that side. I have six at home in a drawer. And since I don't wear a fake eye, my eyelid collapses and my eyelashes turn in. See that?" I pointed to the lashes. "There's nothing they can do about that if I don't wear the fake eye." I stopped then, feeling self-conscious and rambling. "That's more than you wanted to know."

"It's not," she said. "I still want to know more."

But she didn't ask, and I was worn out with talking.

"You look good," Carlos said.

I smiled. As we sat finishing our coffee, I wondered how old Natalie was. Midthirties, I guessed. Or younger. I wished I'd put my hand on hers when she'd been touching my forearm; you can tell a lot from the length and contours of fingers.

"Good morning, pequeño," Carlos said.

Ray's quick steps approached. When I felt his small hand on my shoulder, I wrapped my arm around him and introduced him to Natalie. His elbow bumped against me as he rubbed his eyes. "Guess what? I remembered a color just now. They helped me imagine orange."

"You did that yourself," Natalie said. "We were just listening."

"I don't know what that means," Carlos said. "You can't imagine color?"

"Do you dream in color?" I said.

"I have no idea," Carlos said. "But listen, honey. You've heard of the rainbow flag? I *must* dream in color."

We all had a good laugh at that.

"Do you see in your dreams?" Natalie said.

"Not in a long time," I said. "My dreams are like my life: I hear noises. People touch me. Or I recognize a smell."

"What can you see in real life?" Carlos said. "Do you see anything?"

As I smiled, Ray beat me to it: "He sees nothing all at once. Neither darkness nor light."

I liked the way he said that, as if seeing nothing were a sudden act. "I see the backsides of dreams," I said. "A world that's disoriented."

"For reals," Ray said.

I hugged him for his predictability and lack of guile. "Most people who are legally blind have some perception of light," I said. "I'm one of the few who can see nothing."

"That turns me on," Carlos said. "But I still don't know what it means."

Natalie and I chuckled. "Why would a color come back to you now?" she said.

I thought about how much to say. Why not tell her I'd been an addict? What did I have to lose? "I've been clean and sober almost two years. Maybe it's part of healing. Maybe I'm just ready."

She didn't even pause. "You remembered orange when you were talking about your house."

"He was talking about the accident," Carlos corrected.

"But he was in front of his house," she said. "Maybe it was the last thing he saw."

I liked that idea, whether true or not—but even now I can't remember the last thing I saw. The last thing I remember before the accident was riding bikes. The rest had been told to me.

"You just need something to trigger your memory," she said. "What color do you want to see next?"

"You think you can control his memory, girl?" Carlos said.

"Come on," she said, the excitement real in her voice. "What color?"

"Green," I said.

"What do you associate with green?"

"Trees," Ray said.

"Money," Carlos said.

"Grass," I said.

"I mean, what specific action or place? A memory."

I sat for a moment, thinking. About a year after my accident, when I was six, maybe seven, I was with Mom, Dad, and Larry at a park we always went to on the Fourth of July. I had to go to the bathroom. "You remember where it is," Dad said at the picnic table, "uphill to the right." He wanted me to strike out on my own now that I was better physically. I'd learned to get around my neighborhood with my hockey stick, but the fear of getting lost in unfamiliar places intimidated me, so I cajoled Mom into going with me. After I went to the bathroom, I was facing downhill, testing the ground with one foot outstretched. The grass was soft and smelled fresh-mowed. Mom said, "Go ahead Kevin, run. Your legs are better now. There's nobody down there." When I told her I couldn't see, she said, "You know this hill. Trust what you know." I reached for her hand, and we started running slowly, laughing. As the slope fell away, we picked up speed. Mom couldn't keep up, so I released her fingers; her laughter rose up the hill behind me as I dashed down it, my legs flying, so that for a moment I wasn't what I'd lost anymore. I wasn't what I couldn't do. I wasn't what I couldn't see. I was my legs and what I had and who I was: movement itself, energy, reckless action, and each precise contact with the earth. The world had no horizon. Beneath my feet, without warning, the hill dropped away and I fell tumbling and laughing. I lay on my back out of breath, facing up toward everything and nothing, panting and laughing as Mom arrived.

"Running downhill," I told Natalie. "I haven't done that since I was a kid. You know, a real let-go run, without holding on to somebody's arm."

"You haven't run since you were a kid?" she said.

"I've run on treadmills. I've run on tracks. I mean run freely, downhill, by myself, where I don't care if I hit something, where I'm out in the open, where I get going so fast my legs can barely keep up. Maybe I fall, but that's fine because I roll and roll. I haven't run like that in years." I paused. "I don't know if I can run like that."

"The hell you can't," she said, all the strain gone from her voice. "Ray, you want to go with us? You want to watch Kevin run so fast he's going to see green?"

"You think it'll work?" Ray said.

"If you can do that, sweetie," Carlos said, "I want you to find me this little golden pot at the end of the rainbow."

I laughed and shook my head. I didn't believe she could make me see green. But I wanted to go wherever Natalie Mick was going. And I wanted to do it before Isa woke up.

I walked down the hallway feeling energized and astonished, my senses aflutter. Already this stranger had seen inside my scars and hadn't flinched. I stopped midway, sure of myself for the first time during the trip. Suddenly and completely, I knew I did not love Isa. And from my newfound distance, I wanted to let her down lightly; I didn't want to hurt her. If I could just avoid her for the time being, I thought, that would be best for us both—but I needed to retrieve my clothes from her room.

As I reached for the door, I found it already open. Isa's slim fingers grabbed my wrist and pulled me inside, as if she'd been waiting. "That didn't happen last night," she hissed, shutting the door behind me.

"Your hands are still shaking," I said as calmly as I could.

"Yesterday I was exhausted," she whispered. "I couldn't sleep at all at Robert's house. Then we drove all day and got in that accident and Patrick flailed around like an idiot—because of those stupid bones. Of course they threw him in jail! When the pastor started talking about God, I honestly didn't know what I had within me except guilt and pain. You don't know it, but I was in a car crash long ago, and I was living that all over again." She went on about seeing the coffin on top of the car—but she sounded better, I thought. I was glad of that.

"What car crash?" I interrupted, and she paused, mute. I remembered her dream then: someone standing by the closet. "Who's Jasmine?"

"Ssshhhh," she demanded. "I was in shock, Kevin. I was scared to death. You shouldn't have taken advantage."

I could feel myself beginning to resent her.

"I'm going to be okay today," she said, her voice full again, as if she were willing herself to have faith.

"I didn't take advantage," I said evenly, without emotion—to show my distance. "I think you planned it. You insisted we sleep in the same room."

"Oh, that's convenient," she said, her voice rising. "Don't be ridiculous. I'm being honest with you. If Patrick finds out, he'll kick your ass and who knows what else. Neither of us wants that to happen."

That made me wonder what he would do to her, and it reminded me of Ray's fears about Patrick—my promise to protect him.

"Has he ever hit you?" I said.

"We have to tell them about Patrick," she said, ignoring me. "You know, the family. We should've said something last night."

"Tell them the truth," I said. "Tell them Patrick's in jail. Tell them I slept in your room—on the floor—because you were still in shock."

After a moment, she tried to pull me to her, to confirm our agreement, I knew. But I shielded myself from her.

"I'm sorry, Kevin," she said. "I still love you. I'll always love you. But in a different way than Patrick. I'm a married woman."

I tried to pity her. Did she honestly think that she'd hurt me? That I loved her? That things could be the same? I found my suitcase on the floor and searched through it with my hands to make it obvious that the conversation was finished.

"I heard you talking with that Natalie," she said, her voice like a breeze now.

I grabbed my shaving kit and kept my mouth shut; I wasn't going to get drawn in.

"She seems nice. I can tell she likes you."

I stood. "How would you know? Where were you?"

"Oh, come on. She was flirting, touching your wrist. And you were flirting back in those surfer boxers I gave you. You looked good."

"I wasn't flirting."

"Don't frown like that. Smile."

I smiled at her.

"Not that fake smile. That's better. Show your teeth. Your smile looks great." She opened the door. "I'm going to take Devon with me to pick up Patrick and get Betsy checked. We'll get the back window covered so the exhaust doesn't come in. You take Ray with you, just like that Natalie said. You run down that hill with her. And after you're hot and sweaty, don't fiddle around with your hands and look away. Hold her. Draw her to you. Kiss her like you mean it. Then we'll be on our way to Florida."

She closed the door. Gone.

I was annoyed and haunted at the same time. How had she heard all that? How had she known what I wanted before I did? I hadn't been able to read her; her hands had been trembling, yet she'd seemed so determined. She was right about the night before, though: it had never happened. We hadn't done anything in that bed. There was no reason Patrick would ever know. Then I thought about the low end of her swings, how needy she could become. How long could she keep a secret?

In a kitchen smelling of garlic and coffee, Andrea and Carlos served scrambled eggs with black beans and fresh tortillas. Isa drifted up to me with her sweet wine perfume, kissing me on the cheek. As we ate, I was edgy—acutely aware of Isa and dreading each word she might say. She wouldn't stop raving about me, explaining that I was a newspaper reporter in L.A., that I could type Braille faster than she could type on a regular keyboard, that I'd read more books without eyes than she had with them, and that I was smarter than the kids' teachers at school. Even though Natalie sat next to me, I could hardly get her to say a word.

Isa found a way to tell about our accident, including her husband getting locked in the county jail for saying he didn't like Texans.

"I don't like Texans either," Carlos said.

"You're a Texan," Andrea said.

"Picky, picky," he said.

"I thought Kevin was your husband," Pastor Curt said.

"I'm a friend," I said quickly. I didn't want her saying she was my caretaker.

"He slept on the carpet in my room last night to help me," Isa said. "I was in shock."

There, I thought. Maybe we could move past last night after all.

Devon and Ray couldn't get enough eggs, which were scrambled with potatoes, cilantro, tomatoes, and garlic. They tasted exquisite inside a homemade tortilla.

Natalie's chair scraped as she stood.

"You hardly ate," Andrea said.

"I've got to get some sleep," she said. Water ran in the sink and then shut off. A dish clinked onto a counter. Then her footsteps crossed the linoleum toward the hallway, disappearing on the carpet.

After a moment, Andrea said, "She doesn't look good."

"She was up all night," Pastor Curt said.

"It's her work," Andrea said. "All the stress."

"It's her ex," Carlos said.

"She was married?" I asked.

"Ex-boyfriend," he said.

I was keyed up about Natalie—but for what, a run downhill?

After breakfast, when Natalie didn't reappear, I figured the plans were off. So I lay down in the garage and dropped into a deep sleep. Natalie and Ray woke me about eleven, after Isa and Devon were gone.

"Bring your suit," Natalie said. "We might meet Isa and Devon at the pool afterward." She was speaking rapidly again, with vigor.

I felt recharged too. "Did you get some sleep?" I said.

"I like Isa," she said. "Lots of energy."

That made me wonder what Isa might have divulged. About me. About her. Who knew? I decided not to let it bother me. I put on my glasses. Out in the living room, I asked Carlos for my hat.

"Sweetie," he said, "I like that hat."

"He's been wearing it," Ray said, giving it to me.

That made me smile. I nestled the hat on my head.

"We've got to get you some new glasses," Carlos said. "Something not so big."

Since Natalie didn't have a car, Andrea let us use her compact, which had a high whine in every gear. Ray fidgeted in the backseat, and I sat in front. When we got on the freeway, I asked about the Voice of God church. Pastor Curt didn't seem like a fire-and-brimstone kind of guy.

"He does get people going in church," she said. "He's also very hands-on, helping la gente. The people." She said she met him when she and her boyfriend started the nonprofit; he was the only minister in the whole county to step forward. "Every month immigrants coming across the border were dying of thirst. So we put up water tanks in the desert, on land where the property owners support us. Curt's congregation took the lead in volunteering, going out to New Mexico and refilling the tanks, over fifteen sorties a week. But this summer somebody started putting bullet holes in the tanks."

"What does that mean, 'sorties'?" Ray said.

A siren came up from behind. As Natalie slowed and pulled to the right, the sound Dopplered by us, twisting.

She explained "sorties" to Ray—but that wasn't what he was interested in after all. He was shocked that there were white people who gave water to the poor coming across the border.

"We're not all like Patrick," I said.

When he didn't respond, I started thinking that standing up to Patrick was not about gaining respect—props. It was about creating a world I wanted—being *for reals*. How many times had Ray and I heard Patrick rail about the goddamned illegals? I had grimaced but had let it pass.

Natalie got Ray talking, in Spanish and English, about his padres, abuelos, y bisabuelos—parents, grandparents, and great-grandparents.

He didn't know much about his father's side of the family, he said, except that his abuelo had been killed by a gang in L.A. when his dad was a boy; Ray's mom had always made sure he knew that, to keep him away from gangs. On his mother's side, his grandparents had come across the border in Arizona to find work and had later moved to L.A. His mom was born in East L.A. in a house Ray used to visit to see his abuela, who would show him pictures of her sisters and brothers—his great-uncles and -aunts—as kids in Cuernavaca, Mexico, where she'd grown up. After his abuela died, he used to look at those pictures with his mom, until everything was destroyed by the fire.

He told Natalie about Tía María y Tío José, his aunt and uncle in Cuernavaca who'd visited a few times.

They'd offered to take him, I knew, when his mom had died. But at that point his dad hadn't been sentenced. And then Ray got set up with us and was afraid to go to Mexico, I think.

"You should visit them," Natalie said.

"And take me with you," I said. I reached into the backseat to poke him, but he slapped softly at my hand, so I tried to tickle his leg, making him squirm and giggle.

"I like your family," Natalie said to me. "It's not your typical parents or kids. Isa told me about Patrick."

What had she said? I wondered.

"Where are we going to run?" Ray piped up. "None of this cactus stuff looks any good."

"Cactus!" I said. "We're running in cactus?"

Natalie laughed. "We're going to a golf course."

I'd been fine talking and thinking about Ray. But now the hazards of running on my own began to needle me. I figured the odds were five to one that I would make a fool of myself—and three to one that I'd get hurt.

We came off the freeway and wound along curved streets, where Natalie looked for a sloping fairway and Ray described big houses with pools that butted up to a golf course.

" 'Butted,' " I said. "That's a good word. Where'd you hear that?"

"It reminds me of 'butt,' " Ray said.

The three of us laughed as the car pulled to a stop and the motor shut off. "Dorado Country Club at your service. Ready to dash downhill?"

I could feel my breath shorten as I fretted. I couldn't help it. What if I fell in a divot and sprained a knee or rammed my foot against a sprinkler head? I'd stayed in shape by swimming in Burbank, but in pools there are dividers between lanes. "I should hold on to your arm or something," I said. "I'm going to need some direction."

"I'm going to point you downhill. You're going to run like the wind." She opened her door.

The sun was blazing; I began sweating insanely as soon as I stepped out of the air-conditioned car. "What if I head for a tree?" I said. I heard men's voices far to my left. "Do you have a short rope," I said, "or a belt?"

She didn't answer.

"I could hold one end with my right hand," I said, "and you could hold the other end with your left. That way I'd have my own stride and all that, but I'd still have a sense of where to go." I'd used that system before in running around a track.

"Okay, then," she said. "We can use my belt. I'll tell you when to let go."

"What?"

She laughed. "When we get to a place that's open and you're going in the right direction, I'll let you know. You'll let go and run as fast as you can downhill. If you fall down, it's the softest grass in West Texas. Tell him how soft it looks."

Ray pulled me from the sidewalk onto a lawn. "It looks like better grass than this," Ray said.

"I'll tell you when to stop," Natalie said. "Now, take off your sandals."

"What?"

"We're running barefoot," she said lightly.

I realized that my voice was the heavy one now, but I couldn't stop myself. "I'm not running barefoot in the desert of El Paso."

"If you want to see green, you've got to feel the grass with your feet, between your toes. That's part of the thrill."

I enjoyed her gentle prodding, but I was nervous. When I took off my sandals and placed them in the car, the pavement was so hot we had to hop back to the lawn, which was cool and thick. Natalie handed me the end of a belt. Could she tell I was becoming a wreck?

We practiced jogging uphill along a sidewalk, then running faster. The belt made me feel connected but on my own too. Ray wanted a turn, so he led me for a while. I decided I didn't have to let go of the belt on the fairway.

"Here's the plan," Natalie said, stopping. "We've just walked uphill along the street. Our car is behind us. We're going to cross over this empty lot onto the golf course. We're going to run downhill on the fairway, which goes parallel to this street. At the bottom of the hill, we'll cut through the empty lot down there, where we parked our car."

I mapped it out in my head.

She took the belt buckle from Ray, and I felt a tug on my end, so I stepped gingerly to my left across what felt like prickles and clods of hard dirt and stones. My feet were tender, and I tried to step lightly, but I felt awkward. I wasn't used to being barefoot. My heart was pounding.

"Slow," she said, "so we don't step on cactus."

"Cactus!"

"I'm glad I have shoes on," Ray said, giggling.

"He does *not* have shoes on," she said.

I laughed. "You better not let me catch you on that hill," I said to Ray.

"You can't catch me," he said.

I wanted to touch Natalie, so I reached for her elbow and dropped the belt. She seemed soft and solid at the same time—stronger than Ray but less angular than Devon's bony strength. Her gait was easy. I liked her feel. "You've got some muscle," I said.

As she flexed, I moved my hand up to feel her biceps. Remembering her laughing wheeze, I felt myself smile.

Ahead of us, Ray rattled something metal. "A fence?" I said.

"It's not high," he said.

As Natalie climbed over it, I put both hands on top. It was a chain-link fence, chest high.

"Be careful of the top," she said. "Don't rip your clothes."

"I was pretty good at this as a kid," I said. "And as a bum. But it's been a while."

"You weren't a bum," she said.

"I was. I lost myself for a while, when I was an addict."

"When was that?" she said.

"When I lived in San Francisco. I've been clean two years next month." I put my toes in the fence, raising myself carefully. I lifted one foot over, balancing and turning before hooking my toes in the other side. I brought my other leg over and turned to face back toward the street as I climbed down.

"Nicely done," she said.

I was beginning to relax; my adrenaline was flowing. "Where's the grass?" I said. "I'm ready."

She led me a few yards farther to where grass was cool and soft beneath my toes.

"Think of all the water," she said.

Ray was rolling around already, moaning. "It's so cool," he said.

"This is soft," I said. I reached down and felt the strands.

She handed me the end of the belt, and immediately I felt a tug. "Who's ready to see some green?" she said. "Stick with us, Ray!" We jogged slowly at first, gaining speed as we headed downhill.

With the wind in my face as I was running, I couldn't hear Ray at all. I heard my own shallow breaths and Natalie's long inhales and exhales. The belt tightened and loosened with each stride, the cool grass massaging the soles of my feet and then beginning to drop away as the hill steepened. As we ran faster, the belt tightened and loosened at odd times.

"Okay," she said, "let go!"

"Hey!" I heard a man yell to our right. "Get off the fairway, you idiots! You're gonna get hit!"

I let go of the belt and my legs churned faster, my knees lifting, my feet coming down just in time to meet the soft ground and move me forward. The ground undulated some, but not enough to throw me. It felt good to let my legs fly.

"Can't catch me!" Ray said from in front.

Natalie laughed to my right. "Okay, slow down," she said. "That's right, slower. Ray, over here."

As I came to a stop, I collapsed laughing on the grass, relieved not to have tripped, not to have hit anything, not to have made an ass of myself. Natalie tugged my hand, pulling me up. She steered us away from where we'd parked the car, it seemed, over to where pine needles pricked my feet.

"How was it?" she said.

We were panting; I had to catch my breath before I could talk. "That was great," I said, not wanting to disappoint. It wasn't a letdown, just not as radiant as the memory from childhood.

Ray laughed and leaned into me. "You should have seen you! I've never seen you run so hard. You run like a crazy man."

I tickled his ribs. "I feel like a crazy man!"

"Your legs go every which way."

"That wasn't long enough," Natalie said. "How about we walk up that longer fairway? Then we'll run down it. And we'll cross over this one to get back to our car. Okay?" Her voice was relaxed, much different from earlier.

I didn't think the length of the run would make much difference. "Sure," I said. "But Ray can't run that far."

"You're the one who can't do it," Ray teased.

The longer we walked uphill among pine trees, the more exuberant I felt holding Natalie's elbow, loving the touch of my fingers against her skin moist with sweat. The smell of pine sap was so alive and strong, I could taste it on my tongue. I didn't care about running. I wanted to stop and pull her toward me and kiss her. Right away. Right then. But I thought of Isa telling me to do that, and I became stupid, self-conscious. Two golf carts clattered by, going the opposite direction we were, downhill. When we stopped, she handed me the end of the belt.

I held her warm hand as well as the belt, and I faced straight at her. "I want to thank you," I said, enjoying the liveliness of her fingers. She kissed me suddenly, inciting my good cheek with her lips. I felt short of breath.

"I like it when you blush," she said, giggling in a way that attracted me even more.

Somebody yelled something down below. Maybe she and Ray were looking downhill, I don't know, but I heard a golf cart jiggle from above, to our right.

"Hey," I whispered, "who's that coming?"

Suddenly the belt was taut in my hand.

"Let's go!" she said.

"Security!" a man yelled. "Stop!"

There's always a skip of heartbeat when I hear the gruff tone of authority. In San Francisco, I'd been harassed by police plenty of times.

Never had I tried to run. Kevin making a getaway? You've got to be kidding.

Yet at the Dorado Country Club in El Paso, I sprinted as fast as I could. My heart was in my throat, pounding. I felt the softness of grass beneath my feet as the fairway sloped away from me. I heard Natalie ahead, Ray farther on, and the bounce of the golf cart well behind us up the slope; we had a good lead. I listened to my own breaths. I felt the strength of my own legs.

I released the belt.

When I walk I'm grounded: before the toes of my back foot lift, the heel of my front foot drops. When I run there's a continuous moment of letting go, of faith, a cycle of movement when my back foot lifts before my front foot touches when I hope the earth will be there: constant. At a steady gait on an even plane, or on a slope I know, it's easy to let go and believe. It's a different feeling being chased by security down an unknown hill with random dips and rises. Yet on that slope I trusted, and for a long time everything fell away except for my motion downhill, grounded yet weightless, outside of time.

My body felt marvelous. My legs took charge as my thighs burned and drove, my knees lifted and straightened and lifted again, my calves thrust and flexed and pressed my feet into the ground, and my feet pushed and yielded. My chest expanded and opened, my arms pumped, my jaw relaxed, and sweat dripped from my brow. I heard again the cart bouncing, still behind us, and now the whine of the electric motor. What could he do, run us down? I felt a stitch in my side. My hat flew off.

"Run!" Natalie said, laughing out loud. "Forget your hat! Look at you run!" She was behind me.

"Hey!" Ray said, behind me too.

As a kid I'd always been the straggler, the one left behind. But today I was fastest.

"Hey, buddy!" the security man yelled, still behind us. "Stop!"

He wanted me! And not because I was the weakling.

The slope steepened, dropping away and then rising suddenly. I fell, rolling on the soft grass, and was back up running downhill before I knew what I'd done, alongside Natalie and Ray now, all of us panting and laughing. The golf cart was almost next to us, on our right.

"Turn left!" Natalie said, touching me. "Across the other fairway!"

I turned. We all did, across a slope that slanted down from left to right.

We were idiots! Fools! Beside me ran a kid who helped me see and a stranger who'd given me my own two legs. I opened my heart, laughed at myself, trusted my own body, and believed in each stride.

EIGHT

Natalie touched my elbow, slowing me. We were at the edge of the fairway, where the grass was rougher before giving way to gravel. The cart stopped behind us. "You better run!" the security guard yelled. We responded by lingering at the edge of the grass. I stood with hands on knees, panting and laughing. At the end of her laugh, Natalie unleashed her outlandish wheeze.

Across the few steps of gravel I held to Natalie's elbow, my feet tender, alert. She rattled the metal fence, and I reached to grab it. Afterward we stood for a moment near the car on the coolness of someone's lawn.

"Look," Natalie said, putting my hand on the inside of her leg, just above her knee, "I'm the one tore my pants on the fence." I explored the tear, feeling with three fingers the taut firmness of her inner thigh.

I threw my head back and howled like a coyote. That was how alive I was.

When I inhaled, her hands startled my hips; she was in front of me, facing me. "You're a lot of fun," she said. "I've never run downhill quite like that before."

As I rested my hands on her shoulders, she turned us slowly on the grass. I drew her closer, reaching and feeling the softness and strength of her upper back. She was a couple of inches shorter than Isa and several inches shorter than I. I liked her compact, solid feel. Our noses touched. Our chins pressed. I felt her breath on my lips. We kissed, holding, still turning. As we drew away and breathed, Ray brushed against me, and I brought him in, the three of us circling until our legs tangled and we collapsed on the grass, laughing and rolling.

I often think of that moment with the three of us in the grass—I wanted to lie there forever.

In the car, Natalie said that when my hat flew off, the golf cart swerved to run over it and almost tipped. I liked that detail: the guard off balance instead of me. He could have caught us if he'd wanted, she said; he was just doing his job, steering us off the fairway.

We were still sweating and poking fun at each other when we jostled through the doors of the air-conditioned swim center in El Paso. I could hear splashing and shouting from the pool inside. Even the chlorine smelled good; I felt like a schoolboy. Ray jumped around, tugging at my arm, telling me about fountains and a long, curving slide he could see. I was holding Charlie as the man behind the counter said, "You can't take that inside."

I ignored him, turning away.

"I said you can't take that inside," he repeated, raising his voice.

I faced him. "The hell I can't," I said. I wasn't going to be put down. Not today.

"He's not talking to you," Ray said. "He's talking to that guy with an inner tube."

"Oh," I said, laughing at myself. "Sorry."

After we changed into bathing suits, I walked with Ray into the pool area, carrying Charlie in my opposite hand, extended but upright.

My glasses were in the locker room, and I felt exposed without them. Water seemed to be gushing everywhere, and before I knew it, Ray had me walking down a ramp with Charlie into a thigh-deep pool, approaching the rush of falling water landing upon itself. I sputtered through the waterfall, laughing. Suddenly I was inside it, up against a metal pole and surrounded on all sides by a circular barrage of falling water, none of it falling on me. I put my hand through the water in several places. We walked out through the deluge and then into fountains spurting up. I got Ray to keep an eye out for Devon and Isa, but he couldn't stay off the slide any longer. I stood on the pool edge with Charlie and listened to him slip down in a rush of free fall and splash into the water, shrieking.

"Watch!" Ray said, going back up.

"I'm listening!" I said.

Natalie joined me, and we sat with legs in the water. I folded Charlie.

Ray howled down the slide, sounding like the coyote I'd been after the run.

"He swims well," Natalie said.

"You weren't listening!" Ray said.

"I was!"

"Don't run," Natalie said.

I marveled at how open and talkative he'd become. I wanted to share with Natalie what Ray had told me the night before about his mother, but I held back.

Someone blew a whistle. "No diving," a woman shouted.

"You didn't see green, did you?" Natalie said.

"That's okay," I said. "I haven't run like that since I was a kid."

The next moment slender wet hands were all over my elbow and forearm, tugging me into the pool. I resisted, but Natalie grabbed my other elbow, and I let myself be tugged and pushed into coolness, loving the surprise and suspension of water, as if the world were altogether tactile, touching me everywhere, supporting me. As I surfaced, I thought of Isa's description of the Gulf beaches of Pensacola, how the saltwater holds you up like a cork, how the warmth brings you back to the womb.

Ray's hands touched my neck, clinging, and we both dipped under, holding our breaths. We fooled around at the slope between the shallow and deep ends, him jumping from my shoulders, swimming this way and that to surprise me, darting like a fish. He loved the water. Another kid came over and jumped off me too.

"You're blind, aren't you?" the kid said.

"That's right. I can see nothing perfectly."

"You don't have an eyeball."

"Yes, I do. This one right here." I pointed to my left eyelid.

"I mean you only have one eyeball."

When Ray and I got out, we walked up the two dozen steps to the top of the slide, much higher than I expected.

"How many twists and turns?" I said.

"It's like a snake." He wouldn't tell me more.

So I sat, then lay back on the slippery surface, feet first, with water gushing from my left side but my right side sticking. As I shifted my weight, I inched downward, sticking, until the friction released and I became water sliding along slickness pulled by earth, turning one way and the other, sliding up high on the side, then dead center until one mesmerizing instant suspended me in air, legs akimbo, all motion yet freeze-framed. Without grace, I'm sure.

I got water up my nose, deep and burning, but I didn't care. I glided beneath the cool, forgiving surface as I flutter-kicked and pulled my own wings up and down effortlessly, my hands cupped, knowing their power to suspend and direct. I stretched my arms forward, reaching for the wall and surfacing just before it was there. I rode the slide again, sitting this time with Ray between my legs, clutching him with an arm, holding my nose with my other hand, circling, laughing, twisting, plunging.

Natalie walked with me to another pool, or maybe the same pool but a different area. The shouts of children reverberated. As we swam laps, each with our own lane, I realized I was in the same time zone as Mom and Dad; I needed to thank them for the note-taker.

After my accident, I used to hate the big indoor pool where Mom took me two or three times a week to rebuild my withered muscles. I felt horribly lost; noises echoed in strange ways above and below the surface of the water, throwing off my sense of direction. When I dipped my head under, I had to reach my weak arms over my head, again and again, sending jabs of pain into my neck. My hip ached. I bumped against lane dividers, hitting my elbows and bruising my underarms against the hard plastic and the coarse ropes. I was terrified of the end, the tiles that I couldn't see approach. For several weeks Mom swam with me, but she stopped after my stroke became more consistent and she found out about tappers used in the Special Olympics. She would hold a long, flexible stick and tap me when I was approaching the end, and I'd glide to the edge, my fingers outstretched. We knew better than to tell Dad about the tapping; he didn't approve of special treatment.

As I fell into the rhythm of lifting my arms and kicking in El Paso, I imagined Mom on the deck watching me: her strong legs and big shoulders, the loose skin above her elbows, and those nimble hands that could baste, sew, knit, change a tire, weed, and lift my chin on a bad day.

At the pool, she would tap me and I would glide, reach for the edge, turn, and push off. As a child I loved knowing that she walked along the pool edge and waited at the end for my approach. After I learned to feel for the lane dividers without stroking into them, I came to love the rhythm, routine, and exercise of the strokes. I came to understand that water was like blindness, filling space, reaching to touch the contours of its shore. I liked to let go and lose myself, waiting for Mom's gentle tap, trusting that it would come. With each tap, I felt her devotion, which was only sharpened when I was alone in the locker room afterward, searching for my clothing with my hands, feeling guilty about her coddling and doting, as if we'd both betrayed Dad.

After my arms and chest healed, as I regained strength, Mom stopped taking me regularly to the pool, and when I did swim, she stopped the tapping at each end—as if she'd indulged me enough. I missed that special attention, that secret accommodation between us. It wasn't until I moved in with Isa in Burbank that I found lap swimming again, at a community pool where I counted strokes so I could time my outstretched glide to the tile.

In El Paso, I counted the twenty-second stroke, stretched my arms, and kicked, confident of the tile. I grasped. Feet up. Pushed off. After about fifteen laps, I pulled myself onto the edge and sat, enjoying the resistance of water as I swirled my legs. I listened to other swimmers, trying to identify Natalie. My neck felt stiff but not sore. I rubbed it.

"We'd be on our own now, you and me," Devon said from somewhere, his voice bouncing off hard surfaces, "if you would do anything for a change."

I cocked my head. "Devon!" I said. "Ray's over at the slide."

"You think he's so great, how he describes every stupid thing."

Just like Devon, I thought: confrontational. But then I wondered if he was jealous about my bonding with Ray. "Did you call Alexis today?" I said. "Are they coming?"

He ignored me. As he sat on my right, his feet swirling in the water, his sweat smelled powerful, alive.

"You should try the slide," I said. "It's not deep there. You can almost touch." Although I knew he wouldn't go in, I wanted to encourage him. I'd tried to teach him to swim several times, but it frustrated him not to be in control. He couldn't let go in the water.

"Isa's back at the jail," he said. "We're supposed to stay at the kiddy pool till she comes."

The sound of her name made me uneasy, but I didn't let it spoil my mood. "Did you see Patrick?"

"He looked like shit. He spent the night in the drunk tank with like ten other guys."

"He's not out yet?"

"They wouldn't let him out. Something about he's not a resident. He has to see a magistrate today or tomorrow."

"Tomorrow!" I said, but the more I thought about it, the more I liked the idea: another day here with Natalie. "Come on," I said, "let's finish that swim lesson."

Neither of us moved. "I hear you're fighting for immigrant rights," he said in a challenging tone. Only then did I hear Natalie standing behind me, breathing. "What? You think they should just come into this country and get school and health care all jelly?"

I laughed because that was pure Devon, going on the offensive with a word she wouldn't know.

"What does that mean, 'jelly'?" Natalie said.

"Means 'on the house,'" he said, his tone authoritative, as if he were the expert. "Free."

"Lots of them pay taxes," she said. "And the rest are willing to, if we let them work aboveboard."

I was surprised that Devon didn't even respond. He just stood up and shuffled away toward the slide. "Don't mind him," I said. "He's been stuck at the auto shop all day."

"He's right," she said. "The way it works now, it's an underground economy."

Natalie led me outside, where we stood for a moment in an enclosure, she said. An adobe wall and fence. Picnic tables. A play structure but no children at play. It smelled oddly of fried fish. The air was so dry the skin of my forearms tightened as beads of water began to evaporate from tiny hairs. When she stepped forward again, I enjoyed feeling the tremor of her biceps as she walked. We sat on scratchy grass in the shade where the sun radiated through a cloth awning or canopy above, I don't know. We were alone, I knew that. Or alone enough. Every now and then a wind I couldn't feel whistled through a tight space nearby. I loved the feel of Natalie's thigh against my own, the sparkle of tingles along my leg.

"Do you mind?" she said, her voice more intimate now that we were beyond the echoes of the public pool. "Can I feel your scar?"

"If I can touch your face too," I said, trying to match her sense of presence.

"You go first," she said, lying on her back on the grass. I propped myself on my elbow and brought my opposite hand to her cheek, where a dimple formed as she smiled. I remembered the feel of my mother's dimples; they always formed the instant her lips curved up. I traced my forefinger along Natalie's lips, which felt saucy as she twisted them for me.

"That tickles," she said, setting off her dimples again. Her eyebrows lined the ridge of her sockets perfectly. I stalled my touch on her eyelids, enjoying the fullness and flickers of her eyes beneath the sheer, pliant skin. I felt for but couldn't find crow's-feet at the outer edges of her eyes. Perhaps the same age as me? I massaged the hollow of one temple, then the other. I gently tugged the tender spots where her earlobes met her jaws.

"That feels good," she said, yawning. "I forgot how tired I am."

Her hair reached just beyond her shoulders, and I ran my hand through it several times, enjoying its lightness as it dashed between my fingers. As I massaged her scalp, I listened to her steady breaths. "I like the way you look," I said.

"Very funny. You can't see."

I hoped she might fall asleep, but she popped up. "My turn."

As I lay back, she knelt next to me, holding my face in both hands. I felt goofy and self-conscious. Her hand against the left side of my face, where my nerve endings are still good, was cool. Whenever someone touches my right cheek near my scar, it feels dull, like the sound of a bell through drywall. She rubbed my eyebrows, eyelashes, and cheeks, her touch lingering along my scar, following its course as it scampered from my forehead through my eyebrow, down into my socket, and up onto my cheek. She traced that fault line several times, top to bottom and bottom to top. Along my cheek, I could feel her fingernail catching on stubble, scratchy.

"It's like a river," she said. "A stream."

I liked that.

"You want me to describe your face?" she said.

I could feel my cheeks flush. "You don't need to."

I thought she would be quick. I knew she would lie. I made my expression blank. No emotion.

Her voice was calm. "You're handsome," she started.

Already she was lying—"striking" was a word I was used to. But I couldn't help smiling. Then I laughed and turned away.

She brought my chin back with her hand, and she stretched out next to me. I loved the heat of her rib cage against my chest, the coolness of her wet bathing suit, and the pressure of her breast. "Your jaw looks strong; your nose is straight. You have a high forehead. Your skin is like cream. On your left side, that eyelid is closed, which makes you look quiet, like you're thinking.

"The right side of your face, it's only you; couldn't be anyone else. You earned it when you were young."

I heard myself breathe.

"You're missing a small chunk of your right eyebrow," she went on, "right in the middle of the arch. Your eyelid and eye socket are collapsed some on that side, but not much. Your scar is like a thin seam, like the line between slices of bread in a loaf. It runs like a *Z* from your eyebrow down—"

"*Z*?" I said. "Everybody says it's an *S*."

"Trace it with your finger."

It was true. I'd traced it thousands of times before. How had I forgotten what it felt like to me? It felt like I was writing a *Z* with soft corners.

"For everybody else, looking at you, it looks like an *S*. But for you, facing out, it's a *Z*. And your ears stick out some," she said, laughing lightly. "Like maybe you would've been kidded about them in school if it weren't for your scar."

I smiled, turning away; I couldn't help it. People had described aspects of my face to me, but not in much detail, not all at once. My mother was always too busy trying to raise my spirits. My father couldn't even say "blind" in front of me. My brother had been wounded too deeply by the sight of my body being crushed. Even my friends and girlfriends were too considerate, and I was too self-conscious to ask. My hands were my only mirror. It felt as if Natalie, in minutes, had seen through my scar to me, and even looked back out at my world.

"Look at your lips!" she marveled. "I hadn't even noticed your lips." She pulled my chin back toward her. "They're smooth and thin, like a baby's. They're the color of roses, especially when you blush." She chuckled again.

I laughed too. After a moment, I said, "Do my eyebrows match my hair?"

"Your hair is light brown; your eyebrows are a bit darker. Your hair is thin, straight. But you know that from the feel."

A whistle blew from poolside. "What happens when I frown?"

She laughed. "You look mean. Impatient. Your right eyelid collapses a bit extra."

"What happens now?" I grinned.

"Dimples appear in your cheeks. Your face softens. You look generous."

"You said my face is handsome," I said, flirting. "Was that your first lie to me?"

"I didn't lie." She kissed me briefly, making me stretch toward her, wanting more. "Your scar is arresting because it's different. Most people are attracted to the beauty they know. But I'm not most people." When she kissed me again, we held each other for a long time and I lost myself in the moisture and heat of her lips.

As Natalie drifted to sleep on the grass, I dozed too—until hunger began to bite. It was well into afternoon, and we hadn't had lunch. I lay beside her for a long time, not wanting to wake her. Finally I stood and opened Charlie. I worried some about leaving her alone, but the area was fenced, wasn't it? And we were just outside the door. I knew I'd be back in minutes.

Inside, I heard Devon's and Ray's voices mixed with the shouts of other kids. I stood near the pool and called softly for Devon, whose long strides came tramping across the concrete. He put his big hand, wet and heavy, on my shoulder. I felt his side: dripping wet. "Swimmer," I said, nodding, careful not to make too big a deal of it. When I asked him if he wanted to get something to eat, he said he was starving.

"I'll come if you want," he said, but his voice wasn't in it.

"Swim!" I said. "Swim."

He said he'd seen a little market right around the corner. As he gave me directions, I drew a mental map. I touched my way into the locker room with Charlie, where I found my clothes on the hook. My shirt was still sweaty from the run, so I rinsed it quickly. I didn't care if it was wet; I didn't want it to smell. After I put my clothes on, wet shirt included, Charlie led me back out to the reception area, where I asked for directions to the market. I wanted to be sure.

"It's easy," a woman said. "Go out the door and turn left. Take a left at the corner. It's at the next corner across the street. It's barely a block."

The same directions Devon had given me. When I opened the front door, I was shocked by the strength of the dry wind. On the sidewalk I paused, registering the sun on my face and the wind driving from the left. It was later in the day than I'd thought, judging by the sun; no wonder I was hungry. I walked into the wind, toward the store. That's when I heard a voice, quiet, demurring, on my left.

"Young man, can I pray for you?"

"Excuse me?" I said.

A woman's quick steps on hard heels approached. "Jesus can heal the sick and afflicted." She hooked my arm and turned me downwind. Her voice was soft, her touch rigid.

"Let go!" I said, jerking my arm away. "I don't need to be healed."

"We all need to be healed," she said.

I turned upwind, incensed. Weren't there enough sighted sinners for these zealots? I hurried away, touching the sidewalk with Charlie, left and right, opposite my brisk steps. Then I slowed, breathed, and tried to relax. Charlie's tip dropped down a curb; I was at a street. The store was one block to the left, the woman had said. The wind was swirling, mostly from my left now. Was it coming around the building? The sun had disappeared: behind buildings or clouds?

I turned left and after fifty paces or so I heard a car pass at a cross street straight ahead, going at a right angle to my direction. I swept Charlie, expecting the curb of an intersection, which I located quickly. I traced the edge of the curb back to the right as it rounded a corner so I could cross the street that I'd been walking along. I listened for traffic, pedestrians, and the mechanical click of a stoplight changing signals. But I heard only wind, which came swirling mostly from the left, whistling around something behind me, a stop sign perhaps. I thought of my cell phone and missed its sense of security.

"Hello," I called. There was no answer. I heard no cars and couldn't locate a crossing signal. Reaching Charlie forward, I stepped into the street and crossed tentatively. At the store I would ask at the counter for some hotdogs and a big bag of corn chips. And some packets of cheese crackers. In my wallet I still had five twenty-dollar bills folded first along the length, then across the width, plus some ones not folded at all.

Before I reached the opposite curb, the sun came out and disappeared quickly. A squirrel barked from above, and leaves rustled in the wind: a tree. I stepped onto the curb and continued straight across the sidewalk to its inside edge, where I tapped into and then grasped a chain-link fence running parallel to the street. Off to the left I could hear a metal door slapping rhythmically against its jamb, a pause and then a clamor: the door of the snack shop. I followed the fence upwind, toward the sound of the door, expecting the fence to end immediately at the intersection and the snack shop to be on the other side. But I found I was midblock: the cross street didn't continue through to this side, which made me distrustful. Streets that jog can mess up directions. In five more paces, at the end of the fence, I paused. I heard the clang of the door straight ahead, perhaps another ten paces. The wind blew a plastic cup or something light in circles by my feet. I paused, listening for familiar sounds: people walking or talking, a car driving by.

"Hello," I called again. There was nothing but the clattering door ahead and the harsh wind coming at me in swirls. I thought of heading back without the food and traced in my head the way back. Again I missed my cell phone and berated myself for having thrown it against the wall in Burbank. I let go of the fence and caned farther than I expected toward the sound of the door, which wasn't a door at all but a garbage bin rolling up against a metal chair in the wind, settling downhill, and then slapping the chair again. I had turned half around to head back when I heard footsteps.

"Hello!" I said, twisting my head. "Hello! Is there a store near here?" I must have staggered a bit in the wind.

"Are you drunk?" a man slurred.

Was he blind? "I'm not drunk!" I said.

He came at me, catching me not completely off balance because I heard his quickening steps. He smacked me with his shoulder to my chest, but I stepped back, deflecting his thrust so I didn't fall. My glasses clung to my head, but I dropped Charlie, who knew where? I didn't have time to panic; the man clung, smelling of liquor and gutters and garbage bins, pushing me.

When I was a freshman in high school, I joined the wrestling team to please Dad. I was pretty good when I could get my hands on the other guy. But most of the kids circled around me on the mat and then shot in for my legs to take me down. Once they had their takedown points, they'd let me go before I could reverse them. And then they'd take me down again. I didn't care at first. What I cared about was Dad kneeling on the living room floor with me, even with his bad hand, just like he used to when Larry and I were little. We pushed the furniture away and wrapped each other up until we collapsed, exhausted, sweating.

Out in the wind, I struggled against the man's clumsy weight. With our arms interlocked, we faced each other. I managed a "Help!" that couldn't have been loud. Moments earlier I'd been wandering around, unsure where I was. Now I was grounded, dead certain what I needed to do: take him down. I felt the advantage now that we were in contact. But he was heavier than I.

I tugged at his coat sleeve with my left hand while I pushed with my right, forcing us to circle counterclockwise. As he pulled back in the opposite direction, resisting me, I shifted my weight to go with his and tugged hard with my right hand, pulling him down and letting go afterward. But he had me in his grasp and pulled me as well. I fell hard on top of him, my shoulder into his chest, so that he groaned with a loud "oomph" and let go. I was lucky that as I rolled off him I brushed my hand over Charlie right there on the pavement. I grabbed my stick and was up faster than the man was.

"Hey!" he said.

I caned quickly twenty or thirty paces upwind on a sidewalk, paralleling a street that was on my left. It seemed I was always going upwind—probably moving away from the pool. I listened but couldn't hear footsteps anywhere. The repeated slap of the garbage can fell behind me. I wasn't sure where I was but assumed I was on a side street. If I took two or three rights, I hoped, I'd be back on the street I'd started on, where the Jesus lady stood. I cursed my earlier impatience: Why had I immediately taken offense at her? Why hadn't I just asked her how to get to the store?

I heard no traffic. The sidewalk ended abruptly at a wall, which dumped me into the street, so I walked along the opposite sidewalk, then crossed back at the next intersection, taking a right. The wind gusted from behind and to the left. I turned right at the next street with the wind fully behind me and the sun out again. I could feel sun on my face, which confused me because it had been on my face when I'd left the pool, but the wind there had been blowing from my left. I listened for footsteps. No traffic. Nothing. What an idiot I was to not have a phone!

"Hello!" I yelled. "Hello!"

There was no answer. Were there footsteps from behind? I couldn't tell in the dry wind.

"Help!" I called. "I'm lost." I waited, anxious about the bum I'd thrown down. But what choice did I have except to take a chance and seek help? A car whizzed by on the street. I waved, but it didn't stop. "Hello!" I called.

I walked forward, caning, striking the edge of a low curb sticking up at an odd angle, which I maneuvered around. I should have turned back to find the street, but I kept on, and ten paces farther on I came to a van parked at a different angle. I shouldn't have edged around the van, but I did. I found myself immersed in a labyrinth of parking stops at odd angles, the wind swirling, all shadows: a parking lot. Without the sun, I lost all sense of direction. It was too late to find my way back to the street I'd just been on. I was furious at myself. I tried to walk straight but got turned this way and that. My heart was racing. My jaws were clenched tight. I took a deep breath. The place smelled of urine, old cigarettes, rotting tangerines. I came across a cushion, a mattress rather, a pile of wet clothes or garbage, who knew?

"Hello!" I said. "Hello!"

No one.

Maybe the world lay open, but fear and claustrophobia fell over me like a plague. I felt trapped and light-headed. Nauseous. I couldn't breathe. I stumbled alongside a car, falling. Something dug into my shoulder before I hit the ground, bruising my upper arm. I got up and staggered on, caning sloppily, my hand shaking, my heart faltering.

Breathe, I thought, breathe! But I couldn't find myself.

Charlie finally struck the side of a building, where I collapsed on the pavement, relieved to have found the means of escape back to the street. I heaved up nothing once, twice. I breathed. I lay on my side, gathering strength. I thought of Natalie waking on the grass without me. I thought of the walk around the block I'd taken long ago with my friend Charlie, when we'd run across those godawful kids on bikes. Thank God for Charlie.

Finally I stood, caning carefully this time along the building back to a street. I walked along a sidewalk toward I didn't know where. It didn't matter about the sun or the wind anymore. I crossed an intersection, turned left at another. What I needed was traffic, a crossroads where I could lift my white cane and be found, where I could display to the world my blindness, my inability to cross a street and go to a store. Who was I fooling by running down a hill? I'm Kevin Layne. I can't see. I have a four-thousand-dollar note-taker but can't make a living as a writer. I've put so much crack into my lungs that I can never escape it. My parents don't trust me. I have a caretaker for good reason: I'm twenty-eight years old, and I'm helpless. I can't support myself. How long did I expect to fool Natalie?

I crossed the street and walked toward the distant sounds of traffic. After another block, at an intersection, I stood on the curb, waving my cane as cars slowed and then sped onward. All I needed was someone with a cell phone so I could call Isa. My hands were shaking; my right foot tapped the pavement. I wasn't sure how long I'd been gone.

I lamented: Why had I let go of that chain-link fence? Why had I come on this trip at all, with this needy family? And how could I have entangled myself with Isa? I groaned aloud at that thought, letting a low howl escape. Of course Patrick would batter me when he found out; I deserved it for screwing his wife. Or he'd berate me for days before smashing my note-taker and leaving me in the desert. Or he'd hit her, wouldn't he—and what would I do, stand in as his witness? What a dupe I'd been, thinking I could stay out of the fray.

Standing on the curb with the cars flying by, I thought about the money in my pocket: How far could it be to the nearest bar? Just one drink, I thought. Who could begrudge me that after what I'd been through? Alcohol was a far cry from crack, after all. I could even call Isa's cell phone from the bar. The longer I stood there, the more I allowed my mind to wander so that I began to crave even more: The little glass tube against my lips. The torch of the lighter's heat—on-again off-again—at the opposite end. And the crackling pops as I rolled the tube back and forth with my fingers. I even longed for the bitterness of burned plastic at the back of my throat before my mouth went numb and all of me drifted like vapor along the tube from the tiny rock melting.

I struck out for a bar in a flurry, scurrying along the pavement after Charlie, who was always happy to lead; he never tried to judge me. I loved him suddenly and completely; I felt grateful to have his grip in my hand and his guidance before me. We got half a block before a car pulled up beside us and stopped. It sounded like Betsy's grumbling motor, but I didn't let myself believe; I wasn't sure I wanted to be found.

"Kevin!" Isa called as doors opened.

When I felt Ray's hand on my wet forearm, I realized how sweaty I was. My heart was racing. I couldn't quite breathe.

"Where's Natalie?" I said, panicked, not wanting her to see me like this.

"She's with Devon," Ray said.

Relief washed over me: the mugging, the claustrophobia, the nausea, the humiliation. I felt weak in my knees.

"What the hell!" Patrick said. "Get in the damn car. We got things to do."

I was glad even to hear Patrick. Ray pulled me to the back door, where he slid in first and I came after.

"How are we supposed to find Devon and that peace-lover activist?" Patrick griped. He gassed the car. Something crackled and luffed behind me. I didn't smell exhaust.

"Go to the pool," Isa said. "They'll return there."

"She's looking for me too?" I said.

"Everybody's looking for you," she said.

So Natalie knew I was a fuckup.

"I got mugged," I said.

"What a surprise!" Patrick said. "Wandering around like that. Why don't you just put that stick up your own ass, save everybody a lot of trouble?"

"Stop it," Isa said.

"Cut the shit, Patrick," I said. "I thought you were supposed to be in jail another day."

"They lowered my charges. But they kept my goddamned bones."

I sagged into the seat, the exhaustion draining me. My upper arm ached and stung from my fall in the parking lot. I was sick of them all. But when Ray grabbed my hand, I eked out a smile. His touch helped me breathe.

"Just my luck," Patrick said. "Rich bastard rear-ends me and I'm the one goes to jail."

"There they are," Isa said, "by that pole."

We sped over and jolted to a stop. I rubbed my neck, which throbbed. "Get in, Devon!" Patrick yelled. "We've got stuff to do. I met this guy."

"What stuff?" Isa said. "Who?"

"Nothing," Patrick said.

"Are you okay?" Natalie said from outside the car.

When Devon opened the door, I got out.

"What the hell are you doing?" Patrick said.

"Isn't our stuff at the pastor's house?" I said.

"So?"

"I'll see you there," I said. "I'm going with her."

"Who the fuck's going to lift the casket onto the roof?"

I ignored him. As I caned around the other car, Patrick said, "Has there ever been a man so unlucky?" He was talking about himself, but I was adrift as well.

I figured Natalie and I had thirty minutes together, tops, until Patrick stopped by the Voice of God church on his way to Pastor Curt's house. It had been easy to talk with her earlier, but now I was myself: self-conscious and awkward. Maybe she was preoccupied too because she didn't speak either. We drove onto the freeway and for another few minutes before I gathered my strength. "I'm sorry I abandoned you at the pool," I said finally.

"Abandoned me?" she said. "You didn't abandon me. I'm sorry I didn't go with you. That you got lost. I can't even imagine what that must be like."

"I'm good at it," I said. "Sometimes I can't do shit."

"Stop it," she said. "Why don't you have a cell phone?"

"It broke before the trip," I said.

"I left mine at home today. I'm sick of getting badgered by work at all hours."

I told her about getting mugged, wrestling the man down, stumbling away.

"You're incredible," she said. "You got away from him, and you're blind!"

Even that comment—her allowance for my disability—made me feel lousy. "After this trip," I said, "I'm going to get my own place. I need to get away."

"You should've seen how upset Ray was about you," she said. "And Devon too. When we were driving around, looking for you, you know what Devon said? He said you saved his life. He said you're the first adult who ever believed in him, who actually listened to him. He said if it wasn't for you, he'd be in jail for doing something stupid."

"Devon said that?" I was shocked.

Natalie slowed and turned onto the crunch of gravel. "Shit," she said. "Tevo's here."

"Who's Tevo?" I said.

"He was my boyfriend," she whispered. As we stopped, I heard the house door slam.

"Where've you been all day?" a man demanded, his footsteps brisk and assured. "I've been calling your cell. We missed our water drops."

Natalie got out of the car. I did too, standing.

His steps came to a halt. "Okay," he said. "I see. Well, tonight we're going out again."

I thought of what she'd told me earlier, at the kitchen table, about Tevo having serious eyes.

"Last night wasn't enough for you?" she said. "What if we get arrested again?"

His footsteps crunched in the gravel, moving right past us. "That's why we can't back down," he insisted. He opened a car door. "But the board is meeting tonight. This is your chance to stop it. Luis will pick you up in thirty minutes." The door slammed, and when the engine turned over, it rumbled deeply—a pickup or SUV, I thought. He drove off.

"He makes me so mad!" Natalie said under her breath.

I should have asked what was going on, but what did it matter? I was leaving in fifteen minutes. Inside, Andrea was making chicken enchiladas that smelled sweet and bitter at the same time. I was sorry Carlos wasn't there; I needed his light humor. When I walked into the bedroom with Natalie, I was startled somehow that this was her room. This carpet. This double bed. As she pulled out a drawer and shuffled things about, I wondered if Isa's suitcase was still beside the bed and whether her thin chemise was visible. By the time Natalie walked out to make some phone calls, I felt guilty, as if I'd cheated on her.

In my suitcase I found my next-to-last clean shirt. Tomorrow would be our fourth day out; we had expected to be in Florida by now. As I rolled up my dirty clothes, I felt something prickly in a pocket of the seersucker shirt I'd worn the day before. Reaching inside, I pulled out a bone: the damn coon bone I'd kept from the freeway. For a second I panicked, thinking about Patrick seeing my suitcase in the same room with Isa's things. Then I realized he hadn't been here yet. I was tempted to walk outside and crush the bone underfoot. What kind of luck had it brought me? Sleeping with Isa. Running downhill. Kissing Natalie. Getting lost and mugged. I decided to let it run its course; I put the bone back in the shirt pocket and rolled up the shirt.

After I showered, when I put my bags in the living room, Natalie was still talking on the phone. I made sure my note-taker was in my backpack, and I laid Charlie on top, folded. I was wearing my glasses; I missed my hat. While I waited, Andrea served enchiladas that I couldn't stop eating, though my mouth was burning and I was downing water. Natalie joined me, but she wouldn't eat much; I knew because Andrea kept trying to push food upon her. The more I ate, the more exhausted

I became; I could hardly hold my head up. I couldn't wait to get in Betsy and sleep.

"I'm sorry I'm not saying anything," Natalie said. "I'm sad you're going. I've never met anyone like you, the way you sense things and communicate. The way you strike out and do stuff. The way you take risks."

I smiled, thinking she didn't know me very well. "Thanks for taking me running," I said. "You don't know how much that helped me."

She scribbled something. "Here's my number," she said, giving me a piece of paper. "What am I thinking? You can't read that."

"I'll figure it out," I said, putting the paper in my pocket. "Maybe we can stop on the way back. I'll call you when we're back in Texas." I wanted to ask for more and promise more. But what would that be?

"You're a very strong person. You helped me figure out what I'm going to do," she said. "I'm going to quit my job. I need to make some changes."

"Well, don't do that on my account," I said, trying to smile. We both felt awkward.

As we waited out front, I dreaded the thought of being with Patrick and Isa again. I was too miserable to let myself kiss Natalie, though that was what I wanted to do. She shuffled about, making noise on my account, I suppose. I didn't know what to do with my arms.

"The sun's hidden behind your head," she said, forcing a slender laugh. "Your head's glowing."

I nodded. Sight is strange, I thought, if my head can blot out the sun.

A car pulled into the driveway, a steady growl rather than Betsy's rumble. As we stood, I ran my hand through my hair, pissed at myself for not being able to step forward and pull her to me. I remembered how good it had felt to howl after the golf-course run. Why couldn't I always be lighthearted and thoughtless?

"Vamos!" someone called from the car. "We're late!"

"Why don't you come, Kevin?" Natalie said softly.

"They'll be here any minute," I said.

"Kevin," she said. She slipped up against me, her hand gripping my arm where I'd bruised it in the parking lot. I tried not to grimace. "Why don't you come with me?" she said. "I need you."

Only then did I realize what she was asking. For a moment, I couldn't speak. Who doesn't want to be needed? Who hasn't wanted to escape? I was aware that my mouth was open.

"What do you mean?" I managed to say, hugging her to me. I wanted to hear more.

"Stay with me. You can come with me to this meeting. I'm going to quit. Then we'll figure out what's next. You said you want to get away. I do too. You can hook up with them on their way back west. Or . . . I don't know. We'll see."

I couldn't believe what she was saying. I thought of the money in my suitcase. I remembered what Devon had told me, that I never did anything, never took a stand. "You're asking me to stay with you at Curt's house this week?"

She brought her cheek against my deadened cheek and nodded her answer.

I was beside myself.

"I like you," she whispered in my ear. "You help me put things in perspective. You help me see things. You make me feel better about who I am. Maybe we could go to the mountains for a few days."

I squeezed her. "I like you too," I said, laughing. "Okay. Yes. Okay." I was so light-headed that my sense of touch exploded; I could feel every detail of her back with my fingers. "I just need to talk to the kids," I said. "I need to tell them I'll see them on the way back."

"You can call from my cell," she said. "We're late already."

I nodded. "What do I need to bring?"

"Don't bring anything. We'll be back here tonight."

"I need Charlie," I said.

"Who's Charlie?"

I laughed. "That's what I call my cane. He's folded on my backpack in the living room."

"I like that," she said, "that you give it a name." She ran and brought Charlie out. I was in a daze when I stooped into the backseat, falling, scooting over as she got in after me. She pressed into me and I pressed back, the two of us hugging and laughing. What a day!

As soon as the door shut and she introduced me to Luis and we were backing down the driveway, I felt a lump in my stomach. I hadn't even left a note—nothing tangible at all. How could I run off, I thought, after I'd talked Devon out of doing the same thing? And after I'd promised Ray to protect him?

I tried calling Isa's cell, but we were in a pocket without reception, so I couldn't even leave a message.

It was not the smartest thing I'd done, this rash act of abandoning the kids. I felt self-indulgent. But I also felt buzzed to be in the backseat of a strange car in Natalie's arms. As I kissed her, her hair flew in the wind, whipping the good side of my face. She pulled her head back for a moment, took off my glasses, and kissed me long and hard, open-mouthed. When we broke away, we both laughed. I caught a lilt in her voice as she spoke in Spanish to Luis, her tone lighter and happier than moments before. His Spanish was soft and lyrical, like a melody. They joked and she laughed, releasing her familiar wheeze. It made me grin. I remembered letting go on the golf course, feeling the surge of strength in my legs. Again I was running. Like a fool. Come what may.

NINE

Devon told me later: after Natalie and I drove off to Pastor Curt's house, Patrick found a Mexican restaurant and bought everybody whatever they wanted. He ordered a burrito that got cold on his plate as Isa, Devon, and Ray ate their meals and tried not to watch Patrick outside, where he spoke into Isa's cell phone, pacing on the sidewalk and gesturing wildly. Devon said his beady eyes and dark stubble made him look like Chuck Norris, but his hair looked goofy, matted on the side of his head and puffed up on top from his night in jail. Inside the restaurant, Isa bit her fingernails and pressed her lips into a thin line, watching him and then jerking her head away every time Patrick walked toward them on the other side of the plate-glass window. Creases knitted themselves into her forehead, above the bridge of her nose. But that was it, Devon said. She didn't ask him anything when he rushed inside with that lame-ass grin they'd seen before—every time he had a fucktard idea.

At the Voice of God church Isa refused to touch the casket. As soon as Betsy stopped, she jumped out and stamped over to the big door in her three-inch wedge-heeled sandals, but it was locked. Devon, still in the car, watched her turn around, dip forward, and reach inside her white shirt to hoist up her tube top. Then she leaned her back against the concrete wall, crossed her arms, tucked her chin, and waited as Devon helped Patrick haul the casket from around back and hoist it on top of Betsy.

One of the ropes had been cut, but Patrick didn't seem to care; he cut a length from the slack and tied the ends together. No one could remember what had happened to the tarp. He was short a towel too, but he didn't curse about that either. He found an old blanket, tore it in half, and wrapped it around one of the ropes.

Patrick tried to show Devon the knots again, but Devon wouldn't listen—all those twists and turns. He hated the damn casket anyway, sitting there tilted forward on the rack, the sun reflecting off it like gold and making the carvings come alive now that there was no tarp. Beneath the coffin, Betsy looked like shit. There was a huge dent in her back end. Her busted-out taillight was covered with clear red tape to make it look red when it lit up. She had no back bumper at all. And a sheet of opaque plastic was stretched across her rear window, fastened with blue tape all around. "We looked like fucking white trash," Devon told me, "carrying a rich man's tomb."

At the pastor's house, Andrea told them they'd just missed me; I'd gone off with Natalie to a meeting in El Paso, and she didn't know when we'd be back. Yet right there in the living room they saw my bags.

Patrick's nostrils flared. His eyes got as big as walnuts. Isa tried to hang all over him to calm him down, but that worked him up even more. She checked her cell, but it was a dead zone and there were no messages from me.

"You know what I thought?" Devon told me. "My first thought was you did tap Isa and you damn better be running—but then why would you leave your stuff? Then I figured maybe you were staying with that Natalie after all. But then why the fuck wouldn't you tell us good-bye?"

As Patrick took a shower, Devon told Ray I'd be back. But Ray glared and said, "Shut the fuck up, chingado," which startled and impressed Devon. So Devon backed off, and they both leaned against Betsy and watched the sunset flame across the sky, electrifying the green field and even the dirt all around the squat cement-block house.

When Patrick came out the front door, his hair wasn't mashed to the side anymore; it was wet and wild and sticking up. "Time to go!" he declared, stomping down the walkway carrying my suitcase and backpack.

Devon stepped in front of him. "You can't steal Kevin's stuff," he said.

Patrick's eyes became slits. "It came with us. It's leaving with us. He didn't even leave a note. I don't give a shit, but look at her."

Devon turned toward Isa, who was wiping her face with a tissue, her mascara streaking her cheeks.

"We can't leave him!" Ray said, right behind Devon.

As Patrick stepped toward the car, Devon grabbed at the bags, but Patrick dipped, Devon missed, and Patrick swung the backpack, hitting Devon on the side of his head and almost knocking him down. When Devon came again, Patrick shoved him off with a forearm to the shoulder. "Save it," he said. "You don't want any part of me."

But Ray came alive. He battered Patrick's arms and legs all the way to the car. Then he ran up and clung to the doorknob, all quiet. Patrick had to grab him around the chest, pick him up, and pry his hands off the door. As soon as Ray was off the doorknob, though, he started screaming "fuck" words in Spanish and English—"Chingado viejo hijo de puta!" and "Motherfucker!" and "Cabrón!" He grabbed the flimsy trellis next to the stairs and pulled it down while Patrick wrestled his wiggling body with one arm and tried to pull the trellis out of Ray's grip with his other hand.

"Gimme some help!" Patrick called, but Devon backed off and shook his head. Finally Patrick pried Ray loose. Ray kicked his skinny legs in the air all the way to the car, but he didn't scream anymore. It looked weird, Devon said, all that motion and no sound—after so much badass shit.

In the backseat, Isa hugged Ray as Devon sat in the front and Patrick backed the car around and spun the tires, kicking up stones as they sped out of the driveway. "Thanks!" Isa called out the window to Andrea, who was standing on the front step, as if she'd just heard all the noise.

"You know what I thought?" Devon told me. "I thought, That's it for Kevin. That's fucking it. So what if he abandoned me, the bastard. He's a grown-up. That's what I expected all along."

As Betsy sped down the street, Devon glanced at Ray, whose expression was blank—except for his jaw, which was set in stone. For all the swearing and loco shit, Ray didn't cry at all. Devon stared back at the sandy-brown house amid those lush green fields under a sky turning toward night. He made up his mind that he was not upset. But the fucking tears started coming on their own.

When we sped onto the freeway in Luis's car, still there was no cell coverage. The meeting was in a beauty parlor south of downtown, Natalie said, about twenty more minutes. I liked that idea, a beauty-parlor gathering: board members swiveling back and forth in salon chairs. "You can get your hair done at the same time," I said.

She didn't think it was funny.

For a while Luis tried to talk her out of quitting, in English as well as Spanish, as she twitched and bristled next to me. I realized only later how anxious she was. She changed the subject, telling me that it was Luis who'd been arrested last night, for trespassing. A few months ago, a group of Minutemen had started patrolling the border west of El Paso, in New Mexico, at about the same time that the water tanks in the desert were getting shot with holes. So Tevo had spearheaded a counterproject called Proyecto Luminoso, where volunteers went out at night and shone lights on the Minuteman stakeouts to warn immigrants. Natalie had fought the plan from the start, saying it was too confrontational for a nonprofit that had been created to improve the dialogue, but Tevo had rammed it through. From what I gathered, Tevo seemed to be in charge of things—maybe executive director—and she was working for him.

Last night the sheriff had been waiting on private property and had arrested Luis and his group. The board was to decide tonight whether to continue Proyecto Luminoso.

"You can't stand back and do nothing," Luis said. "Silence is consent."

"There are choices beyond silence," Natalie said.

I couldn't help thinking about Patrick's tirades. How many times had I remained silent?

Finally the cell phone had a signal, but my call went straight to Isa's voice mail, where I left a message saying I was staying with Natalie for now; I'd see them on their way back west. When I hung up, it didn't seem near enough, a tinny recording for the kids on a phone.

During the meeting, I waited outside the salon, leaning against the building as snatches of conflict and canned fragrance drifted from the open door. The air conditioning inside was busted, which probably added to the tension. But with the sun just down, the heat was beginning to drop outside. I called again and again from Natalie's phone, but it went to voice mail each time.

After about fifteen minutes, Isa reached me in a fevered pitch that made me stand stiffly. I tried to tell her I was sorry and I'd see them on their way west, but she spoke in circles about Patrick bringing my suitcase and the trellis coming down and Ray all over him, fighting.

"Ray?" I said.

And Devon had taken a swing at Patrick, she said, when he'd dropped them off at the Laundromat, and it was getting dark.

"You dropped off the kids?"

Right now they were standing in a neighborhood that looked strange, waiting for Patrick.

"Who's standing?" I said. "Who?"

She couldn't take it anymore, she said. He was doing something with the coffin, God knew what this time. She didn't want any more bones or anything else. Why had I abandoned her and the kids, for God's sake?

I tried to get her to talk about the boys, but she rambled on about Patrick's crazy schemes landing them all in jail, as if it were already a fact. I remembered what he'd said in Deming about smuggling in El Paso. What the hell had he talked about—guns or merchandise or what? Why did he do this shit? And how did he get the money?

"Tell him we don't want to see him," I heard Devon say—which meant she was with them, thank God. Devon and Ray weren't waiting at the Laundromat alone.

"The kids want to see you," Isa said. "You could at least tell them good-bye if you don't care about me. And you might as well come get your note-taker. Patrick got that too."

I didn't know who to loathe more just then, Patrick or his enabler.

Natalie was on top of the world when she came outside, stepping lightly, moving quickly, hugging and touching and telling me that the vote hadn't gone as she'd wanted. The board had sided with Tevo, so she'd resigned on the spot, and what a relief already! It wasn't just about the work; thank God she didn't have to deal with Tevo anymore.

Before I could tell her about the Laundromat, Tevo came outside, and they spat in subdued tones back and forth. He told her the board wouldn't accept her resignation after hours, and she said she wasn't waiting until tomorrow; she was resigning tonight, in protest of this decision. They argued until Natalie, frustrated, refused to talk anymore and walked off; I didn't know where.

"That's enough," I said. "Leave her alone."

Tevo shifted his weight, which made his shoes squeak. "So you're blind," he said.

"You got something to say about that?"

"No," he stammered. "More power to you."

I didn't respond. When he asked me how long we'd been together, Natalie and I, I told him we'd met today.

"Today!" His shoes squeaked again. "Today!" he repeated, as if the concept were difficult to understand.

After a moment, he drew a breath and said, "Listen, Natalie's maybe the smartest person I know in dealing with people. Getting people together. Helping people work stuff out. I never could've pulled it off. But she gets in over her head sometimes. I want you to know that. She takes on things she doesn't know much about."

I could feel my muscles tense. But I spoke slowly: "You're saying I'm a cause for her. She's in over her head because I'm blind."

He exhaled through his nose. "Don't be so defensive. I'm saying take care of her. I'm saying she gets involved in lots of things, and she forgets about her own needs."

Oh, I wanted to say, and you know what she needs.

But I kept my peace.

When Luis, Natalie, and I pulled up to the Laundromat and got out of the car, Ray's steps scurried up to me. I opened my arms and got ready to apologize. But he battered my chest with the sides of his fists, hitting me hard, shocking me, hurting me, making me fall back against the side of the car. I had to protect my torso with my arms.

"Pendejo!" he blared. "I hate you. I hate you!"

"Fuck you for leaving us!" Devon said from several paces away. "Fuck *you*!"

"I'm sorry," I said, trying to pull Ray to me, but he wouldn't settle—his arms kept flailing. Finally he'd had enough, and he broke away. I scurried after him with Charlie, trying to follow his quick steps for half a block along the sidewalk, away from the others. I wanted to tell him what had happened and how I'd tried to call and how I would join up with them in only a week or so—on their way back west.

But he wouldn't listen and told me to get away. He didn't trust me, he said. He didn't want to see me. He didn't want to talk to me anymore.

As if that weren't enough, I didn't make it back to Luis's car. As I lost track of Ray's steps somewhere down the block, Natalie came up and pulled me aside. That was how quickly Isa could work.

"Do you still love her?" she hissed in a voice hard as stone.

I panicked. The hairs on my neck stood. "You're talking about Isa?" I said.

Ray's steps scurried past us, back toward the others.

"Is there someone else?" she said.

What had Isa told her? How had I not seen this coming? "No, I don't love her."

"She just told me you two are lovers. You made love in my bed last night. In my bed!"

There it was, out in the open—and not Patrick but Natalie.

My jaws didn't clench. I didn't stop breathing. I just felt rotten, like my stomach was dropping out. I struggled to find something redeeming to say. I wanted to explain, but I didn't know where to start; my relationship with Isa was too convoluted. "I'm sorry, Natalie. I don't love her—"

"You're sorry about what?" she interrupted. "That you slept with her? That you don't love her? That you led her on? That you led me on?"

"I didn't lead her on. I didn't lead you on."

"You did lead me on. You made love to her last night in my bed!"

"That was an accident. A mistake. It was before I met you. Today has been—"

"Don't talk about today! You just ruined today! She's married, for God's sake."

Everything seemed to be falling away from me. I reached, but she brushed me off. "It was right after the car crash," I said. "There was no other bed for me. I should've slept on the floor. I was going to sleep on the floor. We were in shock. I was trying to console her, but things got out of hand. You see how fragile she is. In the middle of the night, she had a nightmare and started hugging me." I struggled for more words, but all I could think of was the act itself, the way Isa's thigh had trapped my penis. "I don't love her," I repeated. "It was a mistake."

A car screeched to a halt in the street beside us; I heard Betsy's rumble before her engine sputtered to a stop. A door opened, and Patrick shouted, "Look who it is! It's Mr. A.W.O.L.-Blind-Man and his lover. You are one popular dude. Is she coming too? Or are you staying here? Hop in, everybody. It's time to get out of Texas!"

Nobody moved. No one said a thing until Isa's sandals stomped across the pavement toward him. "What did you do?" she demanded. "Where'd you get that blue tarp? What's in the casket, damn it? What's in that thing!"

Patrick ignored her. "You fucking broke the kids' hearts," he said to me. "I hope you're proud of yourself."

"Fuck you all!" Devon yelled from down the block. "This is such bullshit."

"Maybe you should go," Natalie whispered to me. "Maybe you should just go."

"Natalie," I said, reaching.

Again she brushed my hand away. "I need some time," she said. "This all happened so fast. I've known you for one day, and you hurt me already."

"I didn't mean to. We can go slow. We'll just . . . I don't know, we'll get to know each other." It sounded so lame.

I reached for her again, and this time she let me hold her, though she was stiff and her face was turned away—a different person than she'd been all day. I tried to fend off the self-hatred and self-pity that were already descending upon me.

She pulled away.

"Natalie," I said.

Her footsteps moved away from me. I almost gave up and got into Betsy, but instead I swept with Charlie back along the sidewalk to Luis's car, which was already starting up.

The passenger door opened and closed. I felt for the window, hoping it was open—and it was. I put my hand on the door frame.

"I've got to go," she said.

"I'm sorry. I made a mistake." I paused, stalling. "How about I stay the week anyway? I'll find a place to stay; I'll see you in a few days."

"No," she said. "There's too much going on. I need some peace. I need some time. You need to go."

It sounded so final that I wanted to disappear.

But I reached into my pocket and found the crumpled bit of paper where she'd written her phone number earlier, at the house. I pulled it out. "I'll call you," I said. "I'll see you on our way back west."

As if I could see.

She didn't say anything.

"We can go to the mountains like you said," I suggested. "If it doesn't work out, then at least we tried. I can get back to Burbank whenever."

Still she was quiet.

"What do you say?" I said.

"So call me," she offered flatly.

The car pulled away, leaving me standing alone with Charlie on the curb, pressing my thumb into his grip so hard that it hurt. I longed for the feel of her fingers squeezing my hand.

There were no crickets here. No breeze. No cars driving by. Just the blind pain I'd let in, again, of my own accord. I don't know how long I stood or whether I sat. I lost all sense.

As a kid I used to hurt myself sometimes. I fell down a ravine on purpose. I rode my best friend's bike into his garage door and broke my nose. I stuck my leg into the grating of a storm drain. Twice I scratched my good cheek until it bled. Hell, I blinded myself. How many times had Mom told me to watch where I was going? Oedipus tore out his own eyes. Samson had his eyes gouged out by others. All of us are warned where to look.

At the Laundromat, Betsy pulled around to where I was and stopped. I gripped Charlie and whacked the casket, again and again, oblivious to Patrick's shouting and Isa's screaming and the front doors opening. It was Devon who herded me and Charlie into the backseat, where Ray pressed himself against the opposite door so as not to touch me. Patrick cursed his luck for being with a crazy blind fucker, and the front doors closed. But he didn't gun the motor pulling out; nobody said a word as Betsy eased along city streets and found the freeway, where she accelerated and the plastic on her rear window rustled and popped in earnest. Charlie lay wounded next to me. I knew Isa should be singing, "Seatbelts on!" Ray's arm should be out the window whistling in the wind. His right leg should be jiggling into mine, oblivious. But he sat still as stone.

Between the kids I sat empty, rudderless, with no core save remorse.

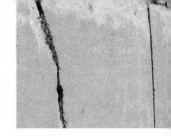

TEN

Well before sunrise the next morning, I stood barefoot with Charlie in a cool creek, ankle deep, waiting for an owl whose hoot had brought me down a sandy pathway prickly with rigid oak leaves. Devon had straightened out Charlie, though he was dented and he folded awkwardly. The riverbed pressed its friendly mud up between my toes. The current dawdled. Itinerant bugs buzzed my ears. The trees above conversed with a breeze I couldn't feel. But there was no owl.

Somewhere along the banks Patrick slept. Despite his rants about fleeing Texas, he'd been unable to drive anymore, which he'd blamed on his sleepless night in the drunk tank.

Ray was stretched out in Betsy's backseat, out cold. He hadn't spoken—hadn't touched me—since we'd left El Paso, though I'd tried to talk with him.

Devon was dozing in the front seat.

Isa was too exhausted and restive to drive. Like me, she couldn't sleep, but I wanted nothing of her. I'd already lashed out as soon as we'd stepped from the car: "You told me to kiss her," I hissed, "and you betrayed me."

"Don't hate me," she said, grasping at me, her hands flickering. "I need you. The kids need you." I pulled away, but she followed, her voice eerie and lost, "Sit with me for a minute," she said. "That's all. Just a minute. Please."

She steered me to a picnic bench, where we both hunched over the table. She didn't brush up against me but came hauntingly close. I thought about the silver cross lying on her breastbone. I could smell the heat of her body, no perfume now, not out here at this time of morning. She whispered about Jasmine and the pain of letting her go.

I remembered that name, Jasmine, from her nightmare after the car crash.

She said she'd been married twice before I'd met her. But I knew that. When she was twenty she had a baby girl, Jasmine Marie, and they used to take her to the beach in Santa Monica. When Jasmine was three years old, they were driving home in the evening after staying too long and drinking too much at the beach. Traffic was awful, but everybody was laughing. Isa was in the backseat with her husband, and she was holding Jasmine in her lap. "We didn't have our car seat with us," she said. "We hadn't planned to go to the beach. I remember brushing away the sand between her little toes." Their friends, a couple, were in the front seat. The car flipped. The world fell in upon itself, she said, and never really opened up again. Jasmine died; everyone else survived.

At the picnic table, her hands flickered onto mine; I could feel her stubby fingernails bitten to the quick.

That's why she hates going to the beach, I thought. That's why she wanted foster kids. She was twenty-three years old at the time, for God's sake. Younger than me.

"If it wasn't for Jesus," she said, "I'd go get a drink right now. I'd drive that car off a cliff. It's Jesus keeps me alive."

She slid closer on the picnic bench, letting me hold her and comfort her and lose myself in the curves of her embrace. I fell into it despite myself, wanting to smother my own loss and failure in the expanse of her needs.

"What can you see, Kevin?" she said weakly. "What can you see?"

I tried to smile, uncertain who I was or what to do next. I couldn't see a damn thing.

"She comes back to me sometimes," she said. "Like last night before we made love."

The stark memory of the two of us in bed together—Natalie's bed—stunned me. I broke away and stood.

"Go sit with Patrick," I stammered. "He's your husband."

I lurched away with Charlie, expecting her to come after me, but she held off. So I wandered, chastising myself for what I'd done with Isa in El Paso. For a long time I lay beneath an oak whose acorns ribbed me no matter which way I turned. I tried to sleep but couldn't calm my mind. I breathed but couldn't get enough air. I tried to remember the precise rhythm of Natalie's laughter, the sound of her wheeze. Why had it surprised me that Isa had driven her away? Isa needed everyone fawning over her, coddling her, confirming her, for God's sake. It was disgusting. And what had I done only moments ago? I'd fallen into her arms at the picnic table.

Sayings from N.A. trapped themselves in my skull: If you always do what you always did, you'll always get what you always got. Familiar misery. Nothing changes if nothing changes.

It seemed everything had changed. Yet I got the same results.

When I kicked off my huaraches, I thought about the boys, and I hounded myself for the way I'd abandoned them. Maybe I should just go, I thought, get away from the mess I'd made, the pain I'd inflicted. I wanted to punish myself for that.

That was when the owl called. I sat up, twisting. The hoot sounded again—a prolonged refrain. I stood and stepped barefoot with Charlie, following another hoot down to the creek.

I shuffled several steps deeper into the stream, listening above, waiting and letting the water's thickness massage and cool my calves. I wondered how deep, how far across? Water knows what to do, when to gather, how fast to run, where to escape. Rivers in Colorado hurry, frothing; in Southern California they slack. This cool current caressed my calves as if enticing me to peace. I could slip in and drift blind, couldn't I, carried beyond failure.

Less than twenty-four hours ago, I thought, I ran barefoot with Natalie. I swam with her in a pool.

Our first stop after leaving El Paso was a gas station where we got out and stretched, all except Ray, who wouldn't budge from the backseat. The pump whined and clicked sporadically when Patrick began to fill up after having paid inside. The dry wind smelled of gasoline, which used to remind me of childhood but now intimated its loss: at the corner station with Mom, gas used to smell of freedom.

Footsteps, boots perhaps, approached, and a man said hello, his voice young and bristly.

"Evening," Isa purred, putting a lilt into one word.

Was she that insecure, I thought, that she needed to flirt? I wondered what the hell she was wearing.

"Not a darn thing going on," the young man said.

What was he, the clerk? Or just some guy standing around?

He let out a thin whistle, half full of air. "That's a casket up there, ain't it." It wasn't a question.

Goddamn Patrick, I thought. What had he bought in El Paso? And why had he put it in the most obvious place: in a coffin on the roof of our car?

"I got a uncle in the memorial business," the guy continued. "He doesn't call them 'coffins' because it sounds too sad. You know what I mean? 'Casket' sounds more distinguished." He whistled again, longer this time, like he was proud of the sound. "How'd you get your rear crashed in? You from California, huh? What you doing with a casket up there anyway?" His tone was cocky and impertinent.

After a short pause, Patrick said slowly, a Southern slant to his voice, "We're sellin' 'em. Handmade. You want one?"

It sounded so unlikely.

"You don't say. That's why you're carting it somewhere this time'a night."

Patrick clanked the nozzle back into the receptacle of the pump. As we opened the doors and slid onto Betsy's seats, the man's voice kept coming. "You know, I've seen this before," he said, his voice grinning from outside Patrick's window. "My uncle manages this stuff all the time. Somebody dies here and you got to transport him over there. Say, over the state line. Are you headed west or east?"

Betsy's motor turned over, died.

"They don't let you drive far, you know. Not with this. Not a chance. One'a them Highway Patrols'll pop ya."

Betsy's motor caught on the second try.

"Listen bud, it's a handmade, one-of-a-kind coffin," Patrick said, working the drawl as if he'd spoken it all his life. "And it's empty. Grand-dad's on his last days, and we got to deliver it. God bless." Patrick didn't spin the tires; I felt my head drift back as Betsy pulled forward, floating into the Mississippi from some tributary. As we picked up speed, the dry wind came at me. I ran my right hand through my hair. We all took deep breaths.

"Jesus!" Patrick said, his voice edgy. "There's no hiding nothin' out here."

"It's on the roof of the car!" Devon said. "In a blue fucking neon tarp!"

Enough, I decided. "We're sick of your shit!" I challenged Patrick. "Tell us what you were doing in El Paso. What's in the damn coffin?"

Patrick waited. He waited. I was about to reach up and strangle him when he said quietly, "That's the beauty. There's nothing in it." Then he launched into a detailed story—proud of himself—about a guy he'd met in the drunk tank who'd connected him with somebody who'd sold him replica watches so cheap we wouldn't believe it. They were in that flat box in the back, beneath our bags.

Replica watches, I thought. Right.

Devon rummaged in the luggage behind us.

"Leave it alone!" Patrick barked. He said the coffin was a perfect decoy; any cop who stopped us would be obsessed with it.

What cop was going to stop and search the back of a family wagon anyway? What a paranoid son of a bitch.

Isa started to speak, but he cut her off, telling her not to worry about the money; he was going to sell the watches in Biloxi the day after tomorrow.

"Biloxi!" I said. "That's where you said you grew up." I didn't trust him.

"It's right on the way. I was going to sell the bones there anyway," he admitted.

The plastic on the rear window complained. The wheels whined. The wind nagged at my hair, swirling. I didn't know what to believe.

I put my hand on Ray's arm, but he pushed it away.

When the tarp on the roof started flapping, Patrick jerked off the freeway and braked, making Betsy skid and kick up dust. He jumped out to adjust the ropes and tuck in the tarp, and then we were back on the road.

I tried talking with Ray and Devon, but neither would speak to me. So we settled in, driving under a lonesome sky and a blanket of stars, Isa said.

I suppose I slept. I dreamed awake and asleep, not quite remembering where or how long it was before the tarp started flapping again and Patrick pulled off so he could untie the ropes and crack open the box and make sure everything was fine inside—that they hadn't cheated him, the bastards!

"Asshole!" I yelled, stumbling out over Ray. I knew he'd been lying. Patrick tried to hold me off, but I pushed him away as I had the bum in El Paso. Standing on Betsy's door frame, I hung on the coffin's edge with one hand and reached in with the other to grab the rifles or handguns— or whatever he was delivering—and throw them onto the ground. But inside the casket, there were no cold metal gun barrels. No wooden stocks. Instead my fingers traced the contours of a body—a naked body laid out cold and hard, with skin strangely loose over muscles gone rigid, like silk on stone. I was horrified to feel across the chest the pattern of my own hairs, the mole on my shoulder. I wanted to wrench my hands away, but I couldn't keep from touching the body's head and face: they were my cheeks—except unblemished, clear and clean, without a scratch. Healed. Cured. I had to know. I had to feel my eyes. Were they whole? Could I see? My fingertips traced my cheekbones and touched two flat silver dollars, cold as metal, where my eyes should have been. I awoke sweating with a start, the wind blowing my hair as we drove. Had Patrick stopped the car and fixed the tarp again, or was that my dream too?

I stood in the creek for a long time with Charlie, listening for an owl's hoot that didn't sound and hearing instead the slow lapping of the stream. "I'm sorry, Charlie," I said. I wiggled my toes in the mud, appreciating the resistance. Far off, a truck rumbled along the freeway. I was about to turn and head upslope to search for my sandals when the owl hooted slowly from across the water. I cocked my head to listen.

I'm staying at Grandpa's for the afternoon just like I always used to before the accident. I'm standing outside, between his house and the pond, waiting for an owl to hoot again down by the water. I haven't been out of the body cast long, and my body aches terribly, especially my hip. I'm learning to walk again after lying in the hospital bed so long. I'm wandering blind for the first time at Grandpa's place, blundering along the path back to his house from the shoreline with my hockey stick, when I hear the hoot and turn to listen, but the owl doesn't hoot again. I turn some more and lose track of direction: Which way is the house, which way the pond? I stand still, waiting, not wanting to venture in the wrong direction. I listen for ducks on the water or waves lapping against the shore, but there's no sound. I'm too embarrassed to call for help because I know the way so well it feels like home. Thinking I'll scare up a flock of birds, I clap and am shocked to hear an echo from the house. I turn in circles, clapping and listening for the house. It's this way. I clap once more just for fun.

I don't know Grandpa is watching. When I approach, he says from the porch, "Why were you clapping?"

I answer, "I was listening for the way home."

After a moment he repeats, "Listening."

I say, "For the echo from the house."

There are always breathers when talking with Grandpa or Dad, so I stand for a while shifting my weight, but this moment lasts longer than usual. Just as I'm about to go inside, finally, he says, "Smart boy." And then the old man breaks down. I don't know what to do because I've never seen or heard him cry before—he's tough as a truck. And I don't understand why he's crying. He just sits on the stoop and says, "It's okay, lad. I'll be all right."

Water splashed as someone approached from upstream. I couldn't help thinking of my promise to protect Ray. I wanted to be the kid I'd been at Grandpa's house—confused, lost, yet intrepid. How had I become Grandpa, helpless against fate, unable to forestall a child's pain?

But it wasn't Ray splashing toward me. "You ditched us," Devon said quietly, standing nearby. "You told us to meet at her house. You told me not to run away, and that's what you did. You're like every motherfucking adult. You say one thing and then do what you want."

My right hand fidgeted with Charlie, sinking his tip in the mud.

I wanted one of Devon's frontal attacks: a strike and retreat. I deserved it. But he jabbed quietly instead, saying that since I always wanted him to describe stuff, he wanted to tell me about the pastor's house when I wasn't there to meet them. How my luggage was piled in the living room neat as shit, but I wasn't there. How he stood up for me. How Ray clung to the doorknob until Patrick pulled him off. How the trellis came down, splintering, and Ray's legs kicked the air as Patrick carried him all the way to the car. How the last light blessed the tan house and the green fields but didn't bless them—two goddamned orphans. "My mom's in prison, but Ray's mom is dead," Devon said.

"I always took his big smile for granted, all those front teeth. But now I miss it. He is one tough kid."

I felt numb. I knew not to touch him, but I did anyway, shuffling over in the water and resting my hand on his shoulder. He threw it off.

"Keep your hands off me," he said.

Instead of apologizing, I took my time explaining what had happened, how I had gotten swept away. I let him know how I felt about Natalie. I told him what it was like to run downhill on my own, chased by a guard. I told him about getting lost outside the pool and how helpless I felt, even after getting mugged and taking down the drunk. I talked about being the kid who was always left behind, sidelined, alone. I described what it meant to let Natalie slip away.

After a while we sat in the sand along the bank talking about Alexis; they'd spoken several times during our day in El Paso. Her mom and dad didn't want to face anybody, so they stayed home and yelled at each other. They both wanted to get away, but June refused to visit Abe in Pensacola, and her dad pretended he had to take care of his father. Neither of them noticed that Alexis wasn't eating. "At least Patrick and Isa get along," Devon said.

A crow squawked and flew from behind us, wings flapping.

"Did you bone Isa?" he said.

I gave him one of Grandpa's breathers. "Think what you want," I said finally. "That's none of your business."

"Ray wants to run away," he said, without even a pause. "He wants to go to Mexico."

I remembered our conversation with Natalie, when she'd encouraged Ray to visit his aunt and uncle there.

"He wants to go right now, from here," Devon said.

"He wants to just go there on foot?"

"It was all I could do to talk him out of it. Isa's with him now, mothering him."

That's good, I thought. That's good for them both.

"I think she's crazy. She's starting to say weird stuff."

We're all crazy, I thought. Everybody except the kids.

"We're going to steal Betsy," he said. "You can come with us or not."

I shook my head. He was old enough to drive but hadn't gotten his license, partly because Patrick wouldn't let him practice on Betsy. "Let me get this straight. Your plan is to drive to Mexico in a stolen car—two minors, without a driver's license or any passports."

He shifted in the sand next to me; a second later there was a slender splash—a stone perhaps. "I can drive," he said. "You don't believe me. But I can."

"I believe you can do anything you want. It's not about that."

"Probably not Mexico," he admitted.

Even without Mexico, it didn't make sense. But I didn't want to take anything for granted, so I told him not to steal Betsy. She wasn't worth it.

"I'm not going back to Burbank," he said.

I didn't argue. I figured he would wait at least until he found out about Alexis, whether she was going to Pensacola.

He stood and rustled his clothes; I didn't realize he was taking them off until he splashed into the water. After a few moments, I joined him in my boxers. The stream was only waist high, but it felt good to crouch down in the coolness, float some, and move about on my hands.

He blew bubbles in the water. "Your stupid swimming lessons never did shit for me," he said. "Ray taught me to swim in about two minutes in El Paso. He kept getting to the ball before I could—so I started lunging after it, kicking my feet, and putting my head under."

"Once a swimmer, always a swimmer," I said, smiling. I wanted to add that I was proud of him, but I knew better.

We left Junction, Texas, later than we wanted because Patrick slept past daybreak. We got stuck in construction before San Antonio and were delayed at Whataburger, where somebody else picked up our order and it took a while to figure that out. Isa bought cheap coffee, and Devon tried to reach Alexis everywhere we stopped, but all he got was voice mail. At a gas station, it heartened me to hear wisps of his voice leaving an upbeat, long-winded message to her. Back in the car, Isa chatted in her caffeine high about Pensacola. She was trying to be cheerful, I'm sure, but she came off zany and childish as she talked about her daddy and how he loved chocolate sundaes with a circle of whipped cream on top. No cherry.

There was no telling what she might blab to Patrick, but I tried to convince myself that it no longer mattered. I attended to Ray instead, offering him pokes and offers and apologies, but he rebuffed me. And all day I tried to produce slivers of hope for seeing Natalie on the way home. But I postponed calling her, fearing the inevitable. I couldn't seem to sleep; somewhere past Houston we entered a new pattern of weather. The air felt thicker. My skin stuck to itself, down by my groin and up near my armpits.

In the afternoon, Isa left a message for Daddy, wishing him well and saying we'd see him tomorrow. "I bet Robert's already there," Patrick said, "telling him not to talk to you, telling him he can't trust you."

"It doesn't matter about that," Isa said abruptly, and then she started chattering about visiting Mommy in Fort Walton Beach, which was about an hour past Pensacola. "We're going home to Florida," she said cheerfully. "And then we're going back home to California."

It pained me to hear her syrupy, childlike voice; it made me anxious and uncomfortable.

"I'm never going home," Devon said brazenly.

Without warning, the plastic on the rear window swept inside in a stunning, debilitating whoooosh, wrapping my head in the panic of the car crash, as if we'd been hit again. My heart jumped into my throat. Ray screamed. Even Devon yelled. I flew into a terror. I fought the plastic and pulled it off my head and down onto the floor in a series of convoluted motions, elbows flying, stomping it like a madman with my feet. I shivered then, convulsing, my thighs shaking. I was panting, lost.

Patrick chortled.

After a moment, I straightened my glasses. I became aware of my rapid breathing. Ray wedged himself against the door. Devon sighed. The car filled with its own exhaust.

"I feel sick," Ray mumbled. They were the first words I'd heard from him since El Paso.

I tried to touch his shoulder, but he pushed me off.

"Lean your head out the window, dear," Isa said.

When his seatbelt clicked off, I was suddenly afraid. I wanted to grip his arm to keep him inside the car.

"Seatbelt on!" Isa said, frantic. "Now!"

It made me feel for her, thinking about Jasmine.

I was surprised at how quickly Ray buckled up.

"I'm hungry," Devon complained.

"Listen, everybody," Patrick growled. "Everything's going to be okay. I'll stop at the next place. We'll get something to eat and tape it back up. We got a late start today. That was my fault. That's what's making everybody anxious."

It was surprisingly helpful to hear compassion from Patrick.

"If you get tired," Devon said, "I can drive."

"If I catch you with these keys . . ." Patrick said. He didn't finish the sentence.

When we pulled off the freeway in Vidor, Texas, my neck throbbed—from sitting upright or from the car crash, who knows? As I lifted my arm to rub my neck, a pain shot from my shoulder, making me wince. In the parking lot outside Wong's Buffet, I smelled hot asphalt, fried food, and a whiff of oranges. There was a funny taste in my mouth, like nails. Bugs droned in the humid air. I moved carelessly and bumped into someone: Isa. I recognized the height and softness of her bare shoulder, and I felt an arm around her back.

"Hey," Patrick said. They were hugging.

It made me wonder, maybe they hugged all the time; maybe that was something he gave her, like Ray offered smiles and Devon grimaces—or so I'd been told. It's hard not to feel irrelevant sometimes.

There was still no peep from Ray.

We were too late for the lunch special, but we got the early-bird buffet for seven ninety-five apiece. Devon ate plate after plate of chow mein, crispy chicken, and beef ribs. I liked the egg rolls and wonton, but not much else. The food helped Isa come down from coffee jitters, I think. When she was walking through the line with me a second time, describing dishes and filling my plate, she admitted in a helpless voice that she was sorry for what she'd told Natalie—everything in El Paso had been a mistake. But she had to keep us all together, that was her job.

Didn't I see that? She couldn't leave me in the middle of Texas, even if I wanted to stay.

I told her calmly that she had no right to talk to me like that; I would stay wherever I wanted. I was about to add that she was no longer my caretaker and I was going to move out when we got back to Burbank. But there she was, serving me food.

When we were back at the table, Isa tried to bring Ray out by telling a story about the first time she and Patrick had eaten out with him. I wasn't there, and it was before Devon was with us. They were at a cafeteria in the heart of L.A., and, somehow, with all his fidgeting, Ray got his head stuck on the wrong side of a turnstile. At first it was funny, but the more he wiggled, the tighter it got. When Patrick tried to pull the bars open, they just got tighter, and Ray panicked, which made him wiggle more. Everybody in the place was staring and circling around on both sides of the turnstile. And then this big guy came out of the kitchen and squatted down. The man grabbed one of the bars with both hands and put his foot on the other, wrenching open a space for Ray to slip his head free. Isa said everybody cheered.

Sitting in Wong's Buffet, I don't know if Ray smiled, but he didn't say anything. I hadn't heard about the turnstile, but it reminded me of when I was a kid and stuck my leg in a storm grate in a rainstorm to get everybody's attention. Once I realized I couldn't get it out, I panicked. A fireman had to pull me free.

Patrick said, "I know a story about your mom."

His words caught us all by surprise, I think. I figured he was talking about Ray's mom.

"Before I was in rehab, I knew her," Patrick said.

"You did not," Devon said.

"She speaks five languages, including Spanish and French. She reads faster than I can. She remembers numbers and can do equations in her head."

The hairs on my arms stood on end; I realized he was talking about Devon's mom, who had moved crack, gotten busted for identity theft, and recently found Jesus in prison, which bugged Devon to no end because she kept wanting to save him. I didn't know much else about her. Patrick knew her how, exactly?

"Your mom wanted out," Patrick said.

"Don't talk about my mom," Devon said, his voice cold, distrustful.

"Think about it," he said. "Your mom dealt and struggled for years and stayed out of jail. She started stealing identities because she wanted out."

"What, did she take money from you?" Devon said, his tone aggressive now. "Is that how you know her? Who the fuck cares?"

"I knew her outside of that," Patrick said.

I remembered what Isa had said in El Paso, that Devon had taken a swing at Patrick at the Laundromat. "Patrick, leave him alone," I said.

"I'm trying to tell the boy something!" he said. "So shut up."

I made myself sit back and breathe.

"Your mom wanted better for you," Patrick said. "That's why she took bigger risks. She wanted out of East L.A., and she wanted to get you out too. But she didn't know how."

"So it's my fault, you're saying," Devon said. "She went to jail because of *me*. Why don't *you* shut up."

"That's not what I'm saying!" Patrick said.

I leaned toward him. "We're all tired," I said. "We don't need this right now."

Patrick stood and stormed off.

I wanted to say something, anything, to help Devon forget this. "What a jerk," I said. "Don't worry about what he says."

"You don't know what Patrick's going through!" Isa griped. She ran after him.

I didn't care what he was going through. As soon as they were gone, I said to the kids, "When we get back to L.A., you don't have to be with Patrick and Isa. We can find you another setup." I realized immediately that I'd misspoken—about finding *them* a setup.

Ray was on me, pounding his fists on my chest.

"Chingado! You never do what you say. You promised you wouldn't leave me. I don't trust you, you shithead. I hate you, you fucker!"

I was astonished to hear him swear, but at least he was talking. The tables around us quieted. He wasn't hitting me hard, so I didn't even shield myself. I figured I deserved it.

Suddenly he grabbed my dark glasses from my head. "I hate these fucking glasses. I hate the way you hide things. You're going to move out when we get home. You've been planning it all along!" I heard my glasses crunch on the floor. "There," he said. "I smashed them, motherfucker! I've got a scar too, you know! I don't try to hide it."

Wow, I thought. The scar on his neck, behind his ear—the one I felt when I put him to sleep. Had his mother hit him there? Was that what he was talking about? I realized he was sniffling, trying to keep himself under control, so I reached for him. He held me off but didn't pull away completely. After a few moments, the tables nearby resumed their chatter.

"When we were in Tucson," Devon said, "you said you were done with Isa and Patrick. Doesn't that mean you're moving out?"

This wasn't the way I wanted to tell them. "It's not going to work for me to keep living with Isa and Patrick."

"That's what I thought," Devon said.

I wondered if that was why Ray wanted to run away, because I planned to move out. "We'll be able to visit each other," I said.

They ignored me. "Ray's right," Devon said. "You act like you're ashamed to be blind. You should be proud of that scar."

I nodded slowly. I'd already given up the cowboy look. I'd left the fedora behind. Now my glasses were gone. "All right," I said. "Deal. I'll be proud of my scar if Ray will let me be his friend again." I reached toward Ray, and this time he let himself fall into my arms. He tucked his head and cried like a kid. We sat there, the three of us, until he was ready to go.

After dinner, we found an Ace Hardware on Main Street to buy duct tape for the rear window. I borrowed Isa's cell phone and gave Ray and Devon two bucks each for candy. As they went inside with Isa, I heard Patrick mutter, still in the driver's seat, "Why can't she button up her shirt?" He jumped out of Betsy and crunched across gravel in quick, determined steps, leaving me alone beside the car.

With my heart pounding, I dialed the number for Natalie that Devon told me was barely visible on the paper scrap in my pocket, I'd been fingering it so much. She didn't pick up, so I left a dawdling message about our day together, what it had meant to me, how she'd already changed me, and how sorry I was to have hurt her.

As I hung up, a stream of people walked by, and I reached to push my glasses up my nose, but there were no glasses. I caught myself dipping my head, facing away. It sounded so easy to be proud of a scar. I turned back toward them, feeling naked, exposed. I'd worn those glasses, I'd always told myself, to make things easier on others.

Before everyone returned, I slipped into Betsy's backseat and leaned into the way-back to feel for the ribbing of my suitcase. I wanted to grab a few fifties; I was down to three twenties, a ten, and some ones in my wallet. After opening my suitcase, I zipped open the inside pocket. It was empty. The money had vanished. I needed that five hundred bucks for El Paso. But I tried not to let myself be shocked; it had to be Patrick. Goddamned Patrick and his watches. He hadn't even bothered to sub-stitute dollar bills folded like fifties—that would have cost him ten bucks.

I closed my suitcase and felt around for Patrick's cardboard box. Fine, I thought, let's see what he got. I brought the box into the back-seat, tore it open more sloppily than I should have, ripped open a layer and then another layer of plastic—and that was when I touched the little brick wrapped tightly in plastic. I leaned over and sniffed the chalky odor, like solvent. Cocaine inside, I guessed. Jesus fucking Christ. Maybe half a key. I dragged a wet finger along the outside of the brick and brought my finger to my gums, but there was no taste, no numbing. The outside of the plastic was clean. But it had to be coke. Was he using again? A half kilo in El Paso would cost him what, seven grand? He could probably sell it in Biloxi for almost double that, even without splitting it up. He had to have gotten a lot more than my five hundred dollars.

An urge reared up to snip a fine line in the bag and snort some. I was glad I didn't have a penknife. I thought about throwing the bag in a garbage bin, closing up the box, and putting it back. Let Patrick realize later that it was missing. But what about my money?

Then I wondered, had he planned this for El Paso, or had he really met a guy in the drunk tank?

That was when I felt two hands on my back. I hadn't heard his steps.

"You bastard!" Patrick said. "You broke the seals." He dragged me from the backseat and threw me up against the car, near the rear wheel well.

"You stole my five hundred bucks, you son of a bitch."

"Keep it down," he hissed. "You'll get your money back tomorrow. You'll get a percentage too."

"What's that!" Isa said, though it was plain enough, I'm sure, sitting on the backseat.

"I don't want a damn percentage," I said. "I don't want anything to do with this."

"That's your problem," he said in a quiet drawl that was doubly annoying for its coldness. "You're always standing back. Doing nothing. You let opportunities slide right by."

I shoved him hard, catching him square, and he shoved me back, throwing me against the car again.

Flip-flops slapped toward us quickly. I said, "No!" but I couldn't step between them fast enough. Devon slugged Patrick: I heard the thud of a fist and then Patrick's grunt. Then Patrick stepped forward and flattened him. Devon was on the pavement that fast, rolling around. And I was upon Patrick, grabbing him from behind, just lucky, wrapping him in a wrestling hold around his torso, a lock using his own wrist and biceps, forcing him to stoop and stagger sideways just to hold up his own weight and part of mine.

"Hold him!" Devon said, getting up.

In my arms was the man who said I couldn't write on my own, who overlooked me every day, who'd taken Isa from me, who'd stolen my money, and who tormented us all. This was my chance, I thought, holding on, gripping. I could let Devon at him right now.

But it was Ray who laid into Patrick's stomach with fists, battering even my arms as I held Patrick from the back.

Isa screeched like a hawk.

I let Patrick loose before Devon got another swing. "Enough!" I said, but I didn't expect anyone to heed me. I crouched with my hands up, protecting my face, expecting to get hit anytime from anywhere. I was panting hard and sweating all over, between my thighs, behind my ears, between my fingers. Let him come, I thought. Let him come.

A siren emitted a sharp burst to my right and then fell silent, startling us all. I heard tires popping across pebbles on pavement.

"Shit," Patrick said, panting.

I thought of the ripped-open cardboard box in Betsy's backseat. Was the half key visible? Was Betsy's door open? My fingerprints were all over that bag.

Betsy's door closed with hardly a sound. But couldn't the cop just look in the window? I could hear Patrick panting.

The patrol car stopped right next to us. The motor died. A door opened and closed. Heavy footsteps crunched on gravel.

"Afternoon, Officer," Isa purred, stepping toward him, trying to head him off, I was sure. Had she buttoned up her blouse?

The officer crunched another step and stopped. "Evening, ma'am. What's going on?" He spoke in a magnificent bass that was calming despite the circumstances.

"This man here," Devon called out. "He hit me."

ELEVEN

The officer's steps crunched slowly, methodically, toward Devon, halting next to him. A horn blared in the distance. I felt helpless, unable to preempt the unfolding of events.

After maybe twenty seconds, the officer cleared his throat. "Did I ask you a question, son?" His bottomless voice was so sonorous it sounded kind. I can only imagine the glare he must have given Devon. After a long pause, the cop continued, "Then why don't you shut your mouth? I saw you hit him first."

Patrick's feet scuffed the pavement slightly as he shifted his weight next to me, unable to remain still with a Texas cop nearby. I could tell he was standing in front of Betsy's closed back door, shielding the view of the backseat.

"We're from Burbank, California," Isa began, "and we're off to visit Daddy in Florida, who's about to die any day, sir. Any day. But we're praying to the good Lord, sir, that we'll see him before he dies. It's been a long trip and we had an accident and the air conditioning doesn't work and we haven't even got a radio, so sometimes these boys, all of them, sir, get a bit cramped in this old car and they say things they don't mean and then one thing leads to another and I appreciate you being here, sir. The Lord Jesus Christ sent you. Just in time, yes he did. And we'll be on our way to Pensacola. We already ate, right over there at Wong's Buffet. All we needed was this duct tape for the window and now we have that too." She took a deep breath, as if she ran out of air and words at the same time.

"Did they hit you?" the officer said calmly, his voice the same as before, low and resonant but not partial to her.

"Oh, no, sir," she blurted. "They've never done that, sir. They wouldn't ever—"

"You," the officer interrupted. I could hear the tools on his belt shift and his steps turn. "Can you see?"

The two-way radio squawked in his patrol car. Then I realized he was talking to me. "I can't, sir," I said. "Not a thing."

"Then why don't you tell me what's going on? What the hell am I seeing here?"

I collected myself for a moment. I think I nodded. Then I took the blame, apologizing about getting Patrick riled up. I said I wanted to stop at a motel in Louisiana and he wanted to drive on through. I said the boys took my side, and tempers got out of hand.

"That's all good," the cop said. His radio squawked again. "I see everybody's all calm. I like that. But what I'm talking about is what are you, a family? Is that her daddy up there in a coffin? And if it is, do you have the certificate and whatnot?"

Patrick cleared his throat and surprised me, setting in slow and easy. "We're a family," he said in the same drawl he'd used back at the gas station the day before. "This here's Isa and I'm Patrick Landry. These are our boys, more than foster boys, Devon Morel and Ray Mendez. I'm trying to teach 'em things—they're good boys, but they don't always listen good. And I ain't the best teacher. This here's Kevin Layne, and he gets around good, you ought'a see him move on his own. He's our guide, you might say, blind as he is. He ain't perfect, but if it wasn't for him we wouldn't be standing here together, that's the truth. And what Isa just said, well that's right: Grandpa's in Pensacola; he ain't up there on the car, though he wouldn't mind riding there if you'd let him. He's ready to go is what I'm trying to say. That's a handmade casket. One of a kind. We're bringing it to him, and it's been one hell of a trip."

I never could quite predict Patrick. I was still furious at him, but that was a shining moment, and I still think he meant most of what he said.

"Untie those ropes," the officer said, walking toward him. "Let me see that it's empty, and you can be on your way."

As Patrick began working the knots, the officer stood so close I could smell cigarettes in his clothing. I couldn't stop thinking of the coke on the backseat. Wouldn't we have to open the back door and stand on Betsy's floor to pull the casket down and unwrap the tarp?

Somewhere in all this, Isa's phone rang—it was Alexis—and Devon wandered off, flip-flops slapping, to talk to her.

"If I were you," the officer said, "I wouldn't be in a big rush. I'd stop at a motel like the boys want. There's a panhandler coming."

"What's a panhandler?" Isa said, all syrup.

"Well," he said, turning toward Isa. The tools on his belt jangled. "It's a hurricane set to blow those Florida beaches up to Alabama— except now they don't know. Maybe it'll hit farther west."

"A hurricane!" she said. "When's it supposed to hit?"

"Sunday night. Or Monday morning."

My birthday had been on Tuesday. We'd left on Wednesday. It was Saturday.

He said it was a category three. I didn't know much about hurricanes, but I knew the rating system went from one to five. From the patrol car, the radio blurted a string of disconnected syllables. "Damn it, Mildred," the cop mumbled, setting off toward his car.

Isa's footsteps hustled to where Patrick was clicking open Betsy's back door. "Texas bastard," Patrick grumbled.

"Ssshhh!" Isa whispered. "Close that up and put it on the floor."

"What do you think I'm doing?" he whispered. Then Betsy's door closed and he finished untying the knots.

"Mildred!" I heard the cop boom in his wonderful bass. "Slow up! I can't tell a thing you're saying." Garbled codes spat out again. I picked up only "I-10 West."

Ray scurried over and leaned against me, grounding me; it felt spectacular. "It's okay," I told him, trying to make him feel better. "We're almost on our way."

Devon's flip-flops came around Betsy.

"Mildred!" the cop boomed again. "Call up Crumfield and tell him to get his ass over there. Not after dinner. Now." The cop started his car. "Never mind," he bellowed toward us. "They're doing a voluntary in New Orleans. All those damn Cajun Creoles are coming to Texas." He sped away, kicking up gravel.

"My mom's part Creole," Devon murmured.

I hadn't known that.

"You sorry Texas son of a bitch!" Patrick yelled after the cop.

"Stop it!" Isa said. "He'll hear you."

Patrick yelled louder the farther the patrol car drove away. "Every Cajun and Creole is better than you! You prejudiced, narrow-minded asshole!"

Devon laughed.

"Don't push me," Patrick said evenly. "That was a stupid thing to do, telling him I hit you. We don't need cops snooping around."

"Why, what are you hiding?" Devon goaded. "Replica watches?"

"Stop it, both of you," I said as firmly as I could.

"Yeah," Ray said, his pitch high but firm. "Stop it!"

"Patrick!" Isa said in a tone so guttural I hardly recognized her. "Are you using? Because if you're using any of that shit, so help me Jesus, we're through."

I got the boys taping the sheet of plastic over the rear window and joined Patrick and Isa up by Betsy's hood, where in snippets of whispers back and forth he was denying that he'd tested the coke.

So it *was* coke. "We're not idiots," I said. "You must have snorted some or they wouldn't have trusted you in El Paso. They would've called you a narc."

"If I'd snorted some in El Paso," he said, "I would've been able to drive through the night. I wouldn't have pulled over and slept in that park. Those guys in El Paso were rookies. They didn't know what they were doing. I should've held out for a better price, but I was in a hurry." He softened his tone. "We need some money, sweetie. That's all this is about. Money."

"Did you use our cash for the trip?" she said. "Did you max out our credit card?"

"He stole five hundred bucks from my suitcase," I said with a sneer.

"You ditched us," he said harshly. "Don't forget that. I thought you were gone for good." His tone turned saccharine again. "I had some cash I've been saving, sweetie. I did use the credit card. I had to. But tonight I'll get it all back—and then some. Biloxi's only six hours away. I know plenty of people there, and it's Saturday night; they'll be up late. I can move the package in less than an hour. We can sleep at Louie's place, or Rico's. We'll stop in and see my parents in the morning and be at your daddy's by noon if we want to. Pensacola's only two hours past Biloxi."

The mention of his parents surprised me, but I was so wound up thinking about the money and drugs that I didn't hold the thought.

Patrick's voice became harsh again. "Here's what I'll do. Tomorrow I'll give you a 20 percent return on your five hundred bucks—at no risk to you. That's a hundred bucks and you don't have to do a damn thing. I'll even give you an extra 5 percent—twenty-five bucks—for every day I'm late. That's how certain this thing is."

It exasperated me, not just the money but also the situation he'd put us in, transporting coke so that now we had to scheme right there in front of the kids. What choice did I have?

"Where's your glasses?" Patrick said, shifting his weight.

I faced him full-on, letting him have a good look. I didn't care about the profit, but I wanted my money. "I want 10 percent a day," I hissed, "for every day you're late." I didn't flinch.

"Deal," he said.

"What about the hurricane?" Isa said, her voice softer than before. "What about that?"

Patrick said he'd find out everything in Biloxi. If it was going to hit near Pensacola, then Biloxi would be fine. If it was going to hit near Biloxi, then we could go on to Pensacola. Either way, it was just a category three. They came toward each other and hugged next to me, so I turned away. She grumbled; I think he kissed her.

At first I was outraged that she'd fallen back in with him. But then a sense of relief washed over me as I realized that I didn't have to save Isa or fix this family. All I needed to do was attend to the boys. Hadn't I made that vow to myself at the start, for different reasons? And hadn't they already reached out to me—all that talk about running away?

"I've got to call Daddy!" Isa said, stepping away, leaving the two of us standing alone.

"I should've just taken his lick," Patrick muttered, referring to Devon. "I had it coming."

I nodded. But I was the one who had started it all by shoving him—and both Devon and Ray had come to my aid. No more fights, I told myself. I'd have to find some other way to stand up for myself and the kids. And if Patrick kept pulling this shit, we didn't have to steal a car. I could get the kids to Burbank by bus. We'd have to explain some things to Children and Family Services, but I could deal with those consequences. I just needed my money back from Patrick. And even if he messed that up, I could call my parents and they'd send me bus fare.

"We're done!" Ray called from the opposite end of Betsy.

Patrick and I stepped around the car. "It looks like a Dixie flag," he said.

"Shit," Devon said. "We look like honkies."

I felt the plastic: the kids had taped a crisscross pattern over the rear window.

"What the hell," Patrick said. "We're in the South. Maybe the cops will leave us alone."

When we got back on the freeway, Isa was complaining about Abe. He wouldn't pick up, and she didn't want to leave another message. His house wasn't on the water, she said, but it was up on the bluff, where it took the blunt force of onshore winds. "I hope Robert's there," she said, "to help him out."

"Abe made it through Hurricane Ivan a year ago," Patrick said. "Didn't even leave his house. And that was a category five."

"Yeah, well, it scared him to death," Isa said.

It occurred to me that Abe could have passed on already. How would we know? The plastic on the back rattled and buckled as the wind swirled in the car. It felt like we were heading into a void.

"Alexis and her dad are in Pensacola," Devon offered. "She was at the airport when she called."

"Why didn't you tell me?" Isa said, annoyed. "What did she say about Daddy? Is he okay?"

"She didn't say anything about that," Devon said. "But she was excited about being in a hurricane."

Ray asked what a hurricane was and Patrick said, "It ain't much."

"It is too," Isa said. "I hate hurricanes."

No one said anything else, so I explained what little I knew: how they form over warm water and how they blow in a circle around the eye. Like a tornado but larger.

"It ain't like a tornado," Patrick said, still in his Southern accent.

"Like the eye that sees?" Ray said.

"Aye," I said, nodding and opening my eyelid with my fingers so Ray could see the redness inside.

"Hell, no," Patrick said. "It ain't like the eye that sees. It's a calm spot right in the middle. If you're in the eye, means you're halfway through it. I been through plenty. Made it through Camille in '69. An oak tree smashed our car. The next day I saw a pine needle sticking straight into a telephone pole."

"You just said hurricanes are no big deal," Devon said.

"Camille's the exception. I been through half-a-dozen hurricanes didn't amount to nothin'."

"When did you move west?" I said.

"When I was twenty-two. I didn't know shit, but I knew enough to get out of Biloxi."

"How old are you now?" I said. I didn't even know his age.

"He's thirty-eight," Isa said.

After a moment, Ray said, "He was two years old in 1969."

"Good math," I said.

"I remember Camille even if I was two," Patrick said. But after a minute, he admitted, "I don't know. Maybe it was from stories and pictures." Then he started quizzing us: What's the Florida panhandle? I knew that answer: the thin strip of Florida running from Tallahassee to Pensacola. Who were the first to explore Louisiana? The Spanish, he told us. Who settled it first? The French.

"You mean after the natives," I said.

He ignored me. Who was Louisiana named after? Louis XIV, pronounced "Louie." Where was the first settlement? Near Biloxi, Mississippi, where we were going. Who were the Cajuns? French refugees from Canada called Acadians. The "A" got dropped off the front and the ending got slurred, like "Injuns."

"You all should to college like Patrick," Isa said.

"Where'd you get your degree?" I said.

"I didn't learn that in college," he said. "I know it because I'm part Cajun. My dad's full Cajun. When he was a kid, they punished him for speaking French in school. He made his money selling supplies to the Army Corps of Engineers. He outfitted every lock from Natchez to Baton Rouge. Now he makes money investing in casinos."

"Your dad has money?" I said. That didn't fit my idea of Patrick.

"We parted ways some time ago," he said.

Suddenly Isa started fussing over the lump on Patrick's cheek and Devon's puffy eye, as if she'd just looked at them for the first time since Vidor. Patrick said his cheek didn't hurt. Devon said the same about his eye. Then she asked me, "Where's your glasses? Did you lose them?"

I squeezed Ray's forearm. "I don't wear those anymore," I said.

After sundown, I reached behind the seat, pulled out my note-taker, and sat for a long time without keying in anything. Eventually I put it away; I didn't know where to start.

We had to slow down plenty between Lafayette and Baton Rouge, but traffic was stopped completely in the other direction, Ray said. As we approached Baton Rouge, we had to stop several times, and it was worse all along I-12. At Baton Rouge, I-10 dips southeast to New Orleans while I-12 heads pretty much straight east, bypassing the Big Easy by going north of Lake Pontchartrain. In Hammond, where we had to exit to get gas, we sat on the off-ramp for fifteen minutes. Patrick was pissed at himself for not filling up before Baton Rouge.

The line for gas was two blocks long, so we left Patrick in line and walked to the food store. Along the way Ray asked all sorts of questions about hurricanes: How big were they? What did the eye look like? What was a typhoon? Again I explained as best I could. "If it's going to be bad, we'll know," I said, trying to comfort him. "We'll go inland."

"I'm not scared," he said. "Does it have lightning?"

I didn't know the answer to that.

"Jesus, save us all," Isa blurted.

Stepping onto the curb, approaching the door to the food shop, I felt exposed without my glasses. But I forgot about it as soon as I walked inside, where people were whooping it up, yelling, cheering, greeting each other. It smelled of cigarette smoke and sweat.

"Do you see?" Isa said.

"What?" Devon said.

"Every bottle of water is gone. Every battery. All the ice."

We stood for twenty minutes in the cashier line with candy and chips and some of the last bottles of soda.

"Should've stayed, if you ast me," a man said. "I been through hurricanes and they're a lot less trouble than this."

"Our whole block stayed. They're having one'a them hurricane parties."

"My brother's coming up tomorrow, soon's he gets off work."

Someone next to me burped onions and beer.

"Ain't gonna be no gas tomorrow."

"We got our cat in the front seat and our dog in the back."

"My sister can't. She's a cop."

"Seen those pictures?"

"Ever' time there's a blow coming, they dredge up them photos of Camille."

"I ain't talking Camille. I mean them moving pictures. It's a big damn blow."

"Where's it supposed to hit?" I said.

"Wherever the damn hell it wants." Several people laughed.

"First they say Florida. Now they don't know shit."

"Could be the one."

"Like hell. Not gonna hit within a hundred miles from New Orleans."

"You did good to get out. Wouldn't do to be blind."

"No, sir!"

"Better *not* to see it, I say. Close my eyes and put my head under a pillow."

"Like hell. You ever try being blind?"

I wondered who had said that. Who had tried being blind?

"It's the noise drive you crazy. Like a freight train coming through. Everything a-shaking and rocking and sucking air this way and that."

"Ain't gonna be no gas tomorrow."

"Ain't no soda today."

"I can handle the noise."

"They gonna have gas up to McComb."

"That where you headed?"

"How'd you get that shiner, kid?"

"Just a fight," Devon said.

There was a pause. "What, did the blind guy hit ya?" Everybody laughed at that, all down the line.

After a moment, they went on. "Wisht I had a room here in Hammond."

"I hear Slidell's got rooms."

"Got a cousin lives in McComb."

"Slidell's gonna be underwater."

When we walked outside, I felt better somehow, more relaxed. But Isa chattered away, nervous.

"We better get some provisions," she said to Patrick as soon as we got back to Betsy.

"We're covered," Patrick said brusquely.

"What do you mean, we're covered?" Isa said, her voice thin, precarious. "They don't have anything left. No water. No batteries. No nothing. Nobody knows where it's going to hit."

Patrick softened his tone. "Get in the car, sweetie," he said. "Everything's going to be fine. I'm just sore because it's taking so long. We can get whatever we need in Biloxi. If we have to go inland, we can do that. We're going to be fine."

"What about your parents?" she said nervously. "You said we'd see your parents."

"Is that what you're worried about, baby?" Patrick said. "Trust me. You'll be fine."

That was when it clicked for me: Biloxi wasn't a detour. This trip wasn't just about delivering a casket to Grandpa or getting into Abe's will or nursing Daddy back to health. We were driving cross-country to see Patrick's parents too. And Isa had known it from the start.

Looking back now, I realize that was why he was so upset when the Texas patrolman confiscated his bones in El Paso. From the time he'd bought those chalky artifacts in the San Gabriel Mountains north of L.A., he'd been creating an excuse to take us to his hometown.

After we were back on the freeway and the traffic eased some, after Ray pressed up against me, sleeping, and Devon dropped into a deep sleep, I relaxed beneath the oblivion of sleep myself, gone even from dreams. When I awoke, we were at rest. My neck was stiff some, my breath sour. But I felt rested. Ray's head and arm were still pressed against me. Waves lapped outside. When I inhaled deeply, I tasted salt. Biloxi, I thought. Pensacola was just a few hours away.

"My eye kinda hurts," Devon said.

I found his cheek with my fingers and gently touched his puffy eyelid.

"Ouch," he said, jerking away.

"Where's Patrick?" Isa said from the front, in a panicked pitch that told me she'd just awakened.

"In there," Devon said. "He said he'd be right back."

"Is it swollen shut?" I said.

"No," he said. "It's not that bad." He told me we were parked in a tow-away zone outside a casino. "There's a big sign that says, 'Closed for Katrina.'" It was one-thirty in the morning, much earlier than I'd thought. A breeze kicked up the hot scent of brine.

Patrick didn't say much when he got into the car, though Isa peppered him with questions. He drove a few minutes, pulled up at another casino, and got out. This one had trucks backed up to the front door, Devon said, and people were carrying out computers and furniture. When Patrick returned, he slammed the door and just sat in the front seat.

"What's the matter?" Isa said.

"Think," he said. "Think! This place is a ghost town. Zeke's gone. Louie's gone. Rico's gone."

Ray stirred beside me but didn't wake.

I thought about my five hundred bucks. "Those are your people?" I said. "Why didn't you call before we got here?"

Patrick didn't answer.

Typical ex-addict, I thought, setting up the conditions for failure.

"What about the hurricane?" Isa said. "What'd you find out?"

"It's not gonna hit Pensacola. It's gonna hit near here. Maybe as far east as Mobile, as far west as New Orleans."

"Where are we?" Devon said.

"Right in between." Betsy started up, pulled back in a curve. "We're gonna sleep at Louie's," Patrick said. "I can't believe he already left. We'll get up early tomorrow and shower. Then we can head to my parents' place. I don't want to wake them up, if they're still home."

"Everybody else is leaving town," Isa said. "We have to get out of here."

"We can leave tomorrow, sweetie," he said. "It's not going to hit until Monday. There's plenty of time."

I'd never felt him drive so slowly as on the way to Louie's place. When Betsy stopped and the motor turned off, crickets and frogs began to harrumph and guffaw all around us. Wetlands, I thought.

Louie's turned out to be a run-down shack that smelled of dirty clothes and mildew. Even I could've found the key hanging on a nail next to the back door. Ray still hadn't woken up, so he slept in Betsy's backseat and Devon took the front. Isa and Patrick crashed on a double bed that took up most of the bedroom. There wasn't a couch, so I slept like a rock on a tattered easy chair until Patrick woke me the next morning, handed me my suitcase, and herded me into the bathroom for a shower.

"Put on something nice," he said.

After my shower, I rolled up my dirty clothes and was feeling in my suitcase for my last button-down shirt when I touched something prickly. From the breast pocket of my dirty seersucker shirt, I pulled out the fragile bone that I'd kept from the car accident. When I came out of the bathroom, the way Patrick was hassling Devon to get in the shower reminded me of my mother getting everybody ready before church. It was Sunday morning, I realized.

As Ray was showering, I heard Isa in the bedroom trying on clothes, taking them off, fussing at herself.

"That looks good," Patrick said. "There. That's fine. Relax."

"Relax! How can I relax with you all over me? Never tell a bipolar person to relax! I can't relax!" She started to cry.

When Patrick came out of the room ten minutes later, he went up to Devon right away. "Do me a favor. Don't tell them we got in a fight. Tell them it happened at school or something."

Maybe Devon nodded. Maybe he shrugged. I don't know. "Why are we always up before dawn?" he said.

As we waited for Isa, Patrick paced; I'd never known him to be so nervous. I opened my palm and closed it quickly.

"What's that?" he said, approaching.

I opened my hand again.

"Coon bone," he said, grabbing it. "I need some luck." But then he handed it back. "Here. It's yours," he said sheepishly, as if submitting to a foreign code.

I found his hand and placed the bone in it. "I've had enough of that luck," I said. "You can keep it."

When we were in Betsy's backseat, Ray fidgeted next to me non-stop, sticking his head out the window, nudging me with his foot, moving his arms about. He told me about the sunrise over the water. "It's not like cotton candy," he said. "It's got skinny orange legs reaching out, like a spider." I tried to picture the orange of my house, as I'd been able to with Natalie, but the mirage wouldn't condense.

Ray described a wide, white beach, seagulls flying, and little waves on the ocean.

"It's not the ocean," Patrick said. "It's the Gulf of Mexico."

"El Golfo de México," Ray said. "Let's go swimming."

It felt great to have him back.

"Where are we going to eat?" Devon said.

Betsy turned to the right. "I told you," Patrick said. "I'll make breakfast. Who knows? My parents might not even be here. I'll make some phone calls. And then we'll figure out what we need to do."

"So what's the big deal about your parents?" Devon said.

Betsy stopped. The motor turned off and ticked.

"I've never met them," Isa said. "They were mad we got married in Vegas."

"You'll be fine," Patrick said right away. "Everybody's going to be fine."

"Why are you stopping here?" she said. "Why don't you pull in the driveway?"

Patrick spoke calmly, quietly, explaining that he didn't want them to see the coffin, so the plan was to carry the casket up the driveway and hide it around back.

The boys opened their doors, and I stepped into the tepidness of morning. I could smell the sea but couldn't taste salt. Devon told me we were a block from the Gulf. "I don't care how we dress up," he said. "The car is all hillbillies."

"Ssshhhh," Patrick whispered.

We carried the casket along a long, straight driveway and around the back of a garage, where we set it down and kept it covered with the tarp. Patrick made us get back into Betsy so he could pull us into the driveway. "Stay here," he said, getting out. "I'll be back in a minute."

After he was gone, Devon said, "Looks like a plantation."

"It does not," Isa said.

"It's a white two-story house," Devon said. "Six big pillars out front. What are those green things called—shutters. There's a porch out front upstairs and downstairs with white railings. Have I ever seen a two-story porch? Hell, no."

"Don't curse," Isa said.

"There's Patrick," Devon said. "What a prick."

"Show some respect!" Isa said. "Especially here at his house. Around his parents."

So this is where he grew up, I thought. It seemed strange.

As we stepped out of Betsy, Patrick was already among us, talking to Isa, "Here, let me hold your hands a minute. That's good; take a breath." I imagined they were hugging; I hoped they were. After a pause, he went on, "I want you all to know, my parents are always pissed at me, so don't expect them to like you. That's all my fault, not yours."

Wow, I thought, Patrick was taking responsibility.

"They just got up," he said. "They're going up to my brother's in Hattiesburg this morning." He took a breath. "You don't have to say much. Tell them 'thank you' and 'nice to see you,' and let it go at that. As soon as they're gone, we'll talk about everything. Leave your stuff in the car. We're gonna make breakfast."

"We need to get out of here too, before it hits," Isa said.

"Didn't I just say? We'll talk about all that as soon as my parents leave."

I'd never seen him so considerate. He orchestrated breakfast with Isa's help as Devon, Ray, and I wandered about the house. I could hear his parents stomping around upstairs, making the ceiling creak. There were five large rooms downstairs: a living room and den on the side closest to the Gulf and a TV room and dining room on the other side. A wide entryway with stairs ran down the middle of the house and into the kitchen, which was at the back. A small bathroom was beneath the stairs; as I walked by it, Isa came out, smelling of woody perfume, making me wonder where that scent had been.

Devon, Ray, and I stood in the living room on a soft carpet beneath a tall ceiling where the acoustics were wonderful; I could tell exactly where people stood from their voices. The chair backs were of fine, soft fabric.

"Look at these pictures," Ray said. "Which one is Patrick?"

"The kid with the baseball," Devon said. "Look how tall his dad is."

I joined them at what I thought at first was a high table. But my hand traced the curve of a baby grand piano.

"You can tell they have money," Devon said. "Look at this place. Look at that necklace on his mother."

"He's got a brother and a sister," Ray said. "He's in the middle."

"You guys are like detectives," I said.

We walked across the wide hallway to the TV room, where we sat on the couch and the kids turned on the television. I was shocked by the coverage of Katrina. As we flipped through channels, the announcers talked about her size and trajectory and destructive capacity. Overnight she'd changed from category three to category five. Landfall was projected for Monday morning, as Patrick had said, which gave us a full day. The mayor of New Orleans was supposed to make an announcement any minute, but so far the evacuations were voluntary.

"Everybody's talking about New Orleans," Devon said, "but look at that. It's headed right next to Biloxi. This is going to be good!"

"It's not good," I said. I had a sinking feeling in my gut, as if time were ticking while we dallied. Forget the money, I decided. If Patrick wasn't ready after breakfast, if he didn't want to come, then I needed to get the kids away. Isa could join us if she wanted. "What do you say?" I whispered to Devon and Ray. "Devon, can you really drive?"

There was a moment of silence, and then Devon slid closer on the couch. "Yes," he whispered. "Yes. We can drive to Florida without them."

I almost said, no, we had to go inland. But I realized I didn't know where we should go. Maybe we *should* drive to Pensacola if Katrina was supposed to hit here. "After breakfast, if he doesn't agree to leave, then—"

"What?" Devon interrupted. "The whole point is to get away from them."

"We can't abandon them without a car," I said. "If they agree to leave—"

"There's two cars in the garage," Ray said.

"That's right," Devon said. "We just have to find the keys."

"I'm not stealing his parents' car," I said. But then I wondered: What if Patrick refused to let us go?

"Patrick!" a woman's voice called from upstairs.

I heard him scurry up the wooden steps.

I tried to imagine past this to what, exactly? What was in the garage, an old Oldsmobile? A Volvo? A Mercedes? I decided it didn't matter. What mattered was getting the boys away from all this. How many warnings did I need? "We'll hear him out," I said. "If he decides to hang around here, then we'll get whatever keys we can."

"Breakfast!" Patrick said. There he was, right in the room, so close I could hear him breathe.

We sat at the dining room table without Patrick's parents. "They'll join us when they're done packing," Patrick explained.

"Bless this food," Isa said, "and your servants before our Lord Jesus

Christ who offers us this day, every day, his blessing of eternal life. We bow our heads to your grace knowing that we have sinned, that every human sins, having lost our way and needing you, Lord, to set us right. We ask your forgiveness in your blessed name, Jesus Christ our Lord, amen."

Patrick served us, walking around the table. "These are grits," he said. "I'm gonna put your eggs right on top. Cut it up and mix it all together with salt and pepper."

He sat down and we dug in. "It's good," I offered. I'd had grits only a couple of times.

"Not a lot of taste to the pinché white grits," Ray said, which got Devon laughing.

"Dip your toast in them," Patrick suggested.

"Look," Devon said, "they're whiter than Patrick."

Even Isa laughed at that.

We were still laughing when the stairs began to creak. Glassware in a sideboard or pantry tingled as sharp heels followed by softer clomps struck the dining room floor. I heard Patrick stand, and he nudged my elbow, so I stood as well, aware of my naked face, but I didn't turn away. I touched Devon's shoulder so he would stand, but I couldn't reach Ray.

"Mother and Dad," Patrick said, "this is Isa."

"So this is our daughter," Mrs. Landry said, not even masking the coldness.

"Pleased to meet you," Isa bleated.

"We're glad to know you," Mr. Landry said, his voice warm and slow.

"She's a lamb," Mrs. Landry said. "Isn't she a lamb?"

"Mother," Patrick said.

"A lamb is nice," she said. "Isn't a lamb nice, Richard?"

"This is Devon," Patrick said, plowing on. "That's Ray Mendez. And this is Kevin Layne. Everybody have a seat. I made some grits."

"I don't have the stomach," Mrs. Landry said. "Not with everything. Not this morning."

"Cynthia," Mr. Landry chided.

Mrs. Landry sat down, and we all did as well.

In the midst of tinkling of silverware on plates, Ray started to giggle but stopped short. I had some trouble spooning up the grits, so I used my fingers. "Mrs. Landry," I said finally, wanting to break the silence, "which one was Patrick's chair when he was a boy?"

"Right there where he's sitting," she said.

"What was he like?" I said, fishing for a story.

"He was always a surprise. Weren't you, Patrick?"

"Is he the middle child?" Ray said. "Is that him with the baseball cap in that old picture?"

"He certainly is. His older sister, Ruth, is a doctor here in town, and his younger brother, William, is an attorney over in New Orleans."

"We're going to meet Billy and his girls up to Hattiesburg," Mr. Landry said.

"I don't know what Ruth is thinking," Mrs. Landry said, "staying here in this hurricane."

"They're going to need her at the clinic, dear," Mr. Landry said.

"Not if there isn't a clinic," she said.

There was an awkward silence that I thought would get Isa talking, but she didn't say a word.

"Good grits," Mr. Landry finally said. "You still got the touch."

"Isa, tell us about the wedding," Mrs. Landry said.

"Mother," Patrick said.

"I want to hear," she said.

"It was beautiful," Isa said. "Patrick proposed to me on one knee, and we drove up there on the weekend and got married in a little chapel. Kevin was our witness."

I remembered the clacks and whistles of slot machines outside the chapel. I also remembered their ebullience all weekend long. I'd had a hotel room to myself; I'd hated it.

"It's not the way we do things here," Mrs. Landry said.

"Devon," Mr. Landry said, "where'd you earn that shiner?" I thought it kind of him to change the subject.

"At school, sir," he said politely.

"Isn't it summer break?" Mrs. Landry said.

"Summer school," Devon said, not missing a beat.

"What do you like studying?" she said.

"History and politics, I guess." He paused, but no one spoke, so he continued, "I'm studying how America is causing wars and making enemies and messing up the world and you adults are leaving us with all kinds of debt."

Mr. Landry laughed, but his wife jumped right in. "Where have I heard that kind of talk?" she said. " 'Question Authority.' Isn't that the button you used to wear, Patrick? Didn't you want to change everything too? And look at you."

"Can we just get through breakfast?" Patrick said. "We have a lot to do to get ready for the hurricane."

She started to cry.

"Cynthia," Mr. Landry said, "don't do this to yourself."

"Fine!" she said, still crying. "You want a nice breakfast, go ahead!" She stood and stormed upstairs.

None of us said anything for a while.

"You have our number up to Hattiesburg," Mr. Landry said.

"Yes, Dad."

"You'll shutter the windows?"

"And we'll put the plants in the garage."

"That garage always floods. Never should've built it there."

"I remember, Dad."

"Everything has to be off the floor. Don't forget the patio. And the lawn furniture."

"What about the garage windows?"

"I didn't have time. There's plywood in the shed if you get to it."

"You might lose that shed. Is there anything you want me to move into the garage?"

Mr. Landry didn't respond right away. "You could have called," he said finally.

"I'm sorry," Patrick said, sheepish. "I didn't know we'd be able to stop."

"Well, it's upset your mother. You can see that."

"There wasn't any good way to do it. Not now. Not later."

"You done with the drugs?"

I thought of the half kilo.

"Clean for almost two years."

Mr. Landry stood. "You stick to it. We're proud of you for that. And for your family here too. I wish I could do more. You know that."

After a moment, Patrick said, "We're doing fine."

"If you'll excuse me, Mrs. Landry, I'm sure we'll meet again in better circumstances."

"Yes, sir," Isa said.

"You got enough gas?" Patrick said. "Pumps are probably empty."

"Filled up the cars two days ago."

As the stairs creaked with his weight, I noted that: the cars were full of gas.

"They're under a lot of stress," Patrick said. "They'll be gone soon, and we'll talk. We've got plenty of time before Katrina hits."

"We don't have plenty of time," I said, but he ignored me.

I did the dishes with the kids as Patrick made a dozen calls, trying to track down somebody named Guidry who was still in town but wasn't answering his cell. Then he tried LeRoi—with the accent on the second syllable, unlike "Leroy"—but no luck there either.

Isa called Abe, but he wouldn't pick up, so she told his voice mail we were in Biloxi and were coming to Pensacola as soon as we could. I wanted to call Natalie, but I put it off until we figured out our next steps.

When I was back in the TV room with the kids, Devon whispered to me on the couch, "His parents' car keys are by the back door on a hook."

A newscaster described footage of past hurricanes, with firsthand accounts that excited the boys and got them talking about waves and winds and destruction. Then the mayor of New Orleans came on and declared a mandatory evacuation.

"They're still talking all about New Orleans," Devon said.

"That's because it's lower than sea level," Patrick said from the hall- way. "We're above sea level here. Two months ago, they evacuated this whole county for Hurricane Dennis. But the storm didn't do a damn thing. It hit the Florida panhandle and messed up some pine trees."

"I want to see a hurricane," Ray said.

"No, you don't," I said.

Mrs. Landry's heels scolded the wooden stairs evenly, purposefully, as she came down to the landing. "We're leaving now," she said. "Could you get my bags?"

I wondered what it must be like for her, to be startled by her wayward son and his foster family on the brink of a hurricane.

"I pulled the Chrysler out already," Patrick said dutifully. As his steps creaked up the stairs, Mrs. Landry's heels struck solidly into our room. Her determined gait reminded me of the Patrick I'd known outside her home. "Be so kind," she said, "as to turn off the television for a moment." The TV popped off. "Before we go, I'd like you to look at this old picture and tell me who it is." She walked next to me and stood in front of Devon. "It's a picture I keep upstairs. Not in the parlor."

I heard the ticking of a clock from the living room—her parlor. Why hadn't I heard the clock earlier?

"That's Patrick," Devon said dismissively. "That's all of you."

"Who else?" she said. Her voice was a higher pitch than her son's but just as declarative and demanding. When she stopped speaking, the steady plodding of the clock was intolerable.

Devon bellowed from deep within. It made my stomach turn.

"What?" I said.

"Let me see," Ray said.

"I don't think Patrick would ever tell you," Mrs. Landry said. "He doesn't have the courage. Or the sense of duty. You both talk big. I bet you can puff up your chest like he can. You're a lot alike, you know. You both . . ." She didn't finish her sentence.

"What's in the picture?" I said. Still I wouldn't let myself grasp it.

Nothing moved save the mechanics of the clock.

"This is my grandson," she said. The clock ticked. Then her heels struck briskly across the wooden floor, into the hallway, and onto the front porch. She was gone.

Devon threw the picture across the room so that the frame struck the far wall and glass shattered onto the floor. I put my hand on his arm, but he stood, releasing his arm from my grip.

"Who was that in the picture?" Ray said. "Who was that maid?"

TWELVE

Mr. Landry clomped in from the hallway. "Now you know," he said, his voice firm but sympathetic. "You've got Cajun and Creole in your veins, son. Can't anybody in this world stop you once you set your mind."

"This man is my grandfather," Devon said, testing the sound of that concept. I knew his mind was racing. I remembered what he'd said about hating his deadbeat dad.

"Brace yourself, son," Mr. Landry said. "You get through this and you'll be the stronger for it. You pass on by again when you're ready. I'll put you to work where you'll make good money and learn a thing or two besides. Right here in Biloxi or up to the river. Anytime. You got my blood, son. I don't give a damn about your skin."

I waited for Devon to lash out at him. Nothing happened.

"I'm serious," Mr. Landry said. "Mrs. Landry, she gets upset, but she'll abide. Truth is, we don't have any other grandson. This part of the country is different than it used to be. This is where you belong. I'll teach you what you can't get anywhere else. You'll see." I heard the clock ticking. All else was still. "Brace yourself, son," he said again. After another moment, he clomped out the front door.

"We're leaving," I whispered. "Now."

"He's my fucking father," Devon said. "And she was right. I'm just like him." He plopped onto the couch.

"Stop it, Devon," I said. "You're not."

"I was gonna tell you when it was time," Patrick said from the hallway.

"Where's Isa!" I yelled. "Isa! Are you here?"

"It's time," Patrick said. "I'm glad you know."

Again I expected an outburst, but Devon sat stiffly, his forearm tense when I touched it. He was processing. Calculating. Laying out steps in his head. That worried me.

"Did you know?" Devon said.

"No!" I said.

"I mean Isa," he said.

"I didn't know at first," she said from the hallway. "He told me two months ago." Her steps shuffled into the room like those of a patient on a sick ward. After a moment, her woody fragrance reached me.

"You dragged Mom west," Devon said.

"We went west together," Patrick said. "I was twenty-two and had just finished college. She'd just graduated from high school and started working for us that summer. We loved each other. She got pregnant, and there was no place for us in Biloxi."

"You were never together."

"We lived together for two years in L.A. You were almost two years old. I was a cook all through college, so I started cooking again, got good jobs working prep for good chefs, but those kitchens were cut-throat. I started doing coke to stay on top of everything, but that sent me over, and I did shit I shouldn't have done. She kicked me out."

"You left her. You gave her no child support. You never gave me shit."

"That's not true. She kicked me out. I gave her money when I could, but I was an addict. I started doing crack. I was homeless for a while. I didn't want you to know me, and she didn't either. She made me promise not to tell you, not to see you, not to hang around. She hated me; you know that. Once I got clean—almost two years ago—she wasn't doing so well. Her health was failing. You were getting in trouble all the time. She reached out to me; that's how desperate she was to get you out of East L.A. Then she got busted and you went to foster care and then Juvie Camp and we were able to get you. I thought we'd get along better if you didn't know. Then I wanted to tell you, but I couldn't find a way to do it. I tried to tell you yesterday."

"You're a coward," I said.

"Life isn't just books," Patrick said. "For two years, I've been raising you the best I can."

"It hasn't even been a year," Devon said. "Fuck you." But it wasn't an explosion, an eruption, a release.

"I always let you have your say," Patrick said.

"That's bullshit," Devon said calmly, evenly. "You dismiss everything I say."

"I never raised a hand against you. Except yesterday. When you hit me, I couldn't stop myself. It was reflex. I shouldn't have done it. I had it coming from you. I still do. I should've let you whip me."

"You have an excuse for everything," Devon said.

"Who has the custody from the state," I said, "you or Isa?"

"We both do," Patrick said.

"So the state pays you to take care of your own child," I said. "How do they not know?"

"I'm not on his birth certificate."

"Is that why you didn't tell him?" I said. "To stay on the state gravy train?"

"You don't have to like me. But you better shut the hell up."

"We love you, Devon," Isa said. "And we love Ray too. And Kevin. We're a family; do you see that now? We *are* a family."

It was so jarring, that statement in this context.

I thought of the hurricane coming. The keys hanging by the back door. The car in the garage. This was our chance to get out of Biloxi—with or without Patrick and Isa.

"What's your plan?" I said to Patrick. "There's a mandatory evacuation. It's time to get out."

"They call those all the time," he said. "The mayor has to do that, or his ass is on the line. See how he waited until the last minute? Besides, I have to sell that shit before I leave. We're maxed out on the credit card, and I've got like fifty bucks left. If you all want to leave now, go ahead. I'll give you the money I've got. Isa, I know you don't like to drive, but you can do it, sweetie. You did it in El Paso."

"Of course we're leaving," I said, leaning forward and sitting on the edge of the couch. "Devon can help drive if he needs to. Which car should we take?"

"You can take Betsy," he said, not even objecting to Devon behind the wheel. "She's got two-thirds of a tank. We can siphon some more gas from Mom's car, but you don't have far to go anyway. Just get off the coast. Wiggins is an hour north. Hattiesburg's an hour past that. There'll be plenty of churches to take you in. I'll be fine here. I've got a freezer full of frozen dinners and a pantry full of canned goods. I've got enough water for a dozen people. There's a generator in the garage. I'll close up the shutters. This old house made it through Camille, which was a category five, winds over one fifty. I'm a goddamned Cajun, and I've been through hurricanes before. I'll catch up with you in Pensacola."

Isa started to hum, not a tune—a monotone.

"Sweetie," he said, "it's going to be fine. If I sell the stuff today, I'll join you by tonight."

Devon stood up. "I'm not leaving." His voice was so even and mechanical it scared me.

"What!" I said, standing.

"You guys go. I'm not scared of any hurricane. I'm staying here with him." His footsteps across the room were steady and short, like a robot: no long strides. He was freaking me out.

"Devon," I called.

He walked upstairs slowly, one step at a time.

I collapsed on the couch, and we all just sat there. The ceiling creaked as Devon wandered from room to room upstairs. That was when it came to me: Patrick had planned this all along, creating excuses to come to Biloxi and introduce his son to his parents—to show them what he had done without their blessing. Their only grandson. How long had he been trying to tell Devon the truth? How many times had he tried? Not just on this trip but over the past year? He knew—he must have known—that his mother would tell Devon. He'd *wanted* her to tell him. That was why we were here. That was why he'd bought cocaine after the bones were gone—to *make* himself come here. For all of Patrick's bluster, he didn't have the strength to tell Devon himself.

I squeezed Ray's hand. "I'll be right back," I told him. Then I got up and opened Charlie. "You should have told him a long time ago," I said to Patrick as coldly as I could.

I found Devon upstairs rummaging through a bedroom closet. As soon as I walked into the room, he said, "Leave me alone."

"We've got to go," I said. "This is our chance. You've been wanting to run. Now's the time."

"I'm not going. And if I did go, I wouldn't take Isa. And I wouldn't come back." Still his voice was flat, measured.

"Fine," I said. "We won't come back."

He tried to brush past me out the door, but I grabbed his arm and held.

"Let go," he said, but he didn't struggle.

"You don't know what hurricanes can do."

"I'm not scared of that shit. You and Ray should go. Isa can drive." He pulled his arm from my grip but didn't move his feet.

"We need you," I said.

"You don't need me. Nobody needs me. Nobody cares about me." It was creepy to hear him say those words without emotion. "My name is Devon Morel Landry, son of Justine Morel and Patrick Landry. I already told you once, if I found the bastard I'd kill him. I've just got to find the gun."

"That's what you're looking for," I said. "A gun."

"My grandfather said it: once a Cajun sets his mind . . ." He didn't finish the sentence.

"You're not stubborn like that," I said. "You're not like Patrick."

"There's a gun in this house. There's got to be."

"Stop it," I said. "Stop it now."

"No!" he yelled. "I'm not going to stop it!"

Finally, I thought. Let it out.

He walked over and slammed the door but stayed in the room. "We both fucked up her life! He screwed her, and I treated her like shit. I used to think I was so smart, I didn't listen to anything she said. She can read a whole book in an afternoon. She can curse in five languages. She can do crazy numbers in her head. And she saw what I was becoming: a fuckup! I fucked up everything, including her life. If she hadn't gotten pregnant with me, she wouldn't have moved west. She wouldn't have stayed with him. He was right. She wanted me out of East L.A. I can see that now. No wonder she turned to God."

"You're a good kid," I said.

"Why the fuck didn't I ask Mom? That's what I want to know. I knew she was Creole, and I thought that meant Louisiana. But I never asked. She used to tell me, 'We don't have any people.' But why the fuck didn't I ask? I didn't want to know, that's why!"

He began pacing back and forth. It was a good sign, I thought. This was the Devon I knew.

"Every time I did something wrong, she told me, 'You're as pig-headed as your father.' Well, I met him, and he's the fucking prick I knew he was. And I'm going to do what *he* would do. He knows he's got it coming. He just told me that! And I see what he means about the history of our kind. Why it's not written down. And why he fucking lost it with every cop that bossed him around, because he was a Cajun himself growing up in Mississippi. He fucked my Creole mom and had to run to California to escape."

As the bedsprings squeaked with his weight, I scooted over, sat down, and put my arm around him. He wasn't twitching or crying; his body was stiff.

He broke away from me and stood. "He's got it coming."

I tried to reason with him: "Patrick knows this house inside and out; he won't leave guns lying around, not now." I tried to entice him by the prospect of driving. I tried to scare him about hurricanes. I tried to lure him with Alexis. I mentioned his mom back in California.

But he wouldn't budge. "You guys go," he said. "I'm staying. Anything can happen in a hurricane."

"You found your dad," I explained. "Now let him out of your life. He's not worth it. You've got a world of choices. You just have to get through this."

"A kid like me?" he yelled. " 'A world of choices'? What the fuck country do you live in?"

For the next hour, I felt like an emissary with a mission nobody would acknowledge. As Patrick waited for callbacks from Guidry and LeRoi, he and Ray carried knickknacks away from windows in the kitchen, pausing as Patrick told hurricane stories, his voice mysterious and wise: "We used to huddle right here in the kitchen and light candles with the power out and the wind howling outside. This is the safest room because the windows aren't so big. Mom would read Edgar Allan Poe as shadows jumped on the wall: 'The Tell-Tale Heart.' Thump-thump. Thump-thump. 'The Pit and the Pendulum.' "

"Is there lightning?" Ray said, excited.

"It's like thunder all the time," Patrick said. "That's how loud it is."

Ray seemed to devour it.

In the living room, Isa slapped her cell phone closed just as I entered. She'd finally reached Pensacola, she said, but Robert had answered, not her daddy, and Robert wouldn't let her speak to him. "He says I'll get Daddy too upset. What does he know?" She paced the length of the thick carpet. "I'm the one he needs. I'm the healer. I'm his daughter!"

I asked if they were getting out of Pensacola.

She put a mug on a sideboard—the clink of porcelain on wood—and shuffled toward me. "The hurricane," she said mysteriously, as if I'd just told her a secret. She gripped my hand with fingers that trembled. I smelled coffee on her breath. "They're closing up Daddy's house," she said.

"He needs you," I said as kindly as I could. "You need to be with them." I told her I had to stay with Devon and Patrick for now, to help them out. Patrick had Betsy ready for her, I said, out in the driveway and gassed up. All she needed to do was drive with Ray east on I-10, and she could join her family

"*This* is my family!" she declared, stepping away from me and pacing again. "We have troubles, every family has troubles, but I've kept us together, haven't I? I've kept Patrick off Devon for months. I've done everything I could, but it's nothing compared with what I owe. I had a child and God took her from me. It's God's will to bring us all together now." She took a shallow breath. "I love Ray just as much as Devon. They're both my children. God works His own miracles." Again she breathed. I started to speak, but she cut me off: "Now that Devon knows, now that we all know—well, we're being put to the test. I know what Devon's doing. He has to own up to who he is. And so do the rest of us."

That was how frenzied she was—rambling yet making a strange kind of sense. "Isa," I said, "I'll come with Patrick and Devon later. We'll all be together tomorrow night."

She stopped pacing, well away from me. "You're done with me," she said defiantly. "I know that. You don't have to tell me. And I know it's my fault. I shouldn't have given in to you in El Paso. Now you don't *respect* me. You see it as weakness. You tried to ditch us—the kids too. But I'm not asking for anything. All this time, almost two years, I've been professional. I've honored your parents' wishes. I haven't abandoned you. I've cooked for you, cared for you, cleaned your underwear. I let down my guard just once—for one night—and now you think I'm nothing. You think that you're the caregiver and I need your help."

Jesus, I thought. I hoped Patrick was outside, well out of hearing.

"Has it occurred to you to ask about me? Like if I'm ovulating? Maybe I'm feeling exposed right now. But no, you don't care about that. It was a one-night deal for you. You think you can just walk away. Well, I have to live with the consequences."

"I'm sorry, Isa," I said. "We made a mistake. It was both of us."

"I chose the wrong man," she said, pacing again, her voice quivering. "Why do I always do that? You always listen before talking. You actually hear what I say. And look at what Patrick's doing: he's dealing again. He's trying to track down those old friends. Just like you were doing back in L.A." She walked up to me, close, and I thought she would fall upon me, grasping, but instead she turned spiteful. "When we left Burbank, you hadn't started using yet. But I could tell you were on the edge. Patrick isn't using yet either. But how long can he stay away from it? How long can you? We caught you in Betsy's backseat about to snort up."

I was shocked. It hadn't occurred to me that she had suspected that. But I didn't get angry. I didn't retreat. I relaxed my grip on Charlie. "Isa," I said kindly, "you can do this. You can drive out of here."

"You think he doesn't need me?" she demanded, her tone accusatory. "Is that it? Well you'll see: he does need me. He loves me. And Devon loves me too. And Ray. You don't see how Ray holds me all the time? How he came to me when you abandoned him, how he smiles for *me?* They all need me, Kevin." She walked past me toward the hallway but stopped and said quickly, "If you go and the kids go, I'll go with you. Otherwise, I don't trust you here with my husband."

I retreated to the kitchen and hunkered down at the table, trying to recover from her madness and trying to get used to the idea of staying through the storm—all of us. It was Ray and Patrick who helped me relax. Patrick gave us tasks to prepare the inside of the house, and he went out back to board up the garage windows.

Ray told me right off that he wasn't going anywhere without Devon and me. He was more afraid of being alone with Isa the way she was acting than waiting out Katrina with all of us. "She keeps moving from one room to another," he said. "Her eyes shift all around. I can't tell what she's going to do."

I said gently, "Don't worry about Isa. She's been through difficult things before. She knows better than anyone how to ward off pain."

The two of us started in the living room, tilting the grandfather clock onto a towel and then sliding it farther away from the windows. We carried precious items upstairs: trinkets from the mantel and photos from the piano. Fine porcelain. Several paintings.

Ray toured me through the rooms upstairs. Along the Gulf side, there was a sitting room in the front corner, over the living room, and a large master bedroom in the back corner. From both of those rooms, Ray said, you could see over rooftops and between branches to the Gulf. The master bedroom opened through French doors onto a small covered porch at the back of the house. There were three bedrooms on the opposite side of the hallway, which ran down the center from the front porch, with a bathroom in between the back two.

Even upstairs I heard Devon's footsteps above me. "He's looking for a gun in the attic," Ray said matter-of-factly.

I felt strange asking him, but I didn't see any way around it. "If you see a gun, let me know. If you see *Devon* with a gun, you tell me where he is, but get away. Okay? You be my eyes, and I'll stop him. But you stay away. Is that a deal?"

"Okay."

"For reals?" I said.

"For reals."

We worked the dining room next, moving the silver and crystal into a closet of sheets and towels upstairs. I settled into the idea of riding out the storm. Here and there I heard Patrick talking with Isa, trying to soothe her. Everywhere I went, I couldn't help reaching into the back corners of chifforobes and bureaus for a gun. I tried talking to Devon when we passed in the hallway, but mostly he avoided us. I kept hoping for a callback from Natalie on Isa's cell. Mostly I gave myself over to Ray, using the senses I had to be aware and engaged.

A friendly cloud cover drifted overhead about one o'clock but didn't lessen the heat or bring a breeze. Ray and I sweated as we carried plants and furniture from the lawn into the garage, which smelled of grass clippings and machine oil. Along the far wall, someone was clanking through tools—rakes maybe, shovels.

"Devon," Patrick called from the driveway, "help us move the casket." But Devon kept at his search, opening and closing drawers—getting to know his grandparents, I thought, as much as looking for a gun. I hadn't heard him speak to Patrick since the scene in the living room that morning.

Behind the garage, Ray and I each grabbed a front handle of the coffin. Patrick picked up the back end, and we hoisted it across the yard, up the back steps, careful as we turned through the kitchen door, and into the hallway. We'd barely set it down when Isa bellowed that she couldn't stand that box in the house. She couldn't imagine her daddy in it. "He's not going in it! He's doing better now. I knew he'd get better. We never should've brought it. We can't give him a coffin! What if his health turns bad again? It'll be our fault. If it wasn't for that thing with those bones and that stupid cocaine, we'd already be in Pensacola."

Patrick had us trudge the casket upstairs, where we put it in the master bedroom, along the far wall. "Go easy on her," Patrick whispered. "Soon as I have the house ready, I can sit with her some." Then he hustled downstairs, where he made several phone calls, not just to Guidry and LeRoi this time.

He was trying.

Ray and I got two Pepsis from the refrigerator and sat out front on coarse St. Augustine grass between the roots of a giant oak. We sat facing a breeze, which brought humid, unruly smells of salt and seaweed from the Gulf. I rubbed away beads of sweat that lay across my forearms and the backs of my hands. Dozens of crickets fretted ahead of us, toward the Gulf, with a few renegades off to our left across the street. Frogs croaked back and forth.

"Why can't I live with you when we get back?" Ray said.

A bug buzzed my face, but I didn't slap. "I wish we could, but the government won't let me."

"Because of your record," he said. "Because you do drugs."

"I used to do drugs."

"You'll do drugs without us."

"Is that what Isa says?"

He didn't answer.

"I have to move out because it's time to be on my own again. The last time I was on my own, in San Francisco, I didn't do so well. But I'm older now."

"I'm not going back to Burbank."

"You're going to stay somewhere out here with Devon," I said, as if I accepted that.

"You could stay too," he said tenuously.

I waited. A car drove by slowly. I got him talking about Mexico, and he told me that his tía María and tío José weren't really his aunt and uncle but cousins of his mom, maybe; he wasn't sure. They were older than his parents; their children were grown. They flew to Los Angeles every other year to visit their daughter. Maybe he and Devon would visit them in Mexico, he said. Maybe they'd both stay down there.

It was unworkable: the money, the distance, their ages. No passports. But I didn't mention any of that. I nodded instead. "You should visit them," I said. "When I get back to Burbank, I'll save that picture of your mom for you. Anything else you need?"

He didn't answer. After a while, he started throwing acorns at a fence post, so I gathered and threw some too. He laughed at how far off I was, but after he told me where to throw, he was surprised at how close I came. He closed his eyes then, I directed his aim, and on the second try he hit something. Ping! But neither of us knew whether he'd hit the target, so we laughed at that and threw acorns at each other. He moved as quietly as he could on the stiff grass and crinkly leaves, but I pegged him a couple of times.

We were still throwing acorns when a bell came tingling along the road. "Afternoon!" a man called. "Last hot meal before Katrina. Best tacos in town."

We hadn't eaten since breakfast.

"You'll get a good price," he called out. "Dollar a taco. Gotta get this thing stored."

As Ray went off to see if others were hungry, I walked with Charlie to the street, where the man was already setting up alongside the pavement and clanking metal pots or spoons. I felt along the edge of a smooth metal counter.

"You as blind as you look?" he said.

"Can't see a thing."

His name was Jamaal; he started chopping something. Onions. "Casinos are closed. I gotta get rid of this meat before she hits. Damn, it's hot, even with the clouds."

Ray's quick steps returned. "You got asado?" he said.

"Yes, sir."

Onions started to sizzle, and a spatula scraped a pan as Patrick's and Isa's footsteps came down the front walkway. "One more coming," Patrick said. "Nice rig."

"She ain't light," Jamaal said. "She's stainless steel."

Patrick gave a whistle of respect. "What are you selling tacos for?" he said. "Where's the red beans and rice?"

The scraping of the spatula stopped, but the onions kept sizzling. "Black man can't sell tacos?" Jamaal said roughly.

Just as Patrick began to respond, Jamaal let out a big guffaw. "Just kidding with you. You can get your red beans anywhere. But not these tacos. Best tacos in town." He chuckled again. "I had you goin'. Did you see his face?"

"You had me going," Patrick admitted. Then he started in, and Jamaal loved it: How much did the rig cost? Do you set up wherever you want? What kind of license do you need? How much do they cost?

Jamaal had an answer for everything: What time of year to buy a license off somebody. Where to set up to maximize the price at a given time of day. How to stay a step ahead of the health inspector and the cops.

Devon joined us; I could smell him behind me. Maybe food would bring him around, I thought.

"What spices?" Patrick said.

"There's the secret," Jamaal said. "Where'd I be if I told you that?"

"Here comes two more customers," Patrick goaded. "What's our percentage, since we brought them over?"

"Like hell," Jamaal said.

A man haggled down the price of two Millers.

"You allowed to sell beers?" Patrick said, but didn't get an answer.

"We need sixteen tacos to go," the man said, his voice thick and slow. "How much?"

"A dollar each today," Jamaal said. He set to it, chopping onions again. After a moment, something slid on the counter in front of me; with my hand I felt a paper plate with a hot taco on top: small, delicate, with moist meat and sautéed onions wrapped in two soft corn tortillas. Ray spooned on some red salsa that had fresh tomatoes, green onions, and cilantro. I ate the taco in four bites.

"These are great," Ray said.

"You're Richard Landry's son, aren't you?" the man with the beer said. "You stayin'?"

"You bet," Patrick said.

"Your parents stayin'?" the second man said. He spoke more quickly, with a nasal tone.

"They left this morning."

"She's fixin' to blow," the first man said slowly. "We're leavin' right now. I hear there's no gas on the road. Not for three hundred miles."

Each time I finished a taco, another one slid onto my plate.

"There's a couple stayin'," the man went on, "Mr. and Mrs. Dexter, and their daughter. They're one door down and across the street."

"I know them," Patrick said.

"Next door to you, there's a lady wouldn't leave. Just so you know."

"Mr. and Mrs. Murphy."

"He's gone. Died last year. And next to her there's a old man with the head of a mule. Wouldn't budge. I don't know who else."

"I'm staying," Jamaal said. "But not over here by the Gulf."

"I been through worse," Patrick said.

"Won't know that till tomorrow." The nasal tone.

"Sixteen tacos," Jamaal said. "That's twenty-two with the beers."

"Man, he made those fast," Ray said.

Altogether I ate five tacos, three with green salsa, two with red. Devon ate eleven and slipped away without a word. Patrick ordered one for Isa, but I don't know if she ate it. I told Patrick it was my treat. "Much obliged," he said. It felt satisfying to pay.

We were walking back up the driveway when Ray said, "Wow. Look at all the birds."

I lifted my face. "Wow!"

"Very funny," he said. "There's lots of them."

"Storm birds," Patrick said, always sure of himself. "You can tell because there's no order. No formations. They're just flying. They get kicked ahead by the upper winds. Look at the heron. Wouldn't be surprised if you found a spoonbill from the Keys."

I'd never thought of birds and hurricanes before.

He opened the back door to the house. "You won't see any house sparrows or turkeys, though. They just hang around and die."

"Don't say that!" Isa said. Her footsteps ran shuffling through the kitchen.

While Ray and I were still in the kitchen, the front doorbell rang. Isa and Patrick had gone upstairs, I thought, so Ray and I walked down the hallway and answered the door.

"You guys got to evacuate," a man said. "Mandatory. This is a flood zone, and it's a category five."

"Who are you?" I said.

"Officer Holmes. Police department."

"We're staying," Patrick declared from above. The stairs creaked as he came halfway down. "We been through Camille. We got our supplies."

"That won't mean nothing in the storm surge," the cop said. "You'll have no medical backup. No food. No water. No police protection."

"We got protection," Patrick said. "We'll keep away looters."

In the pause I heard the stairs creak again and the tick of the living room clock.

"Yes, sir," the cop said. "Now put it away."

"What's he got?" I whispered to Ray.

"A shotgun."

Jesus, I thought: Patrick and cops.

"You got a neighbor next door," the cop said.

"Mrs. Murphy," Patrick said. "And the Dexters across from her."

"Check on 'em when you can."

"Will do," Patrick said.

The officer's boots struck the porch sharply as he walked away. Ray closed the door.

"Put the damn gun away!" I said. "Where's Devon?"

"Right here," Devon called from upstairs.

"Give me the shotgun," I said, walking toward Patrick.

"Not a chance," he said. "I know what I'm doing. Nothing's going to happen except what that boy wants to happen. It's for him to decide. You'll see."

I felt for Devon—not just the menace that lay ahead but the fact that this man was his father. "Don't put this on *him*," I said.

Patrick came slowly down the rest of the stairs. He stood so close I could feel his breath on my face.

I relaxed my jaw, relaxed my hands. I didn't draw back.

"I know what you did with my wife," he hissed. "I'm a forgiving man right now—but only because she needs you."

"She needs *you*," I said.

The pain of the blow felt like a two-by-four against my chest. Was it the butt of the shotgun? It felt too solid to be his forearm. I staggered back against the wall but didn't fall. After a moment, I was able to stand and step toward him so that I felt his hot breath on my face again, sour now. I didn't raise my arms to protect myself.

Go ahead, I thought. I'm stronger than you now. Do your worst.

He turned around and walked out through the kitchen.

If he was planning some kind of revenge against me, so be it. At least my deceit with Isa was out. What I cared about was keeping that gun out of Devon's hands. I walked upstairs and tried talking to Devon, but all he would do was grunt.

I came back downstairs and told Ray, "Next time. For reals. Tell me the instant you see that gun." Then I retreated into the bathroom and, wincing, felt my sore chest. I could barely touch my breastbone, where a knot was already swelling.

The rest of the afternoon and evening, I was between worlds, preparing for turmoil I couldn't envision. Patrick avoided me for a while but then acted as if nothing had happened.

Before the sun went down, I walked through every room with Ray, latching shutters. There were two on the first floor that wouldn't clasp from inside, so Patrick hammered them shut. On the second floor, I felt the first sprinkles of rain as we stood at the railing of the wide front porch, but by the time we walked onto the small porch behind the master bedroom, it had already let up. We left the big shutters open over the glass doors to the front and back porches, to let some light in. But with the shutters closed elsewhere and the lights off downstairs, it was spooky dark, Ray said, his voice excited. He liked the way thin bands of light filtered through, once his eyes adjusted.

I called Natalie from an upstairs bedroom, leaving an upbeat message like the one I'd heard Devon leave for Alexis the day before. I described the clamor of crickets and the salty taste of the Gulf air in Biloxi. I told her about the acorn battle I'd had with Ray; I knew she'd like that. I let her know that everything was out in the open, that Patrick knew and had forgiven me, though that was a stretch. I told her there was a hurricane coming, Katrina, and if she didn't call me back, I'd leave her another message tomorrow and let her know about it.

When I hung up, I thought about calling my parents, but I didn't want them to worry.

After sundown, Patrick started cooking everything in the refrigerator and some meat he'd thawed from the freezer in case the gas lines got disrupted. I filled two bathtubs with water. Ray packed a cooler with ice. We set out candles, lanterns, fuel, flashlights, and batteries.

Rain came for a while. When it let up, Patrick took me outside to show me the gas shutoff and fuse box.

"What about the shotgun?" I whispered to him. "Where's that?"

He closed the fuse box.

"What if something happens to you?" I said. "What if we need it?"

"After we get back to Burbank," he said gruffly, "you move out."

"You leave Devon alone on this trip," I said, "and I'll move out."

He walked off. When I got back in the kitchen, he was cooking again, calm as ever. Devon avoided him completely. All evening, footsteps wandered the house: Isa's light shuffles; Devon's thumps. It was as if they'd become new people, with different sounds. Later, as I came around a corner, Devon startled me with the smell of his perspiration. When I spoke, he was gone without a noise. I couldn't help thinking, He's like Patrick, stealing up even in this creaky place. Where were the thumps he'd been making just moments earlier?

Upstairs, Isa wouldn't go in the master bedroom because of the coffin, so Patrick closed the shutters to the back porch and Devon took over that room. Ray and I chose the room across the hall, at the back of the house away from the Gulf.

After we piled our bags in the corner, Ray walked me over the layout of the room and the two of us played Blind Man's Bluff. I was better at chasing than being chased, since I couldn't see either way. Ray liked the running part because he got to pester and taunt me, then squeal and jump across the bed when I was onto him. My chest was still sore, but the swelling had subsided some and the pain wasn't as sharp. I kept hoping Devon would succumb and join us, but he didn't. We ate a late snack in the kitchen, beef in a sauce that melted on my tongue, it was so delicious.

When Ray lay down after we brushed our teeth, I sat on the bedside. I hadn't put him to bed since the night of the accident—since before I'd abandoned him and Devon. As I was about to rub his back, he said, "Where'd you get this?" He touched a thin scar on my palm, a scar that wraps from between my thumb and forefinger and follows my lifeline.

"No one ever notices that scar," I said.

"How'd you get it?"

"When I was in San Francisco, I got lost one night. Charlie caught on a vent in a sidewalk and dropped down. I fell onto a sharp slice of metal." I felt a jolt of panic and shame at the memory of being lost in an alley and coming down from crack. When Casey had rescued me, I'd blamed him and battered him.

"You were on drugs," he said.

Never, I thought. Never did I want to go back.

I felt along Ray's neck beneath his ear. "How'd you get your scar?" I said.

"I kind of told you," he said effortlessly. "After Mom hit me, I fell back against the corner of a heater. She didn't mean to. I was always falling down and hurting stuff anyway."

He rolled over, away from me, yawning, and I rubbed his back.

"The last thing we really did together was go to the beach," he said. "She felt bad about what happened, so I got to skip school one day that week and she took me to Santa Monica and we ran in the waves."

Santa Monica, I thought. That was where Isa had gone the day that Jasmine died.

"She was the way she used to be; she didn't have that look in her eyes. I wasn't supposed to get my neck wet, but she let me anyway. I remember digging a hole in the sand for water to come into, but the tide wasn't rising fast enough. That's when she said we're like sand, la gente. There's so many of us, we come in every color: dark, light, brown, yellow, red. What matters is who we are and what we do."

I focused on rubbing his back.

"She said she wasn't happy with who she was, and she was going to change. I'd helped her see that. I was the one who gave her strength. She said she was proud of me."

I waited a while, but he didn't say more. "I'm proud of you too," I said.

When he shifted his legs and took a deep breath, I realized he hadn't been twitching or fidgeting at all. I waited for his cue, and though it didn't come, I started in anyway. "Close your eyes and take a big breath . . ." I began.

"You don't have to put me to bed," he interrupted.

"What?" I said, though I'd heard him clearly.

"I'm too old for that."

I felt a sense of loss, as if I'd been uninvited to a family dinner. "Okay," I said weakly, but I kept rubbing his back for a bit and then brought my hands away, unsure what to do with them. I couldn't stop myself from pulling the cover up over his shoulder; he tugged it back down.

I wasn't ready to stop putting him to bed. Not then. Not that night. But he was.

I thought about going out on the front porch or checking on Devon, but instead I walked around the bed and got under the covers, not feeling tired or expecting sleep. As soon as I lay down, I realized my arms were sore from carrying things all day, my chest was throbbing, my leg muscles were tight, and I was drained from the trauma of too many revelations and contingencies. Before I fell asleep, I remembered the pleasure of lying in the grass with Natalie and Ray after our run. I heard rain on the roof—and wind in trees. I tried to imagine the eye of Katrina approaching from the Gulf.

Eye. Aye. I.

I wanted to be that calmness at the center, that darkness within light, that light within darkness, inside the spinning turbulence. That was how little I knew about hurricanes.

THIRTEEN

I woke feeling pressure not just in my ears but also in my gut, a low vibration as the walls crackled and pinged, bracing themselves against the storm. Outside, an eerie growl bellowed in a dissonant key. Rain hit the roof like buckshot. When I reached over, my arm outside the sheet, to check on Ray, I winced from the pain where Patrick had struck my chest. Ray was still sleeping.

I had to stand still a while in my pajamas, getting my bearings against the maddening snarl outside. I smelled dampness and tasted brine. My heart raced; I tried to calm my breathing. I'd never heard walls moan like that, a deep sound from the studs within. As I walked to my suitcase with Charlie, the floorboards no longer creaked from my weight; the structure was bearing other burdens. Suddenly the old house settled as the wind howled outdoors, less threatening because it was a sound I knew. Then I felt pressure in my ears again and trembling beneath my feet as rage gripped the house and the growl redoubled. A dresser came alive, rattling. Shutters clattered in their casings.

When I was dressed and at the bathroom sink, one of the walls vibrated and hummed against my palm—an exterior wall. The other walls were still.

Back in the room, I pushed our bags into the closet, making sure my note-taker was in my backpack, and opened the door to the hallway, where the jumping of shutters and the bracing of joints all along the front of the house unbalanced me. The hurricane was battering us already, it seemed, and where was everybody? Now that I was in the hallway, the thundering roar seemed inside the house as well as out. Was it daybreak yet? I didn't know. When I took a deep breath, a kaleidoscope of flavors greeted me from downstairs: garlic, onions, bacon, potatoes. Patrick was cooking.

As I walked toward the stairs, Charlie found an object against the wall just as I smelled too much perfume. "Isa?" I said, reaching.

"Daddy won't pick up the phone." She sniffled and brought her hand, all aflutter, along my arm.

"You know he's not there," I said, trying to sound soothing and calm. "You spoke with them yesterday. They drove east." I remembered the first time I met her, alone on the walkway in Channel House, where she'd helped me feel at home by letting me touch her. I put my hand on her back; when she felt my touch she jumped.

"We're too late," she said, panting more than breathing. "He said I'd be too late."

"Your daddy's fine," I said. "Robert would have called—"

"Robert's a liar!" She grabbed my elbow. Her nails were bitten to the quick, but her fingertips dug into my skin.

"Breathe slowly with me, Isa. Breathe."

"Why didn't you love me, Kevin, when we lived together, you and me? All that time? I could've loved you then, if only you'd asked. You didn't want me, did you? That's what it was. So you never asked." She released my arm. "Everyone else wanted me. But not you. And now it's too late. He said I'd be too late."

I found her hands flitting about and held them between my palms. "Let all that go," I said. "You're with Patrick. Patrick loves you."

"Patrick," she said wistfully. "I'm always so stupid. I make the same mistakes. He said we'd stop in Biloxi on the way home. But no. We had to stop here first. And now I see where he grew up, I know his mother. How can a mother make her children so confused? How can a mother—" She stopped suddenly, so that the rain and wind seemed to pound the house harder.

"Did you sleep last night?" I said. "Have you had anything besides coffee?"

"Why did I take her to the beach that day?" she said quickly. "Why the beach? We could've gone to the park. Or we could've gotten the car seat before we went to Santa Monica. Jesus, God, if only I'd made the right decision then. That moment. I'd still have Jasmine. Everything would've worked out. That's when it started, all the bad decisions I've made. Why couldn't I die instead of her?" Isa fell to her knees, and I thought she would start praying. I laid my hand on her shoulder. But if she prayed, she kept it to herself.

The roof timbers banged: rat-a-tat, rat-a-tat. She stood suddenly. "What was that?" Her hands darted across my chest like sparrows. "How could I do it? How could I bring Devon and Ray into this storm?" She panted in shallow breaths I could barely hear for the roar from outside.

"It wasn't just you," I said. "You've done what you could."

"But it's my fault," she said. "It's always been my fault. I've done my best, but he won't listen. Devon's as stubborn as his father."

"Don't say that. It's not true."

"Then why is he in the master bedroom where he was conceived?"

Jesus, I thought. That was where he'd been conceived. Patrick Landry, fresh-cheeked from college, and quick-witted Justine Morel.

"I'm your caretaker," she said in a panic. "I'm the caretaker for you all. You don't think so, but I am."

I reached, but she'd slipped along the hallway. I had to stand several minutes to gather my strength.

Charlie found the door to the master bedroom. I knocked quietly, waited, and then stepped inside, closing the door behind me. If Devon was sleeping, I didn't want to wake him. As in our room, shutters jangled their casings and the walls chattered and groaned. Rain blasted the roof. The smell of saltwater was thick. The roar persisted but seemed to have withdrawn outside. This was the Gulf side of the house, so I'd assumed the winds would be bashing this wall—yet it seemed calmer than the hallway, which opened onto the front porch.

"Patrick's right," Devon said from across the room somewhere. "You shouldn't write this shit down."

So he *was* awake. I tried being tough: "Spare me the Patrick lectures. Are you in bed? Did you sleep?"

He walked over and put a wooden object in my hand, a handle of some kind. A kitchen knife, I realized, as I felt the steel blade. Maybe six inches.

I shook my head. "Devon," I said, "you're smarter than this. Patrick will kick your ass."

"He won't expect it," he said.

I thought he'd ask for the knife back, but he didn't.

"Feel this," he said, bringing my free hand to his arm; he was wearing a long-sleeved shirt. Expensive material. Linen maybe. "It's his dad's. Fits me perfect."

I felt his torso. "Too big in the belly."

He walked away from me. "He'll bring out that gun at some point. I'll be ready. You know how long I've planned this?"

"What kind of shotgun was Patrick holding?" I demanded. "Pump action? Bolt action? Lever? Do you know how to load the chamber? Or if it's loaded? Do you know where the safety is, and how to take it off? Was it even a shotgun? Or was it a rifle?" I'd fired shotguns and rifles lots of times with Dad out at the ranch. He would point; I would shoot. Or sometimes he'd tell me where to point. Lots of times I hit the target.

"I know what to do with a gun," he said.

"Patrick knows guns backward and forward," I said. "And he can fight. You've seen that. He'll be on you in a flash."

Devon paced back and forth. "I'm not scared," he said. "I'm his fucking son."

"You're smarter than that."

"Fuck you!" he said. "You don't belong with us anyway. You're not like us. And it's not because you're blind. It's because you have money. That settlement thing and those fucking monthly payments. Where do you think Patrick and Isa got the money for those clothes you're wearing? And for this trip? Why do you think she's so nice to you all the time? They're swindling your parents, that's what. Most blind people are hard-up as hell, trying to make ends meet. That's the truth. You're jerking your head now because you know I'm right. Stand there and face me. I don't care about your goddamned scar. You're lucky, even with all the shit you have to deal with. You just won't admit it. You've got money to fall back on anytime, all the time. After this trip, you're gonna write about all this, aren't you? Like we're one big project. You're gonna write what you want no matter what Ray describes—all about how you helped everybody and you're the hero. So go take care of Ray and Isa while they pretend they need you and you pretend you need them. I know what I have to do. I'm not your fucking project anymore."

Still the shutters banged and the walls groaned and the roar kept coming and the air smelled like brine. I gripped the knife in my hand. I thought about what Isa had said yesterday: he had to own up to who he was, and so did we all.

"Fine," I said. "I can't stop you from whatever you're going to do. But think about Ray today. He looks up to you. He learns from you. You're his big brother."

There was a series of loud smacks from outside, like a row of shovels battering wood.

"I'm hungry," he said suddenly. He stormed across the room, and as he opened the door the hurricane's madness came alive in the hallway.

I slipped the knife into a drawer.

Devon was barely out the door when he said kindly, "Hey, Beavis Butthead. You doing okay?"

"Hey," Ray said from across the hall.

"It's blowing like shit, huh?" Devon said.

Maybe Ray nodded. Maybe he smiled. Maybe he scrunched his shoulders.

"Whoa!" Devon said. "There go the lights."

I didn't notice any difference; I couldn't hear or feel the air conditioning kick off.

"It sounds like a ghost movie," Ray said, his voice vibrant, not anxious.

"Is it dark?" I said. "Can you see with the shutters closed?"

"The sun's not up," Devon said. "We can't see shit."

I had no idea it was that early. "What time is it?"

"I don't know. It's not six yet."

Ray's hand found me, and I squeezed him to me. "You okay?"

"Sure," he said.

"That smells good," Devon said. "Let's go eat."

As Charlie led us toward the stairs, Ray held my elbow, his grip firm but not clinging, and Devon held to Ray. I dragged my hand along the hallway wall; even the interior walls were trembling now. On the stairwell, the banister vibrated as we approached the blast that was hitting the front door full-on. At the bottom of the stairs, the roar sounded like an open furnace; I didn't trust the strength of the door. To my right, toward the Gulf, the living room clattered and clanged. A whiff of Isa's woody perfume came to me. Where was she? As I turned around the base of the banister to walk along the hallway to the kitchen, the floor shimmied. The wall wavered. The house, from foundation to roof, was twitching.

Ray released my elbow; as we entered the kitchen, I smelled candles.

"Better eat," Patrick growled. "Everything's gonna be fine, but get your fill now. She's kickin' up."

Kicking up, I thought. How much worse could it get? Every few minutes the roar seemed to deepen and build and change into new specters that had no source. I felt seasick sitting still.

"Told you it was gonna be like thunder," Patrick said to Ray.

"It's more like a train," Ray said, excited. "And ghosts." He was hearing the same things I was but seemed to be taking it in stride. He had all kinds of questions for Patrick: What was that bang? That whistle? Why couldn't we open a shutter and look out?

"I thought the wind would come from the Gulf," I said. "From the south and hit that side of the house. I thought Katrina was moving north."

"She's blowing counterclockwise," Patrick said. "That makes the wind come from the east as she moves north—if you're close to the path of the eye. The wind's hitting the front porch pretty much dead-on, though she's hitting all the living room windows on that front corner too, making the shutters jump on the Gulf side. It means the eye's not gonna be far from here. She's gonna push the storm surge right into Back Bay."

Something brayed outside. The house braced itself. My jaws clenched.

"That sounded like a cow," Ray said.

As we ate eggs, bacon, potatoes, and toast, I couldn't smell the food anymore. It tasted of the salty air, and the room felt hot and stifling without air conditioning. The back of the house seemed to throb. Every now and then something would bang or smack against the front of the house or roof. Someone's doormat? A branch? A wheelbarrow? I couldn't tell. The kitchen shutters vibrated, not quite rattling. The floor trembled. A shrill whistle sounded: wind in a tight place. Then it stopped just as abruptly. I put down my fork, walked to a window, and held my palm on glass; a high-pitched whine, which I hadn't known I'd heard, halted. The glass bowed in and out. I released the glass, and the room whined again. A screech sounded and stopped. Everything was alive and confounding.

"Isa!" Patrick yelled. "Quit wandering around. Come in the kitchen and eat."

When Devon went to corral her, I said to Patrick, "Have you talked to him yet? Have you told him you're sorry?"

"It ain't about talking," he said as gruffly as ever. "He's got to get through some things. Isa's the one. She didn't sleep. She hasn't eaten. She's pissed at me."

"Have you talked with her?"

"Of course I talked to her. She talked all night."

When she and Devon came into the kitchen, Patrick spoke kindly to her, urging her to eat. Then he explained that this room was down-wind—the leeward side of the storm for now. He wanted everybody to stay in the kitchen until the eye passed. "You too, Devon," he said. "No more wandering off."

"You're always fucking telling us what to do," Devon said.

It's about time, I thought. I wanted Devon and Patrick to have it out now, in the kitchen, without guns or knives.

Patrick didn't respond right away. "This isn't a joyride," he said. "You can think what you want. But let me say it real nice: everybody better do the fuck what I say today. Tomorrow we'll see."

We all waited, but Devon didn't say a thing. He didn't make a sound.

Something big slammed against the front of the house, up high, yet the floor shuddered. It dragged all along the roof before it flew off the back. I could hear four pitches of disarray: two sopranos, an alto, and a thundering bass. I found myself clenching my fists. My shoulders were scrunched up against my neck. I tried to breathe.

"Look what you've done!" Isa screamed. "Look where you've brought us with that coffin and that cocaine! I can't stand it anymore!"

Ray was against me fast, and I put my arm around him. The hurricane he could weather; it was people who scared him.

A series of cracks came from outside, not in our yard, maybe, but not far away, a strange creaking sound like wood ripping apart. A shriek almost human made me cringe: the twisting of metal?

Isa sobbed and ran from the kitchen. I thought Patrick would go after her, but he didn't. "We'll get through this," he growled. "We'll get through this. Save the candles. There's light coming through the shutters. Let your eyes adjust."

Just as the lonesome smell of blown-out candles came to me, the phone clanged on the table—much louder than it should've, startling everybody and making us laugh uncomfortably. Even Patrick chortled. "This old phone is beautiful," Patrick said. "No electricity."

"It's Daddy!" Isa said, bustling back into the room.

But Patrick had already picked up. We could all hear a woman's voice calling out. "Hallo!" she yelled. "Hallo!"

Ray held to me, not clinging but firm.

"Hello!" Patrick said.

"Richard Landry?" she yelled.

"Patrick Landry!" he said.

"It's Marybeth Murphy! I can take the wind. Is there water there?" Her voice was unnerving.

"My cell has no signal!" Isa shrieked.

"It's rainin' like hell," Patrick shouted. "'Course there's water."

"I'm talkin' seawater. It's rushing all along my right side. My corner's pitching. But you're up a bit higher. You got seawater?"

"I don't know. Just a minute." He plopped the receiver onto the table and ran to the back door. "Damn!" he said. "Help me open it." Ray came with me as I hustled over; I was surprised to find Devon there too, helping. He and I put our hands on top of Patrick's on the doorknob. All of us yanked at the same time to get the door open. Immediately the pressure in my ears abated. The roar outside was deafening, with screeches, bangs, and squeals. It felt like we were standing at the edge of an abyss.

"Jesus!" Patrick said. "The shed's already gone. The fence is gone." He kept muttering things I couldn't hear as he stepped outside and I stood on the threshold next to Devon and Ray, where I felt a draft coming through the house, going out the back door.

"He went down the stairs," Ray yelled, no longer clinging—actually pulling me outside now, but I resisted. "Come on," he said. With the back door open, the storm was so loud I could barely hear him, though he was standing right against me. I knew there was a concrete stoop out back, with four stairs leading left, toward the Gulf, where the storm surge would come from, I imagined.

I succumbed and stepped onto the back stoop, where we joined Devon at the wrought-iron railing. I'd expected wind to be gusting like hell, but the air was calm. We weren't even getting wet. I could've lit a lighter.

"Look at everything shake and move!" Ray yelled. "But it's so still here."

"Look at the trees bend," Devon shouted. "The rain's getting blown over the house, away from us. It's going sideways." I was relieved to have him with us again, doing things. I heard a tumbling bang, a thwack.

"Look at that metal go!" Ray yelled. "It looks like a candy wrapper."

There was no seawater in the backyard, Devon said, but it was rushing up the driveway, toward the garage, which was behind the house some and to the right of us, away from the Gulf. But it was lower than most of the yard. To the left of us, toward the Gulf, Devon could see water beyond the house next door—Mrs. Murphy's house.

Patrick rushed back past us and into the house. Stepping from the stable concrete stoop, I felt the wooden floor of the kitchen quiver. The house wouldn't stop shuddering. As I was closing the door, the wind slammed it shut, dampening the roar from outside. I inhaled.

"Mrs. Murphy!" Patrick said. "Stand inside your side door. The one on our side. When I get there and bang on it, you open it. You hear me? I'm bringing you here."

"I can't do it!" she yelled. "There's water coming. I got a bad hip." She was sobbing.

"Yes, you can, Mrs. Murphy. Do it for Ernie. You hear me?"

"Ernie's passed on," she said.

"That's what I mean!" Patrick growled and hung up. "Her house won't make it. It's tearing at the foundation."

I was standing bolt upright, biting my lip, clenching my fists. I realized Patrick could bluster all he wanted. None of us was in control. Not by a long shot.

"Okay," Patrick said, his voice curt, all business. "Call the Dexters and Old Man Hurley. Their phone numbers are in that drawer. No matter what they say, tell 'em to get ready. I'm gonna bang on their door, and I'm not waitin'. Tell 'em don't bring nothin'. And be quick about it. Call 'em before the lines go down."

"Why is this house better?" I said.

"We got two floors," he said. "We're a bit higher up. And they're on blocks. We got a better foundation."

"You want me to help?" Devon said.

He was offering to help Patrick, and I was afraid Patrick might say yes. Devon had chased a ball in a pool, maybe, but he couldn't really swim.

"I'll go!" I said, standing.

"Devon, you help with Mrs. Murphy. That'll get me over to the others sooner."

"He can't swim," I said.

"The hell I can't!" Devon said.

"The boy's a Cajun," Patrick said. "It's in his blood. And it's clear between here and the Murphys' anyway." Then he called, in a nicer tone but just as loud, "Isa, sweetie! Get in the kitchen and stay away from the windows." I didn't realize she'd left.

"Devon's not going!" I said. "I'll go. I can swim. Mrs. Murphy can be my eyes."

The back door opened, releasing a howling roar from outside. The floor shivered. Dishes and glassware rattled. We converged at the threshold.

"How come it's easy to open now?" Devon yelled.

"Because the pressure hasn't built up again," Patrick yelled.

"Look at Betsy," Ray shouted. "She's floating. She's gonna hit the garage door."

"Jesus!" Patrick shouted, before us on the landing.

"Fuck!" Devon yelled, out next to Patrick.

Ray and I stepped into the uncanny calm of the back stoop. "It's gone!" Ray said.

"Betsy's gone?" I yelled.

"The garage!" Ray said.

"The roof blew off," Devon shouted.

"It opened up like an orange peel."

"The whole thing's gone."

I listened, but I couldn't distinguish any difference in sound, just an all-out blasting roar. There were all kinds of whistles. The clash of something against our house. Smacks and pops from upwind. The storm shutters rattling. The moans of walls. But I couldn't hear the disintegration of a garage forty feet downwind.

"Jesus!" Patrick shouted again.

"That was fast," Devon yelled.

I thought of Mrs. Murphy's house, already pitching. What was going to happen to Devon as soon as he got out in this wind and water, with plywood flying? He wasn't going to make it back.

"That driveway is in a dip," Patrick said, as if he knew what I was thinking. "We got to get there and back before the surge comes." He was already at the bottom of the steps. "Go on back," he yelled at me. "There's no reason for all of us to be out here. Devon can bring her back while I go to the Dexters'."

I followed them down the steps anyway, holding to the wrought-iron railing, which felt flimsy suddenly. The ground was soggy, but there was no water flowing.

"I can do this," Devon shouted, ahead of me.

It occurred to me that this was what they wanted, this test of resolve as father and son. Moments before, Devon wouldn't even speak to his dad. Now he was walking into a category five hurricane, trying to save an old lady he didn't even know. And here was Patrick Landry rushing to save his parents' neighbors.

I let them go, the two of them. Standing at the bottom of the stairs, I listened to Patrick bark instructions: "Head down. Shoulders down. Face away from the wind. When we get past the corner, it's gonna sting like hell. If the surge comes, grip the ground with your feet. Arms out like this. If it takes you, you go with it. But that won't happen. I'll get you over there, and you get her back fast before the water comes."

That was all I could hear. It came to me that this was what Patrick had been after for months: Devon's attention and respect. He was teaching his son. Was Devon still wearing his grandfather's shirt? Then I wondered: Did Devon have a kitchen knife? Was that his plan, to go at Patrick in the storm?

When Ray and I came back inside, again the suction slammed the door shut—which meant air was leaking in somewhere in front. Ray found the phone list. As I sat at the table, I put the receiver against my ear, and he dialed the Dexters. My heart raced, my shoulders were tense, and my gut was unsteady.

"It's too late!" Mr. Dexter yelled on the phone. His voice was so loud I had to hold the receiver away. "Carlton's place is gone."

I took a deep breath. "You be ready when he knocks," I yelled.

"Ain't no way he can get upwind to us. Not across that street. It's gonna be a river. And we can't get the baby over there, not with Patrick, not with nobody."

There was a baby? "He's coming right now," I yelled. "If you have a life jacket, put it on." I hung up.

When I called Old Man Hurley, his phone just rang.

Isa screamed from out in the hallway, "Look at the water! It's coming in."

"Get in the kitchen," I yelled, but both Ray and I hurried along the wet hallway to where she stood at the bottom of the stairs. Rain and wind pummeled the front door and the outdoor siding. I didn't trust the door, which shuddered and jumped, but I bent down and felt water racing over the threshold and brought some to my mouth. "It's rainwater," I said, trying to sound calm. "It's not coming from the Gulf."

Ray and Isa found towels that we pressed against the threshold, but they got soaked immediately. Ray brought my hand beneath a windowsill, where water was flowing down the wall. Then he had me kneel down; water wasn't just leaking in beneath the baseboard but also spilling over the top of it like a spring.

"The pressure," I said.

A howling crash came from the Gulf side. Jesus, I thought, was that Mrs. Murphy's house?

We got Isa seated at the kitchen table, and then Ray and I opened the back door to look for Devon. "Here he comes," he shouted. "They're in our backyard, but there's water now."

Holding to the railing, I walked to the bottom of the steps and was surprised, somehow, at the water's warmth. Ray stayed behind me, a few steps up. The water swirled over my toes; we seemed to be on the lee side of the current as well as the wind. But every now and then a little swell would surge in, over my ankles, from a different direction, straight from the Gulf. It threw me off balance, surprising me with its power, coming and going like an agitator in a washing machine. I felt awkward in my sandals. I couldn't imagine what it must be like where Devon was, out in the wind. I held to the railing.

A current rushed in. Something heavy brushed my ankle and hit the wrought-iron railing, wedging against its base and ripping it out in one motion. I lost my balance, falling and splashing, losing my grip on the railing and flailing downcurrent, away from the house, shocked at the power of the flow, shallow as it was.

Ray screamed.

I took short breaths, panicking, until I could grip the ground with my fingers and dig in with my feet. I gathered my legs beneath me and stood against the current that rippled over my feet. If I'd had Charlie with me, I would have lost him. I realized I had to move fast to get back to the stairs before another surge came. Ray yelled to me as I stepped as quickly as I could without losing contact with the earth, back toward the concrete, where he grasped my outstretched hand. I yelled, "Get up;

get up the stairs!" But by then he was gripping my hand and wouldn't let go. With his other hand he was holding the railing, which, I realized when I got back to the stairs, was hanging loose. We stumbled up the concrete together, panting. If the water had been deeper, I would have been gone.

"Oh, my God!" Devon spluttered, behind me.

We hustled upstairs and into the house; the back door slammed shut behind us.

"Oh, my," a woman said in a breathy voice. "Oh, my."

As we sat Mrs. Murphy at the table, Devon began shouting, his voice excited: "It's crazy shit out there. The rain stings like bullets. The current's rushing one way, and the waves are coming another. And the wind. So fucking punk. I didn't think we were going to make it back." He paused to pant. "I got over there okay with Patrick except for the wind ripping and the crap blowing by. Jesus! There wasn't much water until the way back. Patrick took off for the Dexters'. He had to go past her place so he could cross the road with the current. God, it's fast. With every wave. On the road the water's rushing from the Gulf, but in the yard it's coming with the wind. And stuff is flying everywhere. I saw a barbecue skip across the water. A stroller almost took off my head. Where does this shit come from?"

"You did a great job," I yelled. We had to shout now to be heard in the same room, even with the door closed.

"She wouldn't come at first, so that took a while. And the water was rising. The deepest part was right by her steps, almost to my calves. We lost it right off, both of us, but I had a good grip on her, and we got to a higher spot. You okay?"

"This boy saved my life," Mrs. Murphy shouted. "If *any* of us live."

"Then the water started coming across our lawn too. What a fucking rager."

"How deep is the water at the street?" I yelled.

"I don't know!" Devon yelled. "He's not gonna make it."

"My house was going," Mrs. Murphy shouted. "The windows popped one after the other."

A banging started out front, wood against wood. Rapid. Erratic. A broken shutter maybe. A tree branch. A loose piece of siding.

"Where's Isa?" Devon yelled.

"Isa!" I called, running up the hallway with Devon; I lost track of Ray. The banging was coming from the living room.

"Isa, get away from there!" Devon yelled. Glass shattered with a loud pop. I ducked instinctively. The wind raged inside the house, swirling and battering everything in the living room that wasn't tied down. Paper flew. Objects banged on the floor and rolled. The pressure in my ears sharpened again. Something struck my shoulder, flew on. The house groaned and creaked, trembled and pitched, rattling. Brine filled my nostrils and the back of my throat. The storm was taking over, I thought, one room at a time. I heard rain pelting inside now. I thought of the grandfather clock—still ticking, no doubt. The photos we'd carried upstairs. The trinkets. Two bathtubs of water upstairs. The generator gone from the garage. Canned food in the pantry. My note-taker in the closet in the back room upstairs. The casket in the master bedroom. Jesus, I thought, we should've left the casket outside.

Devon gathered Isa, and we all stumbled downwind, Ray next to me now, into the kitchen, where we sat at the table breathing hard. In the sea-salt turbulence, I couldn't smell Isa's perfume.

"It was the big window," Devon said in a voice I barely heard. "It's raining on the piano."

That seemed almost quaint, rain on a piano. I felt his bare arm; he had taken off his grandfather's shirt.

"We should go upstairs," Mrs. Murphy yelled.

The phone rang, but it didn't surprise me this time; it didn't seem as loud as before. I felt for it, picked it up. "Hello!" I yelled.

"Hurley here! Did they make it? Are they there? I don't think they made it. Last I saw, they went down."

"Patrick?"

"Yeah, and the others. Big piece of siding just about tore him in two."

"Devon, look outside," I yelled. "See if he's coming."

"I can't open the door," Devon yelled.

"They'll make it!" I said to Hurley. "He's coming for you next. Get by your door and open it when he knocks."

"Me?" he yelled. "I ain't goin' nowhere." He hung up.

"They've got a baby," Mrs. Murphy yelled. "He can't make it with a baby."

"A baby!" Isa shouted. "What's a baby doing in a hurricane?"

"The current's coming with them," I shouted. "He got over there, so he'll get back."

"We can't open the door," Devon yelled again.

"You got to open a window on this back side," Mrs. Murphy yelled. "With all that wind coming in the front, the pressure'll blow off your roof."

So Devon and I struggled with a kitchen window, with Ray helping too. It had opened easily the day before when I was latching the shutters, but now it wouldn't budge. On the count of three, we slammed upward with the butt of our palms on the wooden frame. The window slid up an inch, allowing wind to screech through. We slammed upward again, driving the window up a foot. The wind howled, the shutters blew open, and things all over the kitchen erupted in mayhem, flying and flapping about the room as the shutters beat against the outside of the house.

Isa screamed.

"There's Patrick!" Devon shouted.

I had to hold on to the wall, things were so unsteady.

"We should get upstairs," Mrs. Murphy yelled again.

I pulled on the back door as someone pushed from the other side, making it fly open suddenly, the wind flashing through that opening too.

"Come on," Patrick yelled. "Get in."

Somebody was sobbing and gasping—it sounded like a young girl—and a baby was squawking as fast as it could fill its lungs.

"I thought we were goners," a man shouted.

A woman was sobbing. The shutters seemed to be hammering the inside of my skull.

After we got everybody inside, the door slammed shut with a boom, making the wind cavort about the room and scream through the open window.

"Those shutters almost hit me," Patrick said. "What the hell!"

"Living room window got bashed in," I shouted. "We had to relieve the pressure."

"I didn't think I was gonna make it over there," Patrick yelled, panting. "All kinds of things were flying. There's wires down over by Hurley. The surge is gushing. No way I could make it there now."

"You okay?" I said. "Did you get hit?" I put a hand on the others, counting: Mr. and Mrs. Dexter and a girl huddled around a baby who wailed in her arms.

"You put a baby through this!" Isa screamed. "Why didn't you get out? You don't deserve a baby." Isa's body brushed mine as she came at the girl.

"Get away from me!" the girl screamed. "Get away!"

"Stop it, you!" Mr. Dexter shouted.

Ray was suddenly against me.

"I just wanted to see," Isa yelled as Patrick pulled her away. "I just wanted to see the baby."

Nobody said a word. I held Ray against my side. We all stood there, recuperating.

"Hurley called," I told Patrick. "He doesn't want you there."

"You're blind," Mr. Dexter yelled.

"Stay here!" Isa shrieked. "Don't go out there again."

"Get on upstairs," Patrick shouted. "Everybody. I'm just gonna look outside. I'll be right back. Devon, help me get out the back door."

"That's just like you," Isa yelled. "Going out there in this."

Ray led the Dexters up the hallway, and I followed with Mrs. Murphy, holding her arm with one hand, guiding her, and feeling along the wall with my other hand, trying to steady myself. It was difficult to walk up the hallway; that was how hard the wind was driving through the house. We splashed in a thin layer of water all the way. As my hand dragged along the wall, I hit a picture frame, and it flew off in a flash behind me.

"Isa!" I said. "Did that hit you?" I didn't know where she was.

"She's over there again," Ray yelled from up the stairs.

"It's judgment!" Isa shouted from the living room. "It's wrath!"

"Isa, get out of there!" I said.

The baby blubbered from the stairwell. I made sure Mrs. Murphy's hand was on the banister and that she'd taken the first step up. Then I turned toward the living room, the wind in my face. I leaned forward but still got pushed back and sideways for every step I took, faltering like a drunk, reaching for Isa.

A big hand came on my back—Devon's—and pushed me forward, into Isa, where I grabbed her and pulled her back, all three of us hurtling downwind back toward the stairs, stumbling and then scrambling up to the second floor. Upstairs the wind inside wasn't so ruthless, though it was loud and turbulent. We got everybody into the back room across the hallway from the master bedroom, the room where Ray and I had slept that was away from the Gulf.

"She's not gonna hold," the girl said, her voice high-pitched and trembling. "What are we gonna do?" Her baby squawked and cried.

"We don't need that kind of talk," Mrs. Murphy said. "Give us hope, Lord. Give us hope."

"There, there," Mrs. Dexter said, trying to soothe her daughter and granddaughter both.

"What was that bang?" the girl said, rushing her words together in a panic. "Did you hear that?" Her voice was disturbing. "I can't take them noises! Kelly's scared."

"Kelly's too little to get scared," Mr. Dexter said.

"Stop it!" Mrs. Murphy said. "All of you. Let's sing a song." She hummed first and began, as if she were used to this. Isa joined in:

> "*Nearer, my God, to Thee, nearer to Thee,*
> *E'en though it be a cross that raiseth me;*
> *Still all my song shall be nearer, My God, to Thee . . .*"

I opened the door, and the boys and I escaped to the stairs.

"Did you see their eyes?" Ray said.

"White people are scary," Devon said.

The three of us struggled back down to the kitchen, where we turned the corner and leaned our backs against the wall.

"It's hot!" Devon said. "What time you think it is?"

I realized I was sweating. "No idea."

"That says five-forty," Ray said.

"That's when the electricity went out," I said.

I was exhausted from the tension, the adrenaline, and the shuddering instability. It got so every bracing of the structure, every moan of the wind, every slam against the siding made me hold my breath. Then I'd gulp and breathe.

"You think he'll make it back?" Ray yelled.

He'll make it, I thought. He's Patrick. But I didn't say that.

"This doesn't change anything!" Devon said.

It took me a moment to realize what he was saying. "Well, there's plenty of witnesses now, that's for sure," I yelled. "You're in Mississippi. You're black. He just saved all these people. You'll go to the chair."

I let that sink in.

"You said you'd run away with me," Ray said, his voice pleading, not frantic. "You said we'd run away."

Devon didn't say anything, and as we stood waiting, I wasn't sure I wanted Patrick to come back. After maybe half a minute, Devon walked around me and hugged Ray, of all things. I squeezed them both.

The back door opened, startling me with the roar from outside. I didn't think it could get louder than the noises already coming through the open window. The three of us broke apart. Then the door slammed shut.

"I'm wiped out," Patrick yelled.

"Where's Hurley?" I shouted.

"Too late! His house is gone. I saw it bust up."

I thought about what that meant. His house had split apart around him.

"I couldn't get there anyway. Water's too deep now. I got stranded in our yard. I didn't think I was going to make it back. I got swept down but got to the lee side of the house, where the current was swirling." He said the water was almost a foot at the back step, with waves coming higher than that.

Jesus, I thought. I'd gotten knocked over with the water barely over my ankles.

"If Mrs. Murphy had called five minutes later," Patrick yelled, "I never would've made it to the Dexters'."

The telephone rang. Old Man Hurley, I thought. Patrick answered it, and a woman screamed. She shrieked and screeched. "The water!" was all I could make out. "The water!" And more screams. It made my stomach turn.

Patrick hung up.

"You know who that was?" I yelled.

"No," Patrick said. "But we're higher up than a lot of people."

"You did great," I shouted, "getting those people here."

There was a shuddering crack out front. The house lurched with a series of crunches. A persistent trembling changed to a series of thuds that I felt in my legs and dreaded in my stomach.

"That oak's over three hundred years old," Patrick shouted.

Just when you think that's it, that you've been through the worst. Just when you think it's peaking. Here comes more.

"What time is it?" I shouted.

"It's early," Patrick yelled.

We sloshed up the hallway. "This is just rainwater," Patrick shouted from ahead. "The surge won't come over the porch. It won't get that high."

We paused at the bottom of the stairs as Patrick checked out the living room, where wind and rain were blasting through the broken picture window. Ray said that the oak out front was down, and a huge limb was beating against the front porch. It felt like a large boat battering a small dock; we were the dock.

At the upper landing, I heard singing from the back room as we turned and hurried into the sitting room, above the living room. One at a time, Patrick and the kids tried to peek between slats in a storm shutter, but we were all pretty much blind with the shutters closed. Each time the oak limb rammed us, the foundation grumbled and the walls complained—until finally there was a wrenching of wood and a shuddering thump. The sitting room staggered. Someone tugged my arm. We ran back as the floor shifted and sank. Window glass exploded. The hurricane rushed in, assaulting us. Papers and books and pictures and wood flew everywhere about us and into the hallway. I got hit in the knee by something. I covered my head. We hovered in the hallway as the sitting room grumbled in a long, whining screech. Were the shutters gone? Were the walls still there?

"What's going on?" I yelled.

"She's sagging, but she's holding," Patrick shouted. "The windows are busted. The Sheetrock's cracked to hell. The corner post must be down."

There were mutterings behind us; I think people came out of the bedroom and retreated back into it. We tried to slide the sitting room door closed, but the frame was so warped that the big oak door wouldn't budge in its grooves.

"Why didn't you tell me you were back?" Isa screamed, behind us. "I thought you were dead."

I couldn't tell if she was hitting Patrick or if they were hugging each other, or both. "Of course I'm back," Patrick said. "As long as the foundation holds, we'll be all right."

That didn't sound promising just then.

"You think this is all right?" Isa yelled, breaking away. "The things we've done. The things we should've done but didn't. Now it's all coming back. There's even a baby. How could that girl put a baby through this?"

"Sweetie, we'll make it," Patrick shouted. "I went through Camille when I was two." They went into the middle room, the one where they'd slept, and closed the door.

From the stairwell, Devon yelled that the water was rising. He said the waves were cresting the porch.

I don't know how long the three of us sat on the upper stairs, where the wind wasn't too bad and where Devon and Ray could watch the water rising a step at a time up the stairwell. The storm surge had crested not only the porch, they said, but also the sill of the living room window, where the sea had poured in and now rolled and sloshed however it wanted, knowing its own level—which for the time being was the sixth step, about four feet, roughly a third of the way up.

The boys were sitting side by side a couple of steps below me. For a while I'd noticed a steady drip hitting my thigh.

"The roof's leaking," Devon said.

I was drained already; how much longer could the forces come? I'd once been in a small trembler, but at least it had been fast. Nothing like this. "We're going to make it," I said, reaching down and squeezing the back of the boys' necks so that they both scrunched their shoulders and leaned away. Something walloped the front of the house, and the structure shifted, screeching.

"How much can the house take?" Devon yelled.

"The front porch is gone," Patrick shouted, suddenly there.

Nobody spoke as we thought about that.

"She's not half over," Patrick said. "The eye hasn't passed us yet, since the wind's not coming straight from the Gulf."

Jesus, I thought, after all he'd done, saving all those people, why not give the kids some hope? The muscles of my jaw felt sore, they had been tense so long. My forearms ached from clenching my hands into fists.

Suddenly Patrick sat next to me on the stairs, almost touching. He told me gruffly that Isa was pacing back and forth, breathing too rapidly, and wouldn't stop talking. She couldn't settle herself down. She wouldn't listen to anything he said. She would come around, he said, but for now he didn't know what to do.

I figured he wanted me to go in and calm her, but he couldn't bring himself to ask. I wouldn't have done it anyway; the kids were my focus. I wanted to yell, What did you think would happen? She said she hated hurricanes. You knew what condition she was in.

I held my tongue.

Another window exploded in the sitting room. The house groaned, trembling. The freight train just kept coming.

Patrick stood. "Come on," he said. "I want to show you guys something out back. Just in case."

I wasn't sure I wanted to know, but I clung to Devon and Ray. As we followed him into the master bedroom and across to the French doors leading out to the back porch, I didn't want to let the kids out of my grip. With the force of the storm coming more from the Gulf, the shutters were drunken pirates now. The furniture was laughing at us, yet the walls barked from the pain of the sagging front corner of the house.

As Patrick fiddled with the doors, Devon pulled his elbow from my grasp; then the casket clasps clicked open one after the other, a few steps away from me.

"There," Devon said.

"That's better," Patrick said. "Thanks."

Pin lights. Now they could see.

Then I heard Devon walk across the room, and I panicked, thinking about the kitchen knife I'd left in the drawer. Had he seen me place it there? Or was there a gun in the casket? My heart raced. I tugged on Ray's elbow. "Did he get something from the casket? Is he getting something out of a drawer?"

Then Devon was back beside me.

"It's okay," Ray said. "He's just standing here."

Suddenly the storm's snarl entered the room, and the shutters over the doorway began to beat against the outside of the house. "Jesus," Patrick yelled. "There's nothin' standing for two blocks."

Again we converged on a threshold behind Patrick. I checked Devon's hands, and he was clean. The shutters stopped banging the wall outside; I assumed Patrick had secured them.

"Look at that," Ray yelled. "It's a boat."

"Oh, my God," Devon shouted. "Look at all the water."

"Look at that pelican," Ray yelled. "Just floating there."

"*That's* what they do," Patrick yelled, surprised. "They hang out on the lee side of buildings."

He pulled us out onto the porch, sliding us along the back wall of the house, Devon first, followed by me and Ray. The backside of the structure wasn't so calm anymore; the storm hurled itself around the corner nearest the Gulf, whipping pellets of rain onto the porch, mostly in front of us but also blustering against us some, though not with its full impact. With my back against the wall, I could feel the porch floor shudder to a different rhythm than the house. I wasn't sure of the size of the balcony—how many paces to the edge?—and I didn't trust the railing, particularly after getting swept off the stoop downstairs.

I tried to push away the fear that Patrick might grab me and hurl me off the porch, for what I'd done with Isa.

Something ripped into the Gulf side of the house and banged into the porch struts on the corner, cracking wood. The floor lurched, making me grit my teeth and clamp my muscles yet again.

"Jesus!" Devon shouted.

"What was that?" I yelled.

"Siding," Patrick yelled. "It broke that post. Look at the ceiling waver." He was somewhere out on the porch, in the deluge along the railing, I imagined. "Listen!" Patrick barked. "This is the place. If something happens and the house is about to go, come out here and jump. The water's plenty deep. You hear me?"

No one responded. We should get back inside, I thought.

"Say!" he shouted. "You hear?"

"Okay!" Ray said bravely.

I squeezed Ray's hand on one side and Devon's lanky forearm on the other. I remembered Devon making bubbles in the Texas creek; no way we could survive this torrent.

Then I thought about the pelican, floating in a becalmed spot.

"If the water rises, no matter what, never go in the attic," Patrick shouted. "There's no way out of there. Come out here instead. It's not far down to the water. When you're in the current, float on your back, keep your feet in front and go where it takes you. Look for the lee side of something to protect you."

Right, I thought, like I could see anything.

"The worst," he shouted, "are trees and chain-link fences. Don't get caught under a tree limb or against a fence. If you come at a fence, get your feet up against it and climb. Don't get caught sideways."

"I could push him over," Devon said in my ear, "but the bastard would probably live." I pulled on Devon's forearm, trying to make a point. He jerked his arm away.

"Ray!" Patrick yelled, still in front of us. "You're a strong swimmer. Don't try to fight the current. Go with it and keep your feet in front of you. Devon! You're a swimmer, goddamn it. You're a survivor. You got it in your blood. But you jump with me. I'll get behind you, and we'll float together. You got to trust, boy! Trust the water. Kevin, you go with Isa. Get behind her and keep her up. She'll be your eyes."

What was it about Isa I couldn't escape?

I'd had enough of this porch. I pulled Devon and pushed Ray back through the doorway, where the wind was raging from inside the house. As we stepped into the bedroom with Patrick behind us, Isa screeched from only a few feet away, "Do you love me, Patrick? Do you love me? Or do you love this cocaine?"

Patrick didn't have time to say a word.

The kids and I were mostly out of the doorway by then, but the powder swirled over us too. We coughed. My eye sockets stung. I tasted the bitter numbness on my tongue, and I admit I wanted more. I worried that she'd already snorted some, but Devon told me later: there was no glass, no mirror, no rolled-up dollar bill. Just the plastic bag that she ripped open, shook, and threw into the gust, covering Patrick with white powder—his hair especially.

The kids seemed to be all right. Devon laughed at the sight of Patrick, though at the time I didn't know why.

I thought Patrick would explode, but I don't think he even moved.

"Devon," Isa shouted, "the casket."

Devon said later that she hadn't set him up to do it. He moved quickly because it was what he wanted to do; it just came naturally. The coffin lid slammed shut. The clasps clicked in unison. There was no struggle, no fight. Once the coke was gone, Patrick's investment lost to the wind, what did the coffin matter? Later Ray told me that Patrick stood aside as they lifted it, Devon on one end, Isa on the other. They hefted it out the door, where it slipped from Isa's grip and landed with a bang that I barely heard in the storm. Devon came around to the back next to Isa and helped her shove the casket into the porch railing, near where the siding had taken out the post. The railing yielded but didn't give. Unprotected from the storm, blistered by the rain, they shoved the casket again. And again. Until it busted through the railing and launched into the Gulf.

I didn't know the particulars at the time, though I guessed that the casket was gone as Ray and I stood on the threshold facing outside and Patrick pushed between us from behind, going out onto the porch.

"Leave them alone!" I shouted. "What's done is done."

"Not yet it ain't," Patrick barked.

Ray squeezed my hand and told me in a voice I barely heard, "Patrick's got the shotgun."

Everything happened even faster after that. The storm dropped away for me. It wasn't the eye; there was no calm. I stepped into the smack of the rain and the wrath of the wind, but I didn't notice the weather.

"Here!" Patrick called. "It's loaded. The safety's off. Fuck up your life. This is your chance. I've been a bastard to you all along. I've got it coming."

"I don't care how many people you saved," Devon yelled, his voice frantic. "You didn't save me."

They were out by the railing somewhere, Patrick over to my right, Devon to my left. Where was Isa? I didn't know. I imagined Patrick staring up the barrel at the son he'd abandoned yet started to raise and Devon staring downbarrel at his deadbeat dad—in this house of all places, outside the master bedroom.

I didn't want to be a blind witness. Or a blundering contender. Hadn't I been enough of both? I stepped out among them, my arms outstretched, my hands lifted, hoping I was between Devon and Patrick. I'm afraid I was off by a yard or so.

"I loved you!" Isa screamed. Her voice came from along the railing. She stepped through the torn balustrade at the same place where the casket had gone through—but I didn't know. I couldn't hear the splash.

Patrick yelled, "Isa!" Then he shouted to Devon, "Last chance!"

A loud blast exploded from upwind, and I ducked instinctively. All my muscles contracted. But it was not the gun; the boom came from too far away.

Next moment Patrick was gone—though I didn't know that either until Ray ran out next to me and shouted, "There's Isa! Patrick's swimming after her."

As awareness came to me, I felt the rain stinging my arms, legs, and face like pellets. The gusts made me stagger. My chest throbbed where

Patrick had hit me yesterday. But I leaned upwind and searched with my arms outstretched until I came to Devon not far from the doorway, where he stood frozen, with the shotgun leveled. I pushed the barrel up and away, taking the gun from him. I felt for the safety and flipped it: on or off, I wasn't sure.

"They drifted that way," Ray shouted. "The same way as the coffin."

Devon collapsed on the threshold. "Another second and I would've shot him," he sobbed.

"No!" I yelled. "You had the chance. You stopped yourself."

"Did you shoot somebody?" Mr. Dexter called from the doorway.

I was the one holding the gun. "Nobody shot anybody," I yelled.

"Then what was that bang? What's that gun for?"

I turned away from him, toward the storm. "Come in, Ray. He'll catch her."

"Who?" Mr. Dexter said.

"Patrick!" I shouted.

"You shot Patrick?" he yelled. "He saved our lives."

FOURTEEN

Gradually Ray and I tugged Devon away from the threshold, into the room, and up against the bed as the storm blustered through the house and out the back door, whipping my hair. I handed the shotgun to Mr. Dexter and asked him to check the safety. Outside, the furnace roared. A crack sounded nearby. Then a foghorn, of all things, forlorn. Inside, shutters thrashed and Mr. Dexter threw out questions that blew away. After he finally gave up, the three of us huddled on the floor against the bed for a long time without speaking, our arms around each other. The loss of Isa and Patrick made me feel empty rather than sad, as if a piece of me were gone. I wondered how it had come to this, the three of us now. How long had we been talking about running? Yet we had stayed and they had drifted off.

Eventually we shuffled across the hall to the bedroom downwind of the storm, where everyone else was sitting and lying about. Before long Devon and Ray had to explain to them what had happened: Isa had jumped first, and Patrick had jumped to save her. I provided some context, saying Patrick and Isa had been arguing. But they were obsessed with the gun: Had I shot anybody or not? Could I even see?

"Sounded like a gunshot to me," the girl squealed.

Devon spoke: "I was the one with the gun. I was pointing it at Patrick when she jumped. And then Patrick jumped to save her. If I wasn't a chickenshit, I would've shot the bastard."

"What the hell for?" Mr. Dexter demanded.

"I found out he's my father," Devon said. "My real father." He emphasized the word "real."

No one spoke for a moment.

"You ought to be proud of that, son. He's a hero. He saved our lives."

"But you're black," the girl blurted.

They didn't ask any more questions, but I'm not sure they were convinced.

The wind came on full from the Gulf for about half an hour, which meant the eye was making landfall west of us, Mr. Dexter said. Eye. Aye. I. The wind blasted and howled, but there weren't so many bangs and booms from outside to unnerve us.

After a while, Katrina began to pummel the back of the house, which made the shutters clatter along that side, so we all moved up the hallway to the front bedroom, across from the sitting room, where everything was sticky and hot. I huddled with the kids next to the bed, and for a while I slept, lying curled on the floor. I woke as the wind began to abate. We opened a window and shutter on the front, which was downwind now, and the others looked out.

"Your upper porch is gone," Mr. Dexter said, as if this house were ours. "Oh, my God. My house is gone."

"There's nothing," Mrs. Murphy said. "Look! Nothing between us and the Gulf."

"The water's going down," Devon said.

Mr. Dexter sat on the bed and cried.

"Who cares about that old house?" Mrs. Dexter said. "Thank God Cathy and the baby are alive. Thank God we're all alive."

The wind was still kicking the back of the house, but not so loudly anymore, so Devon, Ray, and I walked downstairs into water that was still three feet deep—the height of the windowsills in the living room. We tugged on the front door, and when it came open, the water rushed out through oak limbs that were piled up against the doorway. Once the water had drained, we tried to push our way out the front but couldn't get through. The door wouldn't close either; it wouldn't fit back in the jamb. We stayed away from the living room, where the house sagged.

By early afternoon, we could walk out the back door, and the boys and I went off looking for Isa and Patrick in the direction Ray had seen them drift. The water had receded, like a tide that had completed its cycle. Heat hung like a vapor, penetrating deep. We searched, calling their names, but could hardly make headway through the morass. Charlie was little help since there were no clear pathways; battered tree limbs and broken structures were scattered everywhere. I held to Ray's elbow, but I walloped my head on a limb as I stooped to crawl over a fallen trunk. The neighborhood had disappeared, leaving concrete slabs and front stairs. Wires were down. Ray stepped me up six stairs that led to nothing. There were few trees left in the whole neighborhood, he said, and the ones that were standing had no leaves. They described mattresses, couches, and washing machines stuck ten feet high, caught in branches. Ray said cars and trucks looked like carcasses in mud. The swelter intensified by midafternoon. Without any shade, we sweated standing still.

We came across several men looking through wreckage. When we asked about Patrick and Isa, they said they'd seen the body of a man over through those trees.

Devon found it and tried to get Ray not to look, but he insisted, which sent a pang through me: before the trip he would have shied away from such things. Or maybe I hadn't really known him then.

"It's not Patrick," Devon said. "He's too old."

Maybe Old Man Hurley.

"That's gross," Ray said. We walked away, and then he had to lean over and vomit. After we walked farther, he said, "He was bent over backward on a limb with his arm twisted in the socket."

I didn't need to hear that.

We talked to two couples from up the street. "The Landry boy?" a man said. "He was a black sheep there, weren't he?"

"He's not dead," I said. "Don't talk like he's dead."

"You all got a gun?" the man said. "You're gonna need a gun if you got supplies."

"We got a shotgun back at the house," Devon said proudly. "Twelve gauge."

"How'd you get that shiner?" the man said.

I did a lot of sitting that day while Devon and Ray searched through and around debris. After a while Ray would come back and get me, bringing me through an intricate maze. As he wandered off again with Devon, I'd sit with Charlie, passing him from one hand to the other, feeling the dents where I'd bent him in El Paso, and exploring the ground through his touch. It felt good to touch things that were anchored to the earth, even tree stumps and posts. I suppose I was in shock. I felt nauseous, listless. Shards of ideas streamed through my head, yet I couldn't hold a thought. I was glad I hadn't stayed in El

Paso—the kids needed me. But how would we get to Pensacola? Should we still go there? I tested the thought of visiting Natalie—but on what pretext? She hadn't even called me back. Try as I might to block it out, my mind kept returning to Isa and Patrick half submerged, their faces underwater. I imagined the feel of the old man's twisted corpse on a branch. I tried to focus on breathing.

Late in the afternoon, I stood up and shook my legs in the blazing sun, missing my hat. My throat was parched. When I licked my lips, I realized they were burned. I worried about sunscreen; did we have any in the house? In the silence, the storm's roar lingered in my head; I was shocked suddenly by the quiet. There were no fretting crickets. No belching frogs. No flies buzzing. Not a single bug. And no chirps from birds. I remembered what Patrick had said about house sparrows and turkeys—how they hang around and die. And I remembered the pelican in the storm, sheltered on the lee side of our house. I felt the sore spot on my chest where Patrick had hit me. I imagined the handmade casket floating empty in the tempest, with so many people drowned. Who knew, maybe the coffin had helped Patrick and Isa stay afloat. A man's voice drifted from somewhere off to my right. I sat down again. How many people had Patrick saved? Five, including a baby. But six if he'd saved Isa too. Seven if you counted himself.

Isa's words from the morning bored in to me—that I hadn't loved her. How could she say that? I'd always loved her back then, from the moment she'd let me touch her. It was she who didn't love me. Yet that was what she had said when she jumped: "I loved you." Who was she speaking to, Patrick or me? If I'd fought for her years ago, could I have won her? Or was she just saying that after she'd lost me? I shivered in the heat. I stood up, sat back down.

I wanted them both to walk up. I wanted to hear his gruff voice.

We never found Betsy.

From news accounts over the next week, we learned that the eye passed about thirty miles west of us, making landfall near the Mississippi-Louisiana border. The tidal surge in our part of Biloxi was twenty-two feet high. The Landry house was about twelve to fourteen feet higher than the Gulf, which meant we had eight to ten feet of water in the yard. On our block, our house was the closest one to the Gulf that was still standing, though it was barely intact. The front corner nearest the Gulf sagged; the windows there were smashed upstairs and down. The two-story front porch was gone, just ripped off.

"It's a miracle the whole roof didn't go with it," Mr. Dexter said.

The back porch was hanging, its underpinnings gone.

Since oak limbs were wedged up against the front, we continued to use the back door but had to beware the broken struts from the porch overhead. We had flashlights, candles, jugs of water, and two bathtubs full of water. We had the food Patrick had prepared and stuck in the refrigerator, which had somehow stayed closed during the storm. There were cans of food strewn all about the house. Everything from the garage was gone, including the generator. The phone didn't work, and neither did Mr. Dexter's cell. I had two twenties in my wallet. The three of us had our suitcases of clothes. We didn't find any money in Patrick's and Isa's bags, or anywhere in the house, though Devon searched all that evening.

That night after dinner, when the Dexters and Mrs. Murphy got into the whiskey cabinet, I almost succumbed. It was the hardest two hours of sobriety I'd ever faced. I retreated upstairs with the kids, where they got sweaty wrestling on the bed and then came over and tickled me—gently at first, and then like they meant it—until I let go and laughed and rolled around on the bed too. Downstairs, Mr. Dexter started to rant about what a hero Patrick was. The hero of the neighborhood! The hero of Biloxi, goddamn it! Mrs. Murphy started wailing about her son, Rusty, who would be down from Hattiesburg first thing tomorrow. Lying on our backs on the bed upstairs, panting from the wrestling, we let the storm blow downstairs.

We drew water from the bathtub to brush our teeth. We wanted to sleep in the same room, so the kids got the bed and gathered some cushions from a couch for me. I rubbed Devon's back first so Ray wouldn't stop me from rubbing his. When I massaged Ray's back, tracing the scar behind his left ear, I realized I was already beginning to miss them. How much longer would we be together?

Ray asked if Isa had jumped because she wanted to die or because she was afraid the house was falling. I thought about it for a little while and told him she was afraid, but it wasn't just about the house. She was upset with Patrick. And she was disappointed in herself too, for bringing us into the hurricane. "She felt bad about that. Plus, I think she wanted him to save her—to show he loved her after he'd done so many things she didn't like."

"No," Devon said. "She was doing the same thing you were doing: trying to stop me from shooting him."

I had thought about that, but I didn't want to say it because I didn't want Devon to blame himself for what she had done.

"So why did she say, 'I love you'?" Ray asked.

I told him that wasn't what I'd heard. "I thought she said, 'I loved you.'"

But Devon agreed with Ray. "She was telling us she loves us," Devon said.

I wondered why I'd heard it my way and they'd heard it theirs. Then it occurred to me that maybe she wasn't talking to any of us. Maybe she was speaking to Jasmine. "Which way was she looking when she said that?" I asked. "Was she looking at us or at the water or what?"

"She was looking at us," Ray said.

I nodded. "Remember what Patrick told us, how to float and go with the current?" I said. "They're going to live."

"So you don't know why she jumped," Ray said.

The next day, Tuesday, felt hotter than Monday, with more humidity. We had no electricity, gas, or running water. No phones. No extra water to flush the toilets. We didn't wash our dishes, just wiped them as clean as we could. Our world was stagnant.

That afternoon we wandered along Howard Avenue, a major east-west thoroughfare, where groups of people gathered on stoops and porches, listening to radios. We asked about Patrick and Isa, but after a while we stopped; there were too many stories about dead bodies and people missing. We had to walk in the middle of the road, where a trail meandered through debris. Everywhere, Ray said, houses and store-fronts were collapsed or bashed in—either by Katrina or by people; sometimes he couldn't tell which.

A group cooking on a barbecue told us New Orleans was gone, flooded. We couldn't quite imagine what that meant.

"I mean rows and rows of people settin' on roofs with everything underwater. That's what I'm talkin' about."

"Look at this! You think this is different? Why don't they say nothin' 'bout us."

"Water's gone here."

"Damn wind."

"Wind didn't do shit."

"Was the water over to New Orleans."

"Them levees."

"Are you blind? You went through that shit blind?"

"You are one brave turkey."

I remembered that I wasn't wearing my glasses. I didn't miss them. "That's the last hurricane I hope I never see," I said.

People laughed. "You got that right," a woman said.

"They're down at the convention center waitin', just like us."

"Who are?" I said.

"Poor people."

"Say it's a war zone on the radio."

"They're sendin' in troops."

"That's why I got a shotgun."

I wondered if the man showed his gun. I expected Devon to talk about the twelve gauge we had back at the house, but he didn't. Mr. Dexter had stashed it somewhere, and Devon hadn't even badgered him about it.

We found a store broken into, so we went in; the shelves were in shambles, with everything piled about the floor, most of it wet. Devon found some diapers for the baby but no bottled water or food. We were thankful for the full bathtubs we had.

That night death and sewage started to putrefy, bringing vile stenches. Yet I slept better than the night before. The next morning, we found mosquito larvae in our bathtub.

After breakfast we decided we'd had enough of Biloxi—Devon, Ray, Mrs. Murphy, and I. The Dexters decided to stay. They kept the family shotgun, and Devon didn't complain. Mrs. Murphy wouldn't fit into Mrs. Landry's slim outfits, so she had to wear some of Isa's clothes, which struck me as funny: there was a different swish with Isa's provocative clothing on Mrs. Murphy. We walked toward Howard Avenue carrying suitcases and two plastic gallons of water, hoping to get a ride to some shelter, some way to get out. By then a few vehicles were coming through Howard Avenue—bulldozers, camera crews, photographers, and reporters. It was a dismal, depressing day. By afternoon the flies were back from somewhere; I don't know how. The streets stank of infection and raw sewage. Rotten eggs. Mildew. We heard the president was coming, but I don't know if that happened. You don't expect to be the ones on television clips, standing around waiting for handouts, but there we were, desolate, sticky, our hair matted, not having showered for days. Devon, Ray, and I were the lucky ones: we didn't live here; we hadn't lost our homes.

People who had food were running out of water. People without food were getting desperate. There was almost no shade. Two aid workers came through and passed out MREs: meals ready to eat. We tried to tell them about Patrick and Isa, but they weren't gathering that information, the woman said kindly. When we asked for a ride to a shelter, she said there'd be buses, though she didn't know when. Her truck didn't have nearly enough water to go around, and people got upset and rocked it, yelling. She and her driver had to lock the doors and drive off. A couple hours later, we were by ourselves along a side road, talking about trudging all the way back to the house, worrying about whether Mrs. Murphy could make it, when a newspaper reporter stopped to ask directions and gave us a ride because Mrs. Murphy knew her way around. We tried to tell him our story, but he cut us short; he had more stories than he could publish, he said. He was exhausted and had to get some sleep. On the way to I-10, he took us to a shelter inland from Biloxi. Riding in his car and feeling the coolness of the air conditioning, we felt blessed to get out, not just from the hurricane but from the desperation.

As soon as we stepped into the shelter—a high school gym—the odor of too many people in an unventilated space overtook me: stale sweat and old food and sickness, with a waft of urine. I'd been homeless before, but this was the first time I'd been a refugee, and there was something hopeless in the coughs and mutterings of people and the shuffles of feet across the floor. I don't know what the place looked like, but Mrs. Murphy broke down immediately, crying and calling out for Rusty, as if she'd expected him to be waiting on the front step. "I've lost my home," she sobbed. "I've lost everything. And he's not here."

I sat with her on the bleachers, holding her, as the kids searched for Patrick and Isa. Devon tried to report them missing, but the volunteers were too overwhelmed to track all that and feed everybody too. Notes and names were posted along a wall that Ray read through. There was no electricity, but two old-style phones were working. Devon called Alexis's number after I waited in line for almost an hour; it was the only number we had. He got excited talking to her, telling how he'd gone out in the hurricane and saved a lady next door.

When I got on the phone, Robert demanded to know what the hell we were doing in Biloxi. Were we trying to kill the old man with worry? I told him Isa had fallen off the back porch in the hurricane—I couldn't bring myself to say "jumped" on the phone. I said Patrick had jumped in after her to save her. They had both been swept away in the storm surge, and we hadn't been able to find them.

After a silence, he blurted, "That's just like her. She'll show up. You think she won't. But you don't know her. She always turns up." He said he'd come get us in the morning; it didn't make sense to drive out there twice, once for us and again for her. "I'm sure she'll be there by tonight."

I told him this was just one of many shelters, but I don't know that he heard.

I waited in line another forty-five minutes to call Natalie, expecting her to answer this time, after all this, so when her recording sounded, I was so overwhelmed with emotion that I got confused about where to start: how we'd gotten there, what our plans were, what number she could reach me at. I knew she was avoiding me. The beep sounded. "Kevin here," I said. "I wanted you to know that I made it through Katrina and the kids did too and we're in a shelter now and we're going to Pensacola as soon as we can and we're doing okay." I made the mistake of taking a breath and thinking about what to say next instead of saying it; I had to hang up because the tears started welling up. Charlie took me to a wall where I crouched down and sobbed silently alone. For a few minutes my mind went blank, no memories; I couldn't stop the tears, so I just let them come. Two people asked if I needed help, but I waved them off. After a few minutes, I could catch my breath again and find my way back to the kids.

Volunteers from all over the country were making meals, doing medical triage, offering counseling. It was hard to relax with people right next to us crying, coughing, sneezing, sniffling, moaning. That evening we inquired again about Patrick and Isa, but the volunteers still didn't have any lists from outside the shelter. We told how Patrick had saved five people, thinking that might bring some attention, but everybody had stories like that. "If you don't have a story," one lady said, "you didn't make it here."

Ray was in his element, running about, distracting people, and making everybody feel better. On the playground outside, he organized a little-kids' hopscotch tournament that didn't have rules; you had to make up your own and explain them to everybody else. We found people playing folk songs under some oak trees, and we escaped for a bit into music, listening to the guitars. A Hendrix riff reminded me of TBone and Casey playing to tourists at Fisherman's Wharf.

When somebody passed around a bottle of wine, instead of gritting my teeth and steeling myself against it, I let my will to drink fall away. I let it go. I knew it would be back, but for the time being I felt content just to sit with Devon and Ray in the muggy heat of night falling. Every now and then I would catch a snatch of Isa's lilting voice—but it always turned out to be someone else.

All the cots were taken, so we slept on folded blankets on the floor, Mrs. Murphy too. She'd reached her daughter-in-law in Hattiesburg but had no direct way to contact Rusty, who was driving from shelter to shelter and calling his wife from pay phones when he could, since cell phones weren't working along the coast. It was a noisy, smelly, clammy night. I tossed on the hard floor until morning, when the stink of backed-up toilets pushed everyone out under the shade of oaks. I appreciated their leaves.

Robert and Alexis showed up after breakfast, which was served late because the supply truck couldn't get in. I heard Robert before Devon saw him. He was badgering someone about the disordered wall of names. "You couldn't organize it worse if you tried," he said.

"We didn't try," a woman said crisply. "We're trying to feed and house three hundred people in a high school gym that doesn't have power."

I hurried with Ray across the floor, following the slap of Devon's flip-flops. When we got there, Devon and Alexis hugged, I think; clothing rustled, and she laughed uncomfortably. She made a big deal about how rotten we all looked and how much we stank, which felt wonderful to hear because it meant there was a world that was normal, against which we looked strange. For how many days had we been falling apart?

"This place stinks!" Robert said. "Where's Isa?"

As we gathered our belongings, Mrs. Murphy broke down. Rusty still hadn't shown up, and we felt rotten for having to leave her behind. "You saved my life," she told Devon. "Without you, I'd be dead."

Alexis made a big deal about that, asking all sorts of questions and making Devon tell about fighting the storm surge in the middle of Katrina. He loved it.

As we walked outside, Robert couldn't understand where Isa could be; he'd convinced himself she'd be at the shelter. "We're going to find her today," he said, retreating to his deep tone of authority. "I'm not going to let her worry Dad anymore." In the car, the air conditioning pulled me into another world—wasteful and wonderful—for several moments. How could anyone take it for granted? But as we entered the destruction, various forms of fetor penetrated our shell in wave after wave: Brine. Excrement. Carcasses. Putrefaction. Carrion. Decay. By the time we got into Biloxi, Robert's outlook had changed. "Oh, my God," he said. He must have said that fifteen times.

"Look where the water was."

"Look at all the cars in that ditch."

"Ugh. What is that?"

"He's got a homemade shower."

"Look at that boat, up in the tree."

"I can't believe that was a house."

"Look at those people, just sitting on the couch. Where are they going to go?"

"How'd that tractor get up on end?"

"That woman has a gun. Did you see that shotgun?"

"Look at that bridge."

"That's not a bridge."

"Used to be."

We couldn't get near the Landrys' street or down by the ocean, where Robert wanted to search for Isa and Patrick. A National Guardsman turned us back at the railroad tracks. "It don't matter if you lost people," he told us. "Everybody lost people. If they're alive, they'll get out. They have to get out. There ain't nothing else but to get out."

Robert stopped at several shelters around Biloxi. As he and the others went inside, I stood in the shade with Charlie, listening to strangers talk about what they'd lost, where they could go for longer than a few days, and what the hell to do. I allowed myself to miss Natalie—her laughter, the touch of her fingers on my face, and the way she'd gotten me running downhill. I wanted to call her.

On the freeway, it felt strange to sit in the front seat with the kids in the back. The rush of wind against the closed windows, even as the car hurled us forward at seventy miles an hour, sounded vapid after what we'd been through. Several sirens passed, speeding in the opposite direction. Here we were, I thought, back on I-10, American river.

When Robert asked what had happened to Isa, we told about the back porch and the face-off with the gun and the timing of her jump. Again Devon had to talk about finding his father, his real father.

"How did that happen?" Robert said abruptly. "You didn't know he's your father?"

Nobody bothered to answer. Finally Robert said quietly, "Isa's like that too. Even as a kid, she always kept me guessing. She would never tell me what was going on. I had to figure it out for myself, or just not know. I told myself two years ago, when she was borrowing money from everybody: never again. I wasn't getting on that roller coaster. So that's that. She'll turn up. She always does." He sounded uncertain.

"How's Abe doing?" I said.

"Much better—if he was ever doing that bad. He's got his oxygen tank and his walker and his doctors and his pills. He has these spells once in a while, but it's nothing like he let on. Remember what he was like on the phone, like he was on his last breath? Well forget that." Robert's voice was forceful again, pressing. "You know why he wanted us out here? Because he wants Mom back. He's trying to go through Isa and me to get her."

It steamed me, after all we'd been through, all we'd lost, to think that the old man had manipulated us into the trip. Yet as I thought about it, I knew that Patrick and Isa had had reasons of their own for driving east. "So is he about to die or not?" I said.

"He could die tomorrow. Or he could live ten years. But he needs help, that's for sure. His house is too big for him. He doesn't need that dinosaur."

"What about the will and all that?"

"Who knows? He writes her into his will. He writes her out of his will. I can't keep track."

I figured that was a lie. He probably knew to the minute detail.

"You want the background?" he said. "Here it is. Dad has an affair with his secretary, and then he can't believe Mom leaves him. Gone. Moves out the same day she found out. Like a Wednesday. He spends most of his life pretending it doesn't matter, chasing everything that moves. Now he wants Rose back. He says she's the only one he ever loved, now that he's about to die."

"What about you?" Alexis said sarcastically. "Mom's filing for divorce."

"Stop it," Robert said. "We agreed not to talk about that."

"You agreed, not me."

"All those charges are going to be dropped."

"I'm not talking about the charges. She's leaving because you don't pay attention to her. You drink too much. And you slept with that woman in Mexico."

"I didn't sleep with her. And this isn't the time."

"It's never the time."

Devon started laughing.

"What's so funny?" Alexis said in a mean, distrustful way.

"It's not you," he said. "It's just funny how everything's the same. I feel like I've been through one of those time tunnels, and now we're out the other end. Like God came down and shook everything up, only it wasn't big enough, it was only one place."

"I thought you didn't believe in God," Ray said.

After a moment, Devon said, "I don't know what I believe."

Robert pulled off the freeway. As he filled up, we piled out to buy soft drinks and snacks. I was stunned to be in a functioning store with food and water on shelves.

"I don't understand," Ray said. "Why don't they bring this stuff to people who need it?"

When we got back on the freeway, it felt strange to enter Florida without Isa.

FIFTEEN

Even after all the preparation and lead time, I was not ready for Abraham Gibbons. As we pulled into his driveway, Alexis said, her voice light, keen, "Here he comes. He's so cute."

A man called out, "Welcome!" and, in a wheezy, determined voice, declared that his house was ours for as long as we needed to stay. "Look at you!" he said, moving past the others and shaking my hand vigorously. "A blind man without dark glasses. I like that. My eyes are failing me too, but nobody gives me sympathy unless I wear those stupid glasses and carry that cane."

That made me chuckle. He was shorter than I expected. And more vibrant. Much more vibrant.

"Aren't you supposed to be frail?" I said.

He gripped my hand and put it flat on his belly, which felt firm even through his shirt. "Hard as a rock!" he proclaimed.

I resented that; I couldn't help it. It wasn't that I wanted him to die; we'd had enough loss already. It just didn't seem right that he was so hardy after all we'd been through.

"Ah, you pull away," he said. "You're impressed."

I shook my head but smiled. "This is Devon and Ray," I said.

"Ray!" he said. He made a short, shrill whistle and did something—

with his hands?—that made Ray laugh and jump back. "And you," he said to Devon. "I've heard you're smart and you're a smart-ass. You're gorgeous cute, whatever that is. You saved a woman's life. And you pointed a shotgun at your dad but were brave enough not to shoot."

Devon laughed. It was an introduction he actually liked.

"I am honored to have you all," Abe said, sounding like a Southern gentleman.

"How did you know about the shotgun?" Ray said.

"Text messages," he said. "Marvelous invention."

"Who sent you text messages?" I said.

"Here, here!" he said. "Gather here, hold hands."

"I sent those," Alexis said, "from the car."

So he was accessible to Alexis on the fly, yet Isa hadn't been able to reach him all across the country.

He pulled us into a circle and declared, "I gave up that Lord-our-God stuff a long time ago, but let's send our compassion to Isa and Patrick. Let's put our hearts together. We know they're someplace where they can't contact us. But they'll find a phone, and they'll call. Isa always pulls through. She's a survivor, I'll give her that. She goes through hell. She puts me through hell. But she always comes out the other side. She means well, and she loves from the heart. So be it!" He clapped his hands, as if that made it so.

Robert said, "Amen."

Abe insisted on leading me, so I took his bony elbow. As he led me up several steps of concrete, he slowed, wheezing and pulling himself up by a railing. Inside the house, in the cool air of the entry, he wanted to know everything, he said, from the start of the trip. But first he wanted to know exactly when and how we'd last seen Isa. I told him we had to shower first; we couldn't say another word without a shower. Next moment he was all over that, organizing rooms, telling us who was staying where.

"Jesus," Robert said. "You didn't roll out the red carpet when *we* showed up a few days ago."

The house had a reverse floor plan, with bedrooms on the first floor and common rooms upstairs. After a shower I drifted upstairs, where Abe accosted me, getting me some water and telling me how much better I looked without the layer of grime. I lay on his couch in a living room with high ceilings and a shag carpet that made for good acoustics. I felt guilty somehow, ashamed to be lounging in a plush world with such devastation nearby. I told him everything he wanted to know, from Burbank to Pensacola. For a long time, he circled around the kids' last sighting of Isa and Devon's pointing of the gun and what she had meant: "I love you." I didn't tell him what I'd heard: "I loved you." I also left out the casket and the cocaine. As I spoke, he got up and sat and stood again, pacing and wheezing. At one point, I heard something on wheels, squeaking, and when I asked, he said it was his oxygen, which he wheeled around on his walker. One moment he would exclaim wildly that it was beyond hope; why did Isa always do this? Then he'd say, "Patience. If that girl has taught me anything, it's patience. And pain!" Then he'd fly off again about his suffering. Before I knew it, he was whispering to me about Alexis trying to keep her parents together. "I got her eating again, thank goodness. That girl shows a hell of a lot of pluck. It's the kids I care about."

Maybe I dozed because the next thing I knew, the kids were bustling upstairs, starving; we'd eaten only snacks since breakfast. As Alexis made herself a salad, the rest of us sat at the kitchen counter eating frozen pizzas that tasted like cardboard. I missed Patrick's cooking. Robert asked Abe when he was going to move, which got Abe complaining: The size of his house! All the stairs! How would he sell it? How would he move everything? He'd been there fifteen years.

He sounded a lot like me back in Burbank.

"Stop it, Dad," Robert said. "That stuff's easy. It's a series of steps, one after the other. You're just upset about Isa."

"It's not easy!" Abe said. "You don't have a breathing condition and macular degeneration. And you're two thousand miles away."

Macular degeneration, I thought. How bad could it be if he'd read text messages from Alexis?

The doorbell rang, just as Alexis offered to stay and help him move.

"Nonsense," Robert said, walking downstairs and muttering about school—which got me worrying. It was Thursday already, and the kids were supposed to start school the following week.

When we heard a woman's voice from below, Abe jumped up. "It's Rose!" He wheeled squeak, squeak, squeak across the room.

"He's hiding his oxygen," Alexis whispered. "He's so cute. He's been begging her to visit."

"You've come!" Abe called out, with a new fullness in his voice. "We're delighted!" He made a big deal about the view over the bluffs. I wondered how much of it he could see.

"What about the stairs?" Rose said. "How do you even get the door?"

"I'm as fit as ever," he said. "What can I get you?"

"I've come to hear about Isa," she said, all business.

Abe herded us from the dining room into the living area, fussing over pillows and footstools. Rose wanted to know everything about the status of lists and what our plans were to search for Isa and Patrick along streets and in shelters. Robert said that was what we'd been doing all day, for crying out loud. He'd take care of it tomorrow too, but they were leaving on Saturday. "That's what vacations are for, to focus on Isa."

Rose wanted him to stay longer, but Alexis said boldly, "He's got to get back. He has to patch things up with Mom."

Her grandmother was already moving on: she had us describe everything leading up to and after the moment on the back porch. She asked more questions than Abe, even, and the kids had to take over: details about the porch struts and the broken railing, the force and direction of the wind, and why Isa had gone out into the hurricane in the first place. Devon let it slip about a casket, so we had to explain that too, why we were bringing it and who it was for. I thought Abe would say something about it, but he didn't.

We managed to keep quiet about the cocaine.

She wanted to know: When had Isa gone onto the porch? How long had she been out there? Who had she been looking at when she said, "I love you"? How had she jumped?

"She didn't really jump," Ray said. "She just turned and stepped off."

We sat quietly then, thinking about that.

Rose said, "I've seen Isa in hurricanes. She would never go out on a porch in the middle of Katrina."

Yet that was what her daughter had done.

She asked if Isa had been depressed at all during the trip. Had she been acting strangely? When we told her about the car accident in El Paso, she said, "I knew it," and she asked point-blank, "Did she say anything about Jasmine?"

I told her she had.

That solved it for Rose. She couldn't imagine Isa stepping off the porch to save Devon or to spite Patrick or to make Patrick save her. None of those reasons were desperate enough, in her mind. She was convinced that Isa had been depressed and had intended to take her own life.

"She's been delusional but never suicidal," Abe objected. "Could *you* live through what she's been through? She's a survivor. She's always been a survivor." He kept on and on, trying to convince Rose that Isa would not have taken her own life on purpose. But the more he talked the less she would say.

It was exhausting.

After Rose left, Abe was devastated. "She didn't even talk to me!" he said. He complained that he couldn't breathe, called for his oxygen tank. "I don't know what I'm doing, hosting all of you! I'm a sick man." He withdrew, with much assistance and fussing, to his room. All that evening, Alexis and Devon were plotting and planning in one room or another. But there was no way, Robert said, that Alexis was staying an extra week to help Grandpa do anything.

I knew I should talk to the kids about what we'd have to do, but I put it off. Maybe Patrick and Isa would show up tomorrow. If not, I'd call my parents, and they'd have to wire me some money. We'd have to take a bus to Burbank, or a plane if we were lucky. There was no way to prevent it: the kids would get new foster homes—maybe they wouldn't have to change schools again—and I'd look for a place to live. We'd go our ways.

I was too depressed to call Natalie.

The next morning, after Robert left early for Biloxi, Abe asked about my scar, every detail from the bike accident to the lawsuit for damages. "What the hell was that driver doing," he said, "backing up a street sweeper over a five-year-old boy! By God, you earned every cent of that money. You're still paying for it to this day."

It felt good to have someone say that.

Devon overheard that part of our conversation, and he started arguing with Abe about how the government was going broke making handouts to the poor, as if that were my story. Abe took the bait and ran with it, arguing that it wasn't government that was bad but the people who were running it. Look what a mess they were making of Katrina.

They fed off each other, back and forth—each of them getting under the other's skin. I was worried that Devon was pushing too hard, but I didn't step in. "That boy's a son of a bitch," Abe told me later, sucking from his oxygen tank. "But he gets me going. He's got repartee. You can't teach that." It made me smile.

Ray and I were thinking cereal and toast for breakfast, but Devon and Abe had bigger plans. They made twenty pancakes, four eggs, and twelve strips of bacon. Devon ate exactly half of everything. I got two pancakes, an egg, and a piece of bacon. Ray and Alexis ate most of the rest.

"I hardly got a damn pancake," Abe complained, but I could tell he loved it.

Afterward, using Abe's computer, Alexis described her Myspace page—all the photos of Biloxi she'd uploaded from her cell phone.

"Even I'm on Myspace," Abe said proudly through his wheeze. "Look."

"That would be difficult," I said, "for me to look."

"You know what I mean," he said. He described the profile she'd set up for him and read some comments from friends. "Not bad for an old man, huh?"

"Those aren't friends," Devon said. "Those are women trying to sell their services."

Abe pulled out his cell phone and showed me how big his text messages were, though he knew I couldn't see a thing. So I went downstairs and came back up with my note-taker, showing them all how I tapped the keys and read the raised Braille. Abe was astonished. "It doesn't have a monitor!" Then he went on and on about how smart I was. When Ray told him I was a journalist, he demanded to know what was I writing, but I tried to keep it vague.

"A story about me," I lied—which was a mistake because he pressed me with a dozen questions, one after the other, along pathways that made me self-conscious and incoherent. He was genuinely interested. But I didn't have any idea what I was writing.

During the afternoon, we changed into bathing suits and Alexis drove the boys and me across the causeway in Abe's Lincoln. The beach was still recovering from Hurricane Ivan the year before; the hotels looked like ghosts, Ray said, with windows missing and the siding torn off. I expected Isa to pipe up and say something; I don't know why. It shocked me that she and Patrick weren't with us.

At the beach, Alexis pulled the car over and let Devon drive along a two-lane road that paralleled the Gulf. With the windows down, I tasted salt and heard waves lap on sand.

Devon was the epitome of self-satisfaction. "Look at them," he said about people in another car. "They see me driving. Roll up the windows so they know we have air conditioning." He insisted on backing up and pulling into a parking space three times until he was exactly in the center.

Alexis and Devon started tussling or something, so I walked barefoot with Ray over dunes that my heels and then toes sank into, step after step, and then across sand so fine and flat and hot it squeaked beneath my arches, massaging my soles. Behind us I could hear snatches of laughter from Alexis.

"They're smooching," Ray said. "They're always smooching."

I couldn't believe how wide the beach was, how far to the Gulf. "I'll never go to a beach without remembering that story you told me about your mom," I said. "How much she loves you. And what she said about all the colors of sand." When he didn't answer, I said, "What color is la gente today?"

"As white as sugar," he said immediately. "As far as you can see."

"I can see nothing a long way."

When I tried to touch him, he started to run. "There's nothing here," he called out. "You can run. But you can't catch me!"

So I ran, following his giggles and the sound of waves. I pushed into the fine sand, pumping my arms, breathing hard, laughing, and trusting the space before me. I lost track of Ray. When I got down near the surf, I yelled, "Look out!" and slowed but didn't stop. I dropped my things, tore off my shirt, and ran across harder, cooler sand into the rippling waves, high-stepping until I tripped, splashing into the water, which felt as warm as the air. And salty. Much saltier than the Pacific. I'd been in the Gulf already in Biloxi, out by the back stoop and inside the house too, when we'd opened the front door to drain the first floor. But this was altogether different.

"I'm going in," Devon said from the beach.

Alexis laughed. "Put me down!"

They splashed and laughed and drifted off on their own.

I played Marco Polo with Ray, who swam like a fish. When I would dive and swim to where his voice had been, I'd thrust out, reaching. He'd be gone. But I often felt the warm currents of his stroke or kick in the water.

Later, when I had a moment to myself, I tried floating the way Patrick had described on the porch, feet out front, head up, alert—but without a current, I sank. Then I let the weight of my head drop into the Gulf, and I floated for a long time, horizontal, buoyed by salt. The gentle swells hypnotized me. With my ears underwater, I heard a ping in the distance. A dock, maybe. A mooring. I thought of Isa.

The next morning, I slipped into a room, braced myself, and called Natalie again. I'd prepared an upbeat message this time. We made it through. We're in Pensacola. It was great to meet you. Come visit if you're in L.A. That sort of thing. Abe and Devon were driving Alexis and Robert to the airport, and Ray was watching TV upstairs.

Natalie answered on the first ring. My God, she demanded, why hadn't I called sooner? She'd been trying to reach me forever on Isa's cell, which rang and rang. She'd been in the mountains over the weekend, out of cell-phone range. When she'd gotten back and heard I'd been in Katrina—in Biloxi, of all places—she'd found out everything she could about what had happened and had been about to fly out to search through shelters for me. Then she'd gotten my message that I was in a shelter, and she had expected me to call back right away. She'd been on the phone nonstop with relief agencies, asking them about a blind man. She'd called the governor's office. What had I been thinking? Why hadn't I called sooner? She was mad at me. Pissed off. That was when I realized she was crying.

I was more than shocked. I was blown away. We talked for an hour.

She wanted to hear everything about the hurricane—but especially about Devon after I told her the saga with Patrick. I told her Robert had spent a long day visiting shelters near Biloxi and had come home humbled and depressed. It had been five days, but we were still hoping Patrick and Isa would show up.

She asked if I still loved Isa.

"I haven't loved her for a long time," I said. "I did a stupid thing with her."

She told me she'd done some soul-searching in the mountains and was glad she'd left her job. She wanted to see me again; she just didn't know how to make it happen. Could I stop on the way back?

"I'm afraid," I said.

"Of what?"

I was scared she wouldn't want me. That my allure wouldn't last. That as she got to know me, I would lose her. "I'm afraid you'll get me arrested at some golf course," I said. "Or you'll get me remembering all kinds of colors I can't see."

"Have you seen any colors?" she said, laughing. I waited for the wheeze at the end, but it didn't come. We weren't that relaxed yet.

We spoke for a while about the kids, and she tried to convince me they needed a real vacation before they went back to Burbank. "Why not take the train?" she said. "It goes all the way from Florida to L.A. and stops right in El Paso. I'll rent a car, and we can go to the mountains. It won't cost much; we can camp. The church has all the equipment. Then you can go on to Burbank and get them back in school. They'll miss just a few days."

I hadn't been camping since I was a kid. Devon and Ray did need a break. I tried to keep my excitement in check. I told her I'd talk to the kids.

"We'll take things as they come," she said. "No pressure. We'll go to Carlsbad Caverns. It's just a couple hours from here. They have wild cave tours, where you climb ladders and crawl into huge caverns on your hands and knees. The echoes are amazing. You'll love it."

I started laughing. "Wild caves," I said. "Why am I not surprised?"

When Abe and Devon returned from the airport, I told Devon we needed to go downstairs and talk with Ray to figure out our options. I tried to sound cheerful. Devon said right away he'd already decided. He was staying put; he wasn't going back to California.

Here we go again, I thought.

The wheels of the oxygen stroller squeaked toward us.

"You can't just stay in Pensacola," I said.

"Abe's going to sponsor me."

"Sponsor you for what?"

"It's a quid pro quo," Abe said matter-of-factly, like it was a business deal he was negotiating. "I need to sell this house. I need to find a smaller place, a condo. I need to move. Devon can learn all about real estate, buying, selling. You name it. He'll be my man on the ground."

"I'm going to get my GED," Devon added. "I'll take some adult-ed classes if I have to. Next semester, I'm going to start at the community college. Just a few classes. And work too." He'd prepared exactly what to say.

"You're a ward of the court in California," I said.

"At sixteen, you're allowed to live on your own. It's called the independent living program. My probation officer told me all about it. They don't have enough houses for all the kids anyway."

He'd known about this program for how long? Yet he'd tried to talk me into running away at least a dozen times. "I don't think living in Florida is part of that program," I said.

"That's no problem," Abe said. "I can take care of it. He'll be eighteen soon enough."

"In a year and a half," I said. I didn't trust him. Was he angling for Rose? That didn't make sense. Was he planning to exploit Devon? Good luck trying, I thought. I had to admit, there was some symmetry to it. Abe was demanding, but he did need help—and Devon was testy in his own way. They seemed to get along. And Devon's grandfather had already promised him a job on the Mississippi.

"What about Robert?" I said to Abe. "Does he know about this?"

"When he finds out, he'll complain. He always complains. But he'll be grateful enough that he doesn't have to help me move."

"Come on," I said to Devon. "Come back with Ray and me. We're going camping in the mountains near El Paso on the way back."

That didn't interest him. "I have more options here," he said, as if he'd practiced that line.

I turned to Abe. "What are you promising, exactly? Are you going to pay him? Are you paying for the GED? For the community college?"

"He'll get free room and board," Abe said. "And educational expenses until he turns eighteen. Then we'll see after that. He has to learn about real estate and do some legwork for me. He has to help me move. He has to get his driver's license. I'll teach him things. But he'll have to get a job—or do extra jobs around here—to pay for anything beyond room, board, and school."

"How's he going to get a driver's license if he's a ward in California?"

"I told you," he said. "We'll take care of that."

"And health," I said. "If he gets sick or something."

"I'll look into some kind of student plan," Abe said. "I'll see what there is."

"You'll fly him back to California," I said, "if things don't work out."

"Agreed," he said.

I turned back to Devon and said as firmly as I could, "Promise me you won't go to Mississippi—to that job—until after you get your GED."

"I don't want that job," Devon said. "If I go to Mississippi, I'll be looking up the Morels, not the Landrys."

"Promise me," I repeated.

"I promise."

I tried to imagine the two of them six weeks down the road: the old codger and the young miscreant arguing. I wasn't convinced it would last, but who knew? It did seem better than his options back in Burbank—and he could always fly home.

"What are you going to tell your mom?" I asked.

"It ain't—" He corrected himself, mocking me: "It is not what I am going to tell her. It is what I am going to ask her. Like: What the fuck? How did she get mixed up with Patrick?"

That made me laugh. "I'm going to call you and check in."

"That's cool."

"Get your college education. You're a good writer."

"I'm studying real estate," he said with an air of self-importance. "You're the writer."

I was shocked that he was staying. I was relieved. I was happy. I was sad.

I hugged him. "I'm proud of you," I said. "You're a good kid. We'll miss you." Then I told him to go downstairs; Ray needed to hear his plans—and right away.

I gave them some time to sort things out, and when I walked downstairs, the television wasn't even on in the bedroom. They were choppin' it up on the bed—talking about girls and music.

"So what do you think about taking the train?" I said to Ray. I sat on the bed and told him about Natalie's idea: stopping in El Paso, visiting caves, camping. He liked it. We had a long conversation, with Devon too, about what it would take to visit his family in Cuernavaca. When to go. How to plan for it. I promised to go with him at Christmas. He liked that too. "So it's set," I said. "First El Paso, then Burbank, then Cuernavaca?"

He didn't say anything, so I repeated it. Still he didn't answer, but he giggled, so I reached over and felt his head. "Are you nodding to a blind man?" I said, trying to wrap his head in my arm as he squirmed away, giggling, and I toppled onto the bed. Devon laughed, so I grabbed a pillow and got in a good swing, knocking him with the downy fluff. We were all at it then, laughing and swinging pillows amid the soft, clean smell of laundered sheets. I wasn't even wearing glasses that I had to take off.

Suddenly they both withdrew and then came at me together, so I protected my head with my pillow and collapsed on the bed. The mattress sank a bit as one of them fell beside me. As I swung my leg over, Ray squealed and squirmed, so I let him go and he rolled on top of me; I pulled him off and dropped him over the edge onto the floor. Devon's big hands came flat onto my chest as he tried to pin me down with the weight of his body, so I grabbed his wrists, using his own weight, and rolled away, pulling, bringing him over me onto the bed. Ray jumped on top of us both then, all of us laughing and panting and catching our breaths. The air conditioner hummed cool.

After a while, Ray said, "I need to go back anyway, to get that picture of Mom. It's next to my bed."

It felt good to call my parents that evening and thank them for the note-taker. I told them not to send any more checks to Isa Landry; I said I wanted to discuss the control of my account, but not today. "No, I'm not using drugs." I said I'd been traveling and had been in Katrina. "Not in New Orleans. In Biloxi . . . Yes, Mississippi . . . It's too long a story for now, but Isa and Patrick are still missing. . . . At her father's house, Abe . . . I need some emergency money from the account." The deeper I got, the more inexplicable it became.

When they asked to speak with Abe and then talked with him for twenty minutes, I didn't take it personally.

Natalie called me twice a day; she found out that trains weren't running between Texas and Florida anymore, not after Katrina. They were going only as far east as San Antonio. So Abe let me use his credit card to buy two plane tickets from Pensacola to El Paso, and when the wire arrived from my parents, I paid him back. Ray and I planned to take the train from El Paso to Burbank after going camping in the mountains.

We had no way to get in touch with Patrick's parents and hoped that the Dexters or Mrs. Murphy would tell them that their son and daughter-in-law were missing.

In odd places, I kept startling myself, expecting Isa or Patrick to say something. It haunted me to think that maybe they *were* gone. In the middle of the night, as I was walking to the bathroom, I heard Abe ranting upstairs: "How could she throw herself into a hurricane? She's trying to get at me. Well, I'm putting her back in, goddamn it. Robert be damned." He paused for a while, then raved on: "But what the hell does it matter? There's no way she's alive, so she isn't getting a cent! How could she possibly be alive? She's a goddamn survivor, that's how. It's just like her to be alive and not call."

I don't remember dreaming that night; I slept until ten-thirty.

On Labor Day we had a barbecue and told stories about Isa. "It's not a ceremony," Abe insisted. "She's going to show up. Probably this afternoon. She's disappeared plenty of times before." Rose stopped by, which put Abe on edge while she was there and sank his spirits when she left.

Devon was in a good mood all day, poking at Ray and spending time with him. I tried to be upbeat but felt melancholy, not just for Isa and Patrick but also for Casey, who had died in an alley on Labor Day two years earlier. He always made the day after Labor Day—my clean-and-sober anniversary—humbling.

On Tuesday Abe and Devon drove us to the airport, where we parked the car and walked in together. Abe wanted to make sure they would let us on the plane, since Ray had no identification and wasn't related to me. But they checked us in and asked his age. That was it.

Walking from the counter to the line for the security check, I held my old friend Charlie in one hand and Devon's strong, bony elbow in the other, enjoying his gait. Ray had bought flip-flops at the beach, so I listened to his quick slaps ahead and Devon's striding slaps beside me. When we stopped, I squeezed his elbow a last time and reached into my backpack, pulling out *Invisible Man*, the one by Ellison. I handed it to him. I figured he was ready for college. After we hugged awkwardly, I turned to go, but he hooked my elbow and placed a small box in my hand. "It's from me and Ray," he said.

I smiled. Leaning Charlie against my chest, I unwrapped the box, opened the case inside, and took out a pair of glasses.

"Ray-Bans," Ray said proudly.

I loved the pun. I put them on.

"They don't hide much," Devon said. "They just look good. Even on you." I appreciated the grin in his voice. When I stood tall and tensed my jaw, he put his hand on my shoulder and shook me gently, helping me lighten up. I smiled again, registering the touch of his big hand.

I couldn't help thinking of Isa: What can you see, Kevin? What can you see?

Devon and Ray did some kind of handshake and promised to see each other online. Devon offered to visit us when he came out to see his mom. A few moments later, Devon's flip-flops slapped away in long strides, the sound reverberating along the corridor.

At the gate, Ray and I had twenty minutes before boarding, so I took out my new cell phone and called Natalie—ostensibly to let her know our flight was on time. But I wanted to hear her voice. I wanted to learn all her inflections and pauses, so I asked for every detail about the tents and sleeping bags. When I asked what she was wearing so I could recognize her at the airport, she laughed.

"You'll see soon enough," she joked.

Then I called our number in Burbank, to hear it ring at the other edge of the country.

I was shocked when someone picked up. A gush of white noise sounded and fell away. It was absurd. "Isa?" I said. "Who's there?"

"She's gone home," Patrick said, gruff as ever.

My gut sank. I knew what he meant: gone home to God.

"You didn't hear my voice," he said. "I sold your stuff. I wasn't here. I'm dead." The phone clicked. My jaws tensed. My laptop!

"Hey!" I said. I wanted to tell him to save Ray's photo, to put it someplace where we could pick it up.

"Who was that?" Ray said.

"Nobody," I said quickly. "The line went dead." Maybe it was the wrong thing to do, to protect him. But I figured we could look for the photo when we got back to Burbank. He didn't have to worry about it now.

I was surprised at how quickly Patrick had gotten back home. But it was just like him, I decided, to close things down and use Katrina to escape his creditors. I was sure he owed much more than my five hundred bucks and a laptop. Then a touch of doubt crept in: Wasn't it just like Isa to get saved? And then to slip away until she could face people? Maybe she *was* heading home.

Our plane vibrated, leaning into a turn. The floor rumbled, and our seats trembled from the lowering of landing gear. An overhead bin rattled and then stopped. Rattled again. The air was parched and stale. We dipped suddenly, making my stomach jump for a second. Ray giggled. I placed my palm on his back; he was still glued to the window. There were thunderstorms in the area, the pilot had promised, and Ray was hoping to see lightning. "Look at the little cars on I-10," he said. "There's Mexico right there." Except for our connector flight into Dallas, he'd never flown before. Neither had I.

The plane jumped, setting off Ray's giggles again.

"Oh, my," a woman said from across the aisle, in a breathy tone that reminded me of Mrs. Murphy.

I felt calm for the first time in weeks. I'd been writing nonstop on both flights, enjoying the freedom of my note-taker, the drafts of words that drifted me along. I didn't care that it was mostly drivel. As soon as we'd taken off in Pensacola, I took a self-indulgent leap; instead of writing about them, I wrote about me. I knew exactly where to start: losing my job in Burbank. Time flew. Space collapsed. We were suddenly in Dallas.

Now El Paso. As I reached for my backpack beneath the seat, Ray called out, "Lightning!" and started to count out the illusion: one–one thousand, two–one thousand.

The woman said, "My goodness." Still the seats shivered.

There was no thunder.

We touched down with a skip and then a solid landing. I held Ray's shoulder as we came through the security gates. He couldn't see Natalie anywhere, but my heart stayed quiet, my breathing smooth. I thought about my pal Charlie, folded in my backpack, waiting. As I listened to the echoes of footsteps along the corridor, I remembered finding my way as a child, when I had been lost between the pond and Grandpa's home, in a place I'd always known. I'd never been to the El Paso airport. I was visiting a woman I hardly knew, hoping for a connection I'd never had. I was taking care of a twelve-year-old boy who needed to get to school a thousand miles away. I didn't have a place to live. I wasn't sure where we were going or when we'd get there. I gripped Ray's slender shoulder and grinned. I couldn't wait.

ACKNOWLEDGMENTS

My grandfather Frank Nodine and grandmother Ida Randall shared their worlds with me before and after they became legally blind. My ex-brother in law, Steven Walle, who lost all perception of light at age five, inspired me and provided all kinds of information. Zane Bock and Empish Thomas reviewed substantial portions of the manuscript. Craig Blackwell, MD, taught me about eye trauma. Carla Miller and the late Ray Westman shared their knowledge of Braille. The Vista Center for the Blind and Visually Impaired offered information and contacts. Michael Pritchard and Joanne Buckley at Pathway Society, Inc., introduced me to recovery.

For many years Kathryn Chetkovich has helped me advance my writing skills. Thanks also to Paul Skenazy, Ken Weisner, Gary Miles, Kay Martin, Abigail Stryker, Lee Glickenhaus, Monte Levinson, Art Konar, Howard Jaffe, Alan Friedman, Kevin Watts, Sara Ramirez, Robin Hayes, Sheryl Bulgalski, Nancy Graham, and Stuart Faison for their insights. Bruce Nodine offered information about hurricanes. Jonathan Franzen, the late James D. Houston, Jeanne Wakatsuki Houston, and Micah Perks provided guidance about the profession. Recognition by the Dana Award for the Novel helped me persevere.

My agent Susan Golomb found a way forward at every turn, from storyline to publication. Fred Ramey took a risk on a debut novel and made it better.

My parents encouraged me, my kids taught me, and my wife, Shelby Graham, believed in me. To all these people, and to more besides, I am grateful.